LIKE A FLOOD

Elizabeth Proske

Published by SET APART Press http://www.setapartpress.com
Cover Design by www.ElmStreetDesignStudio.net
Interior Design by Penoaks Publishing, http://penoaks.com

Scripture quotations taken from:
THE HOLY BIBLE, NEW INTERNATIONAL VERSION®, NIV® Copyright © 1973, 1978, 1984, 2011
by Biblica, Inc.™ Used by permission. All rights reserved worldwide.
New King James Version®. Copyright © 1982 by Thomas Nelson, Inc. Used by permission. All rights reserved.
Kings James Version. Copyright Public domain.

Song lyrics taken from:
Song ID: 26898
Song Title: God Of Wonders
Writer(s): Marc Byrd, Steve Hindalong
Copyright: © 2000 New Spring Publishing (ASCAP) / Never Say Never Songs (ASCAP).
All rights for the world on behalf of Never Say Never Songs administered by New Spring Publishing / Storm Boy Music (BMI) / Meaux Mercy (BMI) (Admin. EMI Christian Music Group). All Rights Reserved. Used By Permission.
Song ID: 27636
Song Title: Here I Am To Worship Light Of The World
Writer(s): Tim Hughes
Copyright © 2001 Thankyou Music (PRS) (adm. worldwide at EMICMGPublishing.com excluding Europe which is adm. by Kingswaysongs) All rights reserved. Used by permission.
Song ID: 27632
Song Title: Forever
Writer(s): Chris Tomlin
Copyright © 2001 worshiptogether.com Songs (ASCAP) sixsteps Music (ASCAP) (adm. at EMICMGPublishing.com) All rights reserved. Used by permission.
Song ID: 32148
Song Title: Blessed Be Your Name
Writer(s): Beth Redman, Matt Redman
Copyright © 2002 Thankyou Music (PRS) (adm. worldwide at EMICMGPublishing.com excluding Europe which is adm. by Kingswaysongs) All rights reserved. Used by permission Cover Photo © 2012 JupiterImages Corporation. All rights reserved – used with permission.

This is a work of fiction. Locations are either the product of the author's imagination or used in a fictitious manner. Names, characters, and events are the products of the author's imagination. Any resemblance to actual persons, living or dead, or actual events is purely coincidental.

PRINTED IN THE UNITED STATES OF AMERICA
Second Edition 2016

"When the enemy comes in like a flood,
The Spirit of the Lord
will lift up a standard against him."

from Isaiah 59:19 (NKJV)

PROLOGUE

Sucre, Colombia

The Bayliner sliced silently through the water, hugging the shoreline.

Every light on board had been extinguished, rendering the vessel almost invisible in the darkness. A sharp whistle, like the cry of a bird, came from the boat.

Immediately, from the dark line of trees, there came an answering whistle with a small but significant variation.

The whistle from the boat was repeated, slightly altered. Again the whistle was returned.

This time the boat eased itself into a crude natural docking area. Several armed men dressed in dark clothing leapt from it.

An equal number of armed men in military fatigues materialized from the jungle, and the two small armies faced each other in silence.

A short, stout man disembarked and stood in the center of his men, his single gold earring reflecting the moonlight. He was bald, and his thick lips turned down at the corners of his wide face, giving him a frog-like appearance. He gave a signal and two of his men approached the black Dodge Ram 2500 truck that was hidden in the darkness.

The camouflage clad men stepped aside but kept their rifles at the ready as the others climbed into the back of the Dodge Ram. They threw off a heavy canvas tarp that had been strapped over the cargo and chose a crate at random from the many stacked in the bed of the truck. The men laid it at their leader's feet, prying it open for him. It was filled with ziploc bags containing a gritty white substance.

The bald man pushed aside the bags on top and dragged one out from the middle. He placed the bag on a small scale one of his men had produced, nodded in satisfaction, then slit the bag open with a knife. He pushed a fat finger into the slit, pulling out some of the contents.

Another of his men held out a vial to him and he dropped a pinch of the white powder into the clear liquid. After shaking the vial, the frog man examined it in the light from a powerful flashlight held by the first man. The process was repeated with three more bags chosen at random, a fresh vial produced for each sample. Finally, the frog man nodded again.

Not a word had been spoken the whole time. Now a small man with a trim mustache emerged from the shadows and spoke calmly in Spanish. "I trust the quality meets your exacting standards as always."

The bald man gave a smile without warmth. "Captain Ortega, my friend. I was afraid you would not be able to keep our appointment."

"Have I ever missed an appointment?" countered Rafael Ortega.

His slight stature and charismatic smile belied a ruthless, calculating nature that had earned him the nickname *El Tiburon*, or The Shark.

"Never," the other man conceded. "But reports say that travel is almost impossible since the recent flooding, and that many roads are still under water."

"Money is a great motivator, Mauricio. My men and I have endured great hardship to make it to our meeting point on time."

Mauricio narrowed his eyes. "I hope this is not your way of asking for more than the price we agreed on."

"Not at all," Ortega assured him smoothly. "I merely wish to emphasize to you that when you do business with *Las Águilas Negras*, you will not be disappointed."

"Your reassurance is touching. However, I fear that due to the damage to the farmlands, you may not be able to meet the demands of the buyers."

"On the contrary," Ortega said with confidence. "The situation is ideal for us to expand our territory. People will be desperate to cooperate with us now rather than to starve to death waiting for the government to bring help to them. We will soon be able to increase production to exceed your buyers' demands."

Mauricio laughed. "Very resourceful of you, Captain. I wish you luck on your endeavors."

"Enough small talk. Let us finish our business." Ortega's words were tinged with impatience.

"Of course, of course." Mauricio's face tightened at Ortega's tone. He snapped his fingers and one of his men brought a briefcase forward.

As the man held the briefcase open, one of Ortega's men began counting the stacks of money under the watchful eyes of both Ortega and Mauricio.

1

Houston, Texas, USA

"You realize the recent flooding in northern Colombia has changed everything," Pastor Jeff Harding announced. He adjusted his glasses and looked out over a sea of eager young faces, a conglomeration of college students from three different churches who had gathered for a missions-themed rally. Over his head, a huge banner stapled to the wall displayed Jesus' directive from Mark 16:15: "Go Into All The World and Preach the Gospel to All Creation."

To wrap up their final session, Jeff was offering the students the opportunity to put what they'd learned into practice. "This isn't going to be the typical mission trip we had originally planned, where we stay with a nice host family and pray and sing songs and play with kids at the orphanage. Because of what's happened there, this trip will involve major inconvenience, hardship, and grueling work, with no time off for fun and games."

"Sounds like one of your Ancient Greek and Hebrew classes," piped up Jeremy, a skinny, curly headed kid on the back row. Several others, the ones who knew Pastor Jeff from the Christian college he taught at, snickered.

Kevin, a dark-skinned guy with a head full of twists, reached over and the two did a peculiar version of a high five.

Jeff allowed a small smile to cross his face. His boyish appearance and laid back personality made him a favorite among the college crowd.

At forty-five, Jeff refused to settle into the comfortable stodginess of middle age, which was one reason he served part time as the underpaid Youth and Young Adult Pastor of Cornerstone Christian Church in Houston. He supplemented his meager church income with a part time teaching position at Woodrow Christian University, which he also enjoyed immensely. The antics of the college students kept him on his toes and made him feel young.

Jeff's experience with college aged kids had earned him the dubious task of shepherding this current group of over a hundred students, most of them from Pure Grace Fellowship, the megachurch hosting the event. Since attendance was strictly voluntary, he knew most of these students were serious about following Christ and ready to do something about it.

Even if they did make smart remarks now and then.

He responded to Jeremy's wisecrack. "The difference is that here, after you leave your air conditioned classroom, you get to stroll down the hall and use indoor plumbing, and then head off to Taco Bell for lunch," Jeff pointed out. "The area we'll be visiting is normally pretty civilized, but back-to-back hurricanes in the Caribbean caused some major flooding. There are no little boy's rooms, no air conditioning, no microwaves, and cell phones more than likely won't work. And if you're lucky, you might get some thin soup with rice a couple of times a day."

There was a visible reaction in the college students' faces as Jeff's words registered. He could pretty much pick out the ones who had already dismissed the idea of volunteering for the mission trip. He also knew which ones were hooked.

Jeremy and Kevin were hooked, in spite of the inevitable sass he knew was coming.

"Pastor, you'd never make it as a used car salesman." Kevin this time.

"You should know," Jeff shot back with a smile. Kevin and Jeremy worked weekends at a used car dealership, albeit as mechanics, not as salesmen.

Jeff turned serious again. "The reason I tell you the hard stuff is because I want you to seriously consider what kind of commitment we're asking for. We need people who are physically and emotionally strong enough to handle some pretty rough circumstances. Once you're there, you'll be committed for the full two weeks; you won't be able to call mommy and daddy to come pick you up if you decide you don't like it. That's why your applications are going to be screened carefully, and not everyone who signs up will get to go."

Some of the students had already tuned Jeff out, allowing their eyes to glaze over or discreetly pulling out cell phones to text their friends. Jeff addressed the rest of his comments to those who were still awake and considering the trip.

"Pastor Sergio Restrepo runs a mission center and a church in *Cuenco Verde*. His buildings were among the few left standing in the rural areas of Sucre, but there was still a great deal of damage. The entire area has been evacuated, but Pastor Restrepo got permission from the government for himself and a few workers to stay there and repair his mission center. The plan is that when the repairs are completed, they'll temporarily house volunteers from a charitable organization along with local labor who will start rebuilding some of the homes that were destroyed in *Cuenco Verde* so people can return to the area.

"Our job will be to help finish the repairs on *La Vida Nueva* Mission Center, so if you go, you'll be doing some important work that will affect a lot of lives. But it does come with a price." Jeff began counting off on his fingers. "Two weeks without running water, two weeks without microwaves, cell phones, and laptops, and two weeks without pizza. Two weeks of hard physical labor with no relief from the heat, doing whatever Pastor Restrepo needs us to do."

He waited for the kids to settle down again, then rested his gaze on a handsome, serious-looking fellow sitting with Jeremy and Kevin. "Daniel Wescott went with our missionary team last year for a similar trip after the hurricane in Honduras. To help you make up your mind, I've asked him to tell you a little bit about it."

Jeremy and Kevin whistled and stomped, slapping their friend on the back. Daniel, looking very uncomfortable, loped to the podium accompanied by rowdy applause from his classmates.

As Daniel bent his head to pick up the microphone, his sandy hair fell forward, and he flipped his head back to get it out of his eyes. This led to more raucous whooping from the audience. Flustered, he fumbled with the mike. Finally, he cleared his throat and looked at the audience.

"Uh, hi," he began awkwardly. "I'm Daniel."

"Hi, Daniel," a flirtatious female voice called from the back corner. More whistling and catcalls came as Daniel flushed a painful red.

Visibly rattled by their teasing, he cleared his throat again to stall, then tried again. "Uh, yeah, like Pastor Jeff just said, I went with the missions team last year to Honduras. And it was just like he said, a lot of hard work, no electricity, no running water, and the food was, well, kinda....not too good." He scrunched up his nose at the memory. "But at least there wasn't much of it."

The kids laughed at his comment, and Daniel's posture relaxed a little.

He explained some of the work they'd done, how they'd rebuilt tiny houses in an isolated village that had been devastated by the storm. His face lit up with passion as he described the Honduran people. "The cool thing was, even in the middle of that crisis, the people there never lost their faith in God. And they were so good to us, and so grateful for what we were doing. They didn't have much, but they tried to give us whatever they had. They treated us like we were special, almost like we were sent from God or something, and we had to be careful not to let it go to our heads, you know, kind of like Barnabas and Paul had to tell those people in, uh... was it Lycaonia?"

Panicked, Daniel glanced at Pastor Jeff, who smiled and mouthed the word, "Lystra."

"Uh, yeah, Lystra." Daniel looked blank for a moment, like he'd totally lost his train of thought. Forgetting whatever he was going to say about Lystra, he stumbled on gamely. "Anyway, seeing the way these people live, and seeing how much they love God anyway, it made me really appreciate how much we have here in America. I mean, here we have all these big, fancy air conditioned church buildings, and worship bands with all the latest songs, and Bibles in decorator colors, and we still can't wait for church to be over just so we can head to Denny's.

"But believe me, even if you don't like Denny's, if you go to Colombia, after the first two or three days of going without real food, you'll be wishing there was one close by." He grinned then, letting them know the food issue wasn't that big a deal. "But it's worth it, because you know you're doing God's work, and you know you made a difference in somebody's life."

Deciding that was a good stopping point, Jeff stood up. "Thank you, Daniel."

He stepped beside the lanky young man, who topped Jeff's 5'10" by four inches. Daniel looked only too relieved to leave the podium.

Jeff stifled a sigh as he watched Daniel slink back to his seat to the exaggerated applause of the other students. Kind, intelligent, and respected by his peers, Daniel was a natural leader, but he preferred to stay in the background. Jeff hoped this trip would give Daniel a chance to develop more confidence.

He brought his focus back to the audience. "Now remember, folks, that last trip Daniel told you about was only one week. We'll be gone twice as long this time, but we'll get you back in time to do your Christmas shopping."

Jeff noticed people glancing at their watches, so he decided to wrap things up. "The trip is limited to ten people, and naturally, I'm one of them. That means only three of you from each church represented here will be going, so make sure you sign up tonight if you're interested. And if your applications are in order, you still have to pass a physical and a psychological evaluation."

Jeff made a face, trying to remember all the prerequisites. "And make sure your vaccinations are up to date and your passports are in order. And come up with your portion of the airline fare. Have I left anything out, Pastor Meyer?"

Jeff directed his question to Evan Meyer, the pastor of the host church, who was seated on the front row.

Pastor Meyer was a distinguished looking gentleman in his late fifties, with neatly groomed silver hair. He adjusted the expensive silk tie that complemented his tailored dark gray suit, then stood and strode confidently to the podium.

"I think you've covered everything, Pastor Jeff," he said with practiced ease, effectively dismissing Pastor Jeff with his words. "Now let's close our service by praying for the people of Colombia."

Campo Dulce, Sucre, Colombia

"Pastor Alvarez does not care about the people of Colombia!" shouted the young militant standing at the front of the little adobe church.

Several armed men had barged into the sanctuary in the middle of a prayer service and now surrounded the terrified congregants under the approving supervision of El Tiburon. Some of the militants had not yet left their teenage years, but the rifles they bore were still deadly.

Sweat poured from Pastor Rudy Alvarez's head as he stood near the crude wooden altar with a gun pressed against his temple, but his face showed no emotion.

The pastor's wife and teenaged daughter cried quietly on the front row, not allowed by the gunmen to move.

Lieutenant Rojas continued his tirade. "Alvarez is spreading lies to keep the Colombian people poor! He wants you to believe in a God who forbids the easiest way to prosper in our country."

No one responded, and the lieutenant sneered at them. If he had his way, he would have blown away the whole bunch of stupid peasants already, but he knew The Black Eagles needed some of the locals to provide free labor to raise their crops of coca plants. Especially since many of the laborers they had previously coerced had either been killed by the flood or had fled the country.

Rojas stepped aside at once when Captain Ortega joined him at the front, allowing his superior to take over haranguing the people.

"We are not asking you to give up your land," Ortega began in a conciliatory tone. "Only to stop growing worthless crops that fail when the weather does not cooperate and that do not bring enough money to sustain you even when the harvest comes. Your pitiful harvest has already been destroyed by the floodwaters. Instead of replanting your useless crops, you have a chance to grow something that will provide a future for your families. We are offering to give you the supplies needed to rebuild your homes. We are offering you a chance for a steady income. What does this pathetic church offer you?"

At Ortega's question, Pastor Alvarez slid his eyes pointedly to the cross nailed to the front of the small sanctuary. Several pairs of eyes followed the direction of his gaze, and some of the people sat up straighter. They all continued to stare impassively at Ortega, and he became frustrated at their lack of response.

"We have given your pastor the opportunity to cooperate with us, but he has chosen to keep you in poverty. This is your last chance. You must choose today. Will you join with us in bringing this country to its rightful place as a prosperous nation? Or will you continue to follow a man who does not care if your children go hungry? If you want to build a future for your families, you must leave this place now!" His voice rose to a shrill screech. "You must choose now!"

At a gesture from Ortega, the gunmen readied their weapons, making it clear what the consequence would be for choosing to remain in the church.

Hanging his head, one man stood and led his family from the building. Slowly, several others got to their feet and trudged out, some with tears in their eyes as they sold their souls for a piece of bread.

Soon only Pastor Alvarez and his family remained, with three other men, two of them with wives and toddlers at their side. Disgusted, Ortega impatiently motioned for those who were still seated to join the pastor at the altar. The children stood wide eyed, clutched by their trembling mothers as they all clustered together under the wooden cross at the front of the church.

"Your followers have left you, Alvarez," the captain taunted. "Do you still choose to die for the sake of a fairytale?"

"We have chosen life," whispered Pastor Alvarez hoarsely. Those who had joined him at the altar stared with silent defiance at Ortega and his army. Ortega spat in disgust and signaled his gunmen.

The sound of the gunfire echoing from the church building would forever haunt those who had chosen to walk away.

Houston, Texas, USA

"Come on, Pastor Jeff, you can't let me down like this," Jeremy wheedled, leaning his rail thin body forward in his chair in front of Jeff's desk. His light brown curls bobbed up and down as he tried to convey the urgency of his request. "You gotta let me come."

Jeff peered over his glasses at the earnest young man in front of him. Jeremy had been in Jeff's office several times over the last month for some serious discussions, but he'd never seen him this intense.

"Jeremy, under the circumstances, there's no way your application is going to be approved."

"But you're one of the ones who makes that decision," Jeremy persisted. "You're the one who's going to go with the team to Colombia. Don't you have any pull?"

"You know I can't be partial in something like this. I can't use my influence to persuade them to let you go when there may be someone else who meets all the requirements."

"Oh, please, Pastor Jeff," Jeremy scoffed. "It's not like your other options are that great. Not that many people applied, and one of them was Lester Simmons. He only filled out the application to impress Sarah, but you know he's afraid to step out of his house after dark. Darryl Henley smokes so much that birds drop dead from trees when he walks by. And Martha Ramirez looks like she could eat a rhinoceros for breakfast – she'd never survive on the rations in Colombia."

Jeff tried not to smile at Jeremy's unkind but accurate assessment of his peers. He was debating whether or not to reprimand him when Jeremy continued his impassioned appeal.

"You know I can afford my share of the cost, my grades are fine, my church attendance is great. Except for that one tiny little detail, you know I'm your best bet. Besides Daniel and Kevin, I mean, and I know they're going."

"Well, Daniel was an obvious choice because he's been on mission trips like this before," Jeff said, almost apologetically. "He also knows how to do this kind of work because he's worked summers for his father's construction company."

Jeremy waved away the pastor's explanations. "Yeah, yeah. Plus, he already has his passport. You don't have to explain that to me, Pastor. I'd be mad if you didn't choose Daniel. And I know Kevin's qualified. So that leaves one slot open, and I'm your man."

"Jeremy, I understand how much spending this time with your friends means to you, but…"

"It's not just that, Pastor Jeff, I swear." Jeremy looked away for a moment, twisting his face as if trying to decide whether or not to say more. Then he turned back to Jeff, his dark eyes fastened on the pastor's. "I feel like I'm really supposed to go on this trip. I mean, like God wants me to go. Please?"

Jeff saw nothing but sincerity in Jeremy's face, and he could feel himself caving in.

Apparently Jeremy could sense it, too, because a slight smile crooked one corner of his mouth. Then he got serious again and threw in one last plea.

"Come on, Pastor Jeff. This is my chance to do something with my life that will make a difference. I need to do something that matters."

Jeff released a resigned sigh. He massaged his forehead in frustration, mussing his thick brown hair. He thought ruefully that the few strands of gray he'd noticed lately were probably Jeremy's doing. Finally he said aloud what they both knew he was going to say.

"Okay, Jeremy, it's against my better judgment, but I'll see what I can do."

Campo Dulce, Sucre, Colombia

Compared to the more northern areas of Colombia, the little village of Campo Dulce, fifty miles east of Sincelejo, had gotten off lightly from the flooding. While water had invaded most of the homes, ruined their crops of plantains and corn, and left the peasants without electricity, no lives had been lost and the homes remained standing.

Many people had left in search of help from the relief organizations that were rumored to be setting up shelters near the larger communities. The optimistic few who remained hoped to salvage some of their ruined crops and repair the damage to their homes; they were accustomed to a lack of adequate food supplies, and few of them had luxuries that required electricity anyway.

They were beginning to adjust to their lives without contact with the outside world, and the men were joining with each other to work on their neighbors' homes.

Then a second torrent of terror flowed through the streets of Campo Dulce, in the form of an army of men clothed in dark green fatigues who stormed through the little village immediately following the assassination of Pastor Alvarez. The black bandanas covering the lower half of the militants' faces gave them an even more sinister appearance.

The peasants gathered their families together and cowered in their small adobe and straw homes, hoping the threat would pass them by. Those hopes were shattered as the soldiers invaded their once peaceful village.

At each home, a group of soldiers kicked down the door, an unnecessary action, since most of the farmers never locked their doors — they had nothing worth stealing. But the resulting noise and the splintering wood added to the peasants' abject fear, which was the main purpose of the raid. And so they kicked down doors with fervor, aiming their weapons at wide-eyed families while they knocked over furniture and yanked out drawers, strewing the contents across the floor as they searched for anything useful.

If any man resisted, or even looked like he might, the militants dragged him out into the dirt street and gunned him down in front of his horrified loved ones. After a few such instances, none dared to stand up to the invading army.

The Black Eagles now owned Campo Dulce.

Since the farmers had little of monetary value, the Black Eagles satisfied themselves with acquiring another valuable resource: new recruits. If there was a teenager or young twenty-something in the family that looked strong and healthy, he or she would be forced at gunpoint to accompany the Black Eagles when they left the house. Parents and younger siblings wept as young people were swept away from their homes to become unwilling members of the paramilitant army.

At one home, however, such coercion was unnecessary.

Bored with life in the village and fed up with the poverty that seemed to follow his humble, plantain farming family, Adolfo Mendoza had heard of Las Águilas Negras, led by the fearless captain known as El Tiburon.

Adolfo had long admired their exploits, imagining them to be brave revolutionaries saving Colombia from itself. He had sought for a chance to join The Black Eagles but had been unsuccessful in finding a way to contact them.

Now, thanks to the flood, the opportunity had fallen into his lap.

When he heard the commotion down the road, instead of cringing in the back room with the rest of his family, Adolfo went out the front door to investigate. It didn't take him long to figure out what was happening, and he quickly grabbed a small handful of belongings. Ignoring his mother's cries, Adolfo stood in front of his house waiting.

When the small army approached, Adolfo met the leader's eyes without flinching. After a tense moment, Captain Ortega smiled and jerked his head toward his army. Adolfo gave a quick nod and fell into step with them, swelling with pride that he was now a part of something bigger than anything his family had to offer.

Houston, Texas, USA

"Mosquito repellant, check. Sunscreen, check. Flashlight, check." Jeremy was perched on the rail surrounding the airport waiting area, happily ticking items off the list Pastor Jeff had given to each of them.

He stuffed the list back in his pocket, then wriggled out of his jacket. "They sure do keep it hot in here."

Daniel, leaning casually on the rail beside him, pointed up. "You're right under a heat vent."

He grinned as Jeremy squinted up at the heat vent and gave it a look of mock horror. Daniel continued, "You might as well get used to the heat anyway. Remember Pastor Jeff told us that it's going to be really hot in Colombia."

Kevin adjusted one of the twists on his head and laughed. "I think he was pullin' our leg."

"It's true. I looked it up on the internet," Daniel told them. "They're right on the equator. Our winter is their summer."

"Hope you didn't bring all winter clothes," Jeremy quipped to Kevin. He shoved his jacket into his huge backpack and pulled a granola bar out of one of the side pockets. He scooted out from under the stream of hot air and munched contentedly on his granola bar, his second one since they'd arrived.

"You keep scarfing those granola bars like that and you'll run out before we even get to Colombia," Daniel warned.

"Not gonna happen, dude," Jeremy assured him. He held up the battered Mickey Mouse backpack, his only piece of luggage. "My whole bag here is full of granola bars, protein bars, and the occasional package of Skittles."

Daniel laughed and shook his head at his friend's bizarre habits, causing a few strands of his blond hair to fall across his eyes. He brushed them back with an impatient swipe. He probably should have gotten a trim before the trip.

Kevin snickered and asked Jeremy, "So where'd you pack your clothes, man?"

Jeremy polished off his bar and slam dunked the wrapper into the nearest trash can. "Who needs extra clothes? Pastor Restrepo won't care how we look as long as we get the work done. I doubt there'll be any pretty girls to impress out there in the mud, so I tossed out the designer jeans to make room for my goodies."

Kevin gave a low whistle. "You might wanna rethink that granola bar thing, man. Check out what just showed up."

A tall, African American youth with a flat top hair cut had entered the area with two girls in tow. The girl who had caught Kevin's attention had silky, shoulder length auburn hair framing an exceptionally pretty face dominated by huge, smoky gray eyes. Her ankle length jeans and pastel button-down sweater accented her cute figure while still giving her a wholesome appearance.

The other one, a petite girl with smooth skin the color of cocoa, had her hair cropped extremely short. She wore baggy cargo pants, a cream colored tank top that showed off the wiry muscles in her arms, and impossibly huge earrings. A heavy camouflage shirt was slung over her shoulder.

Jeremy jumped to his feet and waved them over. "Hi, you guys part of the team?"

The young man stuck out a hand for Jeremy to shake. "How ya doing? I'm Terrell, and I'm the only one of my group that actually deserves to go."

The beautiful girl with red hair giggled at his comment, but a fierce scowl marred the Black girl's heart-shaped face.

Her annoyance only egged Terrell on. He pointed to the redhead first. "Mindy here is just along because she's the pastor's daughter, and he let this other one come because he was afraid she'd beat him up if he didn't."

The Black girl curled her lip in disgust at Terrell's remark.

"You jerk," she snapped. "I don't hit pastors."

The expression on her face hinted that she could gladly thrash Terrell with no compunction, however. Then she turned to the three friends with a dazzling smile that nearly blinded them. "I'm Resha."

Daniel recovered from her megawatt assault first. He blinked a few times, then stammered, "Uh, I'm Daniel. These two guys are Jeremy and Kevin."

Jeremy and Kevin each waved weakly in turn. The pretty redhead giggled again, her full, pink lips parting to reveal perfect teeth, and offered her hand to each of them. She spoke in a breathy, little girl voice. "Pleased to meet you all. My name's Mindy."

Is this girl for real? Daniel wondered if she'd already forgotten that Terrell had just told them her name, but he decided the airhead bit had to be just an act. She wouldn't have been approved for this trip if she was that dumb, pastor's daughter or not.

From the lovesick way Jeremy and Kevin gawked at the girl, it wouldn't have mattered to them if she had the IQ of a doodlebug.

Daniel grinned and looked at Terrell, who was nearly as tall as he was but not quite as thin.

Smiling back, Terrell shrugged and rolled his eyes. "That's the reaction Mindy usually gets."

The last group to arrive included a stocky Hispanic boy named Manny and his older sister Selena, a tall, thin, dark-haired beauty with a mischievous glint in her eyes. Her skintight jeans and pointed cowboy boots didn't seem like the best choice for construction work — Daniel hoped she'd brought something more practical in the bulging suitcase she was dragging.

A short, ebony skinned Nigerian named Samuel with a perpetually sour expression rounded out the third team. He barely acknowledged their introductions.

Manny was friendly enough, though, even if he looked like he already had jet lag. Selena and Mindy immediately began discussing how the work in Colombia would affect their manicures.

Resha looked bored by it all, but her watchful eyes continually swept the waiting area. She studied Samuel with a suspicious frown when he sidled away from the group and sat in the far corner.

Campo Dulce, Sucre, Colombia

It was with great anticipation that Adolfo finally laid his hands on the AR-18 rifle. He felt a rush of pride remembering how he and El Tiburon had made eye contact when the Black Eagles had stormed his village, as if Ortega recognized that Adolfo was different from the rest.

Adolfo's goal was to become a part of Ortega's elite team. He didn't understand the reluctance of some of the others who had been recruited that day. The Black Eagles had treated them well, feeding them and providing them with a decent place to sleep.

Unlike their homes in the village, the Black Eagles had running water and electricity provided by huge generators at the warehouse they had seized. It was also promised that the recruits would soon be able to send some of their profits to the kinfolk they had left behind so they could rebuild their pathetic village.

Adolfo doubted they would really be allowed to contact their families, but it didn't matter to him. Any money that was forthcoming would go into his own pockets, not to the relatives who had wept when he was tapped by the Black Eagles. How dare his pitiful family resent him this chance to better himself?

He hefted the weapon in his hands, enjoying the feeling of power it gave him as he stood in formation with the other new recruits. With his sturdy build and impressive height, he looked older than his eighteen years. The jagged scar that ran from his temple to his cheekbone, caused by a run-in with a farming implement, added to his mystique. Adolfo knew he made a frightening picture, and he intended to use his intimidating appearance to his advantage.

Today, they were learning how to clean and load the firearms, and Adolfo practiced with enthusiasm. Captain Ortega had promised that tomorrow they would begin training exercises with the rifles, and soon they would be an active part of his army.

Adolfo could hardly wait.

Beside Adolfo was a recruit a couple of years younger, and a lot less eager. Ramiro Vasquez had never visited Pastor Rudy Alvarez's church, but he had met the man a few times in the village. He had been shocked when he learned of what had happened to the pastor and his family, and even more shocked that he was expected to join the group that had done such a terrible deed.

It seemed Ramiro had no choice in the matter, however, so he dutifully tried to make the best of it, loading the rifle with ammo and awkwardly hoisting the heavy weapon onto his shoulder the way they showed him. Soon he no longer felt like just an inept clod.

He felt like an inept clod with a gun.

Houston, Texas, USA

As Pastor Jeff made his way to the waiting area, he could see that the college students had already assembled there.

Watching them, Jeff felt a rush of pride. He knew he'd been given an exceptional team. These young people had been chosen from dozens of applicants based on their grades, attitudes, and physical acumen.

He'd known Daniel, Kevin, and Jeremy for years, and couldn't have asked for a better group from his own church. He had watched Daniel and Jeremy grow up and develop into fine Christian young men, and he cared about both of them deeply. Kevin had joined ranks with them a couple of years ago, a convert of Daniel's and Jeremy's, and the three were now inseparable. Kevin, with his ready smile and clumsy but sincere efforts to change, had quickly found his way into Jeff's heart as well.

Jeff had agonized over his decision about including Jeremy, and his senior pastor, Robert Davenport, had been no help. Because Jeff was better acquainted with the young people, and since he was the one who would accompany them to Colombia, Pastor Davenport had left the decision in Jeff's hands.

Wanting input from someone else, Jeff had enlisted Pastor Evan Meyer from Pure Grace Fellowship Church to go over the applications with him. They had agreed without question on Daniel and Kevin, but filling the third vacancy was more difficult.

Jeff had explained Jeremy's situation to Pastor Meyer, and after considering a few minutes, Pastor Meyer told Jeff, "If the boy wants to go so badly, maybe God really did put it in his heart."

Meyer held up the paltry stack of remaining applications with a rueful smile. "In light of your other prospects, I say we give Jeremy a chance and trust God to take care of him."

And so Jeremy would be laboring in Colombia beside his two best friends.

Because Pure Grace Fellowship was such a large church, there were dozens of applicants from Pastor Meyer's college group, and Pastor Meyer had requested Jeff's help interviewing the top choices.

After joint interviews with several applicants from Meyer's church, they had settled on Terrell Stevens, Resha Cummings, and the pastor's daughter Mindy.

Pastor Jeff had been the one to recommend Mindy, thinking her first aid experience might come in handy. Pastor Meyer was reluctant. "Mindy is a very sensitive girl. I hate to expose her to such difficult circumstances."

"Letting her experience hardship might toughen her up," suggested Jeff. "Besides, she may already be stronger than you think."

Terrell Stevens was a computer whiz, but that skill wouldn't mean much in a country with no electricity, so his main qualification for this trip was his athletic ability. Active in several sports, Terrell would certainly have the strength and stamina needed for the difficult work ahead of them. Right now, Jeff saw that Terrell was fraternizing with the other three guys as if they were all old friends.

Resha Cummings had seated herself a couple of chairs away and was watching the rest of the group through eyes that were sharp and alert in an otherwise expressionless face. Pastor Meyer had told Jeff she was something of a loner, so he wasn't surprised. But Meyer had also given her a sterling recommendation based on her integrity and willingness to grow as a Christian.

Before her interview, Evan Meyer had told Jeff, "Resha has done an excellent job of separating herself from her old, negative relationships. My concern is that she hasn't developed any new relationships in the church to replace her old ties. Even though she seems to be doing well spiritually, she mostly keeps to herself. I'm hoping that spending time with people her own age who genuinely love the Lord will help her get past her trust issues."

After interviewing the girl, Pastor Jeff had agreed the trip would be good for her, and her disciplined determination would be ideal for the task. Her fluency in Spanish was an added bonus.

In the waiting area, Pastor Meyer's daughter Mindy chattered away to a girl that Jeff assumed was part of the team from Greater Truth Tabernacle, the third church that participated in the rally.

The team from Greater Truth was an unknown quantity as far as Jeff was concerned. Pastor Andrew Domingo had insisted on selecting a group without any input from the other two pastors involved. At least Domingo had faxed them copies of their applications, so Jeff knew the three members from Pastor Domingo's church met all the qualifications, on paper at least.

Still, he would have felt better if their selection had been a joint effort like the others.

He studied the group from Greater Truth. The girl talking to Mindy must be Selena Gutierrez. She and her younger brother Manuel, who went by Manny, came from a well-to-do family in Kingwood, a ritzy area not far from Houston. They seemed to be blending in, talking and laughing with the others.

Samuel Adebayo, a Nigerian several years older than the rest of the group, had deliberately separated himself from everyone. Unlike Resha, who at least stayed near the group, Samuel had moved all the way across the room and turned his back to the rest of the team as he read a magazine.

That disturbed Jeff. They would be spending a lot of time together over the next two weeks, and he'd hoped they could all at least develop a friendly acceptance of each other.

Jeff's enthusiasm from a few moments ago dimmed a bit as he considered the magnitude of the responsibility he'd undertaken. He decided he'd wasted enough time observing his charges. It was time to announce his presence and get them started on the long, difficult journey ahead of them.

He strolled into the waiting area, pretending a confidence he did not feel.

2

Day 1: Sunday

After a four and a half hour flight, the plane touched down at the José María Córdova International Airport in Medellin, the only major airport that had reopened since the flood.

A wave of heat greeted the missionary team, the sticky warmth a sharp contrast to the late November chill they'd left behind in Houston. The Colombian sun was shining brightly and the airport was bustling with people. Cleanup crews had efficiently wiped out all signs of flood damage other than some cracked and buckled asphalt, and dark water stains on the buildings that bleach and sandblasting couldn't quite remove. It was hard to believe that torrential waters had wreaked havoc here only a few short weeks ago.

The group lugged their meager belongings onto a bus that would take them as far north as Montería, in Cordoba. Beyond that, the roads were still too damaged for any commercial venues to risk the travel, so someone from the mission center was to meet Pastor Jeff and his team in Montería.

The bus ride, which normally would have taken less than four hours, was a nonstop, six hour torture session because of the condition of the roads. At last the harrowing journey through the steamy tropical wilderness ended when the bus rattled into a weather-beaten station.

After a brief pit stop, the group went searching for their ride to their next destination, La Vida Nueva Mission Center in Cuenco Verde, which was still another eighty miles away.

"Who are we looking for?" Daniel asked Pastor Jeff.

Jeff gave a wry smile. "I have no idea. They just told me someone from the mission center would pick us up."

"What about those two guys Resha's glaring at?" Jeremy blurted, pointing.

Following Resha's intense gaze, Jeff spotted two Colombian men in work clothes standing idly beside a couple of rusted pickup trucks across the street from the bus station. One of the two men was looking their way hopefully, so Jeff approached them while the rest of the group waited in the shade of several palms next to the station.

The older of the two men, a stocky mustached man in his forties, stepped forward with a friendly smile, twisting his floppy straw hat nervously in his hands. He offered a tentative greeting in Spanish and was visibly relieved when Jeff responded in kind.

The two men shook hands, making it obvious to the young people the two laborers would be their ride to Cuenco Verde. The students joined Jeff, dragging their belongings.

The younger Colombian man greeted the students with a nod, then stood back wearing a vague smile that didn't reach his eyes. He was tall, not quite thirty, and wore nondescript, loose fitting, work-stained clothing. He remained silent, but studied each of the team members closely while pretending to look at the ground.

After a few minutes of discussion, Jeff turned to his group. "Team, this is Luís and Antonio. We're going to ride with them to the mission center, so we'll split up and ride five to a truck. I'll be in this truck with Luís. Daniel, you and your two buddies can ride with us, and, uh...."

Jeff paused, remembering too late that he'd intended to mix up the groups so they could get acquainted. It was so natural to see the three friends together that he'd grouped them automatically, and now he was faced with the option of changing his instructions or choosing one person from the other groups to ride with them.

Resha solved his dilemma. Without a word, the stone-faced girl hauled herself onto the bed of Luís' truck and plunked herself down in the corner.

Relieved that the issue was settled, Jeff shrugged and climbed into the passenger seat beside the friendly, heavyset man while the boys joined Resha in the back.

The other five clambered into Antonio's truck, with Manny riding shotgun. That was a good arrangement, Jeff decided, since Manny probably spoke enough Spanish to communicate with the driver if necessary.

While Resha had been glad to bail out Pastor Jeff by jumping in the truck, her main motivation was to get away from Mindy's incessant chatter. The redhead's voice reminded Resha of a mother cooing at her toddler after a successful potty training session.

The three guys had tried at first to include her in their conversation, but Resha refused to be drawn in, preferring to learn what she could by listening to their banter. She pretended to study the verdant landscape while she surreptitiously scoped out the men who would be her co-laborers for the next two weeks.

Jeremy was too thin, but full of life, with dark eyes that sparkled and took in every detail. His sharp nose was longer than it needed to be for his face, but he'd probably grow into it. A simple silver stud in his left ear peeked through his unkempt curls when the wind blew.

He kept the others laughing with his ridiculous observations, but Resha suspected there was more to him than his clowning indicated. He looked familiar to her, but she couldn't place him.

Kevin was quieter than Jeremy, but he held his own with the smart remarks. In spite of his ghetto lingo, Resha wished he would talk more because she liked his deep voice. He would have been cute if it wasn't for that awful hair. The twists and the ghetto talk must be some skewed attempt to prove his identity or something – he couldn't possibly think they were attractive.

She remembered the tall blond one from the rally. Although Daniel was slim, his build gave testimony to regular workouts, but he didn't try to show it off the way most guys did. He seemed a couple of years older than the other two, who seemed fresh out of high school. He was more serious than his buddies and was often the target of Jeremy's affectionate teasing. The three were obviously close.

Laughing at something Jeremy had said, Daniel glanced her way to share his enjoyment and caught her looking at him. His smile turned awkward and he turned away quickly, blushing.

A college guy who could still blush. Amazing.

Done with her assessment of her three seatmates, Resha turned her attention to the two men conversing in the cab of the battered pickup.

The farther they got from the airport, the worse shape the roads were in. The bumpy road, combined with the lack of suspension in the old truck, made it too difficult to keep up a conversation with his friends any longer, so instead Daniel tried to focus on the discussion that Jeff and Luís were having.

He could hear them well enough because the back window of the truck had been broken out, but his Spanish was too patchy to follow the rapid fire dialogue. It was easy to see that Pastor Jeff was getting agitated, though, and he wondered what was disturbing his normally easygoing pastor.

Across from him, Resha watched the passing scenery, but Daniel suspected the small, sullen girl was also listening to the two men.

As the two trucks passed through Sincelejo, the capital of Sucre, the students could see that the city was making a slow recovery. Groups of repairmen worked on the power lines, operating out of trucks that looked remarkably like their American counterparts. A few antiquated mini-buses were making their rounds through the water-blighted streets, but they were practically empty of passengers, as few businesses had been able to reopen yet.

Once they got past the city, they saw fewer people with each passing mile. The aftereffects of widespread flooding were more evident in the low-lying rural zones, and Luís' and Antonio had to leave the damaged road several times because the water was still deep in some parts. They drove off the scarred pavement and forced the trucks through the mud wherever the ground looked highest, and Daniel gnawed his lip, hoping the tires wouldn't get stuck.

Two uprooted trees blocked the road at one point, their exposed roots jutting higher than the roofs of the trucks. As Luís and Antonio maneuvered around them, Daniel marveled at the power the raging currents must have carried to inflict such damage.

There were a few structures still standing, though uninhabitable, with doors and windows washed away. Several of the small homes had been swept clean off their foundations and now perched haphazardly wherever the capricious tide had carried them.

At some of the dwellings, people searched through the wreckage to salvage whatever they could. Several men were working together to pull down the useless framework of one wrecked house, probably hoping to reuse some of the building materials. A little girl sat on a moldy pile of adobe bricks, all that was left of the home she had lived in. She cuddled a mud-caked doll while a skeletal dog sat listlessly at her feet and her parents sifted through the sodden rubble for whatever remained of their previous life. No one looked up as the trucks rattled past.

Soon even these small signs of hope and life evaporated as they entered the area that had been hit the worst, and the unearthly silence was broken only by the sound of their own vehicles.

None of them spoke as they took in the remains of splintered homes, the sodden clothing and belongings strewn about in the mud, the abandoned and sometimes upturned vehicles. Waterlogged mattresses and furniture lay in fermenting puddles. There were pieces of clothing and other debris clinging to tree branches, an indication that the water had even reached the treetops at some point.

Slimy mud clung to everything, and a putrid stench hung in the air. Some areas were still under water, with rusting roofs of ruined vehicles peeking above the fetid surface of the brackish pools. The only evidence of life was an occasional swarm of insects.

An air of desolation hung over the area, its tentacles wrapping Daniel with a feeling of hopelessness as he took in the disheartening sights. His friends' long faces indicated they felt it, too.

Once, Mindy became excited and pointed at a group of people moving about in the distance.

But the team's relief at seeing human life turned to dismay as the people's purpose became obvious.

They were shoveling dirt onto what appeared to be a makeshift grave, hastily dug on the only patch of high ground to lay another victim of the flood to rest. All around the little circle of mourners, Daniel could see more fresh mounds of dirt adorned with makeshift wooden crosses.

He watched despondently as the trucks went past, realizing that the grisly task of recovering bodies had still not been completed, even though it had been weeks since the disaster.

Pastor Jeff had shown them a slide show with images from the devastation to prepare them for what they would encounter, but pictures couldn't convey the enormity of the catastrophe or the depressing atmosphere of oppression and abandonment.

The trucks rolled over a weather-beaten bridge and Daniel hoped it wouldn't collapse under the weight of the trucks, sending them all into the swollen, angry river beneath them. Beyond the bridge, the road began a gradual uphill climb.

The Americans all breathed a sigh of relief when the mission center came into view as the sunlight was starting to dim. Compared to the devastation they had just witnessed, La Vida Nueva Mission Center rose up like an oasis in the midst of the ruins.

Daniel knew a few people had been working nonstop to restore the compound, and although it was obviously still in disrepair, much of the debris had been carted off and stacked several yards away, and pools of standing water had been filled in with dirt to discourage mosquitos. He could hear the hum of a large generator, and a lone man with a black ponytail was pushing a wheelbarrow toward the back of the compound, creating a sense of normalcy.

The images he had just seen would not be easily erased, however, and as they disembarked from the trucks, everyone was subdued. Even irrepressible Jeremy was uncharacteristically silent, and Mindy had tears streaming down her cheeks.

Hearing the rumble of heavy vehicles approaching, Captain Ortega stood up in his jeep and tensed in anticipation. He glanced behind him to make sure the drivers of two other jeeps that accompanied him were alert and waiting for his command. Each jeep held three men armed with automatic weapons, but Ortega preferred to carry a pistol. Satisfied that his men were prepared for action, El Tiburon turned back to his vigil.

"Get ready," he barked into his walkie talkie, peering between the trees that his jeep was hidden behind.

Looking into the clearing, he could now see the two trucks from the Mexican Red Cross lumbering in their direction, heavy canvas covering their cargo of food, medicines, and building materials. He had deliberately chosen a stretch of the dirt road that was wider, with enough space on either side for him to carry out his plans.

In response to Ortega's order, the black Dodge Ram half a mile down the road started its engine. Three men accompanied the driver of the Dodge, each of them armed with an M4A1 assault rifle.

As the relief organization's trucks passed Ortega's hiding place, he signaled to the men who were with him and called another order to his comrades in the pickup. When the Red Cross trucks were several yards away, Ortega's jeeps fell in behind them, remaining a discreet distance back for now.

As soon as the black pickup shot from behind a row of trees to park sideways across the road in front of the first vehicle, Ortega and his men pulled the jeep alongside the lead cargo truck, while the other two jeeps came in on either side of the truck in the back.

Both truck drivers braked to a stop, staring in stupefied silence at the commandos who had accosted them. Several soldiers jumped out of the jeeps and yanked open the doors of the trucks.

"Get out of the trucks!" Ortega yelled, waving his gun.

The driver of the lead truck was a rugged looking Mexican man in his thirties. His younger passenger wore a slick black goatee that did nothing to make him look older. Both clambered out of the truck with their hands held high.

The older one murmured reassuringly to the young one, "It will be okay, Oscar. Just do what they tell you."

"Shut up!" Ortega screamed, and the man complied.

The second truck had been driven by a chunky, middle aged Caucasian man in a baseball cap and a polo shirt with the name "Andy" embroidered over the pocket. Andy's mouth hung open as he struggled to haul his bulk out of the driver's seat.

Ortega had no patience.

"Hurry up, *estúpido!*" he yelled, cocking his pistol. The man practically fell out onto the ground in his rush to comply.

Two of the soldiers motioned for the three volunteers to stand together to one side of the trucks while the other commandos began cutting and ripping the canvas off the trucks to expose the crates of supplies.

"*Por favor, Señores*, we are volunteers, and we are trying to deliver goods to help your people," the lead driver pleaded, still keeping his hands up.

"Shut up!" Ortega yelled again, striking the man sharply on the head with the butt of his pistol. "Do you think we are stupid? We know who you are and we know where you are going."

The man staggered back from the blow, and would have fallen to the ground if the overweight volunteer had not steadied him.

"You okay, Pablo?" he asked, and Pablo managed to nod.

The one they'd called Oscar looked near tears as he begged, "Please don't shoot us."

Reveling in the fear he was causing, Ortega stepped right up to the dark skinned young man and placed the barrel against his forehead.

Like his namesake, El Tiburon had a habit of circling his prey before the kill. Not only did he enjoy toying with his enemies, he had learned that sometimes patience paid off with useful information. Today, he tormented his victims for the mere satisfaction of it.

He could see sweat pouring down the kid's face. Just to get a reaction, Ortega cocked the pistol again.

The young man slammed his eyes shut when he heard the click, and the fat one shakily said, "Here, here, now, there's no need for that."

While Ortega entertained himself with the captives, his men had uncovered the trucks' cargo. One of the men called out something to Ortega in Spanish, momentarily distracting him from his game of instilling fear in his hostages. Then Ortega turned his attention back to the three volunteers.

"Give me the keys," he demanded, holding out his hand.

With reluctance, Andy and Pablo handed over bulky key rings, which Ortega tossed to the soldier.

Pablo, still holding his head where he'd been struck, tried again. "*Señor, por favor*, these are donations that were sent to help the Colombian people."

"We are Colombians," Ortega sneered. "So do not worry, your generous donations are reaching their intended recipients."

Ortega's men started the trucks and began to pull away, the jeeps falling into formation beside them. One of the jeeps approached and Ortega climbed into it.

Andy finally closed his mouth, then opened it again as realization hit him. "Wait a minute! You can't just leave us out here with no way to get back!"

From his seat in the jeep, Ortega pointed the gun at him again.

"You are right. That would be cruel."

After talking with Luís in the truck, and seeing the shell-shocked faces of the students, Jeff questioned the wisdom of bringing the inexperienced young people here for such an overwhelming task. It was his responsibility to keep them on track, though, so he pushed aside his doubts.

He briskly herded his travel-weary team toward the front steps of what he assumed was the main building, since it was the largest one of several in the compound. The wooden cross atop the single story stucco building was another clue. Judging from the blackish water stains that climbed a third of the way up the outside walls, the building had been partially under water but seemed dry now.

A man with a slight build and a thick mustache hurried down the steps to greet them, all smiles. His energetic movements made him seem charged with electricity.

Walking behind him at a more sedate pace was an attractive, slender woman in her late twenties, wearing a simple light blue T-shirt and jeans. Her hair hung loose around her shoulders and her wide mouth yielded a pleasant smile.

The woman was accompanied by a young boy of nine or ten who was all agog with excitement as he peered at the Americans. The family resemblance was impossible to miss, although the pastor's hair was coal black and the other two had a faint reddish tint to their dark hair.

"Welcome, welcome," the man said to them in heavily accented but grammatically flawless English. He greeted Jeff with an enthusiastic hug, as if they were old friends. "You are Pastor Jeff, *verdad?* I am Sergio Restrepo, the pastor of La Vida Nueva Mission Center."

Pastor Restrepo rapidly shook each of their hands in turn, not giving any of them a chance to introduce themselves. He threw an arm around the woman and the boy who were with him and pulled them against him, causing the woman to gasp in surprise and the boy to squirm. "This is my sister Paola, and my younger brother Matéo. Please, come inside so you can refresh yourselves from your journey."

The energetic little man turned and bounced into the sanctuary, pulling his siblings along with him. Bemused, Jeff and his charges followed, dragging their belongings behind them as Luís held the door open for them. They were greeted by the strong smell of bleach and pine cleaner, which could not quite mask the stubborn undercurrent of mildew.

The inside of the building showed more evidence of the recent flooding. Chunks of soggy plaster were piled in one corner, some of it dissolving into a sticky gray powder, and bare bamboo studs were exposed where someone had started to remove the ruined material. The wooden floor showed dark, uneven stains where carpet had been ripped out. Most of the wooden pews had been removed, and Pastor Restrepo had put out an assortment of mismatched folding chairs to accommodate his absent congregation.

The only part of the sanctuary that appeared untouched by the flood was the wooden cross hanging front and center. The cross was plain in design, just two boards nailed together, but it had been lovingly sanded and polished until it seemed to glow in the dim sanctuary, which was currently lit only by a single light bulb hanging from the ceiling and attached to a long extension cord.

The pastor walked rapidly to the front of the sanctuary, then hopped up onto the small raised platform, which was empty except for a lopsided wooden lectern and a piano that had been shoved against the wall. He whirled around to face his guests again.

"Sit, sit," invited Pastor Sergio, waving both arms in a downward motion. Dizzied by Sergio's constant movement, the team obeyed, arranging themselves in the rusted chairs.

Luís whispered a few words in Sergio's ear before going back outside. Sergio frowned in consternation. He turned to the team with a sober face. "Pastor Jeff, Luís has asked me to apologize for him because he did not warn you and your team that we would be driving through the more heavily damaged area. You see, we have become accustomed to the sights now, and he did not consider how it would affect you. *Lo siento*."

Jeff acknowledged the unnecessary apology with a dip of his head, but Mindy still seemed disturbed by the desolation she had seen.

She asked, "It's been over a month since the flood. Why hasn't the government done something?"

"Cuenco Verde is only a small farming community, and has never brought in much income. The Colombian government is concentrating on the more important cities such as Medellin and Bogota, and of course Sincelejo, which is our capital here in Sucre," Sergio explained with no trace of resentment. "These cities normally attract tourists, so it is important for our country's economy that they be restored as quickly as possible."

"What about the U.S. government?" Mindy persisted. "Why aren't they helping?"

"Many other countries, including your own, have been wonderful, sending people and supplies to help the Colombian people. But until recently, the nearest landing strip that was able to open was in Medellin, and the roads have been impassable, so there has been no way to get supplies to many of the outlying areas such as this one."

Pastor Sergio smiled broadly now as he continued speaking in his rapid fire fashion. "I do have some good news. Some missionary friends have been delivering a few food supplies to us by helicopter, and we have been able to share with those who come by looking for help. Also, since more roads are open now, Luís and Antonio were able to pick up some supplies and two generators that were provided by a shelter *La Cruz Roja* has set up in Sincelejo. So your visit will be more pleasant than first expected."

The little man paced back and forth on the six-inch high platform while he spoke, his frenetic movements causing Jeff to feel like he was watching a ping pong game.

"To save fuel, we only use the generators at night, but we are able to operate a few lights and a radio to contact the outside world. The second generator is being used to power our water pump, so you will have some running water. The holding tank is large, but when it runs out, we have no water until we run the generator again the next day, so please use it sparingly. It is not for drinking, only for bathing and washing clothes. For drinking, we have a tank filled with purified water in the kitchen."

Thankfully, his discourse was interrupted when a short, sturdy older woman with salt and pepper hair worn in a long, thick braid appeared from the back, giving Jeff and his crew a few seconds to digest some of the information the pastor had just dumped on them.

The woman, who appeared to be in her seventies, wore a wide, faded, flowered dress that reached her ankles. A ragged shawl was draped over her shoulders, even in the heat. She carried a tray loaded with glasses of something that looked like tea. The wooden tray had to be heavy, but the old woman did not bend under its weight.

"Ah, Abuelita, *muchas gracias*." Sergio took the tray from her.

She nodded and gave the newcomers a shy, toothless smile. Sergio began walking among his guests, handing out glasses to each of them.

"You must try some *aguapanela*, one of our favorite drinks here in Colombia. It is made from sugar cane and a little lime. Drink, drink, it will refresh you from your journey."

The old woman left in silence, and Mindy stared after her with a delighted smile. After she accepted her glass from Pastor Sergio, Mindy thanked him, then asked, "What is her name?"

"We do not know. She does not speak," Pastor Sergio explained, shaking his head sadly. Immediately, his face cracked open with another big smile. "We call her '*Abuelita*', which is a respectful word for 'Little Grandmother.' We believe she was left homeless by the flood, and she has been living here with us until we can locate her family. We have set up a bed for her in the kitchen here in the main building. She has been a great blessing, working tirelessly to stretch our meager food supplies to feed us a hot meal every night. Of course, now we will be able to obtain supplies more readily since the airfield has been opened, so her job will be easier."

As Pastor Sergio talked, he made extravagant gestures with his arms, causing the tray to tilt precariously. Paola discreetly took the tray from her brother and took over the task of passing out the tall, icy glasses.

The diminutive pastor did not seem to notice her intervention – he kept up his enthusiastic monologue without pausing. "You have already met Antonio and Luís, our drivers. Antonio also lost everything in the flood and came to us seeking shelter. His hard work here has been an incredible blessing to us. Luís has been faithful to our ministry here for many years. He has family near Cordoba, but he is staying to help us rebuild."

As he tried to absorb all the information Sergio was pouring on them, Jeff took a tentative sip of his drink. He flinched a bit at the overpowering sweetness of it, but the drink was cool and refreshing after the long drive in the unairconditioned truck.

"The only one you have not met is Stefan," Sergio continued. "He has been with me here for just a few months, but he is a tremendous helper. I believe he is working in the other building right now and did not notice your arrival. You will meet him soon. He has a fascinating testimony of how Christ has changed his life."

Behind Sergio, Paola's eyes lit up at the mention of Stefan.

Mindy must have noticed, too, because she smiled at the pastor's pretty sister. Her question was directed at Sergio, though. "Do you have a family, Pastor Restrepo?"

A shadow fell over the pastor's face, but only for a moment. "My wife and our two sons were visiting her parents in Caltera when the floods came. There was no warning, no time to prepare. Their bodies were never recovered."

The news reports had described how the storm surge had engulfed the shoreline of the small coastal town, sweeping houses and people out to sea, but Jeff hadn't realized his host had been affected. Mindy gasped out loud and everyone else looked dismayed.

Sergio did not allow the team to dwell on his loss. With an effort, the little man brightened again. "I miss them, but I know they are with our Heavenly Father and I will join them some day. For now, I have been blessed to have Paola and Matéo here to help me. They are staying here because our mother's home in El Cerrito was destroyed."

After his previous revelation, no one dared ask about his mother. Sergio answered the unspoken question for them. "Our mother is safe; she is staying with her sister in Montería for now. Paola and Matéo came to me because they wanted to help. The work the Lord is doing here is important to them.

"As you have probably seen, there is much that needs to be done before we can open the mission center again," Sergio continued briskly, taking their focus away from the gloomy news he had just delivered about his wife and children. "But our work will wait for tomorrow. Pastor Jeff, you will of course accept the hospitality of my family and stay in my home with us. It has been cleaned after the flooding and is quite comfortable. Come, come, let me show you where the rest of you will be sleeping."

He walked abruptly out of the room, gesturing with his arm for them to follow him down the same hallway Abuelita had come from.

Jeff and the others looked around in momentary confusion, wondering what to do with their half finished drinks. Paola smiled, a rock of stability in the wake of her brother's erratic behavior. She began collecting the glasses from them as they quickly filed out the door to catch up with Sergio.

"The back of the building has less damage, so we have set aside a room for the ladies here," Pastor Sergio explained. "It is a small room, but there are only three of you. See, it is all set up, and there is a full bathroom nearby, at the end of that hall. The cots were provided by the Red Cross also, with the understanding that they will be used later on to accommodate some of the people from the area whose homes were destroyed, and possibly work crews from a volunteer organization once our own repairs are completed."

The pastor flung open a door, allowing them to peek into a plain 12' x 12' room. Three cots with mosquito nets draped over them were the only furniture. The flooring had been ripped to reveal a water-stained wooden floor but other than that and a faint lingering damp odor, the room seemed fine. Someone had nailed a gilt-framed mirror to one wall and a small fan stood on the floor at the entrance, plugged into a long extension cord that meandered down the hall to points unknown.

An open window at the back of the room allowed in a glimmer of fading sunlight and fresh air to dispel some of the moldy smell. A faded sheet had been nailed across the top of the window to serve as a curtain, but it was held to the side with a clothespin. There was a door next to the window, and Pastor Sergio led them through it now.

The door opened into a storm-battered courtyard. The flood waters had loosened the paving stones, and many of them were cracked, jutting up at awkward angles. Near the back edge of the courtyard stood what must have been a fountain at one time; it was now a pile of broken concrete, the casualty of some heavy debris carried by the rushing flood waters.

Sergio nimbly navigated the uneven stones as he took them across the courtyard to a smaller stucco building with a wavy red roof. The building appeared to have been built at the same time as the sanctuary they had just exited, since it matched in style and material. A crude wooden bench sat outside the arched doorway.

"This was our Sunday School building where we taught the children," Sergio explained with a hint of pride. "For now, it will serve as a dormitory for the men. When your group leaves, the classroom will provide more temporary shelter for families to stay while their homes are being rebuilt."

A rusted metal desk and several brightly colored plastic chairs had been pushed to the back corner at the right side of the large room. The arrangement allowed room for the six cots that were lined up in a neat row with about four feet of space between each of them.

"I am sorry there were not enough mosquito nets for the men." The pastor hung his head as if the situation was a great tragedy. His exuberance returned at once and he marched to the left rear corner of the room to tug open a narrow wooden door, revealing a rust-stained toilet and sink nestled in a closet-sized space.

"The outside plumbing was ruined, but Stefan has been working hard and has connected everything in your building to the water supply. This is only a half bath, so the men will have to make arrangements to shower in the main building. Again, please remember to use the water sparingly."

Back outside, the Colombian pastor indicated a small, square cinder block structure that stood a few feet behind the building the men would be using. "That is our storage shed where the workmen keep most of their tools."

Now Sergio turned and bounced back toward the main building they had originally come from. He pointed out two rectangular buildings nestled between some trees in the back of the compound.

Newer in design than the sanctuary, the wooden frame buildings had probably been added later to accommodate the growing needs of the mission center. Both structures had suffered in the recent disaster – the faded gray paint was peeling and the windows, swollen from the moisture, were ill-fitting.

The building on the right, farthest from the sanctuary, had obviously been hit the worst by the flood. Thick green fuzz covered the sagging steps, and some boards near the bottom had been washed away. Black mold crawled up the side and the roof had almost caved in over the rear part of the building.

"There is an arroyo there, beyond those trees, and it overflowed. The larger building was used as a classroom for adults, and it can be repaired. The smaller one was used to store the food and clothing we gave out to the community. It was partially under water for several days, and all the supplies were ruined. That building will have to be torn down, and we will build another one to take its place. Our three workmen sleep in the classroom building for now."

By the time they returned to the main sanctuary, the team was trudging, their sluggish movements a stark contrast to Sergio's peppy stride. Although the time difference between Houston and Colombia was minor, their activities had taken a toll on them.

They had flown over two thousand miles from Houston to Medellin, endured a punishing six hour bus ride, then traveled another eighty miles in trucks with no air conditioning and no shock absorbers. The *aguapanela* had perked them up some, but the sugar rush was wearing off.

Pastor Sergio obviously wanted to continue the tour, but he must have noticed their glazed expressions, because he took pity on them.

"Of course, you will all want to get settled into your rooms. You have two hours to rest before Abuelita serves the evening meal, so please make yourselves comfortable. Tomorrow we will discuss the work you will be doing."

With a collective sigh of relief, the students gathered their belongings and made their way to their assigned areas, where they plopped onto their cots in exhaustion, duffel bags and backpacks strewn about the floor and forgotten for the time being. Jeff followed his host out to the small house that stood several yards behind the mission compound.

Refreshed from a short nap, Daniel joined his friends exploring the rest of the sanctuary before they gathered for the meal they had been promised.

Across the hall from the room the girls had been assigned to, a door led into the dining area, which was currently furnished with three rickety folding tables and more of the rusted chairs. A long counter separated the dining room from the kitchen. Between the chipped white stove and rusted refrigerator was a door leading outside to a carport in back of the main building.

Kevin and Jeremy looked delighted when Mindy and Selena squeezed between them to peer over the counter into the kitchen. Daniel shook his head at his friends' sappy smiles.

The third girl brushed right past them with no interest. Mindy called after her, "Resha, don't you want to come look?"

"It's a kitchen." Resha's flat tone conveyed total indifference. Kevin and Jeremy snickered.

"It's a Colombian kitchen," Mindy coaxed.

Resha didn't bother to respond as she made her way to the middle table, sitting at the far end.

Mindy hurried after her, choosing the chair next to Resha, and Selena settled beside Mindy.

True to form, Jeremy made a beeline for the three girls and parked himself directly across from them. Kevin and Daniel followed to sit on either side of him. Terrell dragged a chair from another table and pulled it up so he could join them, although he made a point of seating himself at the end farthest from Resha.

The two pastors occupied the table in front, and Samuel settled at the end of their table. When Manny came in several minutes later, rubbing the sleep from his eyes, he looked around, then plunked himself at the last table with the three laborers, since it was closest to him.

Paola and Abuelita served them a light supper of soup and something Sergio called an *arepa de huevo*, a gritty bread made out of corn flour and filled with scrambled eggs.

After eating the light meal, the group milled around in the sanctuary, where Pastor Jeff had told them they would have a short meeting before retiring for the evening. The two pastors had stepped into Sergio's office, which was nestled in one corner of the sanctuary.

That was half an hour ago. Still tired from the journey, Daniel slumped in his chair at one end of the front row. He looked around listlessly at the others as they waited.

Mindy and Selena huddled together at the other end of the front row, chattering about some TV show they were going to be missing while in Colombia. Terrell sat behind them, listening with a superior smirk on his face and inserting an occasional wisecrack.

Samuel sat alone in a corner working a crossword puzzle, his hostile expression warding off any attempts to approach him. Manny was stretched out across several chairs in the back row, sleeping.

Daniel felt sober as he listened to the low murmuring from the room the two pastors had shut themselves in. Pastor Jeff wouldn't keep them waiting like this unless it was something serious.

Beside him, Jeremy didn't seem at all concerned. He bobbed his head to music only he could hear, drumming out a rhythm with his thumbs on the back of the chair he was straddling.

Kevin cocked a worried eyebrow toward the closed door. "What you think they talkin' about?"

Daniel shrugged morosely.

Jeremy stopped drumming his chair and announced in an earnest voice, "They're talking about the gestational habits of miniature gerbils."

Kevin and Daniel both turned to him, staring at him as if he'd grown another head.

"Really. Scouts honor." Jeremy stood up with his right hand raised in front of him in the sign of sincerity. The only problem was, his fingers were crossed. Jeremy looked down at his own hand, acted surprised and quickly put it behind his back, fingers still crossed. He raised the other hand in front instead.

There was an unladylike snort from behind them and the three friends turned in surprise to find Resha sitting two rows back, smothering a laugh.

With three sets of eyes staring at her, she gave in and guffawed. "Sorry, must be jet lag, because that was nowhere near funny."

All three of them laughed with her then, more from the shock of seeing mirth from the sullen girl than from the humor of her comment.

Resha sobered quickly. "They're probably talking about the same thing Pastor Jeff was talking to Luís about on the ride here."

Remembering the tense discussion he had witnessed in the truck, Daniel was instantly intrigued. He and his two friends clambered over the row of chairs separating them from Resha and arranged themselves on the chairs in front of her.

"What were they talking about?" Daniel wanted to know.

Resha narrowed her eyes at him. "You should know. You were listening, too."

"I was trying to listen," Daniel admitted, embarrassed that she'd noticed him eavesdropping, "but I didn't understand much. My Spanish is pretty basic, and they were talking too fast for me to follow."

Resha acknowledged his explanation with a short nod, then lowered her voice so the other students wouldn't hear. The three friends leaned in closer to listen. "They were talking about some paramilitant group that's been causing problems around here."

Daniel had read a little about the drug trafficking factions that terrorized parts of Colombia, but he hadn't thought they were active in the area they were visiting. He asked, "You mean F.A.R.C.?"

"No, but it sounded like the same kind of thing. They call themselves *Las Águilas Negras*, the Black Eagles." Resha snorted in derision. "Cute, huh? Loser drug dealers, just like back home in Houston, except these guys wear soldier clothes instead of gang colors."

"What's all that got to do wit' Pastor Jeff?" Kevin asked.

Resha shrugged, as if what she was about to say was no big deal. "Your pastor was upset because Luís told him the Black Eagles just sent some kind of message to the mission center."

The three friends looked at each other. That sounded ominous.

"Pastor Jeff, I have no desire to put you or your people at risk. We only learned of the danger yesterday, and by then it was too late to contact you." Pastor Sergio's eyes were sincere and full of concern.

Jeff tried to quell his frustration with the situation. He knew the young Colombian pastor would never have knowingly allowed them to be placed in danger. "Exactly how serious is the threat?"

Pastor Sergio pulled a crumpled piece of paper from a drawer in the rusted desk. "It is not exactly a threat. At least it is not worded as such. But now that Las Águilas Negras have made contact, it is evident that they want to use this mission center for themselves."

Jeff studied the piece of paper, which was inscribed at the top with a crude line drawing of an eagle and a cross. His limited skills of interpretation gave him an idea of what the letter said. He looked up at Pastor Sergio in confusion.

"They are offering you assistance?"

"It is more like a bribe." Sergio's smile was tight. "They might supply materials that they have confiscated from the relief efforts in other areas, and provide forced labor to speed up the repairs, but that assistance would come with a price. In exchange for their help in rebuilding Cuenco Verde, they would expect us to cooperate with them."

"Cooperate how?"

Sergio sighed. "The Black Eagles are drug traffickers. They would force the local people to grow their coca crops, and they would use our mission center as a cover for smuggling cocaine out of the country. I am sure that they would use our buildings to process and store their 'product,' and to house their people whenever they wanted lodging."

Sergio's eyes met Jeff's, his voice passionate. "We could never allow that to happen. This mission center is dedicated to God's service. We cannot compromise the gospel in that way."

Jeff understood Sergio's dilemma. For him to agree to their requests would keep his people safe, maybe even provide financial stability for them, but at the price of their own souls. "What happens if you don't cooperate?"

Sergio's jaw tightened and he lowered his eyes, but not before Jeff had seen the anger in them. "The Black Eagles have murdered several pastors who would not cooperate, and even some of their congregations."

"They're singling out Christians?"

"No, they are targeting anyone who resists their efforts. Christians offer the most resistance; that is why we are so often victims to the Black Eagles."

Pastor Sergio hesitated, and Jeff could tell there was more Sergio hadn't told him. He waited.

Finally, Sergio admitted, "Pastor Jeff, it is only right to let you know that already they are putting pressure on us. A Mexican charity group was scheduled to deliver some supplies for us, but they did not arrive. I just received word that the trucks are missing and the bodies of the drivers were discovered on the side of the road a short time ago. They had been shot."

Sergio's expression reflected his anguish that people had died on their way to bring help to him.

Jeff was also saddened at the loss of life, and the information added to his urgency to remove his team from the area. He saw an opportunity to exit gracefully. "Does that mean our arrival here will put a greater strain on your food supply? We don't want to exhaust your resources."

As quickly as Sergio's face had clouded over, the sun came out again and he smiled. "God is our source, not The Red Cross. He has made other arrangements for us to have food and supplies delivered. But I needed to make you aware that the threat is serious."

Jeff was quiet now, allowing the news to sink in. If he had known about the risk, he would never have brought these students here. But they were here now, at great personal expense to them and to the church. Leaving now would mean all the time and paperwork and money invested would have been for nothing.

And what message would that send to the young people right after the church had presented a three day conference about the importance of doing God's work? Still, how could he possibly risk their lives by keeping them in such a potentially dangerous situation? He massaged his forehead, trying to ward off the headache he knew was coming.

Sergio frowned with a mixture of guilt and concern. "Pastor Jeff, you must do what you feel is right. We will understand if you cannot stay, but if you choose to remain, I believe that our Father will guide and protect us. May I make a suggestion?"

Jeff looked at him hopefully, willing to hear anything that might make his decision more clear.

"Why do you not ask your young people to help you make the decision?"

At last the two pastors left the small office to rejoin the students in the sanctuary. Jeff felt like he'd just eaten something unpleasant.

All conversation ended abruptly and the students gathered closer to the front as Pastor Jeff walked to the water-stained wooden podium at the front of the room. He cleared his throat, stalling as he looked at the young people who waited expectantly for him to speak.

The girls sat on the front row, while the three from his church, along with Manny and Terrell, had settled in the row directly behind them. Samuel remained alone on the back row, but he had folded up his crossword magazine and set it aside to listen.

"I'm afraid I got some disturbing news this afternoon on the ride here, and I wanted to verify it with Pastor Sergio before I mentioned it to you all," Jeff began. "Unfortunately, Pastor Sergio confirmed what I learned, and, well, I guess you all have a right to know what's going on."

Jeff paused, looking for words that would convey the gravity of the situation without causing them to panic. The students were shifting impatiently, so he hurried to satisfy their curiosity.

"Today I learned that Pastor Sergio and his mission center have been targeted by a...terrorist group, for lack of a better term. There is the possibility that we could be in great danger if we stay as planned."

"What kind of danger?" Terrell asked suspiciously.

Jeff explained what Sergio had told him. The team was silent, absorbing the news, and they waited for him to continue. "The bottom line is, I think the wisest thing would be to cancel this project and make arrangements to fly you all back to the U.S. right away. But I want to make sure you're all okay with that plan."

"I'm not," Jeremy declared. Several of the others murmured in agreement.

Surprised at their immediate reaction, Pastor Jeff frowned in puzzlement. "Look, we don't know what this group is planning, but we do know that people have already been murdered in connection with the mission center here. The danger is real."

"We knew this trip could be dangerous when we signed up," Daniel pointed out.

"Yeah, that's why we all signed a waiver, so we can't sue the church if something goes wrong," Jeremy reminded Jeff flippantly.

Jeff stared at Jeremy over his glasses, wondering if any of them recognized the seriousness of what he'd told them. "There's a difference between the danger of being exposed to malaria or work related injuries and the danger of being attacked by armed terrorists who have no qualms about killing people."

Daniel chewed his lip. "Pastor Jeff, we all prayed over this trip for a month, we're already here, we're ready to work, and these people are counting on us. I think we ought to stay here."

Jeremy nodded his agreement. "That's right. What kind of Christians are we if we wimp out at the first sign of trouble? Like the man said, we already prayed about us being here. Either God heard us or He didn't."

"I think God would'a warned one of the pastors before we wasted all that money on the plane tickets if we wasn't s'posed to come," Kevin pointed out.

"If we leave now, we're letting the enemy scare us off." Resha's emphasis on the word "enemy" made it clear she wasn't referring to The Black Eagles. "I say we stay and trust God to protect us."

Mindy looked up at Jeff with her big gray eyes. "These poor people need our help more than ever now."

Samuel, Terrell, and Selena didn't look as convinced as the others, but they didn't object to staying. Manny was asleep again, so he didn't offer an opinion.

Although Jeff was still leery of the dangerous situation, he felt proud that his little group was willing to stay the course. He glanced at Pastor Sergio, who was beaming from ear to ear at the young people's dedication. Jeff decided to honor their insistence on remaining at the mission center.

"Okay, okay, we'll stay here and do the work as planned," he conceded, fully expecting a cheer from the team. He wasn't disappointed. "Now let's go over the ground rules."

The cheer quickly gave way to a collective groan, but it was a good-natured groan. Jeff let them have their little fun, then prepared to spell out some basic expectations.

Looking more like a panther on the prowl than a common laborer, Antonio crept along the shadows beside the damaged storeroom, carefully feeling his way in the dark. He reached under the building and pulled out an object that had been wrapped in a tarp and tucked out of sight behind some discarded lumber.

Moving swiftly, he uncovered the communication radio, which was powered by a car battery. He crouched beside the radio and keyed up the mike, keeping a wary eye over his shoulder.

"The Americans have arrived," he said without preamble as soon as the other side responded. "They know of your 'interest' in the mission center and have decided to be heroes and stay to complete the work anyway."

El Tiburon made a disgusted sound. "I had hoped they would be scared off. We cannot clear out the pastor and his family with the gringos there, because there would be an outcry from their government."

"I do not understand why we did not just get rid of Pastor Sergio and his people as soon as we found out that traitor Stefan Guzman was here,"

Antonio grumbled. "I was ready to do it as soon as you decided to take the mission center for yourself."

"You are too impatient, too trigger-happy," Captain Ortega snarled. "I only put up with it because you are one of my most skilled and loyal men, but do not question my judgment."

Remembering the fate of the last man who'd dared to argue with Ortega, Antonio adopted a conciliatory tone. "I am only concerned because now your plans are delayed."

"We will take care of Guzman when the time is right, but I wanted to give Sergio a chance. It is always best when they cooperate," Ortega explained, still sounding impatient. "If they cooperate, there are no bodies to dispose of, and we have free labor. How many gringos are there?"

"Ten of them, but they are no threat to us." Antonio spoke with contempt. "One of them is a pastor, and the others are all young and stupid, with stars in their eyes. They think they will change the world with their good deeds."

There was a pause while the captain considered the situation. "Maybe we can use their 'good deeds' to our advantage."

Antonio frowned in the darkness. "How?"

"We'll let them do all the work for us." Ortega laughed maliciously. "We wait until the repairs are done, and when the Americans leave, we move in to a completed complex, without any effort or cost to us. But if they are going to be wandering all over the place while they work, you had better take care that they do not find your radio. Move it far from any place that they might be working."

"I will move it somewhere safe tonight while they are all dreaming their sweet dreams," Antonio assured his boss.

"Good." Ortega seemed in a better mood now that he had a plan. "And maybe we can use them to keep track of the good Pastor Restrepo. We need to know if his resolve to resist us remains strong, and we need to know where his contacts are so that we can keep them from joining forces against our cause."

"Agreed, but what does that have to do with these American students?"

"They can be our eyes and ears. They will be around the pastor more than you are, and he will probably talk freely around them. Watch the young people. See which ones are not as eager as the rest, see if any of them look discontented. Then target those and use one of them to keep you informed."

"Why should they do that?" Antonio was frustrated at what his superior expected of him.

"Promise them something," Ortega snapped, as if it should have been obvious to Antonio.

At a loss, Antonio demanded, "Like what?"

"It doesn't matter," Ortega barked. "Whatever will buy their cooperation. Once they go back to America, how will they make us keep our promise?"

Antonio smirked. This could be fun after all. "I'll see what I can do."

Daniel settled in to listen to Pastor Jeff's recital of the rules they would be expected to follow.

Jeff stood beside the old wooden lectern, casually leaning one elbow on it. "First, let me remind you about some safety precautions. I hope you all brought mosquito repellent like we told you, because you'll need to use it every day. Also, I know it's hot, but it's better to be uncomfortable than to come down with malaria or dengue fever, so wear long sleeves and long pants as an added protection from the mosquitoes."

Kevin leaned over and murmured to Jeremy, "Pastor Jeff ain't worried about no mosquitoes. He just don't want us checkin' out the girls in shorts."

"You got it backwards, dude," Jeremy whispered back. "It's the girls he's worried about. They'll never concentrate on the work if us guys go around showing off our hot bods."

Kevin snickered. "I dunno, man. I ain't sayin' girls don't like you, but I don't think seein' yo' skinny body without a shirt is gonna make 'em go crazy for you."

Daniel shushed them both.

Pastor Jeff threw them all a hard look, then continued his speech. "You'll be working hard out in the hot sun, so if any of you feel overheated, stop what you're doing and rest in the shade. Drink plenty of water, but remember Pastor Sergio said only the water from the tank in the kitchen is safe to drink."

Feeling the sting of his pastor's disapproval, Daniel nodded to indicate the warnings had registered in spite of their inattention. The rest of the students nodded, as well, and Jeff made a subtle shift from safety to their conduct.

"Pastor Sergio already explained that supplies and water are limited, so naturally, I hope you'll respect any rationing without complaint. I also expect us to maintain high standards as Christians. We already gave you the rules in writing before we left, but I'd like to review them so there's no confusion. No profanity, no dirty jokes. None of you are smokers or drinkers, or you wouldn't have been accepted, so let's make sure you don't suddenly develop any nasty habits."

Daniel grinned to himself, picturing Mindy with a cigar in her mouth. The other students smiled and traded glances, obviously having similar thoughts about each other.

Pastor Jeff continued. "I also understand that you are young men and women who are used to socializing, and you'll have plenty of time for that, but in order to avoid temptation, we have to establish some boundaries. Ladies, under no circumstances are you to be in the men's quarters at any time, and likewise, the men will stay out of your room. No boys and girls mingling at all after lights out each night."

Terrell leaned forward with a smirk and murmured, "You hear that, Resha? You're going to have to control yourself and stay away from the men's quarters."

Resha turned around in her chair and hissed, "You can relax, Terrell. If I want a man, I won't be looking in your bed, because you don't qualify."

Daniel blinked at her unexpected venom, and the retort left Terrell gaping and speechless.

Not so Kevin and Jeremy, who both gave an appreciative "oooh".

Jeremy leaned over to give Resha a high five, but she'd already turned to the front again.

Jeff hadn't been able to hear the words, but it was easy to decipher the tone of the exchange. He cleared his throat. "We're going to be spending a lot of time with each other, and it's natural that disagreements may come up. If you have any grievances with each other I expect you to handle them maturely. If there's a problem that can't be resolved in a civilized manner between you, bring it to me or to Pastor Sergio. Understand?"

There were nods all around. Pastor Jeff allowed his stern look to relax.

"I won't be watching you every second, so you'll be on your honor, but remember," Jeff wiggled his eyebrows menacingly, "God is watching."

The young people all smiled again, which was the reaction Jeff had hoped for. Rules were necessary, but he didn't want the students to feel he didn't trust them. They were adults, after all, even if he still saw them all as kids in need of guidance.

He transitioned into the schedule he and Sergio had worked out for them. "Each morning we'll meet here after breakfast for a brief prayer time, and to get our assignments for the day, and we'll have a short devotional here each evening after we finish the work. For tonight, let's spend a few minutes getting to know each other better, since we'll be spending the next two weeks together."

Jeff asked them to move their chairs into a semicircle so they all could face one another. When they had done that, Jeff obeyed an impulse to push Daniel out of the nest. "Daniel, why don't we start with you? Tell us your testimony."

Daniel looked at Jeff as if he had just asked him to poke out his own eyes. As a matter of fact, that suggestion would probably have been more acceptable to Daniel. "Uh...uh...."

Predictably, Jeremy piped up, "I'll start!"

Daniel sagged with relief and threw his friend a grateful look, but Jeff suspected Jeremy had done it more to get attention than to rescue Daniel.

"I got saved at a Vacation Bible School when I was nine years old," Jeremy announced, standing up to ensure all eyes were on him. It didn't take him long to turn the spotlight elsewhere, though. "Guess who had dragged me to that VBS with him?"

He turned and grinned at Daniel, who narrowed his eyes suspiciously. Jeremy returned the scowl with an even bigger grin and went on. "See, we lived down the street from each other then, and Daniel here was a couple of years older, so I went along just because I thought it would be cool to hang out with this older kid. But he wasn't interested in being my friend as much as in getting me saved from eternal damnation. He kinda 'encouraged' me to respond to the altar call, and then made sure it stuck. So, see, if it wasn't for Daniel here, I wouldn't be the fine, godly man I am today."

The others laughed as Jeremy pretended to preen. Then he gave a subtle nod to Kevin, who took that as his cue to add to Daniel's embarrassment.

Kevin spoke in his low, deep voice. "Yeah, well, I met these two guys about five years ago, but I wasn't interested in church at all. Me an' Jeremy hit it off right away, 'cuz Jeremy likes to cut up and have fun." He grinned and added, "In a godly way, of course."

"Of course," Jeremy emphasized, as if there could be no doubt.

Kevin moved to stand behind Daniel, who gritted his teeth as Kevin gestured toward him as if he were Exhibit A. "But, tell you the truth, I didn't much care for this guy at first. He was always quotin' scriptures and prayin' for people and askin' me to go to church. I didn't like hangin' around him. I guess he made me feel guilty. But him and Jeremy was a package deal, so I had to put up with him. And Daniel just kept on livin' out his faith and pesterin' me with that 'Jesus' stuff, so I finally gave in and got saved. I been livin' for the Lord for almost two years now, thanks to this man right here."

He clapped Daniel on the shoulder a bit harder than necessary to make his point.

"Oh, that's so sweet!" Mindy bubbled. "So that's why you guys are such good friends."

Resha rolled her eyes at Mindy's comment, but the others studied Daniel curiously. He fidgeted, uncomfortable with the attention, then blurted out, "Come on, guys, stop trying to make me look like some kind of saint."

Without missing a beat, Jeremy said, "You're right, Daniel, they need to know you're just a wicked ol' sinner like the rest of us. Kevin, remember that summer after Daniel graduated and you and I were about to go into tenth grade..."

The deer-in-the-headlight panic on Daniel's face was priceless and Jeff had to smother a chuckle. Jeff doubted Jeremy would really reveal anything incriminating about his friend, but maybe it was time to step in before Daniel stroked out right there.

Resha beat Jeff to it, interrupting Jeremy. "I sure hope we're not going to have to get up and confess all our sins here, because I've done a lot of things I'm not proud of, and I'd rather not bring it all up again. It's gone anyway, right? Under The Blood and all?"

"That's right, Resha," exclaimed Mindy in her little girl voice. Resha rolled her eyes and clamped her lips together as Mindy continued. "I think it's so wonderful that you've allowed God to change you so much."

Thankfully, Mindy turned her attention to Daniel before Resha got up and slapped her. "And Daniel, I think it's wonderful the way you let God use you to share Jesus with your friends."

Daniel looked absolutely sick now, so Jeff decided to step in after all. "Thanks for sharing your testimony, guys. How about you, Mindy? What's your story?"

Mindy shared how she'd been raised in church, naturally, since her father was the pastor, and she'd given her heart to Christ in Sunday School when she was eight or nine. No surprises there. She sniffled as she recounted how she'd lost her mom in a car wreck several years ago, but other than that, her life had been pretty uneventful.

Terrell volunteered his story next. He'd been saved as a young teen, but hadn't taken it seriously and had done his own thing for a while. After getting tired of his own rebellious escapades, he'd rededicated his life to God in his senior year of high school and was now a solid Christian.

Resha seemed reluctant to share, which was understandable considering the things she'd told Jeff and Pastor Meyer during her interview. She gave the students an edited version. "Like I said earlier, I did a lot of things I'd rather forget. If you can think of it, I was probably into it. I met some women from Mindy's church when I was at a real low point, and they told me how to get forgiven and let God turn my life around. That was about three years ago, and all I can say is, accepting Jesus really made a difference for me. I've got a long way to go, but at least I'm headed in the right direction now."

Mindy got all misty eyed again as she listened to Resha. She probably knew more of the story than Resha had shared, since they attended the same church, but all she said was, "That's beautiful, Resha."

Everyone looked at Selena next, since Manny was still asleep and Samuel's glare discouraged anyone from asking him anything.

Selena looked startled. "Who, me?"

When she realized they were waiting for her to speak, she said, "Oh. Well, I wasn't a bad kid or anything, but I never went to church. Then some friends invited me, and my mother thought it was a good idea if me and Manny went. I really liked it. The people were nice, and they had a lot of fun stuff to do. So me and Manny joined, and we've been going to church for a couple of years now."

Jeff exchanged an uneasy look with Daniel, who he knew would recognize there was something missing from Selena's testimony.

Resha nailed it with her pointed question. "So, when did you get saved?"

Selena looked puzzled. "I told you, I've been going to church for about two years."

"Yeah, yeah, we heard that." Resha dismissed the comment impatiently. "I asked when you got saved. You know, born again? Washed in the Blood?"

Selena laughed nervously, as if she wasn't sure what Resha was asking.

Jeff was frustrated at Selena's pastor. One of the requirements for coming on this mission trip was that the person had a solid relationship with Christ – apparently her pastor accepted church attendance as proof of that. In Selena's case, it seemed to prove nothing.

Jeff wondered if he should allow Resha to continue her aggressive probing or try to address the issue more discreetly later on, but the decision was taken out of his hands when the sound of a helicopter drowned out the possibility of further conversation.

Matéo burst in through the side door, waving his arms in excitement.

"They are here! The Novaks are here!" he cried before running back outside.

Pastor Sergio and Paola were already rushing out the side door.

"Quickly, plug the outside lights into the generator so they can land," Sergio called back to Luís, who ran to obey.

The students looked at Pastor Jeff hopefully. Since Pastor Sergio was all smiles, Jeff assumed whatever was happening was a good thing. He shrugged and waved a hand at the door, indicating they could follow the Restrepos if they wanted to.

They wanted to. The students seemed to have forgotten their exhaustion as they hurried after Sergio. Jeff followed at a more sedate pace and found them clustered in the field beyond the mission center, a few yards from where Stefan and Luís stood with Pastor Sergio and his siblings.

Jeff joined his team, and they watched a small helicopter hover over the field to the left of the complex in preparation for landing. The wind from the blades ruffled their hair and made them squint as the chopper began to descend, its blades beating out a steady thwup-thwup-thwup.

Sergio began running toward it before it had quite touched the ground, ducking low as his hair blew wildly in the wind from the spinning blades.

When the little chopper finally steadied itself, a ruddy faced man in his late fifties climbed out and clasped the pastor's hand in a firm shake. His pale red hair was streaked with white, but his stout body looked strong, as if he was accustomed to physical labor.

He turned to help a woman about the same age and build as he was from the helicopter, and Sergio quickly moved to her side and took her other arm. She smiled and accepted their help graciously, but she didn't look as if she needed anyone's assistance as she hopped from the chopper with the confidence of an athlete.

As the trio walked towards the waiting group, Paola trotted towards them and gave the woman a quick hug.

Sergio proudly announced, "Pastor Jeff, this is Brother Russ Novak and his lovely wife Helen. They have been an incredible blessing since the flood. He came to check on us when we were unable to get in touch with the outside world, and he made the Red Cross and other agencies aware of our presence here so that we were able to get help from them as soon as they could get through. His endorsement of our mission center helped convince the government to give us permission to remain here and rebuild. He is also the one who set up our radio so that we could communicate with you and others who have donated generously to us during this crisis."

Novak gave Pastor Jeff's hand a hearty shake. "Don't let him fool ya, Pastor. He's the one who's been a blessing. When the wife and I came to Colombia as missionaries a couple years back, we didn't know anything about the customs over here. Pastor Sergio here was kind enough to teach us, kept us from making total idiots out of ourselves. Now we got our ministry going pretty good over in Cucuta, but we wouldn't have lasted more than a month without this man's help."

Novak clapped Pastor Sergio on the shoulder with a meaty hand, making the smaller man sway, then turned to look at the students. "So these are the young people who are helping you out, Sergio?"

Sergio's smile encompassed all the students with pride. "Yes, yes, they have just arrived and are ready to go to work."

The pilot had unloaded several large cardboard boxes, and Luís and Stefan quickly swept them away from the helicopter, stacking them next to the building. Manny and Selena joined Matéo in inspecting the contents of the boxes, but the rest of the team listened as Pastor Sergio talked with Mr. Novak and his wife.

"God bless you for what you have done, Señor Novak." Sergio buzzed around the opened boxes of donated food, peering into each one as if looking for something. "We appreciate so much all your efforts and generosity."

Novak opened his hands apologetically. "Now, Pastor Sergio, I know it ain't much, but we can't fit a whole lot in the chopper."

"It is not that," Sergio was quick to reassure the missionary, looking embarrassed that his disappointment had been evident. "Your gift to us is very generous. It is just that..." he hesitated, frowning. "...we were hoping that the shipment would contain Bibles."

"You want Bibles, Pastor?" Novak asked in surprise. "We still got a few Spanish Bibles up at the church. We probably won't be able to get any more for a while because of the flood and all, but most of our people are set, so you can have what we got. We just thought that since food's been kinda hard to come by in your area, you'd want to meet that need first."

Sergio smiled broadly. "But the Word of God is also a need, Señor Novak. 'Man does not live by bread alone.' Without food, the body will die. But without the Word of God, the spirit will die. Which is more important?"

Novak returned the smile. "You got a point, there, Pastor."

"The people here understand this, Brother Novak," Sergio explained. "We are accustomed to going without food sometimes. When people show up at the mission center, they will gladly accept food if it is offered, but the first thing they ask for is a Bible. Most of the people lost theirs in the flood and are desperate for the hope God's Word offers them."

"Well, then, we'll just have to come back later this week, with all the Bibles we can find."

Sergio waved his hands vigorously, as if to ward off the very notion. "But you cannot make another trip so soon."

"Pastor Sergio, it's not as bad as you think any more," Novak assured his friend. "Cuenco Verde and the other villages around here are pretty isolated, but a lot of Colombia is getting back on its feet. Most of the major roadways are cleared now, and shipments are starting to come into the country. It's still kind of hard to get food and water, but it's available if you know where to look. Me and the Missus will be glad to come back if it means putting God's Word into the people's hands. That's what we're here for."

Sergio grabbed Novak in a zealous bear hug. "Thank you, thank you."

Novak laughed and returned the hug. Apparently he'd experienced Sergio's exuberance before. The two men continued talking as Sergio dragged his friend towards his house, with Helen and Paola trailing behind. Matéo ran ahead of them, sucking on a lollipop Novak had slipped him.

As Jeff and the students watched the happy group enter the building, Daniel remarked, "Hearing how these people feel about the Word of God kind of makes me ashamed of the careless way I tossed my Bible into my duffel bag."

Jeremy scrunched up his face guiltily. "Yeah, I just stuffed mine in there between the granola bars, kind of as an afterthought."

"You guys feel bad?" Kevin said. "At least you brought Bibles!"

The others laughed at his comment, but Mindy looked concerned. "Kevin, you can borrow my Bible if you want to. I'm sure Selena will let me share with her."

Jeff took pity on Kevin and spared him from having to answer.

"Listen, it's been a long day and we'll be getting up early, so why don't we all turn in for the night? I'm sure Pastor Restrepo and his friends have a lot of catching up to do, so they won't miss us."

The group nodded in relief. The brief nap before supper had allowed them to stay awake for the meal, but their fatigue was catching up to them again and they were ready for some rest.

The rickety fan in the girls' room did nothing but blow random puffs of hot air as it rattled through its noisy oscillation. Resha hadn't bothered to gather the mosquito net around her, and it shimmied every time the fan wobbled in her direction.

Fed up, Resha tried turning the fan off, but the switch broke in her hand. She yanked the plug from the extension cord, then waited to see if the other two girls would object. Mindy and Selena remained silent. Either they were asleep, or they were scared to say anything. Good.

Resha flung herself fully clothed onto the cot she'd chosen, against the wall farthest from the door. The odor of mildew wafted from the lumpy pillow.

Without the noise of the fan, Resha could hear Mindy snoring softly on the cot between her own and Selena's. The girl had fallen asleep almost the moment her head hit the pillow, and Selena's stirring had quieted not long after. But Resha was wide awake, and she fidgeted on the creaky cot. She'd always had a hard time going to sleep in a strange place, and the stifling heat added to her restlessness.

After what felt like hours, Resha decided to put the time to better use than staring at the dark water stains on the ceiling.

She sat up and began praying silently. She prayed for the pastors who were being harassed by the Black Eagles, especially Pastor Sergio. She prayed for their own protection, and she prayed that God would give them courage.

Still not sleepy, Resha felt confined sitting on the cot, so she stood up, trying not to wake the others, and began pacing quietly beside her cot. While she paced, she prayed under her breath for Pastor Jeff, who seemed to be having misgivings about coming to Colombia, then she prayed for each member of the team by name. She even prayed for Terrell, not realizing that she had begun whispering the words out loud the more involved she got in her prayers.

At last, Resha felt her eyelids grow heavy, so she crawled back into her cot and pulled the sheets up, unaware of Selena's silent scrutiny.

When Resha's pacing had awakened her, Selena had been uneasy at first, wondering what the strange, belligerent girl was up to. But even though she couldn't understand the words, after a while Selena realized that Resha was praying.

It felt strangely soothing, kind of like when her mother used to tuck her in at night when she was little. Selena was almost disappointed when

Resha at last grew silent and went back to bed, but then she fell into a contented slumber, feeling wrapped in a cocoon of protection.

3

Day 2: Monday

A faint, steady beeping woke Daniel. His eyes popped open and took in the unfamiliar surroundings. He was confused for a moment, not seeing his alarm clock, then remembered he had set the alarm on his watch and quickly silenced it. Still wearing his jeans and T-shirt from the day before, Daniel was surprised he'd slept so well on the flimsy cot.

He sat up quietly and looked over at the other cots. The rest of the men were all sleeping, as he had hoped. Jeremy sprawled on his back on the cot next to Daniel's with his mouth wide open, and he had one leg draped over the edge of his cot on either side. Daniel grinned at the sight as he grabbed his sneakers and a denim work shirt. He tiptoed out into the courtyard, careful not to wake anyone.

He sat on the rough wooden bench outside the door to put on his shoes, then tugged the denim shirt over his plain white T-shirt. He stood and looked around, eager to start his morning jog. No matter what part of the world, there was something about the early morning air that was invigorating and full of promise. After muttering a quick "good morning" prayer, he took a deep breath and set off at a slow pace to warm up, enjoying the unfamiliar cries of tropical birds.

Daniel didn't relish the idea of jogging past the temporary graveyard they had passed yesterday, so he headed down the rutted dirt road in the opposite direction. Pastor Sergio had said that more homes were still standing that way, and that some of the villages several miles east had not even been evacuated, although they were still without power.

Sure enough, even though Cuenco Verde was deserted, most of the tiny adobe homes scattered under the canopy of palms and flowering fruit trees looked almost livable in spite of the black mold crawling up the sides.

Others, however, had been partially under water for too long, and the lower part of the walls crumbled. The wooden houses would have to be gutted and reframed, while the little straw and mud huts were beyond hope, nothing more than soggy piles of rubble.

Daniel picked up his pace. Twenty minutes into his run, he started to wilt. The sloping road and the hot, humid air made his daily routine more challenging than he'd expected. Jogging lightly in place, he removed his outer shirt and tied it around his waist.

As he pushed back the sweaty hair that was sticking to his forehead, Daniel heard what sounded like gunfire in the distance and cocked his head to listen.

Sure enough, he heard it again.

Glancing at his watch, he decided he'd had enough of a run. He turned and jogged back in the direction he'd come from.

Jeremy and Kevin were sitting on the bench outside their dorm when he got back, Kevin with a steaming coffee mug he had begged from Abuelita, and Jeremy with a granola bar and his canteen of water.

Kevin shook his head in disbelief as Daniel wheezed up to them. "Man, I thought for sure you was gonna give up on that while we was here. Look at you, sweatin' all over the place!"

"Forty minutes..." gasped Daniel, throwing himself to the ground beside the bench, "...seems a lot longer in Colombia than it did in Houston."

"Different time zone," Jeremy suggested, handing Daniel his canteen.

Daniel paid no attention to Jeremy's absurd remark. He grabbed the canteen and guzzled half the contents, then handed it back, wiping his mouth with the back of his hand. "Thanks."

Jeremy shook the canteen and frowned at the meager amount Daniel had left him.

Oblivious to his friend's displeasure, Daniel untied the shirt from his waist, mopped his face with it, and began a series of crunches.

"You're makin' me tired, man. Stop already," Kevin complained.

A loud whistle came from across the courtyard, and the three friends looked up in surprise to see Selena standing in the girls' doorway with a hairbrush in her hand.

"I sure hated getting up this early, but it's worth it for the show," she drawled, looking Daniel up and down.

Daniel flushed and sat up hurriedly, tugging his denim shirt back on.

Selena laughed at him and dragged the brush through her long black hair. "You know, you and that Resha girl are two of a kind."

Kevin looked at her like she was crazy. "Oh, yeah?"

"Yeah, she's in there now doing some kind of weird martial arts stuff." Selena struck a comical pose to demonstrate.

"I think Pastor Jeff said she's a kickboxing instructor back home," Jeremy remarked.

Mindy appeared in the doorway beside Selena, her hair done up in two perky ponytails. "I took a kickboxing class once," she offered brightly.

"Not that kind of kickboxing, Mindy," Resha snapped, popping up behind both of them. "The real kind, like self-defense stuff."

Trying not to squirm under the scrutiny of the three girls, Daniel looked at his friends for help. Jeremy smirked, and Daniel couldn't tell whether his friend planned to rescue him or turn the knife.

Both, it seemed.

"Don't you ladies have something better to do than stand around and ogle Daniel's physique?" Jeremy asked.

Selena laughed, Resha snorted, and Mindy gasped in horror at the very idea, her big eyes getting even bigger.

"Come on, Mindy," Selena tucked Mindy's arm under hers and led her toward the front of the building. "We can ogle these guys anytime. Let's go find some hot Colombian guys to ogle."

Daniel could hear Mindy spluttering as the two girls walked away. Resha rolled her eyes and went back into the dorm to finish her routine.

Jeremy howled. "Daniel, you should see your face!"

"Yeah, man, I didn't know you could turn so red." Kevin chuckled.

Disgruntled, Daniel stood and brushed the dust off his pants. "I'm red because I've been running in this heat, guys. Now let up."

Kevin peered at him more closely. "You know, you really do look ragged out, man. Maybe you oughtta lay off the joggin' for a while."

Daniel nodded. "Well, next time, maybe I'll cut it a little shorter. It got kind of weird out there, anyway." He wiped sweat off his face with his sleeve.

"Weird, how?" Jeremy asked.

"I'm not sure." Daniel frowned thoughtfully. "I know there's nobody around for miles, but I could swear I heard gunshots."

As soon as the sun had risen, Captain Ortega had marched the new recruits, freshly outfitted in army gear, to a field just outside the village of Campo Dulce. The crop of plantains had been ruined by the flood, and rotting fruit lay scattered about, flies hovering in clouds over it. Soon, the field would be recultivated with a more profitable crop of coca plants, but for now, the mud and odor would serve to teach the trainees to be ready for action even in adverse circumstances.

Their first exercise was simple target practice. Working in pairs, the new recruits hoisted their weapons onto their shoulders, then fired on command at the makeshift targets, crude cardboard cutouts meant to represent the Colombian president and law enforcement authorities.

Eagerly waiting for his turn to fire his newly issued firearm, Adolfo was pleased to see that the female recruits had joined them for the exercise, suited up in dark green fatigues just like his own. One recruit in particular caught his attention, a tall girl with wavy black hair and cold, calculating, green eyes.

Adolfo pushed his way through his fellow trainees, arranging it so that he would be paired with the girl, whose name he had learned was Gloria. When he and Gloria both successfully completed their first session with the rifles, their rounds hitting the targets with impressive accuracy, they exchanged smug smiles, and Adolfo knew he'd found a kindred spirit.

Eager to escape the confines of the girls' quarters, Resha was the first to enter the dining area. It didn't take long for Mindy and Selena to find her, though, and they joined her at the center table they'd shared the night before. Soon the three guys she'd ridden with in the truck showed up and sat across from them, and Terrell pulled up a chair to sit on the end again.

When everyone had been offered a mug of rich Colombian coffee, Abuelita and Paola brought in trays laden with scrambled eggs and some kind of bread made out of corn flour, as well as a large clay bowl filled with strange looking fruit.

After Pastor Sergio said a blessing, Paola smiled and set her platter in the center of the table. "I hope that you all like eggs, because you will be eating plenty of eggs during your stay. We have been blessed with many chickens, and while our other supplies may run low sometimes, we have never been short of eggs."

"That's fine with me. I like eggs." Daniel happily scooped a large serving onto his plate, along with some bread and a spiky greenish fruit, which he eyed curiously.

"Dude, you like anything edible," Jeremy scoffed.

Kevin poked at the spiked fruit on Daniel's plate. "Yeah, but is that thing edible?"

Daniel cut the fruit in half with a knife, exposing a milky white center peppered with tiny black seeds. Without hesitation, he picked up one of the halves and scooped out some of the fruit with his teeth, grimacing a little as he chewed.

Paola laughed. "That is a *cherimoya*. They normally get ripe a little bit later in the year, but the flood and the extremely hot weather have caused the trees to drop the fruit early. The neighboring farms have been abandoned and are mostly neglected, and the fruit will spoil before the owners get back, so we are helping ourselves to it so that it will not go to waste."

Daniel scooped out another bite as the rest of the group watched in fascinated horror. "It's not bad once you get used to it," he told them with a shrug.

Selena wrinkled her nose and shook her head when Paola offered the fruit bowl to her. Resha also declined, but Mindy gingerly selected the smallest cherimoya. She set it on her plate, staring at it fearfully, as if it might grow legs and attack her. It was still on her plate at the end of breakfast.

As soon as they had done eating, Selena gave a tremendous yawn. When everyone looked at her, she straightened up defensively. "What? I can't help it Resha kept me up half the night, pacing around the room."

Resha frowned. She hadn't realized anyone had noticed her movements.

Mindy looked from one to the other. "Really? I didn't hear anything."

Not over your snoring, Resha thought, but she managed to bite it back before it slipped out of her mouth.

Terrell was not so successful in keeping his mouth shut. "What's the matter, Resha?" he jibed. "A little leftover crack in your system keeping you up at night?"

Resha clenched her fists under the table to keep them from flying into Terrell's face.

"I think she was praying," Selena offered.

Everyone turned to look at Resha, who felt like anything but a praying woman as she sat with her teeth clenched, nostrils flaring, and her eyes flashing with anger.

She was glad when Pastor Sergio stood up to address the team, giving them a list of chores to be completed.

The team's first task was to remove the sodden carpet and other waterlogged materials that were scattered in piles throughout the mission complex. They finally met Stefan, the third laborer who was helping Pastor Sergio, when he was assigned to show them where the damaged materials were located, as well as the spot a hundred yards from the mission center where they were to pile it all to await pickup by a government detail some time in the next few weeks. At least moving it would get the foul-smelling, moldy remains away from the buildings so the rest of the work would go more pleasantly.

Stefan, a muscular man in his early thirties, wore his faded jeans tucked into work-stained brown boots. Daniel couldn't help noticing how Paola couldn't keep her eyes off Stefan's long, wavy black hair that was pulled into a ponytail, accenting his chiseled features. A small, neat mustache topped the laborer's friendly smile.

Stefan's English was spotty, but he managed to communicate with the team by supplementing his conversation with liberal gestures that seemed to delight Sergio's young brother Matéo, who could have translated but preferred seeing the spectacle. Daniel suspected Stefan exaggerated his gestures just to amuse the boy, which, of course, scored brownie points with Matéo's pretty sister.

Donning thick work gloves, the group went to work. Jeff and Sergio began at the house, pulling off boards near the bottom that had been under water. Samuel observed the two pastors for a few minutes, then went to the other side of the building and started prying off damaged boards by himself with a crowbar he'd found in Luís' toolbox.

Terrell and Daniel started dragging heavy rolls of wet carpet from where they had been piled next to the buildings. Each time they shifted one of the cumbersome rolls, clouds of odor and swarms of mosquitoes were released, causing Selena to squawk and run away.

The two guys laughed good-naturedly at her and Mindy, who was squealing as she slapped at the mosquitoes. Only Resha stood impassively, reeking of mosquito repellent and shielded by her thick jeans and heavy camouflage shirt.

Pointing at Resha, Terrell said to Daniel, "Those mosquitoes know better than to bite Resha; they might get high if they suck her blood."

Daniel frowned. "They're leaving her alone because she's wearing long sleeves like Pastor Jeff told us to."

"She has to wear long sleeves," Terrell laughed, undeterred. "Got to hide those needle tracks, huh, Resha?"

Daniel responded by giving a sharp tug to his end of the carpet. "Come on, this thing is heavy."

He wanted to get Terrell away from Resha before she exploded, since she was glowering at him with revenge in her eyes.

Terrell smirked at Resha one last time as he and Daniel hauled their heavy load to the designated dump site.

Resha glared at Terrell's back until a nervous laugh from Selena brought her attention back to her companions.

Mindy seemed unaware of any tension as she cheerfully suggested, "Let's go see if we can help the other guys."

Resha accepted the distraction. The girls followed the sounds of banging into the main building and found Jeremy and Kevin using hammers to knock out more mildewed plaster, adding moldy chunks to the piles already accumulated on the floor.

The two guys had made a contest out of the process, each trying to see who could break off the largest chunk without it crumbling. They egged each other on with friendly insults.

Resha propped open the doors with a couple of chairs, hoping to allow the breeze to circulate in the suffocatingly hot building, but it did little to help. She scowled as she watched the guys work, twisting her mouth to one side, then decided, "Let's go find some boxes or something to put this stuff in so we can move it out of their way."

The girls managed to round up several heavy cardboard boxes that had held donated food supplies, and they started shoveling the chunks in with their gloved hands. Selena and Mindy made a lot of faces and choking sounds as they worked, but Resha had tied a bandana around the lower part of her face to filter the dust and some of the smell.

Manny wandered in, halfheartedly tossed a few chunks of plaster into a box, then left to get a drink of water.

He must have been awfully thirsty, Resha thought facetiously after an hour had passed and Manny still hadn't returned.

Manny was bored. The main reason he'd agreed to sign up for this trip was to get his mom off his back, but he had also hoped it would be an adventure.

He'd pictured himself lounging in a hammock, meeting lots of cute Colombian girls, who would all be ever so appreciative that he'd come all the way from America just to help them in their hour of need.

Instead, he was actually expected to work hard, and so far the only Colombian females he'd seen were Abuelita and Paola, both way too old for him. Paola was pretty enough, but she had to be nearly thirty, and besides, she was obviously hot for that Stefan guy.

Speaking of Stefan, Manny spotted him working in the distance with Luís and Antonio. They were digging some kind of deep trench, using shovels, and Manny idly thought how much faster the work would go if they had a back hoe or something. He leaned against a building to watch them for a while, then eased himself to a sitting position, where he dozed off, unaware that Antonio was watching him speculatively.

After a couple of hours of working in the sweltering sanctuary, the teasing banter between Jeremy and Kevin had given way to silence and the occasional grunt.

Selena sat down wearily on the floor between the boxes the girls had filled, her hair hanging in damp strings and clinging to her forehead. Mindy was flushed from the heat and her ponytails drooped, but she had managed to finagle a broom from Abuelita and was sweeping up the smaller bits of plaster.

Resha had grown tired of bumping into boxes of discarded plaster as she worked, so she began putting the heavy cartons outside while the other two swept up. She was hot, exhausted, and hungry, and the boxes were heavy and awkward. Some of them came apart as she tried to move them, but she valiantly struggled with each one until she managed to get it out of the way.

As Resha was depositing a bulky carton beside the others she had already stacked outside the door, Terrell and Daniel walked past after delivering a load to the dump, their sweaty faces and clothing streaked with mud and mildew.

Terrell took one look at the bandanna covering her face and spouted, "Jesse James lives again. Didn't you already get sent up once for bank robbery, Resha?" Terrell gave a mock sigh and turned to Daniel. "I guess some people just never change."

Daniel didn't answer him. He was walking a few steps ahead of Terrell so Resha couldn't see his face, but she saw him shake his head almost imperceptively. Maybe he didn't think Terrell was funny, either.

Terrell looked disappointed that Daniel didn't laugh at his cleverness. With one last taunting look at Resha, he picked up his pace to catch up with the blond guy.

Resha didn't think twice about what she did next.

Terrell jumped, startled at the sound of a mini-explosion right behind him. He spun around in time to see that a large chunk of plaster had shattered on the wall where his head had been a moment before.

"Oops, sorry," Resha said in a totally flat voice. "Must have slipped."

Both Terrell and Daniel looked in shock at Resha, who stood with her arms crossed over her chest, her eyes daring Terrell to challenge her. After a stunned silence, Terrell curled his lip in disgust and muttered, "I thought that interview process was supposed to keep the crazy people out of this trip."

He shook his head and walked away, but Daniel stared at her a moment longer, his expression unreadable. Resha's satisfaction wilted a bit under the scrutiny of those guileless blue eyes.

Okay, so her behavior had not been exactly Christ-like, but she wasn't going to back down. She kept her chin tilted defiantly until Daniel had turned away and rejoined Terrell. Then she rushed back into the building, thankful the other two girls had missed the exchange.

Sorry, God, sorry. I'll try to do better, I promise. I need some help, though, okay? Because this fool Terrell is working my last nerve.

Daniel had been trying to figure out whether the girl had actually intended to hit Terrell or not. Probably not, he decided, seeing the satisfied gleam in her eye. If she had really been aiming for him, Terrell would most likely be nursing a concussion right about now. Daniel realized he was staring and turned away from her quickly – it wouldn't do for her to see the amusement in his eyes, or an entire box of moldy plaster might be heading his way next. For such a tiny girl, she had a lot of spunk.

Daniel caught up to Terrell, who still looked angry. His new friend didn't mention the incident again, though, so Daniel left it alone, too.

They were both relieved to find they were down to the last roll of wet flooring. After plodding back and forth with the cumbersome burdens all morning, they were ready for a break.

The two of them had just maneuvered the final unwieldy, oozing mass onto the dump pile when Pastor Sergio came outside, clapped his hands together to get everyone's attention, and announced that Abuelita had lunch prepared for them in the dining area.

Everyone dusted themselves off the best they could and trudged inside with relief. Even Manny materialized from somewhere, looking cleaner than the rest of them.

Although the food revived Jeff, the dining experience was less than enjoyable for him and his team. Apparently the ice in the aguapanela last night had been a luxury to welcome their arrival, and the sweet drink they were served today was lukewarm.

Even with the windows open, the room was hot and stuffy. The stagnant heat intensified the smell of mosquito repellant mingled with sweat, and flies took advantage of the open windows to swarm around their plates.

Jeff was glad none of the students complained, especially since Sergio's family and the three laborers did not seem to notice or mind the discomfort as they hungrily devoured the arepas de huevo and rice that Abuelita served.

But at the end of the meal, Mindy innocently commented, "You know, now that we've got all that moldy stuff out of the building, everything looks so clean and shiny now. It's a shame we have to come in and track all this dirt back in."

Her face brightened, as if she'd just had a great idea. "Maybe we should eat our lunch outside tomorrow so we can keep the church clean. It would be just like having a picnic!"

The rest of the team quickly murmured agreement, and Pastor Jeff smiled knowingly. Maybe Mindy was smarter than they gave her credit for.

As they stood to leave, several of the students began trying to clear the table, but Paola shooed them away as she and Abuelita collected the dirty dishes from them.

When the two women left the room, Pastor Sergio explained, "Please allow them to do this service for you. Paola's health and Abuelita's age do not allow them to do some of the heavier work that all of you are doing now. This is their contribution, it is their way of thanking you."

Hours later, with all the flood damaged material dragged to the dump site, the girls had gone inside to get cleaned up before their evening meal. Rather than waiting for a turn at the shower inside the main building, Jeremy and Kevin rigged a short hose to the water pump and sprayed each other down outside, clothes and all.

"That looks like a good idea," Daniel observed, so Jeremy turned the hose on him, getting him full in the face.

Laughing and spluttering, Daniel grabbed the hose away from Jeremy.

"You rotten little punk!" he yelled, making a nozzle out of his thumb so the water would spray harder as he deluged Jeremy.

"Save the water! Save the water!" Jeremy squawked, ducking away from the spray while the others laughed at his plight.

Reminded of the water rationing, Daniel quickly ran the hose over his own hair and arms before handing it to Terrell. The refreshing spray felt wonderful as it washed away the sweat and grime of the day's toil.

It wasn't until all four of them were completely drenched that it occurred to Daniel that they couldn't very well go inside dripping wet.

Thankfully, Matéo came running out with a stack of faded, threadbare towels.

"Abuelita said to give you these," he panted.

Daniel sheepishly accepted the towels and handed one to each of his friends, embarrassed that their antics had been observed by the old woman.

Was that his imagination, or did the curtain in the girls' room just drop back into place? Mortified, he realized Mindy and Selena might have been watching, too.

"Thanks, Matéo," he managed. "And please thank Abuelita for us."

Matéo nodded eagerly and ran back inside to pass the message along. The boy seemed happy to be useful.

Daniel dried off the best he could, but his clothes were still soaked. "We can't go inside like this."

"It's gonna take too long for our clothes to dry in this humidity," Kevin grumbled.

"Let's find a way to pass the time, then." Jeremy began snapping his wet towel at the others, and soon they were all engaged in a playful four way duel.

Sitting in Pastor Sergio's living room after the long day, Jeff felt guilty seeing the young men trying to clean up with the water hose.

Here, he had the luxury of sharing a shower with only three other people, even if they were forced to severely restrict their time to conserve the water stored in the tank.

Still, he reminded himself, he had warned them before the trip that they might not have running water at all, so the meager supply from the water pump was a blessing they all appreciated.

Jeff turned away from the window and glanced at his surroundings.

The room was small but neat. Since the house was elevated, the water had not done too much damage, other than leaving a stained, bare wooden floor where wet carpet had been ripped out.

The wooden legs of the sofa Jeff had slept on the night before showed evidence that a few inches of water had entered the house, but everything had been thoroughly cleaned and smelled of bleach rather than mildew.

Jeff had waved away Sergio's apologies for not being able to offer Jeff a bed or a room of his own. The worn sofa had been more than adequate last night, and he would gratefully accept it for the remainder of their stay.

On the coffee table in front of the sofa was a large Bible that had been spared from the tide. This Bible was not there for decorative purposes; it had obviously seen much use, because the gilt edges had worn off the dogeared pages, and the binding was creased from being opened so often. Jeff had read from it himself the previous evening, comparing the Spanish version to the small Bible he always carried with him.

Jeff had noticed the cluster of framed photographs on the wall behind the sofa last night, but he'd been too tired to study them. Now he recognized one as a wedding picture depicting Pastor Sergio standing beside a radiant young woman. There were photos, obviously done at a cheap photography studio, of two young boys, one about age seven, the other a toddler of three or four years. There was one picture of the entire family standing together in front of the mission center.

Remembering what Sergio had revealed to them about his family, Jeff felt grieved for the other pastor's great loss. When Sergio came into the room moments later, Jeff turned compassionate eyes on him.

"You had a lovely family, Pastor Sergio. You must miss them terribly."

Sergio dropped into the armchair across from Jeff, and his eyes passed lovingly over the pictures.

"There are times when I wonder how I can go on without them," he admitted. "I feel as if the very heart has been ripped out of my body."

"I'm very sorry," Jeff said, knowing no words could really offer comfort.

Sergio accepted Jeff's condolence with a nod. After a moment, he said, "My grief is for myself, not for them. I truly do know that they are in a much better place. For now, the work of rebuilding keeps me occupied so that I do not have time to think too much about it. And God has graciously allowed my sister and my little brother to be here during this time. Having family with me is a great comfort."

Jeff sat respectfully still, his silent presence conveying his commiseration.

After a moment, Sergio shifted his gaze from the pictures to Pastor Jeff. "What about you, my friend? Do you have a family?"

Jeff hesitated. To simply say "no" would be rude, especially to this man who had just bared his soul to him. But to admit that he was also a widower would invite sympathy to which Jeff wasn't sure he was entitled.

Jeff and Michelle had married during Jeff's last year of seminary. Michelle was a Christian, but apparently not as sold out to the faith as her new husband. When Jeff accepted a low-paying position as associate pastor at a small church, Michelle had quickly discovered that being married to a pastor meant more sacrifices than she was willing to make.

Too little money to spend and too little time with the man she'd married had taken a toll on the marriage within a few short months.

Michelle was not willing to share her husband with the elderly widows and troubled youths who seemed to expect the couple to be available twenty-four hours a day. A 3:00 AM phone call with news of an aging member's passing had pushed her over the edge.

As soon as the call ended, Michelle had sprung out of bed, ranting at Jeff. "Mr. Foster was ancient and he's been on the brink of death for the last month. We all knew he was about to kick off. His wife couldn't have waited until some decent hour to call you? It's not like you can make funeral arrangements in the middle of the night!"

Jeff had tried to placate his young bride before hurrying to the grieving widow's home, but when he got back home hours later, Michelle had already packed up her things and left.

Michelle had insisted it was a "trial separation," and then immediately found solace with an attractive executive who could lavish her with the money and attention she craved.

At the senior pastor's suggestion, Jeff had taken a leave of absence to protect the unsullied image of the church "until the situation gets resolved," and so Jeff was left to suffer alone with his emotional upheaval. Three months later, when Jeff was served with divorce papers, he'd already come to terms with what he knew was the inevitable end of his marriage, and now his biggest concern was how being divorced would affect his future in the ministry.

Ironically, the day he'd finally resigned himself to signing the papers that would dissolve his marriage, Jeff received word that Michelle had been killed in a car accident while vacationing in Florida. Her lover, who had been driving the luxury sports car that was crushed by a runaway semi, had survived the wreck but had been rendered a paraplegic.

Jeff had done his grieving when Michelle had walked out on him months ago, so all he felt upon hearing the news was a vague sense of relief that he would not have the stigma of being divorced after all.

Having a pastor who was a widower was more acceptable to most Christians, after all, than having one who was divorced. He'd put the divorce papers in the shredder and calmly started making funeral arrangements.

His congregation had showered him with sympathy cards and good will, never suspecting that Jeff had reconciled himself to the loss of his wife long ago. Because Jeff and the senior pastor knew the truth, they mutually agreed it would be best for Jeff to move on.

Jeff found a teaching position at Woodrow Christian College with little effort, but his call to the ministry was still strong. Before long, he had cut down his hours at the college and accepted the low-paying, part time position of Youth and Young Adult Pastor and general gofer that he now held at Cornerstone Christian Church. Between teaching at the college and the demands of ministry, Jeff had little time to miss the companionship of a wife.

Bringing himself back to the present, he realized he still had not answered Pastor Sergio's query. Finally, he said only, "I was married once. She died before we could have children."

Now it was Sergio's turn to say, "I am sorry, my friend."

"It was a long time ago," Jeff told him quickly, deflecting sympathy and further questions by turning away.

The two pastors sat in silence for a while, lost in their own memories. Masculine laughter floated in from outside, and the men cast an amused glance towards the open window.

Sergio smiled. "God has given you sons and daughters anyway."

Jeff recognized the truth in Sergio's words. He'd always considered Daniel, Jeremy, and Kevin special, but he now realized he'd already gotten attached to Terrell and the rest of his charges as well, even in the short time he'd known them. He nodded. "Yes. God has never given me a reason to regret not having children of my own. I just hope I'm up to the responsibility He's trusting me with."

"Do not trouble yourself over things you cannot control, Pastor Jeff," Sergio advised. "It is easy to see that your dedication to the young people causes you excessive worry. You are a fine example for the students, and it is clear that they respect you greatly, but they are in God's hands. It is up to Him to see to it that His will is accomplished for them. Your job is simply to give them the Truth and be available to them when God calls you to be."

Jeff accepted Sergio's advice with a nod. Even though Sergio was a decade younger than he, Jeff recognized that the Colombian pastor's faith and wisdom were strong. Sergio had been through the fire and came out a finer vessel.

After their evening meal, Pastor Jeff announced the students would have an hour of free time before they settled in the sanctuary for a short devotional. Since there was no place for them to go, of course, no television to watch, no CD players or video games, Resha suspected the pastor wanted them to spend the time getting to know each other.

Uninterested in socializing, Resha left the dining area and headed for the sanctuary, where she sat on the end of the front row of chairs to wait. She'd hoped for a little peace and quiet, but Selena and Mindy saw her and joined her as if she'd been saving the spot next to her just for them.

Oh, joy.

Plopping into the chair beside Resha, Selena woefully dragged her fingers through hair that was still damp with sweat and whined, "This humidity is ruining my hair."

Mindy nodded in commiseration, although her ponytailed auburn tresses looked as silky and bouncy as ever. She gazed in admiration at Resha's neatly shorn head. "Resha, you look so good with that hairstyle, but I think it would look terrible on me. I wish I could wear my hair like that while we're in Colombia."

"Did you think this haircut was a fashion statement?" Resha couldn't keep the contempt out of her tone. "I wasn't worried about whether it looked good or not. I did it because I didn't want to have the problems you two are having, not to mention lice."

"Lice?" Selena looked horrified as she frantically began fingering strands of her hair to see if anything had attached itself to them.

As Selena continued her timorous inspection, Jeremy, Kevin and Terrell meandered in and spotted the girls. They sat on the edge of the short platform in front of the girls so they could pass the time flirting with Mindy and Selena.

Manny somehow found the energy to join them, sitting a few feet away to listen, but his eyes kept closing and his head kept lolling to the side as he dozed off.

Bored listening to the meaningless repartee, Resha looked around the sanctuary to see if anything more interesting was happening. The two pastors had vanished into Sergio's office, no doubt to discuss ancient Jewish customs or something equally fascinating, and Samuel was sitting by himself on the back row, working a crossword puzzle in a thick magazine.

Resha had just caught sight of Daniel about the same time Selena asked the three guys in front of her, "Where's your friend?"

Jeremy gave her a knowing smirk, but he asked innocently, "Who? Pastor Jeff?"

Selena frowned. "Are you kidding? He's old!"

"Are you talking about Samuel?" Jeremy continued his charade, keeping a perplexed look on his face.

"Oh, please!" Selena wrinkled her nose, making the three guys laugh.

Jeremy smacked himself on the head as if he'd just figured it out. "Oh! You must mean the tall, good-looking, blond guy."

"That's the one," Selena admitted with a giggle.

Jeremy looked from Terrell to Kevin with his arms spread wide in an exasperated gesture. "Can you believe this? Three great looking guys right here in front of them, ready to do their every bidding, and they still have to look for Daniel."

Terrell laughed at Jeremy's tragic expression, and Kevin snickered. "Story of our lives, Jeremy."

With a huge sigh, Jeremy made a show of looking around, shielding his eyes with one hand as if searching, even though he'd probably known all along where his friend was. "Let's see, is that him over there in the corner?"

Mindy and Selena followed Jeremy's gaze to where Daniel sat on the floor in the back corner of the sanctuary, totally absorbed in a book. Selena had to know, "What's he doing over there all by himself?"

"Reading his Bible, what else?" Jeremy shrugged, as if it were the most natural thing in the world.

"Are you serious?" Selena scrunched her nose up again. "Does he always do that?"

"Nah. Just once or twice a day," Jeremy grinned.

Terrell shook his head in disbelief while the two girls gawked at Daniel, who was so immersed in his reading that he didn't even notice that all eyes were suddenly on him.

Resha wasn't impressed.

He's probably got the latest issue of Playboy hidden in there, she thought cynically.

Exactly one hour later, Pastor Jeff asked the students to gather closer to the front. All but Samuel assembled themselves on the first two rows of chairs. The Nigerian man stayed on the back row, his only concession to close his magazine and lay it on the seat beside him.

"We'll be using our two weeks in Colombia to learn what God has to say about loving others," the pastor explained with a small smile. "I suspect it's a lesson that will be sorely needed as we spend a lot of time in close quarters with each other."

"For tonight's devotional, we'll be looking mainly at two scriptures. The first one is Colossians 3:13. Daniel, would you please read that aloud for us?"

Daniel flipped right to the verse and stood to read it. "'Bear with each other and forgive one another, if any of you has a grievance against someone. Forgive as the Lord forgave you.'"

Pastor Jeff asked Jeremy to read the next one, and the curly headed guy bounced up to read Ephesians 4:32. "'Be kind and compassionate to one another, forgiving each other, just as in Christ God forgave you.'"

Still embarrassed about her plaster-throwing tantrum, Resha wondered if Pastor Jeff had chosen those scriptures just for her benefit. Everyone else but Mindy looked equally convicted, though, so she relaxed and listened.

Resha found she enjoyed Pastor Jeff's style of teaching. Instead of spoon-feeding it to them, Pastor Jeff had them look up the scriptures for themselves, then he asked questions to make them think about what the words meant.

Her own pastor, Mindy's dad, was an engaging speaker who kept his congregation entertained with his well-modulated voice and amusing stories, but Resha usually left the service feeling vaguely dissatisfied. She heard the other churchgoers raving about the "great message this morning," and figured she was just too pig-headed to get anything out of it, so she tried to study the Bible on her own. Now she was actually learning from Pastor Jeff, and was disappointed that he ended his session after only about twenty minutes.

To close out their devotional time, Jeff encouraged them all to gather at the front for a group prayer. The students stood in a circle and joined hands, heads bowed as Pastor Jeff prayed briefly for each one of them by name. Then he invited them to add their own prayers or prayer requests.

After an awkward silence, Mindy chimed in with a prayer that her dad wouldn't be too lonely while she was gone, and for his church.

Jeremy added a prayer for his own family, with a specific request that God take care of his sister Natalie. No one else was brave enough to pray in front of the group yet, although they all remained respectfully reverent while their peers prayed, and Resha prayed under her breath for every request mentioned.

As he closed with a final prayer and dismissed them, Pastor Jeff graced them all with an affectionate smile, seeming pleased with their response to their first session.

The group dropped hands reluctantly, and Resha was surprised at the feeling of kinship she felt toward the others after praying with them. In spite of her exhaustion, the mellow mood followed her as she headed for the girls' quarters for the night,.

Mindy seemed to be basking in sentimentality, too. "Wasn't that wonderful? It was so nice praying with everybody, don't you think?"

Selena, who had stood between Mindy and Terrell during the group prayer, murmured dreamily, "Oh, yeah. Did you notice how strong Terrell's hands are?"

Resha tuned out the rest of their conversation and plopped onto her cot, committing to memory the prayer requests the others had mentioned. It would give her something to occupy herself with during another sleepless night.

Since they couldn't take the shortcut through the girl's room this time, the men trudged out the front door of the sanctuary, then made their way across the courtyard to their own dorm.

The day before, Manny had been the first one to enter the dorm, so he'd automatically gone to the cot on the far end. He figured the others would just grab a cot in whatever order they entered the room, but Samuel evidently didn't like being sandwiched between Manny and Terrell.

When the men returned to their quarters after the devotional, Manny found that his belongings had been placed on the next cot over. The one against the wall that he'd used the previous night was occupied by Samuel, who had already settled into it with his back to them.

When Manny saw the new arrangement, he gaped in surprise, then shrugged, crawled onto the cot Samuel had put his things on, and went to sleep. As long as Manny had a pillow and some sheets, it didn't matter to him where he slept.

4

Day 3: Tuesday

In spite of his claims to the contrary, Jeremy had made room in his backpack for a few changes of clothes along with his stash of granola bars. The next morning, he replaced his stained work shirt from the previous day with an oversized T-shirt bearing a full color picture of a smiling Tweety Bird on the front. He'd personalized the shirt by adding freckles and a Groucho Marx mustache to Tweety's face with a Sharpie marker.

Terrell took one look at the T-shirt, curled his lip in disgust, and walked out of the room shaking his head. Jeremy cracked up, delighted that his artwork had gotten a reaction.

As they headed to the dining area for breakfast, Jeremy noticed the piano that had been shoved into the back corner of the platform in the sanctuary. He couldn't resist inspecting it more closely, checking the legs and crawling underneath it to look at the bottom.

Seeing Matéo walk by, Jeremy popped out from underneath the piano and grabbed the boy's ankle. "Hey, Mat, was this thing underwater?"

Matéo gasped in surprise before answering. "No, only the legs got wet. But it does not sound right any more."

Jeremy bounced to his feet and flipped up the piano's lid, exposing the reeds inside. "Probably just needs to dry out more. The humidity makes the wood swell."

Matéo looked bewildered, but he nodded as if he actually understood the strange person's muttering. Jeremy grinned at him and ruffled his hair. He pressed a key and the piano emitted a pitiful quavery note that made both of them laugh.

Mindy and Selena walked in and the piano was promptly forgotten as Jeremy jumped off the platform to greet them.

"Ladies, allow me," he said, offering an arm to each of them.

Giggling, they each took an arm and allowed Jeremy to escort them into the next room.

Behind him, Daniel and Kevin looked at each other and rolled their eyes.

"If I tried somethin' like that, they'd report me for harassment or somethin'," Kevin grumbled.

"Nah, they'd probably just laugh at you," Daniel told him.

Terrell added his two cents worth. "My advice is, don't try it."

"Jealous, jealous," Jeremy called back to them, winking at the girls.

When they were seated at the usual table, Mindy got a good look at Tweety Bird. "That T-shirt looks so cute, Jeremy," she cooed. "Did you do that yourself?"

Jeremy looked down at his T-shirt and feigned a hurt, indignant look. "No, when I woke up this morning, Terrell was standing over my backpack with a marker in his hand. I think he must have done it while I was asleep. Can you believe that?"

Mindy turned to stare at Terrell in shock.

Terrell laughed and shook his head. "Jeremy, you are really something." Unconcerned, he shoved a forkful of scrambled eggs into his mouth as Mindy continued to gape.

Selena looked a little confused by the exchange, while Daniel and Kevin grinned in appreciation. Resha ignored them all, cutting her eggs into little pieces with a knife.

After breakfast, Sergio announced to the group that Antonio and Luís would be driving both trucks to Sincelejo to pick up a load of supplies to replace the ones that had been confiscated en route to them. "I feel it is safer to travel if there are two people in each vehicle. I would appreciate it if two of you would ride with them."

Manny was the first to volunteer. As Antonio motioned for him to follow, Jeremy whispered to Kevin, "Bet he just wants to get out of work."

Samuel stood without a word and nodded at Luís.

Kevin snickered. "And ol' Sammy just don't wanna be around us."

Uneasy with their whispering, Daniel frowned at his friends. "Guys, do you want Pastor Jeff to get after us again?"

Pastor Jeff's attention was on Sergio, though. The little Colombian pastor was whirling around as if looking for someone.

When Stefan walked in, already dripping with sweat and carrying a tool box, Sergio's face lit up. He said something to Stefan in Spanish, then turned to the three young women. "Ladies, Stefan will show you where to find the painting supplies so that you can begin your next project."

Stefan smiled at the girls and held the door open for them to pass through first, and Selena all but fell over herself to get close to the handsome laborer. Resha's lip curled in disgust at Selena's blatant admiration of the Colombian workman, and Mindy just giggled.

Once the girls had gone, Terrell, Kevin, Jeremy, and Daniel were the only ones left without an assignment. Sergio told them, "We must take advantage of the dry, sunny weather we have been blessed with to complete the repairs to our roofs. Daniel, Pastor Jeff tells me that you have experience with construction work?"

Daniel shrugged. "A little bit."

Sergio seemed satisfied with the uncertain response. He nodded vigorously as he rubbed his hands together. "Good, good. Perhaps you will take charge of the roofing repairs."

Daniel hesitated. "Uh...I've never worked with those clay roof tiles before. All the roofing I've done was with regular shingles like the ones on your house and those other two buildings."

Ever the optimist, Sergio brushed aside Daniel's concerns. "The process is very similar. I have no doubt you will figure it out quickly. Antonio and Luís should be back soon with the materials. Before they return, would you please start by removing the tarps and plywood that we used to temporarily patch the damage? You will find a ladder behind the storage shed."

And with that, Sergio was gone.

Daniel blinked. Apparently Pastor Sergio had more confidence in Daniel's abilities than he did. He dragged a nervous hand through his hair and looked at his friends helplessly, but they just grinned back at him.

With an impudent smirk, Jeremy goaded, "So what's next, Boss Man?"

And so their work day began.

After the flooding, Paola had watched most of her neighbors give up all hope of rebuilding. Many people had abandoned their homes in search of dry ground and a fresh start even before the government-mandated evacuation. Other than herself and her two brothers, and Sergio's faithful workers, the village of Cuenco Verde was void of life, human or otherwise.

When most of the water had receded, however, many of the chickens that had literally flown the coop to escape the floodwaters returned in search of their familiar shelters and regular feeding. Unfortunately, their coops had been obliterated by the raging tide, and their owners were nowhere to be found.

The chickens seemed so helpless and confused, clucking uncertainly as they pecked at the ground where their homes had once been. Paola began gathering the chickens together, luring them with grain that had been donated to the mission center. She felt sorry for the forsaken fowl, and hoped that they could contribute to the mission center's scant food supply.

When she succeeded in rounding up more than a dozen of the feathered creatures, Stefan built a hodgepodge chicken coop for them out of materials he had scavenged from the abandoned neighboring farms. Paola took responsibility for raising the chickens, and to her delight, they began producing eggs prolifically. The success of her endeavor released her from some of the guilt she had felt at not doing more of the physically demanding labor.

With the Americans here now, supplementing their food supply with the eggs was more important than ever. It was still early in the morning and already Paola could hear the young missionaries hard at work.

She finally finished collecting the eggs, cleaning the coop, and setting out feed for the chickens. She stepped outside, carefully carrying a canvas sack filled with freshly laid eggs, stretched her back, and watched as the American college students worked on the other buildings.

It was such a relief to have their help. Before they had arrived, Paola had been overwhelmed by the amount of work that had to be done. She wanted so much to do more than raise chickens and help prepare food, but several childhood bouts with malaria had rendered her permanently frail and susceptible to illness. Much to her frustration, Paola tired out easily whenever she tried to do some of the heavier chores, and Sergio had relegated her to helping Abuelita in the kitchen. Antonio, Luís and Stefan had taken some of the burden from her brother, but now that the American team had arrived, Paola noticed that her brother seemed much more relaxed.

She enjoyed having their company, too, even though she hadn't learned most of their names yet. Sergio evidently planned to keep the boys and the girls separate during their working hours, giving the girls what he considered the "easier" chores. The two pretty girls were so cute, always watching the boys and giggling while they worked. The little dark one wasn't very friendly, but Paola liked her anyway. The girl rarely smiled and mostly kept to herself, but she worked harder than the others.

Paola could understand the girl wanting to be left alone. Paola felt the same way; living with her brothers was a blessing, but sometimes she wished she had more privacy, especially now that the American pastor was staying in the house, too. Her chicken coops were her only sanctuary these days, and the incessant clucking made it difficult to think deep thoughts.

The two tall boys, the white one and the black one, had paired up again and seemed to be getting the most done; they were both strong and worked together well.

Then there were the two silly ones that were always laughing, again a white one and a black one. They did their share of the work, but they made a game out of everything and kept the others upbeat. She couldn't always understand their jokes, but it made her smile just to see them laughing and teasing each other, especially when the white boy's curls bounced as he laughed.

Paola thought the young Hispanic boy was lazy, always finding an excuse not to work – a drink of water here, a lost hammer there, a longer restroom break than seemed right. She knew he'd gone on the supply run with Antonio just so he wouldn't have to do the work on the compound. But he was the youngest of their group, so maybe he wasn't used to working hard yet.

She didn't care at all for the last member of the team, the dark-skinned man who seemed older than the rest. Paola thought she'd heard the others call him Samuel, and he usually worked alone or with her brother and Pastor Jeff. Samuel didn't mind working, but he acted as if he didn't like or need any of the others. She sometimes wondered why he had bothered to come, since he seemed to have no affection for any of them.

Stefan and Luís walked by, carrying a load of lumber. Stefan smiled and released his load with one hand to blow Paola a kiss, and she forgot all about the college students as she waved at him, her eyes sparkling.

That morning, the girls had been assigned to work in the room they slept in. Mindy was stirring gallons of paint while Resha scraped the remnants of carpet glue from the floor. Selena was painting the windowsill, a job Resha suspected she had taken just so she could watch the guys working on the roof of their building across the courtyard.

Through the window, the girls could see Daniel and Terrell on the roof, spreading rolls of tarpaper into place. Jeremy was pulling stacks of red clay roofing tiles off the back of the truck Luís had parked in the courtyard, and Kevin was moving up and down the ladder hauling supplies with him. Daniel stood and stretched, then took a swig from his canteen before moving on to the next section to work.

Resha hoped Selena's eyeballs wouldn't ruin the paint job when they popped out of her skull.

"Why is it," Selena wondered, "that when men don't shave it looks sexy, but if we don't shave our legs, it's just gross?"

Resha shook her head to dislodge the imagery Selena's comments had created, but Mindy appeared to be seriously pondering the question.

"You know, I never thought about that, Selena, but you're right!" she exclaimed as if Selena had raised an issue worthy of deep philosophical discourse. "Maybe it's because we can wear pants and hide our legs, but the guys can't really cover their faces."

Even Selena had to bite her tongue at that one. She changed the subject to one that was equally deep. "All those cute guys, just ripe for the picking. Which one do you guys want?"

"I already have a boyfriend back home," Mindy told her primly as she pried the lid off another can. "We're getting married after I graduate."

Selena was not deterred. "But what if we got stuck here forever and we could never go home? Then we'd have to pick from these guys. Stefan is the best looking one, but I think he likes Paola, and Luís is too old and too, you know, too Colombian. Antonio looks good, but he's not around much. And he doesn't even try to speak English. So I'll have to settle for one of our own guys. Resha, who would you pick?"

Resha snorted. She was getting used to the other two and their bizarre conversation, but she refused to encourage Selena's fantasies.

"We're not going to get stuck here, Selena," she said flatly.

"I know, but just pretend," Selena insisted, not the least bit dissuaded from pursuing her train of thought. "Mindy, who would it be for you?"

Mindy stopped stirring and twirled her hair on her finger as she considered the options. "Oh, I don't know. Maybe Jeremy. He's only nineteen, but he's really cute."

Selena turned to her in surprise. "Not hunky Daniel?"

"Well, he's cute and nice, too, but Jeremy is so funny. Besides, I just love his curly hair."

"My brother has curly hair," Selena pointed out.

Mindy scrunched up her face as she tried to picture Manny in her mind. "Manny's hair isn't curly, it's more like wavy. Besides, he's even younger than Jeremy."

"Okay, so it's Jeremy for you." Selena nodded as if the matter were settled. "Daniel would probably end up with Resha, anyway."

Resha, who'd been listening with half an ear while she worked on a particularly stubborn patch of glue, turned and squinted at Selena. "Why would you pair me off with a big blond boy scout?"

It wasn't that the idea was repugnant to her, just improbable.

"Well, opposites do attract, you know," Mindy offered.

"Oh, they're not so opposite, really," Selena remarked. "They're both exercise freaks. They're both kind of quiet. And Daniel's always sneaking off into some corner to read that Bible of his, and Resha's always stalking around the room at night mumbling."

"It's called 'praying', Selena," Resha snapped. She had forgotten Selena was a light sleeper.

"Exactly!" Selena exclaimed in triumph. "See what I mean? You both take the God stuff so seriously. You two belong together."

Resha snorted, shook her head, and went back to scraping. She couldn't believe she'd allowed herself to be sucked into one of their inane conversations.

Selena and Mindy moved on to a discussion about hair styling products.

As per Mindy's suggestion the day before, Abuelita and Paola had prepared plates for the group to take outside at lunch time. Daniel picked up a plate and a glass from the kitchen and carried his meal to a shady spot between the two wood frame buildings, where the others already sat crosslegged on the ground under a canopy of palm trees.

The mosquitoes and flies were just as bad, but it was a lot cooler than it had been inside, and the air was fresher.

Jeremy had borrowed a durag from Kevin to confine his unruly curls, exposing the silver stud in his ear. Terrell pointed at it. "Hey, Jeremy, did that earring come in a pair?"

Always a glutton for attention, Jeremy turned his head this way and that so the sun would glint on his earring. "Yeah, I thought of getting two holes in my ear but I chickened out, so now I've got a spare. A spare earring that is, not ear."

"Maybe you should lend the extra one to Resha," Terrell raised his voice to make sure the girl in question heard him. "She could wear it in her nose."

Jeremy's smile froze and he nervously cut his eyes sideways to see Resha's reaction.

She was visibly clenching her jaw as she refused to look Terrell's way. The dig was mild compared to some of the things Terrell had said to her, but Resha had to be getting tired of his taunts.

Daniel wondered whether Terrell had forgotten yesterday's incident, or if he thought there was safety in numbers, or if the guy was just plain stupid. He gave Terrell a pointed look.

Terrell pretended not to notice, but at least he dropped the subject.

Mindy didn't have enough sense to drop it, although there was nothing but innocence in her tone as she commented, "Resha, I didn't know your nose was pierced."

Resha's eyes rolled heavenward in an unspoken plea for patience. She shoved a large bite of food into her mouth, stifling whatever response she wanted to make. When Mindy realized Resha wasn't going to answer her, she pouted but stayed quiet.

Kevin and Jeremy grinned at each other, amused by Resha's restraint.

"Man, girlfriend got some discipline," Kevin whispered to Jeremy, who nodded in admiration.

They might have felt differently if Daniel had told them about the plaster incident, but that was something he chose to keep to himself. He wondered idly if her nose really was pierced.

Jeff peeked out the window to see how his crew was doing with their outdoor dining. They seemed much more relaxed than they had been inside, although he didn't understand how they could be comfortable sprawled out on the hard ground. Ah, to be young again!

But then again....

Jeff was aggravated to see Daniel absently scratching his ribs while Kevin slapped at a mosquito on his neck. How hard could it be to remember to put on repellant?

At least Jeremy wasn't scratching, but he'd obviously forgotten his sunscreen; his cheeks were much too pink and his nose was flat out red. Resha was the only one still heeding his advice to wear long sleeves, the others having shucked off their outer shirts in favor of cooler, short-sleeved T-shirts, their bare arms an open invitation to hungry mosquitoes. Jeff shook his head in frustration and reminded himself one more time that they were adults, not children.

Manny wasn't with them, but Jeff had seen him slip into the men's quarters with his plate, and he assumed the boy was going to sneak a nap after he ate. Then Jeff realized Samuel wasn't with them, either.

Glancing around, Jeff saw that Samuel had pulled a folding chair into the shade created by the cinder block shed and was eating his lunch alone. The pastor sighed, took one last sip of his aguapanela, and walked outside. He approached Samuel and offered a friendly wave, which the Nigerian acknowledged with a curt nod.

"It's a lot cooler out here," Pastor Jeff commented, hoping to open a conversation with small talk.

Samuel merely nodded and took another bite of his *arepa*.

Jeff felt awkward towering over the Nigerian man, but there wasn't another chair for him to sit in. Finally, he crouched beside the man, keeping his face toward the arroyo so he wouldn't come across too strongly. "I was hoping the whole group would sit together for meal times."

"We are all more comfortable if I sit here by myself," Samuel said in his thick accent. He offered nothing else and Jeff swallowed another sigh.

"Samuel, you seem very unhappy here," Jeff prodded.

"I did not come here to be happy. I came to work." Another bite, followed by a long swig of his drink.

Jeff fought off his irritation, but he couldn't hide it entirely when he asked, "Samuel, I don't understand why you signed up for this project if you didn't want to be a part of the team."

Samuel took his time finishing his arepa, then crumpled his napkin and placed it on his empty plate. Jeff wondered if the man was going to bother to answer him.

Finally, Samuel spoke, looking off into space. "Ten years ago, I was still living in Nigeria. There was a terrible drought. My family was dying because there was no water for our crops, no water for us to drink. A group of Christian missionaries from Australia came and helped our village to dig water wells and saved many lives.

"Once our bellies were full, we were ready to listen to their message. My family and I became Christians because of what the missionaries did for us. When I was finally able to come to America three years ago, I prayed that one day I could do for someone else what those missionaries did for my family. By being a part of this work here, I am hoping to give back in some small way what I received from them."

That didn't answer Jeff's question, but it was the most he'd ever heard Samuel speak, and he was humbled by the Nigerian man's story. Jeff hadn't realized before how heavily accented Samuel's English was, and he wondered if that was the reason he didn't like speaking with anyone. He also understood now why Samuel was older than the other students – he hadn't even come into the country until recently.

While it certainly didn't excuse the man's rudeness, Jeff was impressed with Samuel's desire to repay a kindness that had been done for his family. After a pause, Jeff said, "Thank you for sharing that with me, Samuel."

Samuel's only response was to stand up and turn his back to Jeff while he folded the chair he'd been sitting on. Jeff took that as his cue to leave. He stood and walked alone back to the sanctuary.

As the team devoured their skimpy lunch under the cluster of shady palms, Paola appeared, carrying a heavy pitcher of aguapanela. Daniel felt guilty at the sight of the frail woman serving them, but he remembered Pastor Sergio's admonition and smiled at her as he accepted a refill.

Suddenly, Mindy gave a delighted squeal. When everyone looked at her in surprise, she pointed excitedly. "Look! A puppy dog!"

The phrase "puppy dog" was hardly an apt description for the poor, mangy creature that was snuffling at the ground near the chicken coop. The pathetic looking brown mutt had patches of hair missing in several places, and its ribs were sticking out.

"'Puppy Dawg' looks hungry," Kevin observed.

Daniel broke off a piece of his arepa and tossed it in the general direction of the dog. Although the food landed a couple of yards short, the soft thud it made spooked the animal, which gave a frightened little whimper and slunk away with its tail tucked under. It disappeared behind the building.

"Oops," said Jeremy at the same time that Selena cried, "Aw."

Daniel grimaced apologetically. "Sorry about that. It'll probably smell the food and come back."

Paola smiled at the kindhearted young people. "Matéo has been trying to catch that dog, and he has been putting out food for it when he thinks Sergio is not watching. He wants it for a pet, but the dog will not let anyone get near him."

Craning her neck to try to see where the animal went, Mindy asked, "Where did the doggy come from?"

"*¿Quién sabe?* Who knows?" Paola replied sadly. "Probably his owners left him behind when the flood came, or maybe...maybe his owners did not survive. So he is all alone now and must fend for himself."

Mindy's eyes filled with tears. "Oh, the poor baby. We have to help him!"

After lunch, Daniel and Terrell hauled the ladder to the classroom in the back to start repairing its roof, relieved they would be working with regular shingles instead of the fragile red tiles they'd had to use on the stucco building.

Kevin borrowed the truck keys from Luís and backed the truck closer to the building so they wouldn't have to carry the supplies as far. He and Jeremy cut the thick straps off the boxes of shingles and began passing them up to Daniel and Terrell.

As Daniel and Terrell dragged a couple of the heavy cases across the roof, Daniel finally had a chance to ask about something that had been bugging him. "Why do you give Resha such a hard time?"

"Because it's fun," Terrell said carelessly.

Daniel kept his gaze on Terrell and waited for more, not willing to settle for the glib answer. They reached the damaged area and began unpacking the shingles. As they continued to work in silence, Daniel assumed he'd been brushed off.

Then Terrell grinned. "You don't let things go, do you? You're a little too introspective for my tastes, but I like you."

"Does that mean you'll answer the question?"

"I don't know," Terrell admitted. "I guess it just bugs me that she's here."

"How's that?" Daniel fished around in his pocket and came up with a fistful of nails.

"It just doesn't seem like she's got a right to be here, you know? I mean, with her jail record and all."

Daniel blinked, surprised to learn that the petite girl with the pixie face really was an ex-convict. He wanted to ask Terrell about it, but it wouldn't be fair to talk about that behind Resha's back, especially with someone so hostile toward her. Instead, he asked, "You don't think God can change people?"

"Well, sure," Terrell was forced to concede. He unhooked a hammer from his belt and handed it to Daniel. "She might have changed some, but she's still got a criminal background. They had to do all kind of extra paperwork to get her passport application approved. They could have saved all that trouble and just picked somebody else."

"Such as?" Daniel probed. He had a feeling there was more to Terrell's animosity.

After a pause, Terrell smiled sheepishly and admitted, "Such as my girlfriend. She applied, and she should have qualified, but they chose Resha instead."

Ah, so that's the problem, thought Daniel. "Maybe they didn't think it would look right for them to send you and your girlfriend on a trip together," he suggested.

Terrell considered the possibility, then shrugged. "I guess. It still just doesn't seem right, that's all. I mean, do you think it's fair that somebody that's been to jail got to come instead of somebody with a clean record?"

"I think...." Daniel took his time positioning a row of shingles just right, giving himself time to consider his response. "I think God had the final say about who came on the trip. I think everybody that came is here for a purpose, and there's a reason Resha is here just like there's a reason the rest of us are here."

Looking thoughtful, Terrell gazed down at the courtyard where the girls were washing out some paintbrushes in a bucket. "Maybe you're right."

After they'd finished the roofing repairs on the men's dorm and the other classroom, the guys started putting things away. Terrell folded the ladder and carried it to the side of Pastor Sergio's house to use the next day. Since Luís and Stefan had already repaired the roof of the main sanctuary before they'd arrived, Sergio's house would be their final roofing project. Kevin and Jeremy unloaded the last of the shingles from the back of the truck and Daniel began stacking the boxes beside the house.

They were all moving a lot slower than they had that morning, but Jeremy looked particularly weary as he staggered under the weight of a carton. Jeremy had never been as athletic as his two friends, but his energy usually made up for what he lacked in muscular strength. It looked like his energy had failed him this evening – his brown curls were flattened with sweat and clung to his heat reddened forehead, and his breathing came in shallow gasps.

Daniel quickly took the box from him. "Hey, Jeremy, take it easy. We're just about done here."

Hearing the concern in Daniel's voice, Kevin took a closer look at Jeremy. "Yeah, man, go sit down in the shade or somethin'. We got it from here."

Jeremy frowned and opened his mouth to object, but couldn't muster the strength to argue, so he nodded and leaned against the truck. After taking a drink from his canteen, he said apologetically, "Not used to working in this heat, I guess."

The other three made short work of the remainder of the cartons, and soon all four of them were washing up for dinner. None of them were up to a water fight this time, so they took turns at the sink in the tiny half bath in their dorm.

Glimpsing himself in the mirror, Daniel turned to look at his friends and saw they were all as scraggly and unkempt as he was.

"You know, sooner or later we're going to have to venture into the girls' domain and use that shower," he sighed.

"Yeah, a shave would be nice, too." Terrell rubbed his stubbly jaw. "It's too dark to try shaving with that little stick razor in this bathroom with no windows. They've got lights over there."

"A shave sounds great," Jeremy agreed, running a hand over his own chin. He was looking more like himself now that he'd rested a bit.

Kevin must have noticed, too, because he chuckled and taunted, "Come on, Jeremy, you know you don't need to shave but once a month anyway."

Jeremy grinned. "Yeah, well at least I don't have to shave my back."

Terrell and Daniel laughed at Kevin's vehement denials. After the scare Jeremy had given them earlier, it was good to see him back in form.

As far as Jeremy could tell, the free time Pastor Jeff insisted on giving them after dinner was a waste of time. It's not like the students were using it to "bond," or anything.

Although Mindy was sure trying.

For a while, Jeremy had amused himself watching Resha try to respond with patience to Mindy's incessant prattling. But after one final eye roll, Resha had given up and stomped off to the girls' dorm.

Samuel had parked himself on the back row with his crossword puzzles again while Terrell tried without success to engage him in conversation. Manny had gone to bed complaining about a sore back when he returned on Antonio's truck with the roofing supplies. Daniel was back in his corner, balancing his Bible on his drawn up knees while he scribbled in a notebook that lay on the floor beside him, and the two pastors had vanished into Sergio's office.

The ultimate disappointment came when Mindy and Selena left with Paola. The girls said Paola was going to show them her chicken coops, but Jeremy suspected they were really just going to dish about Stefan. With no one to flirt with, Jeremy would have to kill time annoying Kevin, and he could do that any time.

The piano lid was still up the way he'd left it that morning, so Jeremy poked his head underneath it.

"Still too damp," he pronounced. "Needs to dry out another couple of days."

He pushed and tugged at the piano to pull it away from the wall a few inches, then sat next to Kevin and tapped his fingers on the chair, drumming out a weird little beat to amuse himself.

Jeremy eyed Daniel, who had set his Bible on the floor beside him and now had his head bowed and eyes closed. If Jeremy didn't know Daniel was praying, he would have thought the guy had dropped off to sleep.

He tore a tiny strip of paper out of his notebook, balled it up and asked Kevin, "Shall I throw spitwads at him?"

"Jeremy, you ain't right, man," Kevin chided, snickering. "Leave 'im alone. He might be prayin' for you."

"I need it," Jeremy muttered under his breath, causing Kevin to shoot him a puzzled look.

Before Kevin could question him, Sergio scurried out of his office wearing an uncharacteristic frown.

"What's up, Pastor Sergio?" Jeremy asked.

"Pastor Jeff and I were going to try to contact Brother Novak, but the radio is not working any more." Sergio was actually wringing his hands in his agitation.

"Really?" Jeremy's attention was immediately piqued. "Was it running off a battery or electricity?"

"We were using a car battery when Brother Novak first brought it to us, but when we got the generator, Stefan changed it so that we can use the electricity."

Jeremy chewed his lip, trying to decide whether his assistance would be welcome. "Want me to look at it?" he finally couldn't resist offering.

Sergio looked at him with surprise. "Of course, Jeremy. I know nothing about such things and Stefan is still working outside, so I would appreciate any help you can give me."

Jeremy followed him back into the tiny office, and Kevin trailed along behind. When Pastor Jeff saw Jeremy with Sergio, he stepped aside with a grin. "I was wondering if you'd find out about it. She's all yours, Jeremy."

Jeremy first played with all the knobs, then checked the connections to the power source, and finally ran his hands along the back of the oversized radio, turning it on the desk so he could see the cables better.

He stopped, frowning in confusion. "You said this thing worked before?"

"Oh, yes," Sergio told him. "It is our only means of communication right now. We have been using this very radio since right after the flood. It is how we arranged for you all to be here."

Jeremy nodded absently, already trying to figure out how to make it work, but he was still puzzled.

Pastor Jeff murmured something to Sergio about giving Jeremy room to work, and the two pastors left the cramped room.

Kevin leaned in closer and asked, "What'sa matter, man?"

"There's a piece missing, see?" Jeremy pointed to a male connector jutting from the back of the radio. "There should be a little co-ax cable right here. There's no way this radio could have worked without it."

"Maybe it fell off?" Kevin suggested.

"Co-ax cables don't just fall off, Kevin," Jeremy scoffed, knowing Kevin didn't have the slightest clue what a co-ax cable was. Still, he dutifully searched all around underneath the table and the radio.

Nothing. Jeremy stood back with his chin on his fist and his other arm folded across his chest, thinking hard. After a moment, he said, "I think I can make it work, though."

He stuck his head out of the room and spotted the two pastors talking to Daniel, who was eagerly pointing out something he'd discovered in his Bible.

Jeremy called out, "Pastor Sergio, is there another radio, like just a transistor radio that you're not using, or maybe a TV that we can take apart?"

An hour later, Jeremy had removed the co-ax cable from a television Sergio had confiscated from his living room. He attached the wire to the back of the radio and tweaked it a bit before declaring it fixed. All four of them held their breath while Sergio tried it out, and all breathed a sigh of relief when the radio crackled back to life.

"Jeremy, I do not know how to thank you." Pastor Sergio clasped Jeremy's hand and shook it fiercely. "What a wonderful gift God has given you, to be able to fix this for us."

"Jeremy can fix anything," Kevin told him proudly.

"Everything except your bad attitude," Jeremy grinned.

In spite of their good spirits, Jeremy still thought the missing cable was peculiar. He had mentioned it to Pastor Sergio, but Sergio seemed unconcerned, so Jeremy dropped the subject.

It probably wasn't important.

Resha tried to pray awhile in the empty dorm, but the afternoon sun had made it unbearably hot and the paint fumes from earlier were still trapped inside. She opened the side door to let the room air out and wandered into the courtyard, not ready to give up her solitude yet.

The sun was just setting, and a slight breeze made it cooler out here. She leaned against the wall, arms folded across her chest, and tried to decide what she should pray about.

There were so many things to choose from.

Matéo listlessly tossed a dirty rubber ball up in the air and caught it. Once his chores were done, he sometimes got bored and lonely after having no one to talk to all day except his older brother and the three workmen. Paola was nice, but she never had much energy to play with him. He wished there was someone closer to his own age around.

He was curious about the American missionaries, too. Why had Sergio told him not to bother them in the dining room? Matéo wasn't going to bother them – he just wanted to ask them some questions. That would be more fun than playing all by himself.

Rounding the corner, Matéo spotted Resha out in the courtyard, and he stopped bouncing his little ball to stare at the strange-looking American woman. He was fascinated by the shiny disks hanging from her ears, and he'd never seen hair that short on a girl before.

This one had a lot of energy – Matéo had watched her working without taking any breaks. He'd never seen her smile, but for some reason, he wasn't afraid of her. He knew that deep inside, she couldn't be as mean as she looked. Or maybe he felt safe because she was not much bigger than him.

She wasn't in the dining area, so he wouldn't be breaking Sergio's rule if he talked to her out here, would he?

To give himself an excuse to get a closer look at Resha, he dropped his ball and let it roll toward her.

Resha's prayers for Pastor Sergio and his family were interrupted by a skittering noise to her left. Without turning her head, she cut her eyes toward the sound. It was only the pastor's little brother, scampering after a rubber ball.

"Good evening, Miss Resha," he said politely, pocketing his ball as he approached.

Resha returned his gaze steadily, without smiling. "Good evening, Matéo."

That was all the encouragement he needed. He skipped right up to her and tugged at her hand. "Miss Resha, come, let me show you the arroyo."

Resha was surprised at his familiarity, but the only indication she gave was a slightly raised eyebrow. "Didn't your brother say it was dangerous?"

"He said he did not want anyone to go around the arroyo alone," Matéo corrected her. "If you go with me, neither of us will be alone, so it will be okay."

Typical male, Resha thought with cynical amusement. So young and already looking for loopholes to get his own way.

Still, a glance at the sun told her she probably had another half hour before the evening devotional, and exploring with Matéo beat watching Mindy and Selena drooling over the men. She nodded her agreement. "Okay, but we need to make it fast. It's getting dark already."

Matéo pulled at her hand eagerly and Resha allowed him to lead her towards the lush line of tropical foliage. He headed straight for a small opening between several flowering plumerias.

From the confident way Matéo navigated a pathway between the trees, it was obvious he spent more time by the arroyo than Sergio realized. Resha could understand the appeal of the forbidden territory to an adventurous boy who had no playmates to keep him entertained.

She was able to keep up with the nimble boy with no problem — climbing in and out of windows of the houses she'd broken into before her conversion had been good training for clambering over the big rocks that lined the sides of the ravine. When they got near the water, the two paused a moment to savor the coolness created by the heavy tree cover, listening to the shrill cries of hidden birds.

The arroyo was wider than Resha had expected, and the bank dropped sharply rather than tapering off. When the rushing waters had subsided, they had left in their wake exposed, gnarled roots that now jutted awkwardly from the jagged sides. The churning water at the bottom ran rapidly toward the river a couple of miles away, and she understood why Sergio had warned Matéo to avoid the area.

"Sergio says the sides used to look like this," Matéo said, moving his hands to demonstrate a gentle slope. "But after the flood, the ground fell into the water, and now it is too deep."

Resha noted how the edges had crumbled, making it a sheer drop into the water below. "Yeah, well, you better stay away from the edges, kid, because they might give way some more."

Matéo looked confused at her words, so she rephrased her comment in Spanish. "*No se acerque demasiado al borde. La tierra podría caer dentro.*"

When Matéo's blank expression didn't change, Resha decided he was just playing dumb because he wanted an excuse not to take her advice. She dropped the subject.

The two of them made their way several yards farther down before their progress was stopped by a tangle of bushes and vines too dense to penetrate. They perched on clumps of snarled tree roots and looked down at the swirling brown water, which carried a film of scum on the surface, broken up by leftover flood debris. The odor of decaying vegetation mingled with a pungent floral perfume.

They sat in companionable silence for a few minutes, swatting at the swarming mosquitoes. After a while, Matéo spoke, keeping his eyes on the rapidly flowing water.

"Sergio says that his children are in Heaven now because they believed in Jesus."

It hadn't occurred to Resha that the loss of his brother's family had affected the lively little boy. She studied him from the corner of her eye and tossed a pebble into the ravine so he wouldn't notice that she was watching him closely. "Your brother is telling the truth. That's what the Bible says, isn't it?"

Matéo nodded his head, intent on the brown foam that formed at the edges of the water. When he said nothing more, Resha asked casually, "Did you know his kids?"

She tossed another pebble.

"I didn't see them very much because they lived too far. They were both too little anyway." He shrugged as if it didn't matter, but his face was somber. After a while, he said, "Rodrigo was only four, and Hector was seven. I used to play ball with Hector when Sergio brought them to visit."

Now Matéo threw a pebble into the water, too, then another. Watching them sink, he asked, "Do you think they can play ball in Heaven?"

Why not? thought Resha, but she didn't think she was wise enough to make that call. To be safe, she told Matéo what she knew for sure.

"Well, we know that God is good, and that He loves Hector and Rodrigo, and since He made them, He knows what they like to do. Jesus promised to prepare a place for us in His Father's house, and the Bible says there's no tears in Heaven, and the streets are made out of gold, so whatever they're doing, you can bet they're happier than they've ever been."

Her answer seemed to satisfy Matéo, because his face relaxed. He let the pebbles he had collected trickle from his fingers and the two remained quiet for a while longer.

Resha decided it was time to move on. She pointed her chin toward the other side. "Is there any way to get across?"

Matéo shook his head. "No, only the bridge that the cars go on, but it is too far." He looked at her hopefully, his melancholy forgotten. "Do you think we could get a little boat and go across?"

Resha hid her amusement at his childish optimism. "That's not a good idea, Matéo. We don't know how deep that water is, and there might be snakes in it. You should listen to your brother and stay away from here."

"Okay," Matéo said.

Resha knew the odds of the little boy keeping his word were miniscule. "Come on, Matéo, it's getting dark. We need to get back."

She turned and headed back up the incline, not bothering to check whether he was following her. A few moments later, scuffling footsteps told her that the boy was behind her.

After the evening devotional, Daniel dropped in utter exhaustion onto his cot against the wall by the door, releasing a grateful sigh.

Two cots away, Terrell groaned in pain as he lowered himself. "I'm sore in places I didn't even know I had muscles," he groused in the darkness. "Tell me again why we're doing this?"

"You mean besides serving God?" Daniel teased. "Just think how good this will look on your resume."

Stretched out on his cot between Jeremy's and Terrell's, Kevin laughed. "Daniel don't need no resume. He gonna be CEO of his dad's company two days after he graduates."

"Come on, Kevin," Daniel objected. "You know my dad would make me earn it like anyone else. I don't even know for sure if I'm going to work for him."

"'Course you are, man," Kevin pooh-poohed Daniel's protest. "You gonna get rich workin' for daddy, and you gonna marry some pretty girl and live in a big two-story house and have lotsa little Daniels and Daniellas runnin' 'round, and you all gonna hold hands and sing 'Jesus Loves Me.'"

A surprised laugh burst from Daniel. "That's ridiculous."

Terrell and Kevin snickered at the absurd image, and Daniel decided to return the favor.

"So what about you, Kevin? Are you going to marry Tameka when you graduate?" Daniel asked, referring to a chubby girl Kevin sometimes dated.

Kevin dismissed the notion with a snort. "Nah, man, I ain't gettin'married anytime soon, 'specially to Tameka. Nah, what I'm gonna do is, I'm gonna take over the dealership and make lotsa money, and then I'm gonna buy me a whole string of Ferrari dealerships, and the rest of you gonna come beggin' me for a loan."

Terrell added his own fantasy to the mix. "And I'm going to develop a computer program that will make Microsoft obsolete, and you guys will see my picture in the paper and tell everybody you knew me way back before I became the richest man in America."

Now it was Daniel's turn to snicker.

Then he noticed Jeremy wasn't churning out his usual wisecracks. "What about you, Jeremy? You got big plans for after you graduate?"

Silence.

He looked over at the cot next to him, but it was too dark to see Jeremy.

Kevin reached a foot over to jostle their friend's cot. "Yo, Jer, you fall asleep already, man?"

After a long pause, Jeremy answered, "Sorry, guys, I guess I was thinking about something else."

His friends were shocked into silence themselves. Jeremy without a clever comeback?

He never did answer Daniel's question.

5

Day 4: Wednesday

"Manny, I need your help, please," Antonio called in Spanish. "I am going to pick up some more supplies in Sincelejo and I need you to ride with me."

Manny groaned. The only reason he'd volunteered to ride with Antonio the day before was to get away from the work at the mission center, but he'd ended up having to help Antonio load heavy lumber and roofing materials. His arms and his back were still aching.

"Can't you ask someone else?" he whined.

Antonio's eyes narrowed for a moment, but his friendly smile was back so quickly that Manny might have imagined it. The Colombian man looked around at the students hovering nearby, then stepped closer so only Manny could hear his words.

"I have been watching you, Manny. You are not like the others. You do not want to waste time doing this kind of work. You have bigger dreams, do you not?"

Manny liked the sound of that, and he puffed up with pride that Antonio had noticed that he wasn't a common laborer.

Antonio continued. "I am the same, Manny. I am not content to build another man's project, especially one that is doomed to failure. I may have a way to help both of us, but we cannot talk about it here."

Now Manny was eager to go along, anxious to hear what Antonio had to say. "Let me go tell Pastor Jeff that I'm going with you. I'll be right back!"

As Daniel rounded the corner, he spotted Abuelita cautiously descending the moldy, wobbly steps of the ruined storeroom, carrying a box that looked much too big and heavy for her.

Daniel knew full well the old woman could manage on her own, but he couldn't stand just watching her struggle with the burden when it would be so easy for him to carry it for her. He approached and held his hands out in an offer to take the box.

Abuelita gave him a toothless smile and placed the box in his arms. Then she bent to pick up two large bags of corn flour she'd placed on the steps and the two of them walked toward the kitchen, Daniel pacing himself to her slower footsteps.

When they made it inside, Abuelita pointed to a cleared space on the counter, and Daniel set down the box that was filled with canned food and bags of rice. Abuelita reached up to pat Daniel's cheek, and he had to bend his head down slightly to receive the gesture of appreciation. He left the kitchen wearing a foolish smile, feeling both pleased and embarrassed.

"Kissing up to Abuelita so she'll give you extra food?" Jeremy needled when Daniel joined them. He and Kevin were pulling heavy plastic off the boxes of shingles. They both had bandanas knotted around their heads to keep hair and sweat out of their eyes.

Kevin snickered. "She already gives 'im the biggest portion, man. You see the way she piles that food on his plate?"

Terrell laughed as he unfolded the long aluminum ladder and propped it up against the house. "If she's serving that canned meat again, Daniel can have mine."

"Looks like I'll be eating your lunch, then," Daniel told him with a grin. "I think that's what was in that box."

He pulled a rolled-up Rangers baseball cap from his back pocket and plopped it on his head as protection from the sun's fierce rays.

Pastor Jeff walked past tugging on a pair of work gloves. He paused when he saw the ladder. "Going to do Sergio's roof today?"

They all made affirmative sounds and Jeff glanced up at the sun beating down on the roof. "It's going to be another awfully hot day, boys. Make sure you drink lots of water." Jeff's words were addressed to all of them, but he focused his gaze on Jeremy.

"We just filled up our canteens," Daniel replied, patting his where it hung off his belt.

"Good." Jeff nodded approval, keeping his eyes on Jeremy. It was obvious to whom his remarks were directed, and Jeremy's face flushed with anger as he looked anywhere but at Pastor Jeff. "If any of you feel like you need to, make sure you take a break, okay? We don't need any of you getting overheated out there."

"What difference will it make in the long run, Pastor Jeff?" Jeremy challenged cryptically, finally making eye contact with Jeff.

Pastor Jeff stared at Jeremy, then sighed and walked away.

Jeremy spun on his friends angrily, glaring at Kevin. "What'd you guys tell him?"

"We didn't tell 'im nothin', man," Kevin insisted, looking at Jeremy like he was crazy.

Jeremy swung his scowl to Daniel.

"We really didn't, Jeremy." Daniel held up his hands placatingly. "You know how Pastor Jeff is. He just knows everything."

Jeremy fumed a moment longer, then suddenly grinned, his ire forgotten. "Yeah. Kinda creepy, huh? Wonder how he does that?"

While the young people tackled their assignments, Sergio and Jeff toiled under the carport with their own project.

The two pastors were refinishing the water-damaged pews that had been removed from the sanctuary, sanding off the water marks on the legs and replacing the nails that were rusted. Soon they would be ready to apply a fresh coat of varnish, but they still had one pew left to sand.

Jeff heard Matéo calling out to someone and looked up to see the little boy dart across the courtyard with a canteen and hand it to Terrell, who nodded his thanks. Sergio waved to get his younger brother's attention, and Matéo trotted to where he and Jeff were standing.

Sergio handed Matéo a square of sandpaper that had been worn smooth and used to the point that holes showed through it. "Matéo, go and ask Luís if he has any more sandpaper like this in his toolbox, please."

"Okay, Sergio." Matéo nodded eagerly and sprinted off again.

It seemed to Jeff that the little boy was always running from one group to the other, fetching tools, passing messages, refilling canteens. He did whatever they asked him to with a seemingly endless supply of energy and without complaint.

"He's quite a helper," Jeff commented. His glasses had slid down on his sweat-slicked nose, and he pushed them back up. "We could all learn from his attitude."

Sergio beamed with pride. "Yes, my little brother has been a tremendous blessing to us here. I was afraid at first that he would just get in the way, but he begged and begged for me to let him come with Paola and help. Our mother encouraged it, also, because she was having a difficult time keeping up with Matéo, so I finally allowed it, and I have not regretted it."

"I'm surprised you were able to get permission for a child so young to stay in the area after the forced evacuation," Jeff said as he turned his own square of sandpaper around and around, trying to find a spot on it that was still usable.

Sergio looked uncomfortable. "They may have gotten the impression that Matéo was older," he admitted.

Amused at Sergio's obvious discomfiture, Jeff pressed, "How would they have gotten that impression?"

"Well, they met me in person when I requested permission, of course, and they met my sister, also," Sergio explained, his eyes cast downward. "When I told them my brother would also be joining us, they must have assumed that he was also close in age and asked only for his name. I did not volunteer any other information."

Jeff smiled at Sergio's obvious embarrassment over his disclosure. Instead of teasing the younger pastor, Jeff changed the subject to one he'd been wondering about anyway. "That is kind of a big age difference between the two of you and Matéo."

"Paola and I were born to my mother's first marriage," Sergio explained. "When my father died, my mother remained unmarried for many years, until God sent her another husband, who is now also deceased. Matéo is the result of her second marriage."

Jeff was mildly surprised. "But the three of you look so much alike, especially him and Paola."

"We all favor our mother, and Paola and Matéo also got their coloring from her. We do not consider Matéo a 'half' brother. He is our brother."

"Of course," Jeff said.

At that moment, the subject of their conversation came bounding around the corner, holding out several sheets of sandpaper. "Luís said this is the last of the sandpaper."

Sergio smiled at his young brother and accepted the paper. "We will be careful not to waste it, then. Thank you, Matéo."

"Okay." Matéo scampered away.

Jeff and Sergio exchanged a smile at the boy's energy.

Resha strode to the cinder block storage shed to gather more painting supplies, with Mindy and Selena nipping at her heels as usual.

Stefan was already there, sorting through some metal pipes. He smiled at the girls and stepped aside so they could get to their paint cans.

Selena was blatant in her admiration for the Colombian laborer, staring him up and down like he was the first man she'd ever seen. As the three of them lugged the heavy cans back to the main building, where they would be painting the kitchen and dining area, she craned her neck all the way around so she could watch Stefan carrying the pipes under one arm. "No doubt about it, Stefan is hot. How serious do you think he is with Paola?"

Resha gave Selena a withering look, repulsed that Selena would even consider coming between Paola and the workman.

Mindy seemed unaware of Selena's interest.

"Aren't they the cutest couple?" she gushed. "Do you see the way they look at each other when they think nobody is watching? It's just so sweet!"

"I guess," Selena agreed reluctantly, but she continued to ogle Stefan until he was out of sight.

Mindy turned her big gray eyes toward Resha, disregarding Selena's less than enthusiastic response. "Oh, Resha, you should have heard what Paola told us last night."

She popped open a paint can and pushed it toward Selena while she continued her tale. "Paola said she was sick when she was young, so she never had a chance to go out on dates or anything. Then later she got stronger, but Matéo's daddy had died, so Paola had to help her mom raise Matéo. She didn't have time to meet anybody, and she said it must have been because God knew she would meet Stefan here! Isn't that just the most romantic story?"

Resha didn't bother to respond, but Selena cut her eyes upward and huffed, then started stirring the paint more vigorously than necessary. Resha squinted at Mindy, suspecting that Mindy's words were intended to discourage Selena's inappropriate crush. If so, they'd hit the mark.

Mindy hummed happily as she poured paint into a roller tray.

Lacking the right supplies to finish his plumbing project, Stefan had started working instead on an old, dark green Chevrolet sedan that had been parked in the grass behind the storage shed. From his perch on Sergio's roof, Daniel could hear metallic clanging as the Colombian man struggled to remove a stubborn part.

When Daniel had hammered the last shingle out of the case into place, Terrell called out to their friends below that they needed another box, but there was no response.

Looking around, Daniel spotted Kevin's legs sticking out from under the Chevy, while Jeremy and Stefan leaned over the hood.

"Looks like we're on our own," he told Terrell wryly, then climbed down the ladder to grab more shingles.

Heading for the bundles of shingles piled in the shade of the house, Daniel found Mindy sitting on the stack with her back to him. She must be taking a well-deserved break from all the painting the girls were doing, he thought, but she was making little frustrated sounds.

"Are you having some trouble there, Mindy?" he asked, amused at her obvious distress.

Mindy turned and held up a cell phone. "This isn't working."

Daniel bit his lip, then explained patiently, "Remember Pastor Jeff told us our cell phones probably wouldn't work in Colombia? All their towers are down, and I doubt T-Mobile has coverage all the way over here, anyway."

"Oh." Mindy pouted in disappointment, and Daniel felt sorry for her. Trying to cheer her up, he reminded her, "But the camera in it should still work."

She brightened immediately. "Oh! So maybe I can send pictures to my friends even if I can't talk to them." She saw Daniel's expression and her face fell again. "I guess not, huh?"

He shook his head apologetically.

Mindy stared at her cell phone as if it had betrayed her. She held it up to him again and he saw that the screen was blank. "It's not charged up anyway. There's an extension cord in our room, and I had the phone plugged in the whole time we were having breakfast, but it didn't do any good."

"Mindy, you have to plug it in when the generator's running." Daniel tried to keep the exasperation out of his voice. She turned big sad eyes to him again, and he melted. "Look, plug it in tonight when the lights are on. There should be electricity in the cord then, okay?"

"Okay, Daniel." She nodded obediently, then said, "Do you really think that will work? I couldn't get it to charge before we left Houston, either."

Daniel shut his eyes and prayed for patience. "Why don't you give it a try, and if it still doesn't work, ask Jeremy to take a look at it." He wondered if he had done Jeremy a favor by sending him the beautiful redhead, or if he was finally getting revenge on Jeremy for the many pranks he'd pulled.

Mindy nodded again, smiling happily. "That's right, I'll bet Jeremy can fix it. Thanks, Daniel."

Daniel managed to smile back at her as she scooted off the stack of shingles so he could get to them, and he grabbed a couple of cases. As he climbed back up the ladder with his load, he blew out a long breath and crossed his eyes.

Terrell took the boxes from his hands and laughed. "Been talking to Mindy again, huh?"

By lunchtime, Stefan and his two self-appointed mechanics had gotten the Chevy running. Jeremy laughed off the Colombian man's appreciation while Kevin wandered away to wash up.

Looked like Daniel and Terrell had finished replacing all the damaged shingles – Terrell was piling up the empty cartons as Daniel carried the ladder toward the shed. Jeremy hurried to catch up with Daniel and grabbed one end of the ladder to help.

Daniel gave him a perturbed look. "Great, now you show up, after all the hard work is done."

"Hey, you don't think cleaning a 1998 carburetor is hard work?" Jeremy protested, wiggling his fingers in Daniel's face to show how grease-stained they were.

Unimpressed, Daniel pulled a crumpled handkerchief out of his back pocket and shoved it at Jeremy so he could wipe his hands on it.

"Thanks, bro," Jeremy said. When his hands were semi-clean, he stuffed the hankie into Daniel's shirt pocket, then reached up and twisted Daniel's cap sideways on his head, causing his hair to stick out at odd angles.

"What kind of perverse pleasure do you get out of doing stuff like that?" Daniel grumbled, but he left the cap askew. "I hope the others realize it's your handiwork and don't think I'm making some kind of statement."

Jeremy cackled as the two of them made their way toward the kitchen to pick up their lunch. Terrell and Kevin had beat them there.

Terrell gave Daniel an odd look when he saw the cap. Then he saw Jeremy trailing along behind Daniel and laughed. "Figures," he said.

Jeremy winked at Terrell, then twisted his friend's cap around to the front again.

Daniel gave a relieved sigh.

What he didn't realize was that in setting the cap straight, Jeremy had made sure Daniel's hair was even more mussed. Kevin snickered and elbowed Jeremy behind Daniel's back.

Resha suspected that Mindy had put the splotch of paint on the tip of her nose just to look cute. Apparently it worked, from the way all the guys were fawning over the redhead as they settled down with their boiled egg sandwiches. Resha considered telling them Mindy's snore sounded like a garbage truck, but managed to bite back a mean remark.

Why was it so hard to put into practice what Pastor Jeff was teaching them about loving each other? To distract herself from her urge to insult Mindy, Resha busied herself shrugging out of her camouflage overshirt, revealing the bulky black T-shirt she wore underneath.

She tied the camo shirt around her waist before she sat on the ground, glad she'd thoroughly doused herself in mosquito repellant so the annoying insects wouldn't buzz around her bare arms.

Kevin pulled off the bandana he'd tied around his head and rubbed his hand over his scalp, fluffing his twists. Selena sat behind him on the ground and plucked at the twists one by one, watching them spring back into place. "They're like little slinkies!" she said in delight.

Kevin ducked his head to avoid her probing fingers, but it was evident from his grin that he enjoyed her attention.

Not one to be left out, Jeremy snatched off his bandana and offered his own head for Selena's inspection. "What about my hair?"

Selena laughed and obliged him by smashing his curls down with her hand and watching them spring back up.

Mindy watched in fascination. "Is your hair naturally curly, Jeremy?"

Jeremy grinned, tweaking one of his own curls. "Yeah. My sister Natalie is jealous because her hair came out real thin and straight, but I don't think she'd look good with curly hair. She looks prettier with her hair the way it is." Jeremy seemed proud of his sister.

"Natalie is the one you're always praying for in our group prayers, isn't she?" Mindy asked. "Is she older or younger than you?"

"You ask so many questions, Mindy," Selena complained.

Mindy pouted. "I can't help it if I'm interested in other people."

Jeremy didn't seem bothered by Mindy's questions. "She's three years older."

Mindy scrunched up her face, and Resha hoped the redhead wouldn't strain too hard trying to do the math. "Oh, she's twenty-two, the same age as me and Daniel! Daniel, did you go to school with Natalie?"

Daniel looked caught off guard, clearly not expecting to be a part of this conversation. "Uh, no. Natalie went to..." Daniel paused before finishing vaguely, "...a different school."

Resha wondered why he'd substituted whatever adjective he'd been about to use. Why would he not want to say....? Something flickered in her brain, and suddenly she remembered a much younger, spindlier Jeremy.

"That's where I know you from, Jeremy!" Resha took her cue from Daniel's discretion in case Jeremy didn't want his family's business aired in front of everyone. "I was at...the same school Natalie went to, and you came to visit her."

"You was at that alternative school with his sister?" Kevin blurted out in surprise.

So much for discretion, Resha thought with irony. Now everyone here knew Natalie had been a problem student.

Jeremy just grinned and squinted at Resha. "Your memory's better than mine – I don't remember seeing you there."

Resha twisted her face wryly. "I looked a little different then."

She didn't elaborate, and no one dared to ask. Resha braced herself for smart remarks from Terrell, but to her surprise, he said nothing, just stared with determination down at his plate. Maybe Pastor Jeff's teaching was getting to him, too.

"Were you friends with Natalie?" Jeremy wanted to know.

"I wasn't friends with anybody," Resha said. "We talked some just because we were stuck in the same classes. She seemed to like you a lot."

Jeremy's smile widened. "Of course. How could she help herself?"

Right before they drove onto the rickety, narrow bridge that would take them across the arroyo and back to the mission center, Antonio glanced behind them in the mirror, then suddenly whipped the steering wheel around, taking them onto the grassy shoulder.

Manny gaped in surprise as the truck bumped along the rocky terrain, heading for the line of trees.

"What are you doing?" Manny asked in a high pitched voice.

Antonio gave him an indulgent smile. "Now that you are one of us, I will have to tell my boss the good news about you. I have a radio hidden here in the woods that I'll use to contact him."

Manny's look of confusion gave way to a proud grin. "Wow. I'm starting to learn all about your secret operations already."

Antonio guided the truck as deep into the trees as he could, cutting the engine when he reached a small clearing well out of sight of the road. As he opened the door and got out, Manny asked, "Am I coming with you?"

Watching the out-of-shape boy try to climb around on the rocks might be amusing, but Antonio was in a hurry. "No, I will need you to stay here and watch the truck. Make sure no one comes near it."

Manny straightened up in his seat, looking proud at being entrusted with such an important task. Antonio dragged a freshly charged car battery from behind the seat, then checked his pocket to make sure he had the cable he had pilfered from Sergio's radio the day before.

He smiled again at his protegé, but when he turned away he allowed the smile to curl into a sneer.

Paola carried a cardboard box out to the tree where the young people had gathered. "Luís brought some things that a temporary shelter in Sincelejo donated to us. Abuelita thought you might like some to go with your food."

She smiled as she set the box down on the ground beside Jeremy and opened it, revealing that it was packed with single serve packages of potato chips. "Take what you want and bring the rest back to the kitchen when you are done."

Glad for a snack to supplement their meager meal, the students closest to the box reached in and grabbed a bag, and Jeremy passed bags out to the rest.

"Here you go, Chief," said Jeremy, tossing one to Daniel, who caught it deftly.

Resha frowned. "Why did you call him 'Chief'"?

Kevin answered for him. "Jeremy be callin' him all kinda things like that. Chief, Cap'n, Boss Man, Mighty Mouse." The group laughed at the last one, and Daniel looked uncomfortable.

"It's because he's so bossy, always telling people what to do, always has to have his own way," Jeremy interjected, but no one believed him.

Daniel's quiet humility was already evident after only a few days, even when Sergio put him in charge of a project. The students laughed again at the absurdity of Jeremy's statement.

"Nah, it's 'cause we always goin' to Daniel for advice," Kevin explained. "He got all the answers."

"The Bible's got all the answers," Daniel corrected irritably. "You guys just come to me because you're too lazy to find them for yourselves."

Jeremy spread his arms and looked to the others for vindication. "See? See? You see how he is?"

"Ewww!"

Everyone turned in surprise to Selena. She was looking at her bag of chips with disgust. "These are expired!"

Daniel inspected the date on his own package, then shrugged. "They're from this year."

He opened the bag and crammed a handful of potato chips into his mouth while Selena looked on, repulsed.

"Not bad," he pronounced around his mouthful.

"The radio is in a safe location now," Antonio told Captain Ortega. "And I believe I have found our pigeon."

Ortega's voice crackled back over the radio. "Good. What is this pigeon like?"

"He is a lazy, fat slob who thinks there are easy ways to make his fortune, and he is eager to hear how special he is, so he was easy to convince," Antonio said contemptuously. "None of the others pay any attention to him, so they will not notice if he is listening to their conversations."

"Perfect," Ortega approved. "What did you promise him?"

"The moon and the stars." Antonio snickered. "I left him 'guarding' the truck now, so he will feel important."

Ortega laughed.

When Antonio got back to the truck, he found what he expected – Manny was asleep.

Antonio slipped in quietly, and the young man didn't stir. Once he was settled in the driver's seat, Antonio slammed his door hard.

Manny jumped and looked around wild eyed.

Antonio smiled at him benignly. "I told El Tiburon about you. He is eager to get you involved in our operations."

Manny smiled back, his usually dull face alight with anticipation.

There was a lull in the conversation as the students finished their lunch. Everyone was hot and tired, dreading another half day's work in the scorching sun, and their fatigue was evident in the listless way they began stacking their dirty dishes.

Well, Jeremy was probably more exhausted than any of them, but that was no excuse to drag around like a slug. Good thing he was around to liven things up.

He ripped open his bag of chips and said, "You know, Daniel, you never did give your testimony the other night."

As Jeremy had hoped, Mindy immediately latched onto his comment. "That's right, Daniel. Why don't you tell us now?"

"Yeah, I want to hear this," Terrell said, settling back against a tree trunk and crossing his arms to listen.

Daniel glared at Jeremy, who smiled back at him serenely. "Go ahead, Daniel. The rest of us got to talk the first night, but you're still the mystery man."

The rest of the students looked expectantly at Daniel. After a final murderous stare at Jeremy, Daniel stalled by pulling off his baseball cap and trying to smooth his tousled hair. Then he took a deep breath. Everyone had to lean in closer to hear him when he finally mumbled, "Not much to tell. I got saved in a Sunday school class when I was about six years old."

Resha gave a skeptical snort. Daniel looked at her and added defensively, "I know some people don't think you can get saved that young, but I really did."

"Oh, we believe it," Terrell laughed. "That's the only explanation for the way you act."

"That's so precious," Mindy burbled. "I'll bet you're so happy your parents took you to church when you were a little boy."

Daniel fidgeted, staring at the ground. "Uh, my parents didn't take me to church. The family next door did."

Mindy was scandalized. "Your parents don't go to church?"

"They do now." Daniel finally glanced up at his friends. "When the neighbors moved away a few years later, I didn't have any way to get to church any more. I begged and begged, and finally my parents took me. My dad found out he could make business contacts at the church, so he started going regularly."

Daniel gave a faint smile as he continued. "The senior pastor, Pastor Rob, preaches a pretty straightforward message that's hard to ignore. My mom got saved first, then my dad a few months later."

"It was so sweet of your neighbors to take such an interest in you when you were little," Mindy gushed.

"Yeah, I'm still thankful for that." Daniel's eyes took on a faraway look, as if he was remembering. "I didn't realize it at the time, but I think they must have known I was in a pretty tough situation."

Resha rolled her eyes. "Oh, please! How bad could your situation be at six years old? I bet you were a spoiled, pampered, little kid. You're healthy, your parents are still together, your family has plenty of money."

Daniel stared at Resha as if she'd slapped him. "There are problems that money can't fix, especially when you're a little kid, and sometimes having your parents split up wouldn't be the worst thing that could happen."

There was no condemnation in Daniel's reply, but Resha looked a little remorseful as she shrugged and looked away. Everyone else kept looking at Daniel, waiting for more, but he had clearly said all he was going to say. He'd retreated into some private world and was staring down at the baseball cap he still held in his hands.

During the uncomfortable silence that followed, Jeremy regretted that he'd pushed his friend to talk. He tried to think of something silly to relieve the tension, but drew a blank until Terrell nudged him.

Terrell was obviously as eager as he was to lighten the mood. "You know all of the man's secrets. What I really want to know is, what was Daniel's horrible sin that you mentioned that first night?"

"Oh, that." Jeremy brightened and sat up straight, ready to make up some wild story. The truth was funny enough on its own, but he wouldn't do that to his friend. "Well, see..."

Daniel came back to life and cut him off. "Jeremy, you realize that if you say another word, you'll be eating those potato chips without teeth." He said it calmly, quietly, without bothering to look up.

Jeremy winked at Resha, smiling broadly, but he kept quiet.

Some lines could not be crossed.

Antonio's truck rattled and groaned it's way up the driveway as the group stood to carry their soiled dishes back to the kitchen. Peering into the truck bed, Daniel could see that it was piled high with boxes of big, clay floor tiles.

Manny hopped out of the truck, more animated than they'd seen him so far. He gave a strange, smug little smile and dipped his head at the team before swaggering after Antonio.

"Brothers are so weird," Selena muttered, shaking her head.

Sergio bounded out of the sanctuary and rubbed his hands together in glee as he checked the load Antonio had delivered. "Ah, now we can finish the floors in the classrooms."

He turned to the team. "Would some of you please help to stack the floor tiles under the carport? We are not quite ready for them, but Antonio is going to need to use the truck again soon."

Mindy and Selena offered to carry all their lunch debris inside, so Daniel and his friends prepared to unload the truck. Resha shrugged and joined the four guys.

As if he'd suddenly remembered something, Sergio spun back to them. "Oh, and Jeremy, Pastor Jeff wanted you to come inside and help him."

Jeremy's jaw clenched and he stormed back towards the sanctuary behind Sergio. Daniel frowned and looked at Kevin, puzzled at their friend's unusual touchiness. Kevin shrugged and grabbed a couple of boxes of tiles and carried them the several yards to the carport. Terrell followed suit.

Daniel and Resha simultaneously reached for the same box of floor tiles. For the first time, he noticed the tattoo of a rose snaking up the front of the girl's forearm.

He tried not to stare.

Great, now I've gone and scandalized the choir boy, Resha thought. Although he looked less like a choir boy today, with his face unshaven and sweaty strands of hair hanging over one eye.

"'Tattoo,'" she snapped, allowing him to take the carton. "It's called a 'tattoo.'"

Daniel blinked. "Huh?"

"The ink." Resha stuck her marked forearm in front of Daniel's face, giving him a chance to stare at the tattoo openly. "Do you know how much it would cost me to get rid of that thing?"

He studied it for a moment before his eyes wandered up to the inside of her elbow. Was he looking for the needle tracks Terrell had mentioned?

She snatched her arm back and reached into the truck for another box before continuing her thought. "It would cost me nearly a thousand bucks for laser removal. I checked into it after I read that scripture in Leviticus about not marking your flesh."

Daniel looked thoughtful as he stacked another carton onto the box he had in his hands. After a moment, one side of his mouth lifted in a crooked smile. "Not too many people read Leviticus, let alone try to live by it."

He looked so pleased, Resha was afraid he was about to jump into a full scale discourse on the relevance of Old Testament law. He surprised her by just shrugging. "I wouldn't worry about it if I were you."

"Oh?" She'd expected the straight-laced guy to be so offended by her tattoo he might offer to sand it off her arm himself.

"Nah. Lasering it off wouldn't change the fact that you did it in the first place; it might hide it from the rest of the world, but not from God."

The comment should have offended Resha, but coming from Daniel, it didn't sound like a put down. Curious, she asked, "So what do you think I should do about it?"

"It's already been done, right? The Blood of Jesus cleanses us from all unrighteousness. Better than lasers." He pointed at Resha's wrist. "So as far as God's concerned, that's already been erased."

She considered his words as she wiped sweat off her brow with a work-gloved hand. "Wow, Chief, that's pretty deep."

Daniel blinked in surprise. Maybe no one but Jeremy ever called him that, but Resha liked the nickname for him.

He recovered quickly and smiled again. "Besides, there are plenty of Christians who don't think there's anything wrong with tattoos. Some people even get so-called 'Christian' tattoos as part of their witness."

"Oh, yeah? Then how about you get a little tattoo of a cross, right here?" Resha challenged, tapping her own upper arm.

Daniel gave her an appalled look. "I didn't say I was one of them."

He picked up the cartons of floor tiles and walked away, leaving Resha with a bemused look on her face.

Interesting guy.

Resha trudged behind Daniel back to the carport, hating that she struggled to carry just one of the heavy cartons while the guys toted two apiece with no problem. She was glad this was the last load.

Mindy and Selena had just about finished cleaning up the lunch area, and Jeremy had rejoined them, wearing his mischievous grin again. As Daniel deposited his cartons on a stack, Jeremy flicked water from his canteen on him.

"In a better mood now, I see," Daniel remarked, wiping the water from his eyes. Or maybe it was sweat.

"Yep. I thought Pastor Jeff was just trying to babysit me, but he actually needed something. Sergio's radio lost reception again, and I had to adjust it a little bit. I fixed it like that." He snapped his fingers in Daniel's face.

Daniel sighed and pushed Jeremy's hand away, then stepped aside to let Kevin through.

As Kevin delivered his final armload of boxes to the stack of floor tiles, he stumbled over the corner of a carton that was jutting from the pile, causing him to drop his load. There was an audible crunch as at least a few of the tiles broke, and Kevin let loose a curse word.

Daniel shot him a look, and Jeremy snickered, but neither one said anything. Terrell, though, couldn't let it go.

"Hey, you ain't in the 'hood no mo', man," he razzed in a crude mockery of Kevin's ghetto slang. "You can't be talkin' like no ghetto rat."

Kevin whirled to glare at Terrell. "You better watch ya own mouth, man. Resha might put up with it, but you ain't gonna do me like that."

Terrell didn't have enough sense to leave it alone. "Oooh, big man gonna protect his honor."

Kevin lunged toward Terrell, but Jeremy and Daniel had been ready for it – they each grabbed one of Kevin's arms to restrain him.

Mindy and Selena gasped and backed away from the guys, clutching at each other as if World War III was about to break out.

Resha stood her ground and watched with interest. Half of her wished they would let Kevin loose so Terrell would get what was coming to him. Terrell might be bigger, but as mad as Kevin was, her money was on him.

"Come on, Kevin, let it go," Jeremy urged, but Kevin kept trying to jerk his arms away from him and Daniel.

"No way, man," Kevin spat, shooting daggers at Terrell, who stood tense and ready to fight if he had to. "This guy been raggin' on people ever since we got here. Somebody need to shut 'im up."

Then Daniel spoke quietly. "Kevin."

Kevin turned reluctant eyes to Daniel, who just looked back at Kevin and shook his head slightly. Kevin let his breath out in a huff and relaxed then, and his friends let him go, although they remained on guard.

Resha raised an eyebrow, impressed by the calming influence Daniel had over his friend. What had he done to merit that much respect from Kevin?

Now that the situation had been diffused, Terrell held his hands up in apology. "Hey, I was just kidding, okay? I didn't mean anything."

"Yeah, man, it's all good." Kevin said it grudgingly, but the two bumped fists and everyone breathed easier.

Things were awkward for several minutes, but as they all worked together to clean up the broken tiles and finish stacking the rest of the boxes, the incident was put behind them.

Pastor Jeff had watched the whole thing from behind the water pump, where he'd been replacing some rusted fittings. He knew the heat was taking a toll on all of them, and minor irritations they might normally overlook could be magnified out of proportion, so he was always alert, ready to intervene if necessary.

He was pleased when the young people resolved the tense situation on their own. Nodding in satisfaction, he turned back to his work.

As the students settled into their routine for the evening meal, sitting at their usual places, Pastor Jeff was glad to see that Terrell and Kevin had put aside their aggressions – the two were talking and joking with each other as if nothing had happened.

Jeff had hoped his group of young missionaries would mingle more with the locals, but there didn't seem to be any snobbery in their segregation – they just sat with the people they were comfortable with. The language barrier might have something to do with it, as well.

The Colombian laborers seemed content to have Manny sit with them, since he usually trudged in late for meals. Antonio even tried to draw Manny out, asking him friendly questions in Spanish.

Samuel sometimes sat at one end of the table with the pastors, sometimes he parked at the end of the table with the workmen. He didn't speak to anyone at either table, in any language.

After his experience with Samuel the day before, Jeff had to admit he had to work on looking past appearances to see others as they really were, good or bad. It was a lesson that would serve them all well, especially during their time in Colombia.

He'd decided to use tonight's devotional time to teach the students about seeing others through God's eyes instead of their own. As he'd prepared for his teaching, his studies had taken an interesting turn, and he looked forward to seeing the students' reactions.

When they gathered in the sanctuary after dinner, Pastor Jeff innocently asked for a volunteer to read a couple of scriptures. Of course, Jeremy bounced to his feet at once, Bible in hand.

"Thank you, Jeremy. Would you please read James 4:12 for us?"

Jeremy flipped a few pages with his usual enthusiasm, but when he found the verse, he cut Pastor Jeff a sideways look before he read, "'There is only one Lawgiver and Judge, the one who is able to save and destroy. But you – who are you to judge your neighbor?'"

"The next verse I'd like you to read is Romans 14:4." Pastor Jeff hid a smile at Jeremy's reproachful look.

Less eager this time, Jeremy found the place and read, "Who are you to judge someone else's servant? To his own master he stands or falls. And he will stand, for the Lord is able to make him stand."

Jeremy looked at the others and made a face. "Is it just me, or is it hotter than usual in here tonight?"

Jeff waited for the nervous laughter to fade away before saying, "Okay, I've got one more."

"You know, Pastor Jeff, maybe we should give someone else a chance to read." Jeremy played up his look of guilt as he slunk back to his chair.

Jeff smiled indulgently, then turned his eyes to the only one in the room who looked blissfully unaffected by the self-consciousness the others were feeling. "Mindy, please find Matthew chapter seven and read us the first four verses."

"Okay." Mindy found the passage, then stood up and read with childlike innocence, "'Do not judge, or you too will be judged. For in the same way you judge others, you will be judged, and with the measure you use, it will be measured to you. Why do you look at the speck of sawdust in your brother's eye and pay no attention to the plank in your own eye? How can you say to your brother, 'Let me take the speck out of your eye,' when all the time there is a plank in your own eye?'"

As Mindy took her chair again, Jeff noticed Kevin sneak a glance at Terrell, then hang his head. Terrell didn't turn Kevin's way, but his ears had turned dark red.

Jeff wasn't surprised to see Daniel slump over and squirm in his seat – the young man had a tendency to feel convicted about everything. Even Resha looked uncomfortable, screwing her mouth to one side and shifting her shoulders as if trying to shake off the guilt.

Jeff doubted Selena understood much of what they'd read, but she looked guilty in general anyway. Jeff's choice of scripture for the evening was hitting more nerves than he'd intended.

"Now all these verses seem pretty self-explanatory," he continued. "They're all saying we shouldn't be judgmental of others, right?"

There were assents all around. Since Mindy still had her Bible open to the scripture, Jeff pointed at her and asked, "What's the very next thing Jesus says?"

"Uh, He says, 'you hypocrite...'," Mindy began uncertainly.

Jeff cut her off. "Exactly! Pretty judgmental, huh?"

The students tittered uneasily, probably wondering where he was going with this. Jeff asked Terrell to read the first part of the next verse.

Still flushed, Terrell read, "Do not give dogs what is sacred. Do not cast your pearls before swine."

"How do we decide who is a 'dog' unless we judge them?" Jeff challenged. "How do we know who is a 'swine' unless we judge them?"

When no one was brave enough to hazard a guess, Jeff went on. "Verse fifteen tells us to watch out for false prophets. How does it say we can recognize a false prophet?"

Daniel's eyes skimmed the next few verses, then he gave a tentative answer. "It says we would know them by their fruit."

"So what does that tell you?" Jeff urged Daniel to carry the thought through to its logical conclusion.

"Um, I guess we have to judge whether their fruit is good or bad," Daniel offered.

"Right," Jeff affirmed. "So how does all that fit with the first few verses that tell us not to judge? Why would Jesus warn us not to judge other people, then explain exactly how to judge?"

The students were quiet, mulling over the question.

Resha frowned in thought and finally ventured, "I guess it depends on whether we're judging by our own standards, or by God's standards."

Jeff was pleased with her conclusion. "That's a big part of it, Resha. Would you mind reading John 7:24 for me?"

Resha found the verse in her New King James and read, "Do not judge according to appearance, but judge with righteous judgment."

She raised her eyebrows in surprise that the Bible confirmed what she'd just said.

"Exactly," Jeff looked around at them. "Anyone else have any ideas what God is telling us in all these verses we've read?"

"He sayin' we got to judge ourselves first," Kevin suggested after a few seconds. "We got to get our own self straight with God, and then we can judge everybody else."

Jeff smiled encouragingly at Kevin's effort, then decided he'd given them enough to think about for awhile. "I want you all to meditate on those scriptures tonight and see if any of you come to some other conclusions as well. Let's go ahead and wrap this up for the night."

With a sigh of relief to be out of the hot seat, the students stood and gathered in their circle for prayer. Jeff was gratified to note the young people were getting more comfortable praying out loud with each other. As they held hands in the prayer circle after the devotional, several of them expressed prayers and concerns while the others listened respectfully or prayed silently along with the person speaking.

Daniel prayed for Pastor Sergio and his family, Mindy prayed for everybody to get along with each other, Kevin prayed for help controlling his temper, and Jeremy prayed for his sister again. After the final "amen", Mindy turned to hug those closest to her.

Jeff felt they were becoming a family, which was what he had hoped for.

6

If Resha heard one more remark from Mindy or Selena about how "cute"
the men were, she was going to gag. Right now they were whining again
about the condition of their hair. Resha wanted to pull out her own hair,
except she didn't have enough to pull out.

Still stinging from Pastor Jeff's message last night, Resha tried hard
not to judge her two roommates. If she could bite her tongue long
enough, maybe they would just go away. She turned her back to the other
two girls and pretended to sleep while they fussed over Selena's hair.

Then it was Mindy's turn – Resha sat up in time to watch Selena try
to braid Mindy's hair in imitation of Abuelita's hairstyle. When Selena was
finally done, she tied the plait on the end with a puffy bow Mindy pulled
out of her bag.

After checking each other's makeup, the two girls headed for the
door. Resha stayed sitting on her cot, pretending to search for something
in her duffel bag. Why wouldn't the others just hurry up and leave so she
could have a few minutes without their incessant jabbering gnawing at her
ears?

"You coming to breakfast?" Selena stopped in the doorway to ask.

"Maybe later," Resha mumbled without looking up. "I'm not hungry right now."

Selena shrugged and left, but Mindy was instantly the picture of solicitude. "Oh, you're not sick, are you, Resha? You didn't drink any water from the tap, did you? Should I see if I can find something for your stomach?"

Resha glared at her and snapped, "I'm not sick."

"Oh. Okay." Mindy shrank back at Resha's sharp tone, then she walked toward the door. Right before stepping into the hallway, she turned and murmured, "I hope you feel better soon, Resha."

Finally, Resha thought when Mindy's footsteps faded.

She tossed her duffel bag aside and stood up, pulling her camo shirt over her tank top. Needing some fresh air, she walked to the door leading out into the courtyard and yanked it open. Maybe she could sit out there and soak in the quiet for a few minutes before heading into the noisy breakfast area.

Someone had beat her to it.

Daniel sat on the ground with his jean-clad legs stretched out in front of him, leaning his back against the wall, so intent on his reading that he didn't hear her come out. It looked like he'd finally had a chance to shave and wash his hair.

Resha squinted at the worn Bible he held on his lap and started to go back into her room to give him the solitude she herself was craving, but her curiosity got the best of her and she walked closer instead.

Standing over the blond man, she had a better view of his Bible. So there wasn't a porn magazine hidden in there, after all. Instead, Resha saw that he had underlined and highlighted different passages, and there were notes jotted in the margins. He had a pen in one hand as if ready to mark whatever else he found interesting, and there was a tablet on the ground beside him, full of scribbled notes.

When she'd seen enough, Resha announced her presence in a flat voice. "You're missing breakfast."

His eyes flew up in surprise and he stammered, "Oh, uh...I'll grab something later. Maybe one of Jeremy's granola bars."

Since he didn't tell her to go away, Resha plunked herself on the wooden bench. "You studying to be a preacher, or what?"

Daniel's brow furrowed, as if he was trying to figure out her motive for asking. She allowed none of her thoughts into her deadpan expression, forcing him to take her question at face value.

"No, it's just that last night I was reading those verses Pastor Jeff told us to study, the ones about judging others, and I couldn't figure out what else he was getting at. I wanted to see if I could get it this morning, while I was still thinking about it."

Resha wondered why it should matter to him. From what she'd seen Daniel was the least judgmental of all the students there. Well, except for Mindy, but she didn't count. "So did you figure it out?"

Daniel chewed on his pen, frowning thoughtfully. "Well, maybe. I had to look it up in some other places in the Bible, too, though."

"Yeah? Like where?"

"Well, there's plenty of scriptures that say not to judge other people, like in Luke, where it says not to judge so you won't get judged." Daniel was getting more animated as he thought about it. He sat up straight and started turning pages. "But check this out. In First Corinthians, I think it's in chapter two, it says if we're spiritual, we should make judgments about everything. Oh, and let me show you this one. In chapter six, it says we're going to judge angels!"

Resha raised her eyebrows. She'd never seen Daniel's face light up like that, and it looked like he was gearing up for a whole Bible study right there. She made herself comfortable on the bench.

This was definitely more interesting than hearing a discussion about what shade of eye shadow would be in vogue when they got back to America.

Taking a quick inventory, Pastor Jeff noticed the group gathered in the dining area was smaller than usual. He wasn't surprised that Manny wasn't around – the chubby young man often slept late, making an appearance toward the end of the meal and gobbling whatever food Abuelita had held back for him.

But the fact that Daniel and Resha were absent was unusual, and the fact that a male student and a female student had gone AWOL at the same time was especially disconcerting.

Jeff didn't want to seem like a mother hen, but he was responsible for them, after all. He discreetly left the dining area and walked down the hall, where he tapped on the door of the girls' room. When there was no answer, he opened the door cautiously and peeked in.

Resha wasn't there. He walked to the window at the other side of the room and looked across to the mens' building.

That's when he spotted them.

Daniel was sitting on the ground beside the bench with his Bible propped up on his bent knees, while Resha sat cross-legged on the bench with her chin in one hand, listening with intense concentration as Daniel explained something to her, his hands flying in excitement.

Jeff should have known.

The one thing that would keep Daniel from food was God's Word, and if anyone else shared his passion for it, it would be Resha. He watched as Resha interrupted Daniel with a question, which sent Daniel into a page-flipping frenzy as he searched for whatever passage he thought would illustrate his point.

Jeff smiled and turned away to return to the dining area.

The Word of God was a much better chaperone than he would ever be.

Abuelita had a plate waiting for him when he returned. Jeff took his place beside Sergio and bowed his head for a quick 'grace' before starting on the scrambled eggs. Sergio seemed to be in an especially good mood, and Jeff wondered if the danger had passed.

"Any more 'communications' from the Black Eagles?" he asked, sipping from a steaming mug of dark, rich coffee.

Sergio shook his head as he mopped up the last of his eggs with a bit of bread. "No, all has been silent since your arrival, and as you can see, we have been able to pick up our supplies with no interference." Sergio beamed with joy. "Perhaps it is because you and your team are here. The Black Eagles may be reluctant to cause trouble with such a large American presence at the mission center, for fear the authorities would get involved."

Jeff nodded thoughtfully. "Possibly. Only one thing concerns me about that."

"What is that?" Sergio asked.

"How do they know we're here?"

Sergio's smile faltered.

Multiple scriptures later, Resha's head was spinning, and Daniel kept finding more related verses with no sign of winding down. It was fascinating to see how everything in The Word of God fit together, but there was a limit to how much Resha could absorb at one time. She decided to put a stop to it before her brain exploded. "So what's your conclusion?"

Daniel blinked as her nonchalant question brought him back to earth. He pondered a moment, then shrugged and gave a crooked smile, "I guess it more or less boils down to what you said last night – God wants us to judge people and things through His eyes, not our own."

Resha was stunned that this guy who seemed to have memorized half the Bible had actually paid attention to her tentative guess from the previous evening. To cover her confusion, she announced curtly, "Pastor Sergio'll be handing out assignments in a minute."

Then she slid off the bench and walked back into her dorm without a backward glance.

Daniel stared after the slender girl, wondering if he'd offended her somehow. He had thought Resha was interested in the verses he found because she'd asked a lot of questions, but maybe he'd gotten carried away and bored her?

Finally her words registered and he glanced at his watch. Oops.

Where had all that time gone?

He reluctantly closed his Bible and began gathering his notes.

When Resha entered the dining area, the others were stacking their empty plates for Paola and Abuelita to pick up. Mindy saw her and rushed to her side. "Oh, Resha. Are you feeling better?"

Mindy had apparently gotten it stuck in her head that Resha was sick, and she wasn't going to let go of the idea. Resha gritted her teeth and kept her voice toneless so she wouldn't yell. "I feel fine, Mindy."

"Do you want me to ask Pastor Sergio if you can be on light duty or something?"

"I said I feel fine," Resha snapped, unable to hide her irritation this time.

Stung, Mindy said in a small voice, "Oh, okay. I'm glad you feel better."

Resha forced herself to suck in a deep breath, chiding herself for her impatience. No need to be nasty. Mindy is just being nice – she can't help it she's such a pain. Don't judge her. Don't judge her.

Abuelita must have seen Resha come in. The old woman pressed something warm wrapped in a napkin into her hand. Embarrassed, Resha thanked her.

Inside the napkin, Resha found a chunk of cornbread and a boiled egg. She guessed they were meant to be served later as part of their lunch, and she felt guilty for disrupting the old lady's plans. She nibbled at the food so she wouldn't seem ungrateful.

A few minutes later, she saw that Daniel had finally put away his Bible and made his way into the dining area. He ignored his friends' questioning looks as Abuelita handed him another little bundle wrapped in a napkin. Daniel grinned his thanks and wolfed down the morsel with no compunction, washing it down with water from his canteen.

Resha had just finished choking down her own improvised breakfast when the two pastors stood up. Pastor Sergio consulted his notebook briefly, checking what needed to be done that day.

"Come, let us pray before we get started on our day's work," he urged, and the team gathered in a circle and joined hands.

As he headed toward the storage building to gather the materials he would need for his next assignment, Daniel saw Jeremy posing happily for Mindy while she snapped pictures with her cell phone.

When she saw Daniel she squealed and waved at him, excited. "Oh, Daniel! You were right! Jeremy fixed my camera!"

He managed a feeble smile and returned the wave halfheartedly, and she clicked a photo of him.

Jeremy grinned and gave Daniel a wink, mouthing the words, "Loose battery."

Daniel wondered if he was talking about the cell phone or Mindy.

Then a wave of remorse hit him as he wondered how that last thought fit in with all the scriptures he'd just studied about judging other people. Before he could sink too deeply into a morass of guilt, Jeremy sidled up to him and punched him on the arm.

"Hey, it's a good thing Mindy came to me before she took your advice." He smirked.

Daniel frowned, puzzled. "My advice? I just told her to plug it in while there's electricity."

Jeremy's grin grew wider. "Colombian outlets look like ours, but they have a stronger current than American ones. Sometimes you need an adapter to plug in something like her dainty little camera phone."

Daniel cringed and raked a hand through his hair. "Oh, no."

"Not to worry, Boss Man, I had you covered," Jeremy reassured him smugly. "I just happened to find such an adapter in Luís' store of goodies."

Daniel was almost afraid to ask. "What would have happened if she'd plugged it in without it?"

"It might have fried her cell phone." Jeremy stared at Daniel, waiting.

A mental image of Mindy, her face twisted in confused dismay as she held up a smoldering phone, played across Daniel's mind.

Daniel tried to fight it but finally had to give in.

He and Jeremy collapsed against each other, laughing uncontrollably.

Several yards away, just out of earshot, Mindy centered them in her viewfinder and merrily snapped away.

Seeing the boys so happy made Mindy smile. She knew they were probably laughing at her – most everyone did. But Daniel and Jeremy were always nice to her, and they were so sweet to help her with her cell phone, so she didn't mind. She just wished she understood what was so funny.

She snapped one more picture, then went to look for Resha to see if she'd let her take a picture of her. Mindy was so glad she was finally getting to know Resha. She'd seen her at church lots of times, but they'd never had a chance to talk to each other.

She knew Resha got mad at her sometimes, but at least Resha never laughed at her. But then, Resha hardly ever laughed at anything.

Poor Resha.

Pastor Sergio had asked the girls to clear the furniture out of the classroom building so the new floor tiles could be laid. The workmen had already moved their bedrolls someplace else, and most of the items were easy to move – two small filing cabinets, a dozen folding chairs, a couple of tables, and a trash can.

Now they were faced with a massive, old fashioned metal desk topped with a thick wooden slab. Resha and Selena tried pushing it, but only succeeded in moving it a couple of inches. Mindy joined them, bracing her back against one end and using her legs for leverage, and between the three of them, they managed to scoot it over a few feet before they needed a break.

"Too bad Luís and Antonio already left, or we could have gotten them to move this thing." Selena panted, leaning against the desk.

"We could probably ask some of the boys to move it," Mindy suggested as she straightened and rubbed her lower back.

Selena liked that idea. "Oh, yeah. We could get Terrell and Daniel in here and they'd have this thing out in a couple of seconds." Her voice took on a hopeful lilt. "It's really hot in here – maybe they'd take off their shirts."

Mindy giggled. "Or Kevin. He's nice and strong, too."

"And that voice of his! Oooh!" Selena rolled her eyes up dreamily.

Annoyed, Resha began shoving at the desk by herself. "We don't need their help. Come on, we got it this far. Once we get it out the door, it's downhill."

Selena sighed. "Okay, okay. I just hope the guys don't laugh at us when they see us struggling with this stupid desk."

Her comment set them off again.

"But Jeremy has such a nice laugh," Mindy said, forgetting the desk.

Selena dropped her arms from the desk as her mind went back to the men. "Yeah, and did you notice the way Daniel's mouth kind of opens a little bit sometimes when he smiles?"

Another giggle bubbled from Mindy. "Yeah, he looks just like a little boy when he does that, doesn't he?"

Resha was so aggravated now that she actually moved the desk a few feet all by herself, causing its legs to make a metallic shrieking sound as they dragged across the floor. "Don't you two ever get tired of drooling over the men?"

"You don't like men very much, do you?" Selena sulked, reluctantly taking her place behind the desk again.

Resha didn't bother to answer, not wanting to get involved in a conversation with them about men.

Mindy, of course, couldn't let Selena's comment go. As she pushed against the desk with her back, she asked, "Really, Resha? Why not?"

The desk was finally at the door, and Selena had a good view of the four in question as they worked on Pastor Sergio's house. "Yeah, just look at them! How can you not like them?"

"First of all, I never said I don't like men, you said that," Resha corrected, standing up straight for another short break. She folded her arms as she leaned against the monstrous desk. "But I'm willing to bet I've had more experience with men than either of you, and...let's just say I don't trust them."

Mindy looked at her with compassion. "But, Resha, these boys are different. They're Christians!"

Resha snorted in derision at Mindy's naivete, wanting to end the discussion. Still, Mindy's comment lingered in her mind. She hadn't been around Samuel and Manny enough for her to form an opinion about them, and Pastor Jeff and Pastor Sergio didn't count – they were older and had dedicated themselves to serving God.

She considered the remaining four. She had to admit she felt comfortable with the trio from Pastor Jeff's church – they treated Resha and the other girls as equals. Oh, sure, Resha had seen them noticing Mindy and Selena, but she'd never caught any of them staring at them in that way some guys did, like women were slabs of meat on display at the butcher shop. And none of the three had tried to bully or intimidate any of them.

Even Terrell, jerk that he was, treated the other two with respect, and he'd stopped picking on her, too, for some reason. All of them seemed sincere in their faith, and Daniel was definitely not faking his love for God's Word.

Could Mindy be right? Did being a Christian make a difference in the way men acted?

Mindy had braced herself against the desk again, but she was still looking at Resha with those big cow eyes, waiting for a response.

To get them off her back, Resha said sourly, "There's one thing I do like about the men. They're probably not standing around gossiping when they should be working."

And she gave the desk a mighty shove, causing Mindy to stumble a bit as the desk jolted out from under her.

Selena got the hint and gave a little huff before rejoining Resha and Mindy in their efforts.

The four men under discussion were putting up long, thick planks of treated wood to replace the ruined siding the pastors had pulled from the side of the house. As they worked, they watched the girls straining to drag an oversized, metal desk from the building.

"That might be a little easier if Selena wasn't wobbling on those high-heeled cowboy boots," Terrell observed, holding up one end of a long plank while Daniel nailed it down on the other side.

"Don't they look great on her, though?" Jeremy eyed Selena as he dragged another new board from the pile.

"Especially with them tight jeans," Kevin added, grabbing one end of the plank. He and Jeremy placed the panel where Daniel could easily reach it, and Kevin continued, "How much you think those big ol' earrings of Resha's weigh? If I was her, I'd be scared they'd catch on somethin'."

"And can you believe that bow in Mindy's hair?" Terrell laughed. He stepped out of the way so Daniel could attach his end of the plank to the house. "How in the world did she find the time to fix her hair like that?"

"Girls ain't got no sense." Kevin chuckled.

Terrell nodded in agreement. "Pretty impractical, aren't they?"

"Yeah, aren't they wonderful?" Jeremy clutched his chest and pretended to swoon, and the other two laughed at him.

Daniel finally had enough of their conversation. He pointed testily at the unfinished project. "If you guys are through gossiping like old ladies, we've got some siding to finish up here."

"I know what your problem is, Daniel," Jeremy told him playfully as he sat on the pile of new lumber and fished a granola bar out of his pocket. "The reason you don't have a girl is because you are way too serious."

"Really?" Terrell looked surprised. "When I first saw this guy, I had him pegged for a jock. You know, the kind with a girl on each arm and one stuffed in his locker for later. Now I figured out that's not his style, but he's got to have a girlfriend. Don't tell me girls don't go for this hunk of meat. Selena and Mindy can't keep their eyes off him."

"Nah, man, it ain't that," Kevin was quick to explain as he dropped down next to Jeremy, talking about Daniel as if he wasn't there. "He got plenty of girls that like him, but he ain't never found one good enough yet."

"Yeah, none of them live up to his standards," Jeremy confirmed.

"They're not my standards," Daniel muttered. No one paid any attention to him.

"I thought for sure that girl he met a couple years ago would stick," Jeremy mumbled around a mouthful of granola bar. "The one with that long brown hair and the big, uh...feet. What was her name? Salamander?"

"Samantha." Daniel gritted his teeth at Jeremy's deliberate mutilation of the girl's name.

"Yeah, her. You dated her longer than anybody. Almost six months, wasn't it?" Jeremy took a swig of water from his canteen to chase down the granola bar.

"Six months sounds serious. So what went wrong?" Terrell stretched his arms behind his head to loosen the cramped muscles.

Daniel felt his face grow hot. He mumbled, "We, uh, had different values."

"That means she didn't get what she wanted from him," Kevin chuckled.

Daniel shot him a reproachful look, hurt that Kevin would so casually spill what he'd only admitted to his two closest friends because they'd pressured him. The look was lost on Kevin, who seemed unaware he'd violated Daniel's confidence.

"You're kidding me, right?" Terrell quirked a disbelieving eyebrow. "This guy can't be for real."

"Yeah, my buddy, the Man of Steel." Kevin slapped Daniel on the back.

Daniel shrugged him off and concentrated on positioning the next plank.

Terrell opened his mouth to say something else, but he must have noticed Daniel's irritation. He shut his mouth and pushed the other end of the plank into place, holding it steady so Daniel could nail it down.

Maybe Pastor Jeff's sermons were getting through to Terrell. Whatever the reason, Daniel was glad his new friend had dropped the subject.

Kevin was still grinning, though, as he stared expectantly at Jeremy. They all knew Jeremy wouldn't pass up an opportunity to tease Daniel.

But Jeremy was staring off into space and said nothing. That was so unlike Jeremy that Kevin nudged him with his elbow and asked, "Yo, Jer, what's up, man?"

Jeremy snapped out of it immediately and grinned. "You know what Daniel needs? He needs to find himself a nice, pretty Christian girl whose parents have kept her sealed up in a bubble."

"Who you got in mind?"

Daniel did his best to ignore them as he and Terrell positioned the next board.

"Well, see, here's what I was thinking." Jeremy settled in for a long dissertation. "Mindy got saved when she was a little bitty kid, just like Daniel."

Kevin nodded wisely.

"And you know what else?" Jeremy began ticking items off on his fingers. "Mindy's an only child, just like Daniel."

"What else?" Kevin egged him on.

"Well, Mindy comes from a nice, well-to-do family...."

"...just like Daniel," Kevin finished for him with a grin.

"And she's twenty-two years old...." Jeremy waited expectantly.

Terrell joined Kevin this time. "...just like Daniel."

Daniel finally had to laugh, his annoyance at Kevin forgotten. "So what are you guys trying to say here?"

"We think you should ask Mindy out when we get back to Houston," Jeremy announced decisively.

Daniel didn't hesitate – he shook his head with equal decisiveness. "No."

"Oh, come on, Mindy is a Christian, she's sweet, she's gorgeous," Jeremy persisted. "And she'll believe anything you tell her. What else could you possibly ask for in a girl?"

Daniel just laughed at Jeremy's question, unaware that his eyes had drifted across the compound to Resha, who was shouting angry orders at Mindy and Selena as the three girls fought to get the bulky desk down the steps.

Kevin snickered behind him. Daniel turned to find that Kevin and Jeremy had followed the direction of his gaze, and he was confused when they exchanged surprised looks.

Then Jeremy wiggled his eyebrows and Kevin laughed out loud, changing it to an unconvincing cough when Daniel gave him a dirty look.

"Come on, guys, quit messing around," Daniel told them. "We didn't come all the way over here for romance. We're supposed to be working."

"Believe me, trying to fix your love life is work," Jeremy insisted, but he shoved the rest of his granola bar back in his pocket and stood up, ending his short break.

Selena was pleased when her brother joined them outside in their shade at lunch time instead of taking his plate and sneaking off to nap in the dorm. As the students waited for everyone to get their food from the kitchen, Manny seemed more engaged than usual, participating in the conversation for once instead of listening halfheartedly.

Once they had all settled down with their food, the group normally bowed their heads while one of them said a quick grace. It was Jeremy's turn, and Selena expected him to make a show of it, the way he did with most things just to get attention. She was surprised when Jeremy simply thanked God for the food and asked His blessing on it and on them.

Selena looked up before he'd said the "amen" and found her brother looking around at them with his lip curled in disdain. She caught Manny's eye and frowned at him, but he just shrugged indifferently and started eating. She wasn't into all this praying and stuff either, but Manny's attitude disappointed her. What did he expect from a mission trip sponsored by the church?

As soon as she had a chance, Selena leaned over to her brother and hissed, "What's wrong with you?"

He looked at her with false innocence. "What are you talking about, Selena? I'm just eating."

"I saw how you were looking at them when they were praying over the food," she accused, keeping her voice low so the others wouldn't hear.

"So what's the big deal?" Manny spoke quietly, too. "If you had been praying with them instead of looking around, you wouldn't have seen me, so don't act like you got all holy lately."

Selena gave an indignant huff, then shook her head. "Manny, if you start making trouble, I'm going to tell Mama when we get home."

"Go ahead, crybaby. I got bigger things going on than to worry about what you tell your mommy." Manny stood up and walked away, leaving his dirty dishes on the ground.

"Manny, get back here and pick up this stuff!" Selena stood up and yelled after him. Manny tossed a dismissive hand over his shoulder and kept going, leaving Selena glaring with her hands on her hips.

She felt the eyes of the others on her and turned to face them sheepishly. "He's such a pesky little brother. I don't know what's wrong with him today."

Mindy, ever the peacemaker, gathered up Manny's dishes and stacked them on top of hers. "Maybe he's just having a bad day. I'm sure he'll feel better tomorrow."

After everyone had finished eating, Mindy scraped the crumbs and leftovers together for the dog. Usually they all cleaned their plates, devouring every morsel of their skimpy rations. Mindy suspected her friends had left small pieces of their sandwiches on purpose today so she'd have something to feed the puppy. They were so sweet.

Once she'd delivered her own and Manny's dirty dishes to the kitchen, Mindy came back out with the leftovers wrapped in a dishrag and called softly.

The others had left Mindy alone so the dog wouldn't be intimidated by seeing so many people, but Matéo had figured out what she was doing and stood silently nearby while she waited to see if the dog would come.

Soon, the dog timidly peeked around the corner of the old storeroom, but it stayed a safe distance away.

Mindy duckwalked closer to it, holding out the dishtowel with the leftovers and making little cooing sounds. The dog watched her suspiciously, but it didn't cringe away like it had the day before. When she got within a couple of yards away, the dog started to back off, so Mindy sat on the ground.

After watching her a moment, the dog sat down, too, eying the scraps in her hand. Mindy began singing "Jesus Loves Me," hoping to soothe the dog, all the while holding out the scraps. The dog took a tentative step closer, sniffing the air, but it couldn't bring itself any closer than four feet away. That was good enough for today, Mindy decided.

"What a brave boy you are!" she praised the dog, and tossed it a scrap as a reward. The dog gobbled it up and looked around the ground for more. Mindy shook the rest of the leftovers from the dishcloth and carefully backed away, leaving the dog to its feast. When she got far enough away that she wouldn't frighten it, Mindy snapped a quick photo of the dog with her cell phone.

As soon as the dog had finished eating, it slunk away. Matéo darted out from behind the decimated fountain in the courtyard, clapping with delight. He and Mindy gave each other a celebratory hug, both of them giggling happily.

After lunch, Kevin and Jeremy laid the floor tiles in the kitchen while Terrell and Daniel started on the floor in Pastor Sergio's house.

The girls were given another painting job. The freshly plastered walls of the main sanctuary had been painted the day before by Matéo and Paola, and Resha was giving them a second coat, trying to correct the drips and streaks they had left.

Selena couldn't figure Resha out. The little thug seemed mad all the time, but she never bothered anybody, and she was always praying. Right now, Resha was perched on an old wooden ladder in the opposite corner of the room, slashing paint across the walls with no regard to her own safety.

Mindy, on the other hand, squealed in terror each time her stepladder wobbled a little bit, even with Selena standing below to steady it.

After one more stroke with the paint roller, Mindy was finished with her section of the ceiling. She handed Selena the paint roller so she could climb down from the ladder. "I wonder if the boys are going to put carpet or floor tiles in here?"

"I think Pastor Sergio said they're not going to use carpet in here any more because it gets moldy too fast in this climate or something." Selena scraped the excess paint from the roller on the edge of the paint tray. "They're probably going to put down those big tiles that came in yesterday."

"It's going to look really nice in here." Mindy looked around as if imagining the finished look. She rolled her shoulders a few times, trying to ease the tension she'd developed from craning her neck upwards to paint.

"What they really need to do is get some AC going in here." Selena fanned herself with her hands. Sweat trickled down her back, and her T-shirt clung to her, heavy and sticky.

Even Mindy looked less than fresh after working inside the stifling sanctuary all afternoon. "I know," she agreed. "I'd love to take a nice, long bubble bath in cool water."

"Oooh, that sounds great, but it wouldn't do any good. As soon as we got out, we'd get all grungy and gross again. I smell like a sweaty pig!" Selena lamented. "What must the guys think of me?"

Resha finished the last section and climbed down from her ladder. She looked at Selena with contempt.

"If they can smell you over themselves, you've got a bigger problem than you think. At least we've got a shower over here."

Resha folded her ladder with a snap and carried it outside, letting the door slam behind her. Mindy and Selena stared at the door she'd gone through.

Selena complained, "She hardly ever talks to us, and when she does, she usually says something mean. Why does she hate us?"

"Oh, I don't think she hates us," Mindy assured Selena. "She just doesn't like to hear us complain so much."

"Well, then, she's just stuck up and rude." Selena started banging the lid back on a paint can.

Mindy looked horrified that Selena would say such a thing. "I don't think she's stuck up at all. I think she's a nice girl. She just doesn't talk very much."

Selena wasn't convinced. "If you say so."

They picked up their scattered paintbrushes and began folding the drop cloth. Resha came back in, grabbed the second stepladder, and left again without a word. The door banged shut again.

Selena sighed.

Even though Kevin had joked that he hadn't brought a Bible with him, Selena noticed he was clutching a dogeared paperback NIV each evening as the students gathered for their devotional.

After a short opening prayer, Pastor Jeff asked, "Kevin, would you mind reading First Corinthians 13, verses four through seven for us?"

Selena perked up. It would be nice to hear Kevin's deep voice speaking something other than "ghetto."

Kevin grunted, then stood and read in his gravelly bass, stumbling over a few of the words, "Love is patient, love is kind. It does not envy, it does not boast, it is not proud. It does not dishonor others, it is not self-seeking, it is not easily angered, it keeps no record of wrongs. Love does not delight in evil but rejoices with the truth. It always protects, always trusts, always hopes, always perseveres."

As Kevin read, Selena caught Mindy's eye and made a face. She wondered who needed tonight's sermon more, herself or Resha.

7

Day 6: Friday

As Daniel panted his way through his last set of crunches, Jeremy stood over him critiquing his technique and munching on a protein bar. Crumbs fell off the bar onto Daniel's T-shirt and he impatiently brushed them off his stomach, grumbling, "You're supposed to eat those things after a workout."

"It is after a workout," Jeremy explained with exaggerated patience. "You just finished your workout, and I'm eating the protein bar. It's all about teamwork, see?"

How could you argue with logic like that? Daniel shook his head and stood up, dusting off his jeans. He pointed at the bar Jeremy was chomping on. "That's why you're never hungry for breakfast."

Jeremy polished off the last bite and licked a crumb off his finger. "I don't hear you complaining while you eat my share of the scrambled eggs."

Kevin chuckled at their good-natured bickering. "You guys act just like brothers, always pickin' on each other."

"We are brothers." Jeremy leaned his head on Daniel's shoulder and linked arms with him. "Brothers in the Lord."

Daniel snatched his arm away and took a quick step back. When Jeremy made a show of stumbling, Daniel rolled his eyes. "Let's go eat breakfast before I lose my appetite."

"Man, it'll take more than Jeremy to ruin yo' appetite." Kevin clapped Daniel on the back as they headed for the door.

Loping along behind them, Jeremy said, "It's a good thing I know you really love me, or I might get my feelings hurt."

Since his back was to them, Daniel allowed himself a tolerant smile. What they'd said was true, of course. As bratty as they were, these two guys really were like brothers to Daniel, and he would do anything for them.

Except admit it.

Why give them more ammo to use against him?

After breakfast, the men stood near the storage shed, selecting their tools from Luís' toolbox. One of Paola's chickens wandered a bit too far from the rest of the brood and Kevin eyed it hungrily. "Think they'll ever kill one o' them chickens an' fry it up for us? I'm missin' my KFC fix."

The others laughed.

"Not likely," said Daniel. "Paola seems to be kind of attached to them."

Kevin grumbled and Daniel looked more closely at him. Kevin had lost weight with all the hard work and the skimpy diet. Come to think of it, they were all looking a bit leaner, especially Jeremy.

In spite of their efforts to keep up with their grooming, the lack of time and resources had made them all look pretty ragged. Some of Kevin's twists had become unraveled in the last week, and his head was an odd mix of twists and little tufts of hair. Terrell's hair was more of a flufftop than a flattop, and Jeremy's curls were more unruly than ever.

Daniel grinned crookedly as he imagined his own appearance. He knew his hair was getting shaggier than usual, and he hadn't washed it or shaved his face for a couple of days now. They had been taking turns slipping into the bathroom in the sanctuary while the girls were out working, just so they could get a quick shower and shave. His next turn wasn't until tomorrow, so he'd have to put up with his scratchy chin and greasy hair for one more night before he had another chance to clean up properly.

The only one who didn't seem bothered by their lack of regular hygiene was Samuel. He had made no effort to control his bushy beard, and had worn the same outfit since they'd arrived.

Daniel watched the Nigerian man carry some boards across the compound, alone as usual. He'd tried to engage Samuel in conversation several times, but the man either answered in monosyllables or ignored him entirely, so Daniel gave up. He wondered what motivated Samuel's tireless work.

"Whoa, check that out." Jeremy's voice interrupted Daniel's thoughts.

Daniel was surprised to see Manny actually helping Resha carry a sofa from the sanctuary back into Pastor Sergio's house now that the floor had been finished. Once the pair had deposited the couch, Manny wandered off vaguely and Resha strode back toward the sanctuary to get another load.

When she passed the four men, Jeremy had to ask, "Hey, Resha, how'd you get Manny to do some actual work?"

Without slowing her pace, Resha turned her head to look him straight in the eye and said, poker-faced, "I told him I would break his fingers one by one if he didn't get his lazy butt out here and do it."

Resha continued on her way and they all stared at her retreating back. Looking baffled, Jeremy asked, "Was she kidding, or did she really threaten him?"

With a bemused half smile on his face, Daniel shrugged. "Hard to tell."

"That girl is scary," Terrell complained. "She never smiles."

"Probably got bad teeth," Kevin joked.

"No, remember that first day we met her?" Daniel reminded them quickly.

At Daniel's speedy defense of Resha, Jeremy cocked a knowing eyebrow at Kevin, but he nodded in agreement. "Oh, yeah. She's got a great smile. Wish she'd use it more."

"Where Resha come from, you got to look hard," Kevin explained. "In the 'hood, if you smile, you weak. She can't be showin' no weakness."

The other three pondered his statement silently. The strategy must work, because Resha seemed anything but weak.

Sitting on the grass underneath a sprawling tree with the other students, Selena scraped up the last of her rice and vegetables and sighed wistfully. "If I were home right now, I'd probably be Christmas shopping."

Mindy's ears perked up. "Where would you go?"

"Macy's, probably. I haven't been to Macy's since before Thanksgiving." Selena's voice was filled with nostalgia, as if it had been years ago instead of just over a week. She dropped her fork onto her empty plate and pushed the dishes aside, reaching for her glass of aguapanela. "And afterward, I'd stop somewhere and get something filling to eat."

Mindy nodded sadly. "I know. If I was home, my boyfriend would probably be taking me to a Christmas party tonight. I bought this cute little sweater outfit to go dancing in. You should see it, Selena, it's got this darling little ruffled collar and puffed sleeves." Her eyes lit up for a moment as she described the outfit, but then her face fell again as she added, "It's much too hot to wear it here."

As the two of them prattled on about how badly they needed manicures, Resha closed her eyes and inched away from them, disassociating herself from the conversation.

Unlike Resha, Jeremy was getting a kick out of their discussion.

After listening to the two girls for a while, he gave an exaggerated sigh in a perfect imitation of Selena's, then said in a breathy voice like Mindy's, "I know exactly what you mean. Why, I haven't had a decent pedicure in days! If I were home, I'd get one of those pedicures where they put little sparkly things on my toes!"

Mindy and Selena gawked at Jeremy in surprise.

Seeing he had their attention, he plunged ahead. "Then I'd drop a couple thousand dollars on little ceramic Christmas angels at the mall, and then I'd pick up a big fat Christmas goose for lunch, and then I'd put on my sequined Santa Claus tie with real fur to wear to the party."

He sighed again. "But instead, I'm here wasting my time, helping flood victims repair a silly old church just so they can spread the gospel, when I could be doing something meaningful, like...going dancing!"

Daniel hid a smile behind his hand, but Terrell and Kevin laughed outright. Mindy and Selena looked at each other sheepishly.

"Is that really how we sound?" Selena asked, wrinkling her nose.

"Yes," all the guys answered in unison, and Mindy and Selena squirmed. Jeremy's playful teasing had effectively pointed out how superficial and spoiled they sounded.

Pink with embarrassment, Mindy said to Selena, "I guess we really should focus on what we're supposed to be doing instead of on what we're missing."

In an obvious attempt to change the subject, Selena asked, "Do you really dance, Jeremy?"

"Do I dance?" Jeremy widened his eyes and leaned back, pretending to be shocked at the question.

"You had to ask," Daniel groaned at Selena as his friend bounced effortlessly to his feet from his crosslegged position on the ground and did a little twirl.

Selena squealed when Jeremy pulled her to her feet, twirled her around, too, then dipped her, tango-style. He released her and backed away in a flawless moonwalk. Selena and Mindy giggled in delight, and even Resha surrendered a small smile at the exuberant display.

"That's wonderful, Jeremy," exclaimed Mindy, fumbling with her cell phone camera. Selena collapsed beside her again as they watched Jeremy show off his dubstep skills.

"You oughtta see him when there's music," Kevin told her as Jeremy spun to a stop, striking a pose.

Jeremy winked at Mindy. "There's always music."

And he took a bow.

While the students were dancing their way through lunch, Stefan and Luís arrived at the compound with several rolls of vinyl flooring piled in the pickup truck. The stack of floor tiles had dwindled away as the team worked to get it all installed, so there was plenty of room under the carport for the workmen to stack the heavy rolls.

Sergio rubbed his hands together happily as he and Jeff admired the fresh flooring. "Is this not exciting, Pastor Jeff? Your team is working so hard, and they are doing such a wonderful job. We are ahead of schedule already!"

"That's great, Sergio." Jeff was amused at the little man's childish pleasure.

"When we are finished, we will have a big celebration for you all," Sergio promised, throwing his arms wide to demonstrate. "Your team deserves some recognition for all their labor."

Jeff laughed. "They're not doing it for recognition, Sergio. I'm sure seeing the finished mission center will be reward enough for them."

Weary of the conversations buzzing around her as the group finished up their meal, Resha tuned them out and scanned the compound with her eyes.

She had seen the delivery of vinyl flooring the laborers had piled under the carport, and assumed that would be one of their next projects. The other truck was now parked across the compound, near the trench where the workmen had been digging up old pipes for the last several days.

Sergio had told them that some of the aging underground pipes had cracked under the weight of the flood water above them, and others had been clogged so firmly with debris from the flood that they would have to be replaced. Since the pickup truck was laden with heavy looking metal pipes, each as big around as one of the rolls of vinyl, it looked like they were now ready to lay the new pipes in place.

Resha watched idly as the Colombian men began unloading the pipes. It took all three of them to move each pipe off the truck, and she wondered if they had wrecked the transmission by hauling a truckload of the heavy conduit all the way from Sincelejo. Then again, the truck was pretty much a wreck anyway, so it probably didn't matter.

Antonio turned away from the truck for a moment to roll up the sleeves on his blue work shirt. Stefan and Luís didn't notice that their coworker had left his post, and the two of them started to lift one of the pipes from the truck bed without Antonio supporting his end. The pipe slipped and headed straight for Antonio.

Horrified, Resha sat up straight. *Oh, Jesus, help!*

It was all happening so fast that Resha felt sure the man would be crushed, but Antonio must have heard the pipe shift. He swiftly spun around to see the pipe coming at him, then leapt out of the way in almost the same movement. His feline agility undoubtedly saved him from serious injury.

Resha raised one eyebrow, surprised at the man's quick reflexes. In his loose-fitting work clothes, Antonio looked unimpressive, but he must have had some sort of martial arts training at one time for him to move that fast. Unusual for a common laborer, she suspected.

At the sound of the men yelling and the pipe crashing onto the ground, the rest of the students turned to look, but by then, the show was over and all they saw was Antonio's friends rushing over to him to see if he was okay.

As the group returned to their own business of picking up their soiled dishes, Antonio turned and glared at Resha as if he'd felt her eyes on him. For some reason, Antonio's look gave Resha chills, but she stared back at him without flinching.

When Stefan called out something else to him, Antonio's menacing scowl relaxed into his usual lifeless expression before he turned to Stefan, and Resha wondered if she'd imagined the hatred she'd seen in his eyes. She'd gotten plenty of dirty looks in her lifetime, but there was no reason for Antonio to feel that much animosity toward her.

With an effort, Resha shook off her uneasiness and carried her plate to the kitchen.

Matéo was thrilled that today he had gotten a little bit closer to the dog before it slunk away. Following Mindy's example, Matéo now held a chunk of day old bread out to the mutt, making little kissy sounds.

"Here, puppy. Come on, boy. Come and get the bread."

The dog looked warily at Matéo, but it didn't come any closer. At least it didn't back away, so Matéo decided to reward the dog the way Mindy had. He broke off a piece of the bread and tossed it gently toward the dog. The dog flinched but held its ground, and after a moment it crept forward and sniffed at the bread. Satisfied that the bread was safe, the dog picked it up in his teeth and carried it several steps closer to the bank of trees before eating it.

Matéo squatted on the ground and waited for the dog to finish, wishing he could get close enough to stroke its matted fur. When the dog had polished off the morsel, it turned hopeful eyes back to Matéo.

Matéo laughed, happy that he had finally made a small connection with the dog. He tossed it the remaining scraps and sat back on his haunches to watch. The dog finished the bread and looked expectantly at Matéo again, so Matéo held up his hands to show that they were empty.

"Sorry, boy, no more. Later I will bring you an egg."

When the dog realized no more food was forthcoming, it slowly turned and wandered deeper into the jungle, closer to the arroyo. Curious where the dog spent its time, Matéo followed from a safe distance, but once he got closer to the ravine, he lost sight of it.

Matéo listened, straining to hear which way the dog had gone, but he heard a familiar crackling sound instead. After a moment, Matéo recognized it as static, the same kind of static he heard from Sergio's radio at the mission center.

Puzzled and a little spooked, Matéo looked around. Still finding no sign of the dog, he whistled for it, and the static promptly vanished.

More interested in the missing dog than the source of the sound, Matéo crawled on all fours closer to the edge of the ravine, trying to see where the mutt had gone. Suddenly he spied something that made him forget all about the missing canine.

There were several thick beams, similar to the supports Matéo had seen jutting from some of the ruined houses nearby, tied together to make them longer. They had been placed across the steep edges of the arroyo to form a crude bridge, supported by the forked branches of a tree growing in the middle of the water. The boards had not been there the last time he had ventured this far.

Matéo couldn't pass up the promise of adventure. He made his way to the makeshift bridge and cautiously began to crawl across the boards to see what was on the other side. Halfway across, he glanced down at the swirling water several yards beneath him and began to get nervous.

That's when it happened. The boards suddenly seemed to lift up behind him and twist, and Matéo lost his balance and fell off with a cry.

He panicked as the cold, foul-smelling water closed over his head. He beat at the water wildly until his head broke the surface, then flapped around in a panic, his arms getting tangled in slimy weeds as the putrid water ran into his eyes.

"Help! Sergio! Help me!"

Carrying a box of floor tiles to the classroom building they'd cleared yesterday, Resha stopped in mid-stride and cocked her head to listen.

Was that the dog barking? Odd, she'd never heard it bark before. Then, along with the barking, she heard a faint cry. She dropped the box and started running.

Mindy, several paces behind, called, "Resha! Where are you going?"

Resha almost ignored her, but decided it might be wiser to have someone else involved. Without slowing down, she yelled back, "Matéo's in trouble."

Mindy's eyes grew round, and she set down her own box of tiles and ran off in the other direction.

When Resha got to the line of trees, she stopped to listen again, but heard only the dog's frantic yapping. She called out, "Matéo! Where are you?"

Again, she heard the boy's voice calling for help, and this time she heard splashing. Great. The kid had definitely fallen into the arroyo.

She sprinted through the trees and fronds, pushing aside the thick hanging vines that grabbed at her, until she came to the water's edge.

The dog ran back and forth near where the ground dropped off sharply. Matéo flailed around in the middle of the ravine, crying as he tried to stay afloat. He was hanging on to some vines to keep from being swept downstream.

The vines seemed sturdy enough to hold him, but the child was hysterical. Resha was afraid he might break the vines if he didn't stop squirming, and then he would really be in trouble.

"I'm here, Matéo. Calm down," Resha yelled as she snatched the earrings from her ears and tossed them aside. Matéo looked up at her but kept thrashing around.

"Miss Resha! Help!" he called frantically.

"Matéo, stay still," Resha commanded in a firm voice. This time he stopped floundering and stared at her, but she could still see the panic in his eyes. "I'm going to come in, Matéo, and we're both going to get out of there together, okay?"

He nodded, his lip trembling as he gripped the heavy greenery to keep the rushing torrent from sweeping him away. Resha screwed up her face at the thought of getting into the filthy water, but there was no time for her sensibilities.

She stepped off the edge and landed in the water, which came up to her chest. Yuk. At least her feet touched the ground where she was. She hoped it didn't get much deeper. She tried not to think about snakes.

Guess I should have prayed first, huh, Lord? Jesus, please help me get this kid out of here.

Her shoes slipped on the slimy bottom, and her muscles strained against the current. Inch by inch, she approached the center, where Matéo struggled to keep his head above water.

Soon the water reached Resha's shoulders. She pushed off with her legs, swimming toward the boy with strong, confident strokes. Her heavy outer shirt dragged at her and she wished she'd taken it off.

When she finally reached the terrified child, he had tired himself out, which was a good thing as far as Resha was concerned. She'd read that drowning victims sometimes lashed out at their rescuers in panic, but Matéo simply went limp and let her grab him. She extricated his arms from the tangled mess of vines and pulled him away.

"Wrap your arms around my neck," she ordered. When he did, clutching at her neck and ears, she began heading awkwardly back toward the shore.

Resha craned her neck to see around Matéo, whose weight had doubled from his wet clothes. At least the extra weight kept them both from being carried downstream.

She'd almost reached the slippery wall of the ravine when she heard the sound of running feet, then Mindy's worried voice calling from the edge.

"Resha, the boys are here."

Hurrah, thought Resha. She didn't bother to look up, concentrating only on her goal of reaching the edge. By now Resha was back in more shallow water, her feet sliding on the slick bottom, but at least she could keep her head above the surface easily.

As she got close to the edge, one of the guys, she couldn't tell which one because Matéo was blocking her view and his hand was grasping one of her ears, called out, "Hand him up here, Resha. We got him."

Sure, stay up there where it's dry. She pried Matéo's fingers loose and saw Terrell and Kevin leaning over the edge, arms reaching down for Matéo.

As Resha handed Matéo up to the two men, out of the corner of her eye, she thought she caught a glimpse of movement in the trees behind them, a fleeting impression of blue. She cocked her head in that direction, searching the trees with her eyes, but there was nothing. Even the dog was gone, probably scared off by the arrival of too many people.

Terrell and Kevin set the wailing Matéo safely on dry ground and tried to distract him from his terror by peppering him with questions.

Resha stood still in the murky water, her chest heaving from the strenuous effort she'd just put forth. Then she realized Daniel and Jeremy were crouching on the ground above her, each holding a hand out to her, ready to help her from the water.

Did they think she was some helpless female floundering around waiting to be rescued? Her first instinct was to slap their hands away and tell them she didn't need their help.

But she saw sincere concern in their eyes and chided herself for her ingratitude. Remembering Mindy's insistence that they were different from other guys because they were Christians, she reluctantly reached one hand up to each of them and allowed them to haul her up.

As they dragged Resha from the arroyo, her wet jeans clung to her, and Daniel's and Jeremy's eyes automatically drifted to the figure no one had suspected she kept hidden under her baggy clothes. They quickly turned their attention to Matéo, but not before Resha had noticed the direction of their gaze.

She raised a cynical eyebrow at the clueless Mindy. So much for Christian guys being different.

Still, Resha had to acknowledge that their quickly averted eyes were a far cry from how her previous male acquaintances would have reacted. She filed that thought away to ponder later.

Well, just let me take my fine self out of here so I won't cause my iron-willed Christian brothers to stumble, Resha thought sardonically.

Now was a good time to disappear. Matéo had forgotten his fear now, and was almost dancing in excitement as he recounted his adventure for the four men.

Resha slipped away with Mindy fluttering and clucking behind her, all big eyes and worry.

Antonio watched from the distance as the Americans pulled Matéo from the arroyo and led the soaking boy away.

That was fine – he had not really wanted to hurt the stupid child. He had only intended to keep his hiding place from being discovered, and he had accomplished that.

Matéo had probably not suspected anything, but Antonio would still have to move his radio from the hollowed out tree he had hidden it in.

He snarled in aggravation – he had already had to move it once, across the arroyo, when the Americans arrived. That was when he had lost a cable and had to steal one from Sergio's radio.

He did not know how Sergio had gotten his own radio working again so quickly, but it did not matter. Antonio did not mind if they used it to communicate, because he could sometimes catch their transmissions on his own radio and follow their movements. That was how he had learned about the Mexican Red Cross trucks that had been coming to Sergio's aid. El Tiburon had been pleased with Antonio and had used that information to his advantage.

But now, because he had assumed no one would be wandering around the ravine after Sergio had warned them of the danger, he had left his makeshift bridge where the boy could find it.

Angrily, he dragged the boards he had yanked out from under Matéo and set them up again further downstream so he could go across. After he relocated his radio, he would have to put the boards someplace where they would not be found easily.

So much trouble, but he could not risk Sergio suspecting his connection with the Black Eagles, because El Tiburon would be furious with Antonio if he were caught.

Adolfo had been looking forward to this day. The Black Eagles were going to begin training the new recruits in hand-to-hand combat. He was surprised to see that the female recruits were there, too, but he should not have been. Aside from keeping them in separate quarters, the girls were treated exactly the same as the men.

Adolfo looked around eagerly for Gloria, but when he spotted her tall figure, he put on an indifferent air. She felt his eyes on her and smiled flirtatiously. Adolfo responded with a cool nod and began to make his way through the line to get closer to her.

"I am getting tired of these children's games," Gloria said in a bored tone when he stood next to her. "I am ready for some real action."

Adolfo considered offering her some action that evening after the training, but there were too many ears around. He did not want word getting back to El Tiburon that he did not take the training seriously. His offer would wait. For now, he said, "Today should be more interesting. I heard that Lt. Rojas is a martial arts expert. Maybe he will teach us some good moves."

Soon, the tall lieutenant with the shaved head appeared and everyone snapped to attention. It had been drilled into the recruits to show proper respect to their superiors, and Rojas seemed pleased with their response.

Rojas had two of his experienced soldiers demonstrate several techniques, then he paired the recruits up for practice. Adolfo was glad he was not matched up against Gloria, because he probably would have gone easy on her. He was hoping for a worthy opponent, someone he could take out his aggressions on, and was disappointed when Rojas assigned him a flabby looking pig named Benito.

Adolfo approached his designated opponent with a confident swagger. He was amused to see Benito swallow hard before they fought.

Striking fear into the enemy's heart was a major step toward victory already.

It was over quickly. Adolfo had his adversary pinned to the ground in plenty of time to watch Gloria's bout. Gloria fought better than Adolfo's lazy opponent had, but she was no match for the sturdy male recruit Rojas had pitted her against.

Adolfo was enraged to see the boy named Dario knock Gloria to the ground, then land on top of her to choke her as the soldiers had demonstrated.

Without thinking, Adolfo grabbed the startled recruit and dragged him off Gloria.

"You want to learn to fight?" he demanded. "Then fight me."

If Adolfo had hoped to intimidate Dario the same way he had Benito, he was disappointed. Dario took up the new challenge with gusto, quickly getting in a fierce body punch the way Rojas had just shown them. Before he could get in another strike, though, Adolfo had grabbed Dario's arm and twisted it, forcing Dario to his knees to avoid having the arm broken.

Someone yelled, but Adolfo was too caught up in the fight to pay attention. Gloria had scrambled to her feet and was watching the show with amusement.

Dario was no slouch, and it took him only a moment to recover. With surprising strength, he freed his arm from Adolfo's grasp. Still on the ground, he grabbed one of Adolfo's legs and yanked hard, causing Adolfo to land on the ground beside him. The two went at each other like mad dogs, forgetting all their training, and the rest of the recruits stopped their own exercises to watch.

Someone yelled again, and again Adolfo ignored it. Finally Adolfo got the upper hand, pinning Dario to the ground with his forearm jammed against Dario's throat. They were both panting from the exertion as they glared at each other, and Dario's eyes held a mixture of fear and fury.

Adolfo was proud of himself until a crushing blow landed on the side of his head, causing him to fall off Dario, who staggered to his feet and backed away. Stunned, Adolfo turned to find Rojas glaring at him with danger in his eyes.

"Never attack in anger, because you will make mistakes, which you just did in allowing me to catch you by surprise. And never, ever go against my orders again, because that will be your last mistake."

Adolfo was humiliated now, reprimanded and threatened by the leader he had hoped to impress. When the lieutenant turned away, Adolfo saw a slight, sadistic smile on his face, giving Adolfo a small hope that Rojas had been secretly pleased by his fearlessness and ferocity.

Gloria did not bother to hide her own pleasure. When Rojas had ordered everyone back to their places, she brushed against Adolfo and purred, "I like your style, Adolfo. Maybe you can show me some more moves sometime."

Adolfo smiled, forgetting his embarrassment. For the rest of the training session, he paid close attention to Lt. Rojas, hoping to win back his favor. Even when he was pitted against Dario for one of the exercises, Adolfo kept a careful reign on his hostility and followed Rojas' instructions scrupulously, careful not to cross the line again.

He would reward himself by finding Gloria when their training session was over.

Resha dropped her wet clothes on the bathroom floor and indulged in an early shower. Washing the filthy water out of her hair, she was once again thankful she'd cropped it so short.

After the luxury of a full six minutes under the spray instead of the usual three she allowed herself, Resha put on the dry clothes she'd brought in, then turned to pick up the wet clothing she'd dropped in the corner.

The clothes weren't there. She hadn't heard anyone come in.

Creepy.

Puzzled, Resha stepped into the hallway. No one was there.

She made her way into the kitchen in time to see the door close behind Abuelita. With growing suspicion, Resha rushed to the window to see what the old woman was up to. Sure enough, Abuelita was carrying Resha's clothing.

Resha was turning the doorknob to follow her when a voice called her name. She spun around and saw Paola sitting at the kitchen table drinking coffee. "Abuelita is going to wash the clothes for you."

Resha glowered at Paola and demanded, "How?"

"She has an old metal tub outside near the water pump," Paola explained. "She has been washing all our clothes by hand. Would you like a cup of coffee?"

Resha ignored the offer and glared at Paola as if the whole thing were Paola's fault. "She doesn't have to do that," she objected angrily, feeling guilty at the thought of the old woman trying to wring out her heavy jeans with arthritic hands.

Paola did not seem offended by Resha's brusqueness. She smiled. "I understand your concern, but Abuelita is a strong peasant woman. She is accustomed to doing such tasks. It is no great effort for her."

Resha was unconvinced. "Are you sure?" she demanded with her arms crossed.

"Yes, I am sure," Paola insisted. "Your men did not bring as many changes of clothing as the ladies did, and Abuelita has been washing some of their shirts for them. It is her pleasure to do it. Especially for you, who so bravely saved my little brother today."

Satisfied, Resha switched gears. "Speaking of Matéo, where is he?"

Paola looked confused by the sudden turn of conversation, but she answered, "He is in the house. Sergio is punishing him for going to the arroyo by making him stay indoors the rest of the day."

"I need to talk to him," Resha demanded, offering no explanation.

Paola stood at once, setting her coffee on the table. "Of course. Would you like to go and see him now?"

Matéo sat on his bed, a picture of misery. With no one to talk to and no electricity, staying indoors in the stifling heat must be the worst type of punishment for the energetic little boy. His eyes lit up when Paola ushered Resha into the tiny bedroom.

"Miss Resha, Miss Resha!" he cried, rushing forward to throw his arms around her waist. "I did not thank you for saving me."

Resha awkwardly patted his back, then carefully stepped away from his clutching arms. "No problem, Matéo. Can you tell me what happened out there?"

Matéo's brow furrowed in confusion. His tone implied that the answer was obvious. "I fell into the water."

Resha took a deep breath and reminded herself that Matéo was only nine. She tried again. "Matéo, I know you fell into the water, but you were in the middle of the arroyo. You were nowhere near the edge. Did the water carry you out to the middle?"

Matéo shook his head, anxious to please her. "No, I fell off the bridge."

Give me patience, Lord, Resha pleaded silently.

"What bridge?" she demanded, knowing there had been no bridge when Matéo had given her a tour of the ravine several days ago.

Matéo's eyes danced with excitement. "It was a new bridge. There were three or four long pieces of wood tied together, and they were placed across the water to go to the other side."

"I didn't see any bridge." Resha frowned.

Matéo's face fell. "I think I broke it. When I was in the middle of it, the boards twisted up behind me, and that is when I fell into the water."

"I didn't see any boards, either," she said flatly, trying to contain her frustration with Matéo's unhelpful responses and with herself. Resha had been preoccupied with getting the boy to safety and had not paid enough attention to the surrounding area.

Matéo shrugged helplessly. "I guess they fell into the water, too."

Determined to learn the truth, Resha pressed, "Will you show me where the bridge was?"

"Sergio says I cannot leave the house again tonight." Matéo's shoulders drooped in utter dejection.

"I meant tomorrow," Resha explained. "Maybe you can show me after we eat tomorrow, when all our chores are done."

With a fearful, sidelong glance at his sister, Matéo nodded his head eagerly. Paola offered no objection.

Resha thanked her, said good night to Matéo, and headed back to the dining area for supper. As she walked past, Resha noticed her clothes, freshly washed, hanging on a crude clothesline that stretched from the house to the water pump.

Abuelita hadn't wasted any time.

During the evening meal, Resha addressed the four men who shared the table with the girls. "Did Matéo tell you how he fell in the gully?"

All other discussion at the table ceased and everyone looked surprised that Resha had initiated a conversation.

Kevin finally spoke up. "Naw, all he could talk about was how you jumped in and saved 'im."

"Yeah," Jeremy added, his eyes twinkling. "He kept telling us how 'Wonder Woman' braved the snake-infested rapids and snatched him from the jaws of a crocodile."

Resha ignored their kidding. "He told me he fell off some kind of bridge. Did any of you see any sign of a bridge?"

They stopped their playful ribbing and looked thoughtful. After a moment, they all shook their heads, and Daniel said, "I didn't see anything he could have mistaken for a bridge. But he's nine years old. Nine-year-olds tend to exaggerate."

"Yeah, look at all those good things he said about you," Terrell said, but his tone was more teasing than malicious for a change.

Realizing the guys didn't have anything helpful to offer, Resha shrugged indifferently and turned her attention back to her food.

Daniel was probably right – Matéo's imagination might be getting the better of him, but for some reason, his confidence that there had been a bridge there bothered her. She wondered if she should mention it to Sergio, but probably Matéo had already told him about it. She would wait and see if she found anything tomorrow.

Resha suddenly became aware that Jeremy had spoken and was holding out something to her in his hand. She frowned suspiciously and made no move to take whatever it was.

Jeremy grinned at her reluctance. He opened his hand and let some gold-colored hoops dangle from his fingers. "I think these belong to you."

"Thanks." A little embarrassed, Resha accepted her earrings and slipped them into her shirt pocket. She'd put on a pair of smaller, more practical disks, but was glad to get her hoops back, even if they were from the dollar store. How in the world had Jeremy spotted them in the rocky dirt she'd tossed them in?

Jeremy winked at her and turned back to the friendly argument he was having with Terrell. Neither he nor Resha mentioned it, but it was obvious that Jeremy had cleaned the mud off her earrings for her. She decided that, in spite of his clowning, Jeremy was an okay guy.

Armed with a screwdriver pilfered from Luís' toolbox, Jeremy retreated to the sanctuary and began tightening the reeds on the piano as soon as he'd finished eating. The piano's wood had finally dried out enough that he could make some adjustments.

He looked like a mad professor with his brown curls flapping wildly as he leaned over the piano and turned his head from one reed to the next, tweaking and tugging. Kevin and Terrell watched with interest.

"Do you actually know what you're doing?" Terrell peered over the top.

Without looking up from his work, Jeremy said cheerfully, "We'll find out, won't we?"

He tapped a few of the keys, cocking his head to listen, then made some more adjustments. The notes sounded less shaky than before, so his efforts were helping. He kept playing with it, occasionally hitting the keys to test the sound, until Pastor Jeff came out of Sergio's office.

Pastor Jeff smiled slightly and shook his head when he noticed what Jeremy was doing. "You can't help yourself, can you?"

Jeremy grinned and closed the piano lid.

Jeff reached the podium and cleared his throat. "All right, everyone, shall we get started?"

The students gathered near the front, except for Samuel, who stayed in the back corner, but at least he put away his crossword puzzles and pulled out his Bible. The rest of the students had pulled out Bibles, too, even Selena, although hers looked fresh and crisp, as if it had rarely been opened. Manny didn't have a Bible, but lately he'd been sitting up for part of the devotional instead of dozing off right away.

It was cool sitting here with his friends, all of them ready to study God's Word. Jeremy settled back in his chair, content.

God, thanks for letting me come on this trip after all.

8

Day 7: Saturday

The chickens scrabbled along the ground, pecking at the grain Paola had tossed there for them. They seemed oblivious to Paola, just going about their business, taking for granted that the food would be there without a thought about where it had come from. She wondered if that was how she seemed to God sometimes, just taking advantage of all the blessings He provided for her without stopping to acknowledge their Source.

She looked around at her surroundings – at the home she was sharing with her two brothers, at the young workers God had sent to help them, at the beautiful lush trees that provided shade to cool her.

She looked down at her own jeans, and at the dusty huaraches on her feet, and the donated green polo shirt that hung loosely on her thin frame, and she realized that she had everything that she needed. All the way down to the chickens that helped provide food for her.

"Father, You are so good to me, even when I don't stop to thank You," she prayed. "You give me so much, and then You even allow me to help care for Your creation."

She leaned against the wall of the chicken coop, watching the chickens awhile longer before turning her attention upward to admire the clear blue sky. Soon she began to sing softly,

"Todo lo creaste
La tierra, cielo y mar
Los cielos son tu tabernaculo
Gloria al Dios Altísimo."

Confident that she was alone with the chickens, Paola sang with more gusto.

"Dios del cielo, maravilloso Dios
Eres santo, santo
La creación muestra su majestad
Eres santo, santo
Dios de la creación
Dios de la creación."

Suddenly a curly-headed elf popped its head around the corner and gave her a toothy grin.

"Great voice," the elf said.

Paola gave a little scream, then laughed. "Jeremy! You frightened me!"

"Sorry," Jeremy said, but the smile he gave her was unrepentant. "I heard the music and had to see who was serenading the chickens. Do you always sing like that when you feed them?"

It took Paola a moment to process Jeremy's question because he had a tendency to talk fast. When she figured it out, she answered, a little embarrassed, "Yes, sometimes when I am all alone and I think about The Lord, songs come to me, and I cannot help but to sing. I feel as if I will burst if I don't give voice to what He has put in my heart."

Paola felt self-conscious that she had revealed so much, but Jeremy's face lit up and he nodded vigorously, and she got the impression that he knew exactly what she was talking about.

"Yeah," Jeremy agreed emphatically. They stood in companionable silence for a moment, mulling over what she'd said. Then Jeremy asked, "I haven't heard that song in while, but I think I recognize it. Can you sing it in English?"

Only because he seemed to truly understand her reason for singing did she consider it. She thought for a moment, translating the song in her mind, then explained, "The words, they are different in Spanish to make it fit the melody."

"I figured that." Jeremy nodded, then repeated his request. "Will you sing it in English?"

Paola laughed at his persistence, then took a deep breath and began shyly,

"God of wonders beyond our galaxy
You are holy, holy
The universe declares Your majesty
You are holy, holy
Lord of heaven and earth."

Jeremy bobbed his head to an imaginary beat as she sang. When she was done, his smile widened. "That's the song all right. I didn't know Colombian Christians sang the same songs we do. Cool."

Paola replayed his words in her mind to decipher them, then smiled back at him. "Yes it is very …cool."

Jeremy winked at her and trundled off, lugging a bucket of floor adhesive behind him and bobbing his head as if he could still hear music.

Americans were very strange, Paola thought. Especially this one.

Even though it was only mid morning, the sun was already beating down relentlessly. Pastor Jeff approached as the four guys struggled to haul a heavy roll of vinyl flooring off the pile that had been stacked under the carport.

Daniel, Terrell, and Kevin acknowledged Jeff with grunts and nods, but Jeremy deliberately turned away. Jeff's mouth tightened for a second, then he asked with forced casualness, "Jeremy, Stefan is going to make a delivery to some friends in La Rosa. Would you mind riding along with him?"

"I know why you're asking me, Pastor Jeff." Jeremy glared at the pastor for a moment, then turned back to the truck with his face flushed.

Daniel and Kevin looked at him, then each other, puzzled. Had they missed something?

Jeff kept his voice studiously calm. "I'm asking you because, as you know, Pastor Sergio has a rule that nobody travels alone because it's safer if two people go. Antonio and Luís took the other truck to Sincelejo, so I thought you might go with Stefan."

"Sure, Pastor Jeff. What's next? Are you going to have me gathering eggs with Paola? Or maybe I'll be cooking them in the kitchen with Abuelita." Jeremy stormed away, stumbling as he tried to drag the heavy roll of vinyl behind him.

His friends stared after him, perplexed. Pastor Jeff rubbed his temple in frustration.

Wanting to keep the peace, Daniel volunteered, "I'll go, Pastor Jeff."

Jeff waved him away in disgust and snapped, "Fine, Daniel. Go."

Then he stalked away, too, in the opposite direction from Jeremy.

Daniel threw up his hands in exasperation. Was the heat making everyone insane?

Kevin snickered. "Guess we better find Jeremy befo' he hurt himself tryin' to move that flooring without any help."

He and Terrell wandered off in the direction Jeremy had gone.

Daniel closed his eyes and took a deep breath, getting a grip on his frustration. Then he turned to Stefan, who sat in his Chevy looking totally confused by the whole exchange.

Poor guy, Daniel thought. He must think Americans are nuts.

He managed to give Stefan a friendly smile and climbed into the passenger side of the car, noting several boxes stacked in the back seat.

"They are angry at me?" Stefan asked in heavily accented English as they pulled away in the hot, stuffy car. All the windows were rolled down, but the warm, sticky breeze wafting through them did little to cool the air inside.

"Nah, they're mad at each other," Daniel assured him, then decided to experiment with his Spanish. He wrinkled his nose in concentration, then enunciated carefully, "*No, ellos estan enojados el uno al otro.*"

Stefan gave a delighted smile. "*¿Hablas Español?*"

Daniel grinned back. "That was about the extent of it, right there."

Stefan's brow wrinkled in puzzlement as he tried to decipher what Daniel had said.

Daniel broke it down for him, speaking more slowly. "I do not speak very much Spanish. I would like to learn more. *No hablo mucho Español. Yo quiero aprender mas.*"

"And I wish to speak more English." Stefan's face brightened with excitement. "We can teach each other!"

"Why not? We've got a two hour drive," Daniel agreed. Seeing the confusion on Stefan's face again, he amended, "*¿Por que no? Tenemos dos horas.*"

Stefan laughed at Daniel's pronunciation, but he understood the words anyway. They agreed that for the rest of the trip, Daniel would speak only in Spanish, and Stefan would limit his responses to English, so they both could practice.

Their plan worked for the most part, although their sentences were sometimes a hodgepodge of English and Spanish, and their conversation was punctuated with improvised sign language as they tried to convey thoughts they didn't know the words for. It was a fun way to pass the time, and they got to know each other better as they practiced speaking an unfamiliar language.

Daniel was surprised to learn that Stefan had been part of the Black Eagles before he became a Christian less than a year ago. He had been forcefully recruited into their ranks as a young teenager and had been brainwashed into believing the Black Eagles had only the Colombian people's best interests at heart.

"But Las Águilas Negras only want what is good for themselves," Stefan explained. "I was growing tired of the violence, of frightening innocent people to make them do what we wanted, but it was the only life I knew. Until a helicopter flew over our headquarters in the night and dropped some little books about Jesus."

"Mister Novak?" Daniel asked.

"I do not believe so, although Brother Novak also gives out little books with words from the Bible. Our leader, a man I knew as El Tiburon, was very angry and had all the little books burned, but I had hidden one in my pocket."

Stefan had prayed the prayer suggested in the tract, but did not know where to go from there. He was desperate for answers and terrified that his newfound faith would be discovered.

Soon after Stefan's secret conversion, his leader, Captain Ortega, decided to eliminate the Christian influence from a certain small village that was resistant to his attempts to cultivate the coca plants. Stefan had been ordered to invade a home that housed a small home church, and to kill anyone inside. Instead, Stefan had begged the people inside the home for more information about Jesus Christ.

Raul, the self appointed minister, and his wife Manuela, prayed for Stefan and gave him a Bible, and Stefan in turn let the family out the back door, claiming they had escaped before he arrived.

Inside the Bible was scribbled an address for Raul's brother, Javier, who had invited Raul to begin his ministry again out of his home in La Rosa. Stefan had secretly attended their prayer meetings whenever possible, and had gotten the courage from them to defect from the Black Eagles.

In an attempt to make Stefan more difficult to locate, Raul sent him to Pastor Sergio. When the floods came, Stefan never even considered fleeing to safety – he felt a debt of gratitude to Raul and Pastor Sergio and planned to help them in any way possible.

It was to Javier's home that they were now delivering the supplies, for the little home church that Raul now ministered to in La Rosa, a small village about fifty miles east of the mission center.

Matéo couldn't wait until that evening for his promised jaunt with Resha. While the team ate lunch, he fidgeted anxiously around the fringes of the courtyard, waiting for Resha to put the last bite of her food into her mouth.

Resha had spotted him, of course, even though he was trying hard to be discreet. She pretended not to see the little boy, but she decided to have mercy on him and ate quickly, then excused herself to put her dirty dishes back in the kitchen. When she came out, she wasn't at all surprised to find Matéo waiting at the door.

"Miss Resha, would you like me to show you where the bridge was?" he offered helpfully.

"Well, at least your experience didn't scare you away from the water," Resha said wryly. Her comment went over his head, so she said, "All right, Matéo. Let's go."

The two of them slipped around the back of the classrooms so they wouldn't attract the attention of the others. The dog was skulking around near the water pump, and when it saw Resha and Matéo, it looked undecided whether to follow Matéo or stay close to Mindy. It finally decided to stay near the food, so it sat down again.

Matéo was so intent on his mission that he hadn't even noticed the dog.

Once they got close to the water's edge, the little boy hesitated, biting his lip as he stared down at the rushing water. Then he turned and saw that Resha was no more than two steps back, and he regained his confidence.

They clambered over the rocky perimeter until they got near the point where Resha had pulled Matéo from the gully. Matéo frowned as he searched with his eyes.

"I think it was over there." He pointed uncertainly.

Resha looked where he pointed, but saw nothing unusual. She peered down at the water, trying to see if the boards he had described had gotten wedged somewhere, but still she saw nothing.

The boards could have been carried away by the water, she supposed, but it seemed more likely they would have been caught up in the undergrowth like so much of the debris she could still see in the water.

"Stay here," she ordered, then began carefully descending the steep edge.

Matéo watched fearfully from the spot where she'd left him. "Be careful, Miss Resha."

Resha didn't respond – her sharp eyes had picked up on something.

Apparently Matéo had miscalculated where he'd fallen in, because several yards away from where he'd pointed, there were deep indentations in the ground where boards could have been placed the way he'd described. The gully was narrower there, so it would be the logical place for someone to try to cross it.

Resha turned her eyes to the opposite shore. Sure enough there was a matching set of marks on the ground there. In the center of the ravine was a tree whose forked branches reached up nearly level with the bank, the perfect support for a makeshift bridge. Still no sign of the boards, though. It was as if someone had removed them deliberately.

Satisfied that Matéo had been telling the truth, Resha quickly climbed back to where he waited.

"Looks like you were right, Matéo," she told him, knowing it would make the boy feel good. "I can see where the boards were."

"Do you think we can build another bridge?" he asked hopefully as the two of them walked back to the mission center.

Resha almost smiled. So that's why he'd been so eager to show her.

"You'll have to ask your brother about that, but I doubt it. The first bridge wasn't very safe, was it?"

He hung his head. "No," he admitted, then brightened. "But we could build a stronger one."

"Like I said, ask Sergio." Resha was anxious to get back now, so she could ponder the implications of what she'd discovered. "I have to start working again. We're finishing up the floor in the kitchen today."

Antonio and Luís had been packing dirt over the new sewer pipes when Antonio saw the pair heading back to the arroyo. He told Luís he needed a break and followed the boy and the American discreetly.

It was obvious that the skinny woman with the man's haircut had seen evidence of Antonio's activities there, but he did not know what she was going to do with that information. He hoped she was not going to tell Sergio.

Antonio cursed himself for being careless. As soon as she was occupied elsewhere, Antonio would go and try to make the marks from the boards less visible. And if he had a chance, he would break her skinny neck for being nosy.

Then he reigned in his thoughts. He could not go around killing Americans for no good reason. Captain Ortega would have his head for calling the American authorities' attention to the Black Eagles involvement in Cuenco Verde.

Antonio would have to be patient – the filthy gringos would be gone soon enough, and then El Tiburon would let him do what he wanted with the Restrepos. For now he would have to settle for making sure that no one would find anything to link him or Manny to the Black Eagles in any way.

Stefan and Daniel arrived to discover that the front porch of Raul's home had caved in, another casualty of the surging water. Since they clearly weren't going in through the front door, Stefan pulled the Chevy all the way to the back of the house.

A tall, thin man with a long face opened the back door before Stefan had even cut the engine. Stefan waved at him enthusiastically, telling Daniel, "That is Raul."

A ghost of a smile appeared under the gaunt man's thick salt-and-pepper mustache and he acknowledged Stefan's greeting with a somber nod. Except for his clothing, faded to a dull gray from many washings, Raul made Daniel think of a mortician.

It was strange to think that God had used this lean, grim-faced man to disciple the gregarious Stefan. Of course, Stefan had probably not always been as affable as he was now. Jesus had a tendency to change people if they let Him.

Daniel offered to unload the boxes and put them on the back porch so Stefan could have a few minutes with his mentor. Stefan agreed gratefully, and he went inside the house with Raul and another man who had also come out to greet Stefan. The brother, Javier, Daniel guessed.

Neither of them noticed Daniel, so he went to work quietly, unloading the back seat and the trunk. It didn't take long to put the few cases of supplies on the rickety porch, but sweat was already soaking his T-shirt when he was done.

He pushed his dripping hair out of his eyes, then sat in the car and studied the ramshackle house that had obviously been hit hard by the flood.

It might be better to tear the whole thing down and start from scratch, Daniel mused.

A faded blue van was parked in the grass beside the house, and Daniel noticed that one of the doors had been recently painted or replaced, because it was a different color from the rest of the vehicle. Telltale rust streaked the lower half of the van, a sure sign that it had been in high water at some point.

A short, middle aged woman with graying hair swept into a careless bun came out through the back door and shyly offered Daniel a bottle of Colombian soda water. Daniel assumed the sweet little woman with the monkey face was Raul's wife. He thanked her and she scurried back inside.

The drink was tepid, but it was sweet and it was liquid, so Daniel drank thirstily as he waited for Stefan to finish talking with Raul.

When Stefan returned to the Chevy, he told Daniel, in a mixture of English and Spanish, "Raul and Javier have much work to do on their home, also. I have promised Raul that I will come again and help him to repair their water pump so that they will have cleaner water. Since the flood, they have had to draw contaminated water from an old well. They boil the water many times, but I am concerned that it is still unsafe. The water pump is not so near the polluted river, and the distance may filter the water some."

As they headed back to Cuenco Verde, Daniel felt comfortable enough with Stefan to ask him about his relationship with Paola.

"Ah, Paola." Stefan smiled dreamily, putting a hand over his heart with an exaggerated sigh. "*Ella is muy hermosa, verdad?*"

Daniel grinned. In his rapture over Paola, Stefan had forgotten his pact to speak only English, so Daniel deliberately chose not to speak Spanish.

"Yeah, she's real pretty," he agreed in an exaggerated Texas drawl, amused at how flat the words sounded in English compared to the lyrical Spanish words Stefan had used.

Switching back to English, Stefan asked anxiously, "Do you think that Paola thinks of me in the same way?"

"*Si.*" Daniel smiled as he stated the obvious.

Stefan relaxed visibly. "That is good. When all the work is finished and Sergio no longer needs us, I will ask her to be my wife."

"That's great, Stefan. *Muy bueno.*" Daniel was genuinely pleased for the friendly couple. They seemed perfect for each other. "I'm sure you'll be very happy together. Uh... *estoy seguro de que va a ser muy felices juntos.*"

"*Gracias.* Thank you, my friend," Stefan said. He became quiet after that, and Daniel figured he was dreaming of his future with Paola.

Daniel was content to ride in silence the rest of the drive home, but his own mind began to wander.

Seeing Stefan lost in his plans to build a life with the woman he loved, Daniel wondered idly about his own future and hoped God had someone in mind for him, too. He thought briefly about the way his friends were playfully trying to match him up with Mindy and shook his head against the idea.

Mindy was unquestionably pretty and seemed like a sweet girl, but he couldn't imagine wanting to spend his life with her. Her naivete was cute at first, but he had a feeling the novelty would wear off quickly. And although she seemed to be sincere in her love of God, the conversations he'd overheard between her and Selena were shallow and pointless.

Daniel was hoping for someone a little more practical, with more passion for God's Word, someone like.....

"We are back, Daniel," Stefan announced, turning down the road that led to the mission center. Daniel was relieved his desultory thoughts had been interrupted before they could fully form. He was here to do God's work, not waste his time in fruitless speculation.

When Stefan and Daniel disembarked at La Vida Nueva, they found that in their absence, the Novaks had flown in with their helicopter and dropped off the requested Bibles and a few more food supplies for Raul's people. Several boxes were piled on the pavement and Pastor Sergio explained that they were keeping half of the Bibles for the mission center to give out, but the rest would go to Raul in La Rosa.

"It figures," Daniel muttered to Pastor Jeff, shaking his head at the irony. "If we'd just waited a couple of hours, we could have taken all the supplies at once and saved another trip. I didn't know the Novaks were coming back this soon."

"Mr. Novak said he thinks we're going to get one more rainy spell before the dry season starts for good, and he wanted to hurry up and deliver this before the rain," Jeff explained.

Stefan had been examining the crates. He said, "I will make another trip as soon as possible. Raul will want these Bibles quickly."

"Should we put this stuff under the carport?" Daniel offered.

Jeff shook his head. "No, you go in and wash up for dinner. I think Paola and Matéo were going to put it in that old storage building."

Daniel nodded and went inside.

While they ate, the others filled Daniel in on what they'd accomplished that day while he was away with Stefan. Kevin seemed proud to report that he'd helped Luís replace the broken window in his truck, using glass salvaged from an abandoned vehicle they'd found on the side of the road. Jeremy had replaced some light fixtures that had been damaged when the roof leaked. All the floor tiles had been installed in the sanctuary now, and the new floors laid in Pastor Sergio's house.

The freshly varnished pews had been carefully lined up under the carport, and in a few days the sticky finish would be dry enough for them to be installed again. A few odds and ends in the sanctuary and a little painting in the men's dorm, and La Vida Nueva Mission Center would be ready to open again.

The biggest project remaining would be to repair or, more likely, to rebuild the storage building that had been nearly destroyed by the flood.

Apparently whatever had happened between Jeremy and Pastor Jeff that morning had been cleared up, because the two of them were sharing their usual camaraderie.

Daniel sat back, enjoying the company of his friends and the knowledge that everything was going so smoothly. He was glad Pastor Jeff had let them stay instead of returning to America without doing the work.

Pastor Jeff was also looking around at his little group with contentment, enjoying the friendly banter going on at the other table. He was disappointed when Manny disappeared sometime after the meal.

It had been encouraging to see Manny getting more involved with the group, even participating in the Bible study some, but tonight he must have gone to take a nap. The overweight boy had probably worn himself out, since he'd been working more than usual the last few days. He hoped Manny would come back in for the Bible Study in a little while.

But as the time for the devotional drew near, there was still no sign of Manny. Jeff decided to look for the boy, to encourage him to come in and join them.

When he opened the door to go outside, an unmistakable smell of smoke rushed in. The others looked up in surprise, and several of them jumped to their feet. Jeff was already out the door, with Sergio at his heels.

"The storage building is on fire!" Jeff yelled back to the others. The students and the workmen all scrambled out behind them. Abuelita followed at a slower pace, her lips moving in anxious prayer.

It didn't seem that bad at first – only the back corner of the building was engulfed in flames. But it was spreading quickly, and Jeff could already feel the heat from it on his face.

"Come, we must put out the fire before it spreads to the rest of the buildings," Sergio urged, voicing a concern Jeff hadn't thought of. Sergio called out an order in Spanish to Luís, who bolted to the cinder block shed and pulled out a long hose tied in a roll. Sergio and Luís ran to the water pump to hook up the hose.

One hose wouldn't be long enough to reach, so Jeff groped around in the shed until he found a second hose. He dashed after the other two men.

Sergio's words about the fire spreading drew Resha's attention to the cans of fuel lined up under the carport. They seemed far enough away from the burning shed, but if the building next to it caught fire, the fuel cans could explode.

"Let's move these cans," she yelled to anyone who could hear her over the roaring flames. She rushed to the cans and started tugging at one of the heavy containers.

Samuel had been last coming out, so he was closest to the carport. The Nigerian moved quickly to help Resha move the containers to the other side of the sanctuary.

Daniel was about to run and help with the fuel cans when Mindy gave a cry of dismay. "Oh, the supplies for Raul are going to burn!"

Jeremy pointed to the side of the structure that was not being consumed yet. "Look, maybe we can save some of that stuff before it gets too bad in there."

"Jeremy, that's not a good i-..." Daniel started to say, but Jeremy was already running for the building. Daniel looked helplessly at Kevin, then ran after Jeremy, squinting against the heat.

Kevin was only a couple of steps behind them. Terrell crept a little closer to the inferno, but stopped several yards away and watched dubiously.

Even though Selena had moved well out of harm's way, tiny black flakes still settled on her eyelashes. The smell of smoke was going to be impossible to get out of her hair. Gross.

Her brother stood a few feet away, looking frustrated and confused as he watched the frantic activity around them. Was Manny thinking about helping the other guys save the supplies?

"You better not go with them, Manny," Selena ordered. "Mama said for you to stay out of trouble."

Manny nodded, looking relieved as he sat on the steps of the sanctuary to watch.

Mindy joined Selena, dragging a terrified Matéo by the hand. The three of them huddled together near the steps.

None of them noticed when Manny slunk away.

The heat inside the shed was incredible. Daniel had to get his crazy friend out of here before the fire reached their side of the building.

Jeremy had made it to the stack of food supplies, and he wrestled a crate off the pile and shoved it at Daniel.

Daniel had had no intention of participating in Jeremy's futile rescue attempt, but he accepted the crate automatically. He rushed it to the doorway, where Kevin stood shifting from one foot to the other and eying the spreading flames.

Kevin in turn flung the crate as far as he could from the burning building, and Terrell grabbed it and carried it a safe distance away before running back for another load. Ignoring the flames licking closer and closer, Jeremy fought to free another crate.

Sparks stung Daniel's face as he took the crate from Jeremy, and the smoke seared his lungs. "Come on, Jeremy, we need to get out of here."

In a panic now, Daniel passed the second crate to Kevin, whose eyes bulged with fear.

With his arms full, Kevin used his chin to point above Daniel's head. Daniel swung his gaze up to see that part of the ceiling was about to collapse on them, which would crush them in a fiery avalanche. Kevin sprinted away from the entrance with the crate, and when Terrell saw Kevin's quick exit, he trotted farther from the flames, too.

"Jeremy, we have to go!" Daniel yelled, nearly gagging from the smoke. He could hear the burning beams cracking above them, but Jeremy stubbornly tried to snatch another crate from the pile. Daniel grabbed his arm and gave him a shove, propelling him towards the door. "Now, Jeremy!"

Jeremy bolted for the exit carrying one last thing he'd managed to grab, with Daniel right behind him. They were barely out the door when the corner of the roof caved in, falling with a fiery crash right where the two of them had been.

They ran toward the horrified group that watched from the courtyard.

Mindy had both hands on her cheeks as she cried, "Daniel, you're on fire!"

Looking down, Daniel slapped frantically at the spark that had caught the edge of his denim overshirt.

Terrell yelled, "Roll on the ground!"

Daniel did, and the small flame was easily extinguished before doing any real harm. Daniel sat up, choking from the smoke and gasping for breath. When his coughing fit ended, he sucked in deep, gulping breaths. Even the hot evening air felt cool to his lungs after being inside the burning building.

He opened his eyes to find Mindy kneeling in front of him, gazing up at him in concern.

"Daniel, are you okay? Are you badly burned?"

Still dazed, Daniel stared at her for a moment. Man, her eyes were gorgeous. If only they weren't so vacant. He shook his head in response to her question. "Nah, it just got my shirt. I'm okay."

Jeremy crouched beside Mindy, still panting from their desperate flight. His flushed face was streaked with soot, and his eyes were red from the smoke. "I'm sorry, Chief, it was my fault."

"Ya think?" Daniel gritted his teeth and ran a hand over his head in frustration. His hair felt greasy and gritty, which only aggravated him more. He threw his hand toward the object that Jeremy still clutched in one hand. "You nearly got both of us killed for that stupid little bag of rice!"

Mindy looked from one to the other, then slipped away without a word.

Jeremy looked pathetically down at the bag, turning it over in his hands. The plastic wrapper had nearly melted from the heat, and the grains of rice were fused together with it. It was obviously useless.

"I tried to get the whole crate, but you wouldn't let me," Jeremy pointed out sulkily.

Daniel set his jaw. No way was the little twerp going to make him feel guilty.

Seeing that his ploy didn't work, Jeremy tried again, saying optimistically, "We did save two boxes." Then he sighed and finally admitted, "I really am sorry, you know."

Daniel wanted to stay mad at his friend, but Jeremy looked so genuinely contrite and worried that Daniel relented. He sighed. "It's not that big a deal, Jeremy. Nobody got hurt. But next time, just....I don't know, just think, will you?"

Looking relieved to be off the hook, Jeremy dropped down to sit beside Daniel and promised, "I will."

Jeremy seemed sincere in his promise, but Daniel knew his impulsive friend wouldn't be able to keep it. Jeremy just couldn't help himself – he couldn't do anything halfway.

The two of them sat and watched as the pastors and Luís used the two powerful hoses to drench the building next to the burning shed. Apparently they'd given up on the shed as a lost cause and decided the first priority was to keep the fire from spreading to the other classroom. When the classroom was thoroughly soaked, the men turned their hoses to what was left of the storage building.

The water supply was running out, and the pressure from the hoses was weak. Thankfully, the flames were already ebbing since most everything combustible in it had been consumed. Before long, all that was left was a pile of wet, smoking rubble and one corner that was still standing.

Pastor Sergio watched with sad eyes as the last of the embers died down. He shook his head. "The building was not important, but Brother Raul needed those supplies. The people in his village have very little food, and they count on Raul's church to help them out."

"Oh, no," Jeremy groaned and smacked his head. "The Bibles!"

"No, no," Paola cried. "The Bibles, they are okay!"

All eyes turned to her. Paola surprised them all by smiling. "Sergio always likes to include a letter directing the people to important passages they should read first. This afternoon, Matéo and I took the Bibles into the house so that we could insert the letters. The Bibles are still there in my room!"

Everyone broke into smiles at the news, white teeth flashing against sooty faces. Sergio laughed out loud. He grabbed Paola and spun her around. The rest of them joined in the laughter, releasing the tension caused by the fire and celebrating God's goodness in sparing the Bibles.

That evening, Pastor Jeff asked Selena to read John 15:13, his base scripture for the evening's lesson.

Selena gave a nervous laugh as she flipped back and forth in her Bible, trying to find the book of John. The rest of the group waited patiently as Mindy leaned over to help Selena locate the verse, but Mindy got confused trying to read Selena's Bible sideways and ended up in First John instead of John. There was more confusion as Mindy tried to figure out why there wasn't a fifteenth chapter, but finally they got it all sorted out and Selena started to read.

"Uh, greater love...." Selena stopped suddenly when she remembered she was supposed to stand up. She gave the others a sheepish smile as she stood, then started over, "Greater love has no one than this: to lay down one's life for one's friends." She looked up at Pastor Jeff. "Was that the right one?"

Jeff smiled at Selena. "Yes, Selena, that was perfect. Thank you for reading."

Selena dropped back into her chair with a relieved little huff.

Jeff had mercy on her and didn't ask her to explain what she thought the scripture meant. Instead, he directed the question to the group in general. He was surprised when Kevin was the first to offer an opinion.

"It's sayin' if you really love somebody, you got to be willing to give up your life for them," Kevin said.

Impressed because it had come from Kevin, Jeff raised his eyebrows and nodded.

"Not bad, Kevin," he affirmed. Then he turned a pointed look to Jeremy. "Of course, that doesn't mean you should risk your life, or anyone else's, for something that might not be worth it."

Jeremy looked at the ceiling, all innocence, as he shifted in his chair.

Jeff smiled and went back to his message. "Thankfully, we're rarely called on to literally give our lives for someone else's sake. So does that mean we can't prove that we love somebody?"

Jeff waited while the students processed his question. None of them volunteered a guess, so he changed gears. "As college students, what do your lives consist of? Now don't give me the Sunday School answer here. Let's assume we're all trying to live for Christ so we don't waste time trying to impress each other with our piety. Aside from that, what's your life all about back home in America?"

Finally, Daniel grinned ruefully. Jeff knew that as Daniel prepared to graduate in a few months, most of his free time was taken up by one thing. "Homework."

The other students laughed, and it broke the ice. Jeremy called out, "Starbucks."

"Girls," admitted Kevin.

"Shopping," Selena contributed.

They added a few more things, having fun now. When they'd run out of suggestions, Jeff said, "And yet you've been willing to give these things up for a couple of weeks to help somebody else. Since these are the things that make up your lives, in effect, you've all 'laid down your lives' to some degree by coming here."

Jeff watched the young people's faces as they contemplated what he'd said, enjoying the different reactions. Now it was time to make his final point.

"But 'dying to self' is not a one time thing. It's great that we all made certain sacrifices to do the work here, but sacrificing our own comfort and convenience for others should be a way of life for us. Paul said in 1 Corinthians 15:31 that he died daily, not just for a designated, finite length of time. I want you all to start thinking about how you can 'lay down your lives' back home so you can demonstrate the love of Christ to the world around you every day."

The playful mood of the last few minutes had been replaced by thoughtful silence as the students considered how the message applied to them. Jeff was touched that they seemed to be taking it so seriously.

He let the words sink in a bit longer, then had them wrap things up in their prayer circle.

The tired students mumbled "good night" to Pastor Jeff, then most of them made their way to their sleeping quarters. Sergio began fluttering around the room, straightening the chairs that had gotten out of line.

Daniel saw him and turned back to help him. "Let me do that, Pastor Sergio. We're the ones who messed them up."

Kevin and Jeremy ambled over to pitch in.

Sergio stepped out of their way, looking delighted.

"See, Pastor Jeff, how they have taken your message to heart already."

Jeff laughed lightly as they headed to Sergio's office to enjoy the coffee Abuelita had waiting for them there. "I wish I could take credit for it, Sergio, but Daniel's always been like that, and whatever Daniel does, Kevin and Jeremy follow."

The two men sat in wooden chairs in the cramped little room.

"Yes, yes, I suppose I have seen that in them already, but they truly do seem to listen carefully to what you teach them."

Jeff glanced skeptically at his three protegés through the open door of the office. "If you say so."

"I have enjoyed your teaching, as well, Pastor Jeff, but you have been working too hard. You labor all day by my side, and then I see you studying late into the night to prepare a message for your students."

Sergio couldn't stay in his chair for long. He jumped up and tried to pace around the tiny area. Jeff hastily tucked his legs under his chair to give Sergio more room. "I am thinking that since tomorrow is Sunday, we will have a worship service in the morning. I have a short message I would like to give to your team if you will allow me."

"I'm sure they would enjoy that," Jeff said, ducking his head to avoid being hit by Sergio's waving arms. It was dangerous being confined in a small space with the energetic little man.

Engrossed in his plans, Sergio was oblivious to Jeff's plight. "And then, we will have a day of rest to honor the Lord's Day."

"That, they might not like so much," Jeff said, edging his chair closer to the wall.

Sergio whirled and stared at Jeff in disbelief. "But why not? They have been working very hard, and they are ahead of schedule. They have earned a day off."

Jeff shrugged. "It's up to you, of course, Sergio, but I think they would rather keep working."

The three young men had finished their chore in time to hear Sergio's plans for the next day. As they walked back to their room, Kevin grumbled, "Man, I don't see us sittin' around all day when we got all this work to do. We don't need no day off. What we gonna do all day?"

"We could play pinochle," Jeremy suggested helpfully. "Boys against girls. Losers have to wash the winners' cars."

Daniel laughed. "Do you even know what pinochle is?"

"Nope, but who cares? None of us have cars here anyway." After a moment, he asked Daniel, "You're not really going to let Sergio do that to us, are you?"

The question surprised Daniel. "What do you expect me to do about it?"

Jeremy shrugged. "I don't know. Engage Pastor Sergio in a debate about Old Testament Sabbaths versus New Testament or something."

Daniel shook his head. "I don't want to waste the day any more than you do, but I'm not going to argue with the man. It's his mission center and we're his guests. Sort of. He can do what he wants."

Kevin and Jeremy looked at each other in disappointment. The three stopped talking as they entered their room, in case the others were asleep, but their minds were still on the distasteful prospect of twiddling their thumbs for a whole day.

To Jeff's relief, Sergio had opted to move to the living room of his house to finish their conversation. There was more room in the house for Sergio's expansive gestures, and Jeff breathed easier as he sat on the sofa with Sergio sitting in the arm chair across from him for the time being.

The discussion turned to the fire that had broken out that evening. Jeff wanted to know Sergio's opinion about how the fire had gotten started, but the Colombian pastor was as baffled as he was.

"The weather has been dry, but not so much that a little spark would set the wood on fire. Besides, no one here smokes, so there is nothing that could have caused such a thing."

Jeff voiced the fear that had been percolating in his mind. "Could it have been the work of The Black Eagles?"

Sergio did not hesitate in his answer. "No, it is not their style to be secretive in such actions. They would have set fire to the entire compound, in the sight of everyone, so that they could strike fear into the hearts of the people. There was nothing for them to gain in something like this."

The two men were silent, pondering the possibilities. Finally Jeff said, "I can't help but wonder if all these weird happenings are connected somehow. The missing cable, Matéo's accident, and now this."

Frowning thoughtfully, Sergio agreed. "There have been too many unexplained events. Only God knows their meaning."

"Then let's ask Him to help us out here."

Sergio nodded and the two men bowed their heads.

Peeking through a crack in his bedroom door, Matéo watched his brother and the other pastor for a moment, then bowed his head, too.

Manny held his reddened cheek where he'd just been soundly slapped, gaping at Antonio in surprise and reproach.

"I thought you hated Bibles," he whined. "I thought you'd be happy they got burned up."

"¡*Burro!*" Antonio snarled. "El Tiburon wanted to know who the Bibles were supposed to go to. If there are no Bibles to deliver, how are we to find out who else is turning the people against our cause with the words in that cursed Book?"

Manny's lip trembled as he promised, "I'm sorry, Antonio. I'll try to find out something for you."

"I have already found out something, *estupido*," Antonio told him. "The Bibles were not in the shed."

"Then why did you hit me?" Manny was dumbfounded. His cheek still stung from the harsh slap.

"Because what you did was stupid. You accomplished nothing, and you could have gotten caught and ruined our plans. Never do anything without clearing it with me first, do you understand?"

"Yes, Antonio," Manny answered humbly, his head hanging.

"I am giving you a chance to make up for your mistake. Find out exactly when they are going to deliver the Bibles and tell me immediately. We will arrange to have them followed."

"All right, Antonio," Manny promised in a shaky voice. "I won't let you down again."

"You had better not," Antonio warned.

9

Day 8: Sunday

The rain started around 4:00 AM.

Resha woke and sat up for several minutes, listening, then padded over to the window and watched little rivers forming in the fractured cobblestones of the courtyard.

A sleepy mumble came from Selena's bed. "Is it going to flood again?"

"No," Resha answered tersely, hoping Mindy wouldn't hear them and wake up.

But she did. Their voices and the sound of the rain somehow managed to penetrate Mindy's cotton candy dreams and she stirred a moment before asking worriedly, "Are you sure it won't flood, Resha?"

What am I, the weather guru? Resha bit back her irritation. "I heard the weather report on Sergio's radio. It's supposed to stop raining again in a few hours. Shouldn't cause any problems. Go back to sleep."

"Oh. Okay." Satisfied with Resha's answer, Mindy rolled over.

A minute later, Resha heard her gentle snores again, and shortly after that, Selena stopped tossing and turning, too. Resha stayed by the window praying awhile, then she went back to bed to try to sleep for that last hour before they had to get up for breakfast.

By the time the students finished breakfast, the rain had stopped, leaving everything smelling fresh except for the faint lingering odor of smoke. The sun had come out again, promising another hot, humid day.

As they assembled for the worship service Pastor Sergio had announced during breakfast, Jeremy noticed his two friends were restless. Daniel and Kevin wouldn't know what to do with themselves if they couldn't keep working.

Well, Jeremy would just have to save the day, as usual. He leaned back to study Pastor Sergio, who stood on the platform marking places in his Bible with little slips of paper in preparation for his message.

Daniel sat on the front row, listlessly thumbing through his own Bible while the other students milled around. Kevin was still grumbling, until Jeremy told him, "Stop griping, dude. I think I know how we can fix this little situation."

Kevin looked at him suspiciously. "Yeah? You know Pastor Jeff won't like it if we argue with Pastor Sergio."

"So we won't argue," Jeremy shrugged. "Pastor Sergio hasn't said anything yet about taking the day off, so it's not exactly disagreeing with him if he hasn't told us yet, is it? We'll just nip this thing in the bud before it even takes off."

Kevin started to grin. "How we gonna do that?"

Jeremy pursed his lips and looked at their walking concordance. "Hey, Chief, isn't there a story about some dude pulling a sheep out of a hole on Sunday or something?"

Daniel smiled and held up his Bible for Jeremy to see, pointing at a section. "I'm way ahead of you, buddy."

Jeremy read a few lines and grinned. "That's the one!"

"Check this one out, too," Daniel told him, flipping to another scripture a few pages over.

Jeremy snatched the Bible, poking a finger into each spot Daniel had showed him without bothering to see what the second passage was.

Putting on a guileless face, he raised his hand. "Pastor Sergio, would it be all right if I read a passage of scripture before we get started?"

Sergio looked surprised, but then he smiled and waved effusively at Jeremy to take the podium. "By all means."

Jeremy trotted to the lectern, cleared his throat theatrically, and began to read from Matthew, "'He said to them, "If any of you has a sheep and it falls into a pit on the Sabbath, will you not take hold of it and lift it out? How much more valuable is a person than a sheep! Therefore it is lawful to do good on the Sabbath."'"

Before Jeremy got through with the first sentence, a look of realization crossed Sergio's features. Obviously he'd figured out what Jeremy was up to, and the more Jeremy read, the more his smile grew.

His face threatened to break in half when Jeremy read from the third chapter of Mark, "'Then Jesus asked them, "Which is lawful on the Sabbath: to do good or to do evil, to save life or to kill?"'"

When Jeremy was done he sat down again and blinked innocently up at Pastor Sergio.

Jeff gave Jeremy a look of disbelieving reproach, but Sergio laughed. "I understand what you are trying to tell me, Jeremy."

Sergio addressed the rest of the group. "I had wanted to honor the Lord's day by allowing you all to take a rest from your labors, but Jeremy has pointed out that there are different ways of honoring the Sabbath day. Would the rest of you like to take the day off, or would you rather keep working?"

In response, most of them called out some variation of "keep working."

Sergio laughed again, throwing his hands up in capitulation. "Very well, I will not object if we continue the work. But first, we will spend some time in worship."

Everyone looked relieved except Manny, who probably wouldn't have minded napping all day. Oh, well, the chubby kid could sleep sitting up, like he did during their evening devotionals.

Sergio asked them to stand while he led them in a brief prayer. After the "amen", the pastor apologized, "I regret that we do not have our musicians here, or even a CD player, but I feel it is important that we start our service with praise to our God. Paola, perhaps you would come and lead us in a song of worship?"

Paola looked panic-stricken – she clearly was not comfortable with Sergio's request.

Jeremy had been waiting for an excuse. He bounced onto the small platform and slid into the chair he'd placed behind the piano, then asked hopefully, "May I?"

Sergio raised his eyebrows and smiled again. "Jeremy, the piano has not been played since the flood, and I believe it may have been ruined, but if you can coax any music out of it, you are welcome to do so."

Pastor Sergio must not have noticed Jeremy tinkering with the piano between chores, but Daniel knew what was coming. He and Kevin exchanged a knowing grin.

Jeremy was in his element now. He waggled his long fingers over the keyboard in anticipation, then put them on the keys. The piano emitted some weird warbling notes, which made Jeremy snicker. After a couple of false starts, the music sounded less off-key and Jeremy began playing a tune that was easily recognizable to the group, although a little faster than the usual version.

Still standing, Kevin and Daniel started clapping in time to the music and soon everyone joined them. Jeremy grinned at their participation.

Tapping out the rhythm with his foot, Jeremy played the chorus through twice to get a feel for the instrument, and then started to sing.

"Light of the world,
You stepped out into darkness,
Opened my eyes, let me see...
Beauty that made this heart adore You,
Hope of a life spent with You."

Jeremy's voice was average at best, but he exuded sincerity. Even though Daniel had heard the song many times before, Jeremy sang the words as if they were his own personal expression of worship. He and the others couldn't help but join in when Jeremy got to the chorus.

"Here I am to worship,
Here I am to bow down,
Here I am to say that You're my God."

Selena sang along, familiar with the song from her own church.

Then she noticed that some of the clapping had faded away. She glanced around in surprise. Daniel, Mindy and the two pastors had stopped clapping to raise their hands in worship.

Selena had seen a few people at her church do that, mostly the older people, and it always made her uncomfortable. It was even weirder seeing people her own age doing it, but it didn't seem to bother anyone else, so she tried to ignore it. She kept waiting for Jeremy to make a wisecrack or do something to make them laugh, but for once, he wasn't trying to be the center of attention.

When the last few notes of the song faded, Jeremy paused before starting another. He frowned thoughtfully and chewed his lip, like he was listening to the notes in his head, then moved his fingers experimentally over the keyboard for a few seconds without making any sound. When he started playing again, the music was slower and had a more reverent feel.

Selena heard a gasp behind her and saw that Paola's eyes had flown open wide, as if she recognized the song Jeremy was playing. After Jeremy had played the melody through, he winked at Paola and tipped his head toward the platform in invitation.

She stepped to the front hesitantly. Paola and Jeremy watched each other for a few seconds, communicating in that universal silent language all musicians seemed to share. On cue, she began to sing.

"Todo lo creaste
La tierra, cielo y mar
Los cielos son tu tabernaculo
Gloria al Dios Altísimo."

Paola's voice was pure and strong, deeper than Selena would have expected from the fragile-looking woman. As her beautiful alto filled the little sanctuary, Jeremy quickly changed keys to accommodate her voice. The humble Colombian woman kept her eyes upward as she sang, as if her praise was an offering to God.

Although Paola sang in Spanish, Selena recognized the melody from the English version of the song. The words didn't seem to matter to the rest of the group. Her new friends appeared lost in the music, their serene smiles indicating that they'd forgotten the exhaustion, the sweat, and all the petty squabbles. Even Selena could feel the sweet atmosphere in the room as Paola led them into God's Presence.

When Paola had sung it through in Spanish, she glanced at Jeremy and tentatively started to sing the words in English. He smiled and began singing softly with her to keep her on track, but he kept his voice low so that her voice was the one leading. Soon the rest of the voices in the room had joined with the unlikely duet on the platform.

"God of wonders beyond our galaxy
You are holy, holy
The universe declares Your majesty
You are holy, holy
Lord of heaven and earth."

No one was clapping now, and Selena saw that most everyone in the room had closed their eyes and lifted their hands towards Heaven as they swayed slightly in unpracticed harmony. Even Samuel, standing alone in one corner, had both hands raised high.

Selena squirmed, thoroughly uncomfortable now. She glanced over at Resha, certain the cynical girl would feel the same way that she did about all this creepy stuff. But sometime during the song, Resha had fallen to her knees in front of her chair and had her head down, forehead resting on the floor.

Okay, I am so outta here, Selena thought, but her only way of escape was blocked on one side by Mindy, who still had her face turned upward and now had tears streaming down her cheeks, and on the other side by Resha's prone form.

So Selena closed her eyes to shut everyone else out and tried to look spiritual, just in case anyone was watching. She envied Manny, whom she imagined blissfully snoring away as he lay stretched across several chairs one row behind her.

The song ended at last. Jeremy, his head bowed, stopped playing and let silence hang in the air, allowing them to bask in the sweet Presence that filled the room. Was Selena the only one creeped out by all this?

She was relieved when, after a pause, Jeremy improvised a peppy little tune, his bouncing curls keeping time.

Paola used that as her cue to step off the platform and walk quietly to the back to stand next to Stefan. Selena saw Stefan squeeze Paola's hand, then drop it quickly, before Sergio could see him.

Jeremy transitioned into another familiar praise song, and Selena was glad most of them started to clap to the music again. Maybe things would get back to normal now.

By the time they got to the second stanza, Selena felt much more comfortable and sang along.

> "...Blessed be Your Name
> On the road marked with suffering
> Though there's pain in the offering
> Blessed be Your Name."

Daniel thought a song about suffering and pain was an odd choice for Jeremy, who usually picked cheery songs about God's goodness and power. But Jeremy seemed to be really getting into it, his eyes closed and his face lifted upward as he played.

Daniel never could figure out how Jeremy could play without looking at the keys. He admired the way his friend managed to take them into God's Presence even in a sweltering sanctuary with an out-of-tune piano.

Daniel turned to glance at Pastor Jeff, expecting their mentor to be glowing with pride over Jeremy's accomplishment. To his surprise, Jeff was watching Jeremy with a look of profound sadness.

Puzzled, Daniel frowned. Kevin noticed Daniel's distraction and turned to see what he was looking at. Seeing the pastor's expression, Kevin chuckled and muttered to Daniel, "Come on, Pastor Jeff, Jeremy's singin' ain't that bad!"

Daniel chuckled, and Jeff heard them and shot them a warning glance. Daniel and Kevin quickly put their focus back on the worship, where it belonged, and the incident was forgotten. They lifted their voices with the others as Jeremy finished up the song;

"...when the darkness closes in, Lord,
still I will say,
Blessed be the Name of the Lord,
Blessed be Your Glorious Name."

Jeremy segued into one of his favorites for the finale, repeating the chorus several times.

"Forever God is faithful,
Forever God is strong,
Forever God is with us,
Forever....."

When the final notes died down, sweat poured down Jeremy's face, but he looked radiant with joy. Out of breath, he whispered, "God is good."

There was a general "amen", and Pastor Sergio walked back onto the platform. He seemed to be still floating from the worship, and it took him a moment to bring himself back to earth. He motioned for them to be seated.

"Jeremy and Paola, we thank you for bringing us into God's presence this morning."

All faces now turned toward Sergio as he continued. "Now if you will give me just a few minutes, I would like to speak briefly about a scripture that I am sure you are all familiar with. Because our workers have joined us this morning, and they are more comfortable with Spanish, I will use both languages if that is all right."

There were murmurs of agreement all around, and a couple of the students turned to smile at the three laborers who had seated themselves on the back row. Abuelita had joined them, also, but chose to stand off to one side, a kitchen towel still clutched in her hands.

"Please turn to Mark 16:15," Sergio requested, then repeated it in Spanish. The students traded knowing glances with each other as Sergio fervently quoted the scripture Jeff had drilled into them at the missions rally in Houston. "'He said to them, "Go into all the world and preach the gospel to all creation."'"

When Sergio asked Paola to read it in their native language, she found the passage and calmly stood to read it. The students all smiled at how different the verse sounded in Spanish, and at the contrast between Sergio's passionate delivery and Paola's placid translation.

"You may believe that what you are doing is not preaching the gospel," Sergio said, walking back and forth on the platform in his usual animated style. "but because of the work that you are doing here at La Vida Nueva Mission Center, you are helping to make it possible for many people to hear the message of Christ."

The rest of the service followed a pattern of Sergio speaking a few sentences, then pausing as Paola interpreted for Abuelita and the laborers.

Pastor Sergio rocked up and down on his heels as he went on to describe how the mission center would be used first to house people who would help rebuild the community, and how Sergio planned to give the gospel to all who came to work. Afterward, the center would continue to hold church services and classes to teach God's ways to any who would come, and to distribute food, water, Bibles, and Christian literature all over the area. Sergio used Scriptures to help explain how their work on repairing the mission center would indirectly impact many lives for Christ.

True to his word, Sergio ended his message quickly, saying, "We are all part of the body of Christ, and no part is more or less important than another. Your own pastor and I may be called to preach The Message in front of a congregation, but without people like you who are willing to help us with the more humble tasks, we would not be able to do it. It takes all of us together to fulfill that great commission."

Mindy was pleased to think that her labors would play some part in reaching others with the gospel. Sergio closed his Bible and asked everybody to stand for a prayer to dismiss them.

"Stefan, would you please close the service with a prayer?" The laborer hesitated, and Sergio added, "In Spanish, if you like. Our Father understands all languages."

Stefan smiled and nodded, then bowed his head. The rest followed suit as he prayed, "*Padre, gracias por el servicio hoy, gracias para nuestros hermanos y hermanas Americanos. Por favor, das Su bendiga y seguridad en todos las personas aqui. En el Nombre de Jesus, amen.*"

Mindy didn't understand a word of the prayer, but Stefan looked so humble and sincere. She thought it was very sweet of him to pray for them, but since she couldn't follow it, she got distracted and began looking around at the others.

Most of them had their heads bowed, but Selena was discreetly tapping an impatient foot and Manny looked like he was asleep on his feet. The reaction that surprised her the most was Antonio's. He was glaring at Stefan with something like hatred on his features. That didn't make any sense to Mindy.

Why would he be angry with Stefan for praying?

Abuelita had slipped out of the service early and had a simple lunch ready by the time Sergio dismissed them. So the team picked up their plates and carried them outside to their usual spot. Daniel ambled out last, stuffing a pale yellow object into his mouth.

Selena wrinkled her nose. "What are you eating now, Daniel?"

"Little bananas," Daniel told her happily, holding up a big bunch of short, plump bananas, each about three inches long. "They're pretty good. You want one?"

Selena cringed and shook her head. "Where did you get them?"

He popped another banana off the bunch for himself before setting the rest in the middle where the rest could get to them. As he peeled it, he explained, "Abuelita gave them to me. She has a whole lot of them in the kitchen. I think Luís brought them from some field over there since there's nobody else around to pick them."

"Those are called *manzano* bananas," Mindy told them, looking smug that she knew something they didn't. "Paola told me that a lot of the farmers around here grew manzanos because they're easy to grow in this climate, and they used to export them, but they didn't get much money for them."

Kevin yanked a manzano off the bunch and offered it to Jeremy, who shook his head. Kevin shrugged and ate it himself.

"It taste kind of like an apple," Kevin grunted in surprise. He took another bite.

"Oooh, look!" Mindy suddenly stood up. "There's Alfredo!"

"Who's Alfredo?" Selena sat up straight and looked around eagerly. "Is there a guy around that I haven't met?"

But Mindy was pointing at the dog, who was standing nearer than it had before. "He needed a name. We couldn't just keep calling him 'Puppy Dog', so I named him Alfredo."

"Alfredo, huh?" For some reason, that tickled Daniel, and he nearly choked on his banana. Kevin clapped him on the back playfully. Mindy just pouted.

After lunch, the only indication that it had rained the night before were a few puddles on the ground. The powerful sun had dried everything out enough that they could work outside again, and the team began the arduous task of removing the burned debris of the storage building.

Daniel and Terrell helped Luís and Stefan to dismantle what was left of the framework while the others carried the blackened boards and other rubble to the dump pile, which was steadily growing with still no sign of being picked up.

Terrell pointed up at the one corner of the structure that was still standing. The roof and ceiling had caved in, but there were still a couple of beams across the top that had been holding up the roof. "How are we supposed to get those things down?"

Daniel stared up at the beams, perplexed. "No idea. I'm used to building stuff, not tearing it down."

"If it had rained yesterday instead of today, this shed probably wouldn't have caught on fire," Terrell observed grumpily as he tugged at the stubborn girder. He stood on a crossbeam about halfway up, holding on to the vertical support with one hand as he yanked on the offending beam with the other.

"Yeah, but we were probably going to tear it down anyway." Daniel climbed up on the other side of the support and found a place to grip the board so he could add his efforts to Terrell's. "It's probably coming apart easier now that it's all burnt."

As if to punctuate his statement, the board came loose unexpectedly, and the two grabbed at each other and did some fancy footwork to keep from falling to the ground with it.

Mindy, who was sweeping up soot and ashes from a corner they'd already cleared, gasped and cried out, "Oh, be careful!"

Once the two men had gotten their balance and caught their breath, Jeremy applauded from the ground. He grinned up at them as he and Kevin picked up the heavy beam to drag it out to the dump.

"Ya'll missed a spot," Kevin told them, pointing at the other beam a few feet away.

"If we aim just right when we pull that next one loose," Daniel remarked, "we could take Jeremy and Kevin both out at once."

Terrell laughed and jumped down from his precarious perch. Daniel climbed down and brushed his hands off on his jeans. It didn't help. His jeans were just as covered with the black dust as everything else.

Stefan called to them in his broken English, "I will show you an easier way to do that if you will help us to move this."

He and Luís had been struggling with a large piece of the roof that had caved in near the back of the building. The big square of singed wood and shingles was still wet from being hosed down the night before and the rain that morning, making it even heavier.

Daniel and Terrell each grabbed a corner, pieces of blackened shingles crumbling off in their hands as they tugged with Luís and Stefan on the other end.

As the four men dragged it from the corner, they saw what it had been hung up on. Several cardboard cartons of boxed cereal and bags of rice, charred from the flames and now soggy from the water, rested under the chunk of roofing. The men stopped to rest for a moment and stared regretfully at the mound of ruined food.

"Too bad, Stefan," Daniel commiserated. "This was supposed to go to your friends in La Rosa, wasn't it?"

Stefan nodded sadly. "Yes, I had promised to bring them more food soon. But you and your friends saved a little bit of the food, and they will still get their Bibles, and that is more important to them."

"When will you take them the Bibles?" Terrell wanted to know.

"I do not want to take the chance that something else will happen. I am going to ask Sergio if I can take them tonight after the evening meal," Stefan said.

"Will you need me to go with you again?" offered Daniel, bending over to grab his corner again.

Stefan smiled slyly. "No, thank you, amigo. I am going to ask Paola to go with me this time."

Daniel grinned and the four men resumed dragging the heavy slab. Daniel backed into something soft and stopped.

"Oops, sorry, Manny, I didn't know you were right there," he apologized to the young man, who was gaping at them as he held a sooty chunk of something in his hand.

Manny backed away, stammering, "Uh, I was just taking this to the junk pile."

He slunk away with his blackened fragment, walking only a few feet before he turned back to see if the others were watching him.

The four men had returned to their struggle and were paying no attention to him. He set down the object he was carrying and scurried away.

Several yards away, Jeremy loosened his grip on his end of a load long enough to nudge Kevin and point triumphantly at Manny. "Look, look, there he goes!"

Kevin turned to see the chubby boy rounding the corner. "Aw, man, I thought he'd last longer than that befo' he took off to go to sleep."

"You owe me five bucks." Jeremy gloated as the two of them continued hauling their pile of charred lumber.

Stefan slammed the trunk of the old Chevy, sealing in the three cases of Bibles. In the back seat were the two boxes of donated food Daniel and

Jeremy had salvaged from the burning shed. Sergio had insisted on supplementing it with supplies from their own store of food.

Now Sergio packed a few more canned goods onto the front floorboard, leaving room for Paola to squeeze into the passenger seat. She stood behind him, dressed in her usual jeans and juaraches, but had put on a rose colored blouse with puff sleeves that made her look more delicate and feminine.

When Sergio was done, Stefan smiled at the pretty woman, who smiled back with starry eyes. "Ready, Paola?"

Only Jeff, Abuelita, and Matéo had joined Sergio in seeing the couple off on their journey, since the rest of them were either still finishing up some chores or had gone to bed. Abuelita's face was tight with disapproval.

So complete was Sergio's trust in Stefan and his own sister that it took him a moment to comprehend what was causing the normally congenial woman to frown at the couple. When he caught on, he said, "Stefan, since you are going to stay in La Rosa overnight, Abuelita does not think it is proper for the two of you to go alone. I agree with her."

His sister's eyes flashed. "Sergio, do not be ridiculous! We are going to deliver God's Word to the people. Do you honestly believe that we would take advantage of this situation to betray Him?"

"Not at all," Sergio assured her. "But we must set an example for our young American guests, and for Matéo. To avoid the appearance of evil, perhaps someone should go along with you."

Stefan looked at the older woman with concern. "Abuelita, I am afraid the trip will be too difficult for you."

Abuelita smiled and shook her head at the notion that she was volunteering her own services as chaperone. Of course, Sergio would not have asked her to accompany the couple, but he was uncertain who to send. Luis was still repairing the water heater in the main building, Antonio would not have patience for such an errand, and it would not be right to ask one of the missionaries to go at this time of night.

Matéo solved his problem, crying excitedly, "I will go!"

Even though the little boy was too young to fully understand the problem, he seemed eager to be a part of what he probably thought would be a great adventure.

Paola looked doubtful, however. "I do not think that is a good idea, Matéo. We will be driving over some very difficult areas."

"I can do it. Please, Paola!"

Paola looked at Sergio, who in turn looked at Stefan. Stefan tousled Matéo's hair. "It should be all right. The drive will be a little over two hours, but the roads have been mostly cleared. It should not be too dangerous."

Matéo could scarcely contain himself as he crawled into the back seat, pushing aside a box filled with bags of rice to make room. His sister climbed into the front seat and waited as Stefan said goodbye to Sergio.

"We will return in a day or two, Sergio, as soon as we have repaired their water pump. Please pray for us, as we will be praying for you."

"God go with you, my friend." The two men shook hands.

The roads were rough and muddy, and there was nothing to see but dark jungle on either side. The novelty of the ride wore off for Matéo after the first half hour. He nestled down between the cartons of rice and canned goods and dozed off.

Paola and Stefan looked at each other and smiled. Soon, she and Stefan were holding hands contentedly as he drove.

The peacefulness of the drive ended suddenly when a jeep exploded from behind some trees in front of them and turned sideways, blocking the road.

Paola's heart caught in her chest as the jeep's driver hit the brakes and three other men jumped out of the jeep, aiming weapons at the little Chevy.

Stefan slammed the car into reverse, but a black pickup truck had appeared behind them, it's headlights in the mirror nearly blinding Paola.

Stefan threw the Chevy back into drive, grinding the gears, and turned the wheel frantically as he gunned the engine, bouncing the car off the road. He swerved around the jeep, his tires spinning in the wet grass, and managed to bring the car back onto the road on the other side, barely missing some trees.

Caught by surprise at Stefan's quick action, the men scrambled back into their vehicle, shouting at the driver.

Stefan forced the gas pedal to the floor and the old Chevy strained to fly over the rutted dirt road. The chrome grille of the Dodge Ram leered menacingly in the rear view mirror as the truck closed the gap between them. The jeep had joined the chase now and was rapidly catching up.

"¡O, Dios mio!" Paola gasped, finally finding her voice. "What is this?"

"It is Las Águilas Negras," Stefan muttered grimly, his jaw set as he fought to stay ahead of the pursuing vehicles.

Matéo sat up in the back seat, clawing at the boxes to keep from being thrown around in the swaying car.

"What is happening?" he cried.

"Stay down!" Stefan yelled at him.

Eyes wide with terror, he obeyed, sinking back down behind the front seat just as the jeep rammed them from behind. Paola's teeth rattled from the impact.

Stefan wrestled with the steering wheel and barely succeeded in staying on the road. The jeep nudged the Chevy again, harder this time, and Stefan fought for control of the car. Suddenly the black truck appeared on Paola's side.

Paola screamed as the truck crashed into her door, but the screeching sound of metal on metal drowned out her terrified cry.

The impact sent the Chevy careening off the road. The tires could get no traction in the mud, and the car spun several times before the driver's side slammed sideways into a tree, shattering the windows.

The collision folded the car nearly in half, causing the trunk to pop open and the cartons of Bibles to be scattered on the ground. The two back doors also flew open, spilling out bags of rice and canned goods.

Seat belts had kept Stefan and Paola from flying through the windshield, but the force of the crash had thrown them around inside the cab. The driver's side door had caved in, pinning Stefan's arm against him, and his head had struck the steering wheel sharply. There were streaks of blood on his face where shards of glass from the broken windshield had cut him.

Paola's own face stung from similar wounds, and her wrist had been sprained when she put it out to steady herself on the dashboard. Her neck felt out of joint, and her whole body was shaken and bruised. She wondered how her little brother had fared in the back seat.

Her own injuries were suddenly forgotten – she swallowed a terrified sob at the sight of the armed men who now surrounded the wrecked vehicle.

"Get out of the car," yelled one of them, a tall lieutenant with a shaved head and a black bandana covering half of his face. "Now!"

The men all pointed their guns at Paola and Stefan. They obeyed shakily, clambering painfully out through the crushed passenger side since the driver's side door was wedged against the tree. Forcing herself not to look behind her to check on Matéo, Paola prayed silently that her little brother would remain hidden.

Dazed and hurting from the impact, Matéo managed to slide his body out through the bent back door frame out of sight of the militants, dropping quietly to the ground. He crawled toward a cluster of bushes, dragging himself through the muddy grass. The bushes clawed at his skin and caught in his hair as he crouched behind them, but he ignored the discomfort – he had caught a glimpse of the guns and knew the prickly branches were a minor threat by comparison.

"Why have you stopped us?" Stefan demanded with a bravado he did not feel. "We are only delivering food to people who have gone hungry since the flooding. Surely you cannot object to that."

The soldier used his gun to gesture at the Bibles that had spilled from the trunk. "Those do not look like food. Do you take me for a fool?"

Stefan had not noticed before that the Bibles had been exposed. Still, he stood his ground. "It is not illegal to distribute the Word of God."

"Whether it is legal or not is not in question. Your primitive propaganda is not welcome here, Stefan Guzman," sneered the commando, dragging out the syllables of Stefan's name as he stepped to within a few feet of them.

Stefan refused to show his surprise that the militant knew who he was. He could not identify the man who badgered them, but it was possible that some of the others, who also had their faces covered, had known him before he defected. When Captain Ortega stepped out of the shadows, Stefan recognized him immediately.

Paola inched closer to Stefan. Although she held her head high, Stefan could see the terror in her eyes. He longed to reach out to reassure her, but he knew better than most that any reassurance he could give her would be false. This situation would end badly, he knew.

He prayed silently for courage to face what would surely come next as he directed his next comment to his former superior.

"That 'primitive propaganda' is the only hope Colombia has. You would do well to read it yourself." Stefan was pleased that his voice was steady, although inside he was quivering from fear.

Ortega laughed out loud at that, a cruel, derisive laugh. "Never. I have seen the damage it can do. It takes good men who are dedicated to our cause and makes them into useless puppets for so called pastors who want to destroy our country with their outdated rules."

"You are wrong, Tiburon. The Word of God opened my eyes to the truth. You are the one who is destroying our country. You are destroying your own soul. Repent and turn to God before it is too late."

Ortega had had enough. His voice rose shrilly. "You are a fool, Guzman! A fool and a traitor to the cause. Do you remember what the punishment is for traitors to Las Águilas Negras?"

"Execution," Stefan replied calmly, amazed at the peace that was settling over him in the face of his own imminent death.

Beside him, Paola gasped.

Her involuntary outburst caught Ortega's attention. Or perhaps he had been waiting for an excuse to step in closer to her. He touched her cheek and laughed when she jerked her head away. He addressed Stefan. "Do not worry about your *novia*. We will take good care of her when you are gone."

Stefan lunged at him then, knowing it was a futile effort. Two of Ortega's henchmen were already there, grabbing his arms and dragging him several paces away. Another grabbed Paola and twisted her arm behind her back, forcing her to watch.

As he was pushed to his knees in the wet grass, Stefan craned his neck for one last look at the woman he loved. Tears streamed down Paola's cheeks, but he was proud that she stood tall and silent. Their eyes met.

"I am sorry, Paola," Stefan said. He knew her fate would be worse than his.

His final, whispered prayer was that God would be merciful to her.

As a single gunshot rang out, Matéo had to bite his lip to keep from whimpering. His view was blocked by the bushes and the ruined car, but he had heard everything and now wanted desperately to stand up from his hiding place to see if his big sister was okay. Another part of him wanted to curl up under the bushes and cry. He did neither, but forced himself to remain still, waiting for an opportunity to help Paola.

He heard the one Stefan had called Tiburon shouting orders to his soldiers, and two men came near Matéo's hiding place, scooping up the spilled food. Matéo pressed himself deeper into the bush, the thorns scratching his arms and face.

"What shall we do with these books?" one of the men shouted to Ortega, and the other man laughed.

"Bring them," Ortega replied. "They may still lead us to the ones who are stirring up the people against us. Or maybe they are worth money to someone."

The two men began gathering the Bibles that had been dumped on the ground along with the food. Soon metal thuds filled the air, and Matéo guessed the men were throwing everything into the bed of the pickup.

Matéo heard the other vehicle start, and when the jeep drove off, he knew they had taken his sister away. He had to find out where.

While the men who had been left behind dragged Stefan's body and shoved it into the wrecked Chevy, Matéo managed to creep closer to their black Ram. He watched from behind their truck as they doused the wreckage with fuel and set fire to it.

As the men watched to make sure the flames caught, Matéo crawled underneath their truck to hide. When the men hurriedly climbed into their vehicle and drove away, Matéo swung himself up and clung desperately to the back bumper, careful to stay out of sight.

As the truck sped away, the flames found the gas tank of the Chevy and the crippled car exploded, sending a huge fireball into the sky.

By the time Paola was dragged into a musty room in the drab, dimly lit building, her tears had dried, replaced by a cold fortitude.

The worst had already happened. Stefan was dead, murdered by the man he had spoken of with fear and regret. What did she care what happened to her now?

She stood numbly in the small, dingy office as two of Ortega's men knocked and came in, carrying several armloads of Bibles they had salvaged from the wreckage. She tried not to cringe at the disrespect they showed for The Word of God when they dumped the Bibles carelessly into the corner.

The two men paused long enough to leer at her before leaving.

When they were gone, Ortega turned to glower at her again.

"Where were you taking the Bibles?" the captain demanded roughly for the third time, as if the sight of the Bibles would loosen her tongue.

"I do not know," Paola answered him just as roughly, also for the third time. Her reply had not changed, but her voice had gained strength.

Ortega narrowed his eyes at her tone. "Surely you knew where you were going. Do not expect me to believe that you got into a vehicle with no destination in mind."

"I was not driving. Stefan was driving, so he knew where we were going, but your men killed him, so he cannot answer you." Her heart was breaking, but outwardly she remained calm and controlled.

"So it seems you are useless to me, since you cannot answer my questions. Should we kill you, too, then?"

Paola shrugged. It made no difference to her.

Ortega tilted his head and studied her as if she were some odd insect. He seemed intrigued by her detachment.

"I know who you are, Paola. Do you think your life is worth anything to your brother the pastor?" He practically spit out the last word.

Again, Paola shrugged.

"I will break your spirit," Ortega promised, a dangerous glint in his eyes. "It is good for you that you are so attractive, otherwise I would have you killed right here where you stand."

He reached out to stroke her hair.

Paola slapped his hand away, and immediately Ortega slapped her back, hard across the face. Paola crashed to the floor, her head banging against the wall. Her instinct was to scream, to cry, to curl up and cower from him. But she refused to dishonor God by giving in to her terror, so she sat up at once and stared at Ortega without flinching.

His face purple with rage, Ortega yanked her up by her hair and spun her around, smashing her face against the wall. His foul breath burned her cheek as he leaned close to her.

"Your brother is not expecting you to return for a few days, so no one will miss you if I choose to enjoy your company for a while. When I am through with you, I will send your brother Sergio a message to see if he wants to make a deal in return for your life. If not, I will take great pleasure in strangling you with my bare hands. But first, you will enjoy my hospitality for tonight."

He jerked the door open and flung Paola through it. She landed on the ground again, between the two men who had been standing in the hallway to wait for Ortega's orders.

"Take her to my quarters and lock her in," Ortega commanded. "She can wait for me there."

From his position outside the window of Ortega's headquarters, Matéo could see the soldiers dragging Paola down a hallway. At any moment, they would bring her outside through the door he was standing beside.

Quickly, he stepped several feet away and flattened himself against the wall, hoping the shadows would hide him. The soldiers never glanced his way as they yanked Paola out the door and to another doorway in a smaller building across the heavily potholed street.

One of them unlocked the door, and the other shoved her inside roughly. As they locked the door again behind her, one made a comment to the other. Lewd laughter followed. Then they stationed themselves on either side of the door to guard it.

Matéo saw no way he could get to his sister. He had to go for help.

10

Day 9: Monday

"Dude, I thought you were giving up on that stuff," Jeremy complained as Daniel came wheezing up to the bench where he and Kevin sat.

"I said I would cut it shorter," Daniel panted, pushing soggy strands of hair out of his face. "I only did..." he glanced at his watch, "thirty minutes today instead of forty."

"You ain't right, man," Kevin told his dripping friend. "Somethin' wrong wit' yo' head."

"You know, I figured out what's wrong with you," Jeremy said as he pulled the brightly colored wrapper off a protein bar. He licked a smear of melted chocolate that stuck to the foil wrapper.

"Besides my poor taste in friends?" Grinning, Daniel pulled a hankie out of his jeans pocket and wiped his face, waiting for Jeremy's ribbing.

Jeremy took a huge bite of his protein bar and pointed the rest of the bar at Daniel for emphasis. He mumbled around his mouthful. "I saw a special on TV once about people who are actually addicted to exercise."

"Oh, yeah?" After stealing a swig from Jeremy's canteen, Daniel lowered himself to the ground and did a few halfhearted pushups.

"Yeah," Jeremy insisted earnestly. "They had to go through rehab and everything!"

Since Daniel didn't bite, Kevin had to ask, "What kinda rehab?"

Straight faced, Jeremy explained, "Well, see, they would chain the addicts to a big, fat, fluffy sofa and force them to watch reruns of Mike and Molly for hours at a time, and feed them nachos and beer."

"You're such an idiot." Daniel groaned at his friend's remark. He allowed himself to collapse from his last pushup and rolled onto his back, laughing.

Kevin looked up and frowned. "Looks like Daniel ain't the only addict."

The other two looked to where Kevin pointed. There was a figure in the distance running in their direction. Daniel stood up to get a better look. The figure staggered and stumbled, but kept coming.

"Uh, I don't think he's jogging, guys," Jeremy said uncertainly.

"It's Matéo!" exclaimed Daniel, concern coloring his voice. He and Kevin hurried forward to meet the youth.

Jeremy quickly shoved the last bite of protein bar into his mouth and trotted to the house to find Pastor Sergio.

Daniel reached out to steady the boy. "Easy there, Matéo. Take it easy."

"What happened, man?" Kevin asked, dismayed by Matéo's appearance.

Matéo's tear streaked face was dirty, scratched, and bruised.

"They took Paola!" he cried out. "They have killed Stefan!"

Daniel and Kevin looked at each other, stunned. This was bad.

"Come on, let's get inside," Daniel said. They supported the staggering boy on either side and jogged with him back to the mission center.

Pastor Sergio and Jeff were already there to meet them, with Jeremy right behind them.

Ortega looked with contempt at the crumpled heap in the corner of the office he'd commandeered as his personal living quarters. "You didn't have to spend the night on the floor. You could have stayed in the bed with me."

Paola did not respond but pushed her face deeper into the corner to avoid looking at him. Ortega saw her straining at the ropes and guessed she wanted to cover her ears, too. The stupid woman should be grateful that he had at least allowed her to get herself together before he'd wrapped the rough rope tightly around her skinny wrists.

He laughed at her feeble efforts as he buttoned his camouflage shirt. "You are making it harder on yourself, Paola. I would not have tied your hands if you had not been so stubborn last night."

He absently rubbed at the long scratches on his cheek, evidence that Paola had not been as submissive as she appeared right now. But she had paid dearly for that, and Ortega had taught her who was in charge.

Now he bent close to her and grabbed her face roughly, forcing her to look at him. "I am preparing for an important meeting today, so I won't get to enjoy your company again until late tonight. When I get back, you will help me celebrate my success."

Ortega enjoyed the way Paola clamped her eyes shut and cringed away from him. It made him feel powerful. To reinforce his own sense of importance, Ortega released her face with contempt and stepped back, curling his lip. "I was going to try to convince you to become one of us, but I can see you do not have the heart for this kind of life."

Paola barely whispered, "My heart belongs to Jesus."

Ortega heard the faint declaration, and he laughed in derision. "Maybe so, but the rest of you belongs to me now. When I am tired of you, I might let my men have you, and then we will get rid of you. Unless your brother decides you are worth something to him."

He finished tucking his shirt in, strapped on his weapon, and rapped sharply on the door. It opened immediately and Ortega left, throwing one last taunting leer over his shoulder.

Paola could hear him giving orders to the soldiers guarding the door as the lock clicked back into place. She kept her eyes shut long after her tormentor's footsteps faded away. Her loathing for Ortega made her almost nauseous.

Jesus, forgive me, but I feel so much hatred right now.

She forced herself to relax her rigid posture, grateful for this temporary reprieve. She turned and leaned her back against the wall, stretching her cramped legs out in front of her.

The ropes cut into the soft flesh of her wrists, but at least Ortega had not tied her feet. She could have gotten up to sit in the armchair to be more comfortable if she wanted, but she chose to remain on the floor even though her entire body ached from the wreck and from the abuse she'd endured. Getting on the bed was an option she would not even consider.

Ortega had not gagged her, either. Paola guessed it was because it would not matter if she yelled and screamed for help. There was no one around to hear her except for the Black Eagles and the peasants who had sold out to them.

She had no intention of screaming for help anyway. Terrified, humiliated, and grieving for Stefan, Paola wanted nothing more than to die and get it over with. She felt abandoned by God, although she knew in her heart that was not true. She had tried to pray last night, but could do little more than whisper the name of Jesus.

Now that she was alone, perhaps she could talk to her Father, but she did not know where to begin. So many jumbled thoughts tormented her that her mind could not form a coherent prayer.

Did Sergio know that she and Stefan had been attacked? Had Raul missed them when they did not show up at his home? Had he somehow contacted Sergio? If so, how worried Sergio must be!

And where was Matéo? Had he escaped? Was he wandering somewhere, lost and afraid? Had the Black Eagles captured him?

Would they harm him, or worse, would they force him to join their ranks as they had Stefan when he was a boy?

Stefan! Each time Paola thought of Stefan, she thought she would go mad. Her heart literally ached when she remembered what had happened to him, and she wondered if a person could actually die from sorrow.

If so, she hoped death would come quickly, before the evil leader of the Black Eagles made good on his threats to return. Because death would be preferable to enduring more shame at the hands of Ortega and his men.

She drew her knees up and rested her forehead on them. "My Father, I do not know how to pray right now. I do not know what to ask You. I know You are with me even here, but I do not feel You with me. Please, do not leave me in this place with these men. I would rather go Home to You than to be here. Oh, Father, please help me..."

Paola's prayer tapered off, incomplete. She waited for the familiar peace to fill her, but it did not come, and she felt more alone than before.

Daniel kept a reassuring arm across Matéo's thin shoulders as Sergio crouched in front of the boy.

The pastor's features were filled with dread. "Matéo, what has happened? Why are you here? Where are the others?"

Matéo started to gasp out his story again, but Daniel interrupted. "Let's go inside before Matéo collapses."

Sergio took a better look at his younger brother, then quickly ushered them all into the sanctuary through the side door, Daniel all but carrying the exhausted boy. Terrell and the girls had heard the commotion and joined them as Daniel deposited Matéo in a chair. Sergio dragged a chair for himself in front of the frightened child.

Resha frowned as she took in the situation, then she went into the kitchen to get a glass of water for Matéo. He gulped it thirstily, almost choking in his haste.

Mindy sat next to Matéo and held his hand as he spoke, while the others seated themselves nearby to listen. Manny wasn't there because he'd gone on an overnight supply run with Antonio, and Samuel had left early that morning with Luís.

Matéo managed not to break down until he'd choked out the whole story, interrupted occasionally by Pastor Sergio's questions. Then he collapsed into Mindy's arms and bawled. She held the boy, stroking his back, her own eyes full of tears.

No one spoke for several minutes as the magnitude of what had happened sank in. Daniel was still trying to grasp that the affable Colombian laborer he'd befriended had been murdered, and the pretty woman who was always happy to serve them had been kidnapped.

Sergio paced restlessly, his face slack with shock and grief. Finally, he sat back down beside Matéo and said wearily, "I had hoped we would be safe for a while longer."

Pastor Jeff, sitting on the edge of the raised platform, had his face in his hands. "They must have known somehow they'd be traveling that way last night."

"Stefan had tried so hard to break away from the Black Eagles, but it still caught up with him," Sergio lamented. "And our poor Paola at their mercy. Oh, dear Jesus."

"Will they ask for ransom for her?" Jeff asked.

Daniel wondered if Jeff could convince their church in Houston to send money for something like that.

But Sergio's response was immediate and firm. "No. They know we have no money. That is one reason they targeted the mission center, because they thought we would be desperate enough for help that we would cooperate with their illegal activities. But I have already made it clear to them that I will not give in to their demands no matter what. They will not bother putting a price on Paola's return."

Daniel was puzzled. "But Matéo said they didn't kill her. Why would they let her live if they know you can't give them any money?"

"Why do you think, choir boy?" Resha snapped.

Daniel blushed at her sharp reply as the implications sunk in. He must seem stupid and naive to the tough, experienced girl.

Speaking of naive, Mindy exclaimed, "We need to go to the police right away!"

Sergio shook his head sadly. "Not only are the Colombian authorities overwhelmed right now because of the flooding, there are other problems. There are many fine men in the Colombian police force, but many of them are also corrupt. Those who are not sold out to the Black Eagles are afraid to get involved in situations like these. It is useless to contact them. We will only be putting everyone else here in danger."

"What about our government?" Kevin demanded. "Don't the U.S. military help rescue kidnap victims in other countries? I read about them sendin' people to get hostages out and stuff."

This time it was Jeff who responded. "The U.S. military only gets called in if an American citizen is involved, or if the hostage is politically important. Unfortunately, things like this go on all the time in other countries, and we just never hear about it unless the victim is high profile."

"Well, we can't just leave her there!" Daniel rose from his chair, feeling an angry flush steal up his neck. The thought of leaving the kind woman with evil men infuriated him. Judging by the despair hovering over Sergio and Matéo, leaving her there was exactly what they planned to do.

"We'll just have to get her back ourselves, then," Resha said casually, as if it were the logical solution.

"But how?" Sergio's question held no hope. "It is too dangerous. The Black Eagles are trained soldiers. We do not have trained men or weapons. We do not know where they have taken her."

"So what are you going to do?" Resha demanded, fury evident in her tone. "Let them keep your sister until they're done with her and hope they let her go? Or maybe you should hope they just kill her right away."

Sergio was not offended, but met her gaze calmly, although the sorrow in his eyes was unmistakable. "We will pray for Paola's deliverance, however God chooses to do it."

"And maybe we're God's answer to those prayers," Resha challenged.

Daniel would have laughed at Resha's cockiness if the situation wasn't so serious. Instead, he actually considered her suggestion.

"It can't be that far if Matéo made it back on foot," Daniel reasoned. He turned to Matéo, whose tears had dried as he listened to the adults. "Matéo, could you show me where they took your sister?"

Matéo nodded eagerly, a trace of hope lighting his face for the first time since he'd returned.

"No, you will not expose Matéo to more danger." Pastor Sergio was adamant. "It is enough that Paola has been taken."

"He won't be in any danger," Daniel promised. "He said they didn't see him, and we won't try anything with Matéo around. I only want to see where the place is, maybe get an idea what it would take to get in. If it looks like we can do it, some of us will go back later and get your sister."

Daniel's plan sounded simple, but they all knew it would be more complicated than that. Resha looked like she wanted to say something, but she clamped her mouth shut and contented herself with glaring from one to the other of them.

Pastor Sergio sat slumped in his chair, for once not bouncing around the room. He shook his head in hopeless despair. "Luís and Antonio have taken both of the trucks out for supplies. They will not be back until later, so there is no way for you to travel right now."

"I saw a motorcycle propped up over by the storage shed," Daniel pointed out.

"Yes," Sergio admitted with reluctance. He seemed afraid to allow himself to believe they could do it. "Stefan found it on the road after the flood and brought it home. He cleaned it up, but did not have time to try to get it to run."

Jeremy spoke up, "I think me and Kevin can make it run pretty quick. We looked it over the other day, and it just has some messed up spark plugs and stuff."

"But we do not know who it belongs to." Sergio's protests were getting weaker. "We do not have any keys for it."

"I can hotwire it for you," Resha volunteered. The others looked at her in surprise and she shrugged. "I told you guys I've done some things I'm not proud of. I picked up a few skills along the way, so I might as well put them to good use now."

"And there are some helmets in the other building," Matéo offered. "I will go get them."

Matéo ran out, anxious to be a part of his sister's rescue. Jeremy and Kevin trundled out to work on the motorcycle. Resha followed, presumably to lend her carjacking talents.

With every obstacle swept aside, Sergio shook his head and turned away, but Jeff had seen a glimmer of hope in the Colombian pastor's eyes. Perhaps he thought God could use these young missionaries to save his sister's life.

Jeff still had his doubts. Listening to Daniel's confident speculation, Jeff felt frustrated and inadequate. As their pastor, he should be the one coming up with a solution, but the whole situation seemed overwhelmingly hopeless to him. He couldn't let them risk their lives like this.

"Daniel, it's not a good idea for you to get involved. This isn't a game. These people are dangerous. You heard what Matéo said. They shot Stefan in cold blood."

"Pastor Jeff, you told us we were here to do whatever Pastor Sergio needed us to do," Daniel reminded him. "Well, he needs someone to get his sister back."

Jeff sighed. He'd wanted Daniel to develop his leadership skills, but he hadn't expected it to be in a potentially deadly situation. Still, Jeff had to admit Daniel seemed more self-assured than he'd ever seen him. Maybe his newfound confidence was coming from Someone else.

Resigned to accept that this was out of his hands, Jeff moved to stand back with Pastor Sergio and waited to see what would happen.

Matéo returned carrying two helmets encrusted with dried mud.

Daniel took them from Matéo and held them at arm's length. "Where did you find these, Matéo?"

Matéo bit his lip anxiously. "One was near the motorcycle when Stefan found it. The other one had washed up by the storage shed. Are they going to be okay?"

"They'll be fine, Matéo. Thanks." Daniel grimaced as he attempted to brush some of the caked-on mud off with his hands. There was a spider web in one of the helmets with dried leaves stuck in it and Daniel blew on the web to try to shake it loose.

Mindy stepped forward and held her hands out for one of the helmets. "Selena and I will get those cleaned up for you."

Selena stared at the helmets in horror. Daniel grinned and thrust the one with the spider web in it at her. She wrinkled her nose but accepted the helmet, and Mindy took the other one. The two girls went out to find some rags.

Daniel crouched to get at eye level with the little boy. "Okay, Matéo, you're sure these guys didn't see you last night, right?"

Matéo shook his head. "No, I was lying down in the back seat, and I came out of the car when it hit the tree. I hid in the bushes until they left with Paola, and then I sneaked onto their truck."

"Good, Matéo, you did real good," Daniel said, and Matéo glowed at the approval of his new hero. "Now when they get the bike fixed up, I want you to ride there with me and show me the last place you saw Paola. Will you do that?"

"Yes, yes, I know exactly where she is." Matéo nodded emphatically.

Jeff and Sergio exchanged a sad look. The location must be burned into the little boy's brain. What other images from last night would haunt him?

"What was the place like?" Daniel asked. "Was it on a main road? Were there other people there, or just the Black Eagles?"

Bombarded with so many questions, Matéo considered them with a thoughtful frown, then answered each query. "It was in a little village. It looked like there used to be a main road through it, but it is torn up from the flood and there are messed up cars on the sides that were left behind. I saw some people there that were not dressed like soldiers, people like farmers and merchants. They all looked scared when the truck drove past."

Daniel nodded in satisfaction. "Good, if there are other people there, we might not be so obvious. But remember, we don't want anyone to know what we're doing, so you'll have to act like we're just riding through the village. No pointing at the building we're looking for or anything like that. We'll work out a way to talk to each other without anyone else being able to know. Understand?"

"I understand, Daniel. I will be very good."

Daniel smiled at the boy's eagerness. "I know you will, Matéo. I know you will."

For the next hour, Jeff, Sergio, and Daniel discussed strategy, with Matéo dutifully answering all their questions.

Daniel and the little boy worked out a plan for communicating while they passed the buildings in question. They had just agreed on a few discreet signals when they heard the sound of a motorcycle revving and a cheer from Jeremy.

"Ready, Matéo?" Daniel asked, offering the boy a handshake.

Matéo nodded and shook his hand solemnly. The group walked outside and found Kevin and Jeremy still tweaking the engine while Resha twisted some wires together near the ignition switch. Mindy and Selena stood by watching, each holding a freshly scrubbed motorcycle helmet.

"It had some water in the gas tank, but we drained it and filled it up with fresh fuel," Kevin told them. "It's prob'ly gonna run rough at first, but once you get goin', it'll be okay."

Daniel nodded and handed Matéo the smaller of the two helmets, then climbed onto the motorcycle and began adjusting his own helmet.

Matéo slid the oversized helmet onto his head, then crawled hesitantly onto the motorcycle behind Daniel.

"Don't kill the engine unless you know how to hotwire it yourself," warned Resha, ever practical.

Daniel cocked an eyebrow at her in amusement. "I guess I'd better not kill it, then."

He revved the motorcycle, his anticipation at riding it obvious.

Mindy looked on, worried. "Daniel, do you even have a license to drive a motorcycle?"

"Not a Colombian license," Daniel admitted with a crooked smile. "So while we're gone, why don't you guys pray that I don't get pulled over?"

Resha didn't return the smile. "We'll be praying for a lot more than that."

As the motorcycle roared away, Mindy gave a sad little wave and murmured softly, "Be careful, Daniel."

Paola shifted on the dirty floor, trying to ease the cramps in her shoulders. The ropes had held her arms behind her in an awkward position for many hours now, and she struggled again to bring her arms around her legs so that she could have her hands in front of her. But the efforts only caused her to become overheated, so she gave up.

There was a ceiling fan above her that had at least stirred the hot air during the night, but it had slowly ground to a stop shortly after Ortega left. Paola guessed that, like Sergio at the mission center, the Black Eagles ran their generators as little as possible. Now, as the morning sun rose higher, the room was becoming unbearably hot.

Paola looked across the room at the only window, which was covered in grime. It had a simple latch which she could easily open if only her hands were free. Not to escape, because she knew she would not get far with the men posted outside the door, but to let in some fresh air. Smoke from the soldier's cigarettes wafted in under the door, making her ordeal more unbearable. She longed for a drink of water.

"God, are you really here in this place with me?" she wondered.

Words from Psalm 139 came to her, and she spoke aloud, her voice raspy. "You said that even if I make my bed in hell, You are with me. Father, it feels like I am in hell. Where are You? I cannot feel You."

She swallowed, trying to moisten her parched throat, and tried to comfort herself with Bible verses. "Oh, Lord, You are my Rock and my Fortress and my Deliverer. You are my Shield and my Strength and my Refuge."

Still, she felt only despair. She knew she felt closest to God when she was doing what He had created her to do, but how could she possibly sing in this dark situation?

The words to a song the Americans had sung two days ago floated through her mind, and she forced herself to sing a few tentative notes, not sure of the words but remembering the meaning.

"When the darkness closes in, Lord, still I will say,
Blessed be the Name of the Lord,
Blessed be Your Glorious Name."

And as Paola sang praises to His Name, the darkness that had closed in on her began to dissipate. The circumstances had not changed, but her outlook had. Her situation did not seem so hopeless in light of God's love.

How she wished her hands were not tied, for she longed to raise them to her Father. In spite of her thirst, Paola's voice picked up strength as she began to sing songs more familiar to her, songs in her own language about God's power and might.

Ramiro, the reluctant young recruit, approached the two men posted to guard the door of Captain Ortega's quarters. He was always nervous around the older, more experienced Black Eagles, but these two seemed uncomfortable, too.

When Ramiro got closer to the guards, he could hear a woman singing from inside the room. From the soldier's conversation, it was obvious the sweet voice was the reason for their nervous fidgeting.

"What is wrong with that woman?" one of them grumbled, hunching his shoulders.

"I think she is demon possessed," replied the other. He laughed a little too loudly.

Mustering his courage, Ramiro stood in front of them and asked, "Is one of you Julio?"

The soldier who had laughed grunted acknowledgment.

Ramiro looked at the ground to show his subservience as he relayed his message. "El Tiburon wishes for you to meet him in the office. He has some instructions about tonight."

Julio spat and went on his way to meet Ortega. "It will be a relief to get away from this relentless assault on my ears."

Ramiro listened to the singing for a moment, wondering at the words he heard, before he dared to ask the remaining guard, "Is that Captain Ortega's prisoner? Why is she singing like that?"

"I do not know, but I am sick of it," the man snapped. "Go and find me a roll of duct tape so I can put an end to it."

Ramiro felt sad that the beautiful voice would be silenced, but he had seen how the Black Eagles punished those who disobeyed orders.

He quickly ran off to find the duct tape.

In spite of their solemn mission, Daniel relished the exhilaration of riding the motorcycle. The powerful machine underneath him gave him a transcendent sense of freedom as he roared over the bumpy road.

At first, Matéo clung to him with white-knuckled fingers, but soon the little boy began looking around in wonder as the jungle flew past.

Daniel wished he could take off the helmet and let the wind rush through his hair, but he didn't want to give Matéo the idea he could do the same.

Besides, Resha had pointed out that the helmet would mask his blond hair, and his long sleeved shirt and work gloves would hide his fair skin. He didn't need to attract attention by being an obvious foreigner.

As they drew near the spot where Stefan's car had been ambushed, Daniel's eyes were drawn to the ruts beside the road where Stefan had driven around the roadblock.

Matéo tensed up behind him, and Daniel berated himself for being so insensitive. He hadn't considered how the boy would feel seeing the scene again while everything was still so raw. The sight of the burned out shell that had once been Stefan's Chevy was disturbing to Daniel – it must be many times harder on Matéo.

He hoped Matéo didn't notice the dark stains on the ground near the wrecked car, and he drove past quickly, not giving either of them a chance to glance inside.

Daniel pointed at a fork in the road just ahead, then raised a questioning hand. Fresh tire marks made it obvious which way the Black Eagles had gone, but he wanted to distract Matéo from the wreckage.

Daniel turned the bike in the direction Matéo indicated and they quickly left behind the grim reminder of last night's tragedy.

Sure enough, a few minutes later, scattered signs of habitation began to appear – such as clothes hanging out on a line to dry, some men working in a field in the distance, even a couple of small children trying to play in the rutted street.

Daniel squinted to see if the field was sown with coca plants, but he didn't really know what a coca plant looked like.

As they entered the small town, Matéo sat up straighter. He nudged Daniel's side with his right elbow, the signal they'd agreed on to let Daniel know which way to turn. Daniel turned right and saw a long, cinder block office building and a warehouse, both old and streaked with mildew, and both seemingly abandoned.

Pressure from Matéo's left hand made him look more closely, though, and he saw that a generator had been set up outside the two buildings, and the locks on one of the doors had been recently replaced.

A man in his thirties, in military dress, stood outside that door smoking a cigarette. The soldier glanced up at them with narrowed eyes as they drove past but did not seem overly suspicious.

Daniel was careful not to show particular interest in the man or the building as he kept driving in the same direction until he'd left the village behind them.

Once they were a safe distance away, Daniel pulled the motorcycle over behind some trees. He'd forgotten Resha's admonition not to cut it off and reached for the key out of habit, but he was reminded when there was no key. He hoped they had plenty of fuel in the tank to get back.

Daniel beckoned for Matéo to follow him several feet away from the bike so they could talk without having to yell over the sound of the engine.

Matéo had obviously been bursting with information, because he didn't wait for Daniel to ask any questions.

"The door where the man was standing is the place where they took Paola," he said with certainty. "They pushed her through that doorway and locked her in. There were two men last night, though."

"She must still be in there," Daniel speculated. "Otherwise they wouldn't bother to post a guard. Was that big warehouse the other building you talked about?"

"Yes, they had first taken her to that long warehouse building, through the door in the front. They took her to a room at the back of the building." Matéo pointed to his left as if he were seeing it in his mind. "The man was asking her questions, but I could not hear what they were saying. Then two other men brought something in, and then they went back out. Then the man hit my sister and knocked her down, then pulled her up by her hair and pushed her out of the room. The two men brought her back out through the door and then made her go into that other building where the man is standing now."

Matéo's voice was shaky again, and Daniel hated that he'd made the boy relive his experience. He stifled his own outrage as Matéo recounted how they'd treated Paola.

Forcing himself to take a deep breath, he gave Matéo's shoulder a reassuring squeeze. "You're being real brave, Matéo. Paola would be so proud of you."

Matéo's nod was uncertain, but he managed to keep his tears in check.

Daniel continued, "Now we have to go through the village one more time, because now that I know for sure that's where they took her, I want to see if there's a way to get in. Then we'll go home and make some more plans to get your sister back, okay?"

Matéo nodded again, the helmet sliding awkwardly on his head.

Daniel straightened the helmet and clapped Matéo on the shoulder to fortify him. "Let's go then."

They climbed back on the idling motorcycle and drove once more through the village, more quickly this time. Daniel wished they didn't have to drive past the scene of the kidnapping again, but he didn't know any other way to get back to the mission center, so he sped up when they got to it.

When they arrived back at the mission center, Matéo's ordeal finally caught up with him. He could barely stay awake, and Daniel had been afraid the boy would slide off the back of the bike, but he'd managed to hang on. Now Daniel handed the exhausted child over to Pastor Sergio, who in turn asked Mindy to take him to the house and put him to bed. Matéo stumbled a little as Mindy led him away.

It was close to lunch time, so Sergio recruited Selena to replace Paola in helping Abuelita in the kitchen while Mindy tended to Matéo. Manny and Antonio were still gone, but Daniel noticed that Luís' truck was back, and there were piles of new lumber stacked near the singed earth the burnt building had rested on.

"After lunch, perhaps you would give the rest of the team the plans you made for the new building so they can get started on the construction," Pastor Sergio told him. Then, in spite of his earlier misgivings about a rescue attempt, Sergio seemed anxious to hear what Daniel had learned. "For now, please tell me what you discovered."

The men assembled in the dining area and Daniel drew a rough map and a sketch of the buildings Matéo had shown him. "I think if we wait until dark, some of us could get her out. But we'd have to go on foot. One of the trucks would be too obvious, especially if they've been watching us."

"But it is too far to go on foot," Sergio pointed out. "I do not believe that Paola could make such a journey, especially if she has been injured. Is there any place nearby to hide one of the trucks?"

Daniel mentally went back over the area he had seen. "There's a turnoff about a mile before we got to the Black Eagle's headquarters." He made a mark on the map he'd drawn earlier.

After another half hour of discussion, they had come up with a tentative plan. Sergio insisted on driving Luís' truck, because he was familiar with the truck and with the roads. Daniel suspected it was also because the pastor wanted to play his part in rescuing his sister.

Daniel would accompany him since he was the one who had scoped out the area. Sergio would let Daniel out at the turnoff he had mentioned and Daniel would make his way on foot to the building.

Sergio would wait thirty minutes, then he would drive the truck in closer, to a spot Daniel had marked on the map a couple of blocks away from the building. They hoped that would give Daniel enough time to free Paola from the room she was being held in.

Daniel wasn't sure yet how he was going to accomplish that part, and discussion turned to whether or not someone else should go with him.

Naturally, Jeremy and Kevin wanted to go, but Terrell looked at them all like they were crazy. Samuel sat in the corner with his arms folded, offering no opinion or advice. Jeff and Sergio just frowned, their apprehension obvious.

Resha strode into the room and announced, "I'm going with Daniel."

Everyone turned to stare at her.

Jeff shook his head immediately. "Resha, I can't allow you to do that. It's too dangerous."

"More dangerous for me than for one of them?" Resha challenged, jerking a thumb at the men. They all looked at Jeff now, waiting to see how he would react.

Before Jeff could stammer out some kind of reply, Resha spoke again. "This was my idea. I want to go."

Jeff looked helplessly at Sergio for reinforcement. Sergio was speechless for a moment. Then Daniel heard him murmur to Pastor Jeff, "I have heard that American women are strong-willed. I do not know how to handle this spirited young lady, but I will try."

He turned to the assertive girl. "Resha, we thank you for giving us hope that we could rescue Paola ourselves. But I agree with your pastor. You should let the men take over from here."

Resha had obviously been prepared for that reaction. She tossed a small object onto the table in front of them. "Fine. Which one of you knows how to use this?"

They all stared at it, perplexed. It looked like a nail file that had been deliberately nicked in several places.

"It's a jimmy to unlock a door," she explained. "Unless you plan to make a whole lot of noise by kicking the door down, you're going to need this."

When no one spoke, Resha picked up the object and pocketed it. "Then it looks like I need to be there. I've got plenty of experience with B & E."

Daniel doubted Sergio knew what "B & E" meant, but the Colombian man asked, "Could you not show one of the men how to use the tool?"

"It's better if someone with experience does it. Different locks need different techniques." Then she played her trump card. "After what she's probably been through, Paola will feel better if there's a woman there."

All the men squirmed uncomfortably. They had no argument for that. Daniel waited to see if Pastor Jeff could counter her logic.

Instead, Jeff gave a resigned sigh. "All right, Resha. If Daniel has no objections, I guess you'll be the one to go with him."

Resha turned hooded eyes to Daniel, her face expressionless as she waited for the verdict.

Daniel raised his eyebrows, studying the slender girl whose head barely reached his chin. Her confidence made up for what she lacked in stature, and more importantly, so did her faith. He finally shrugged. "I'm okay with it. Since I have no idea what I'm doing, somebody with experience will be helpful."

"Fine." Resha's voice was casual, but Daniel caught the gleam of triumph in her eyes as she turned away. "Let me know when you're ready to leave."

And she walked out.

The men all looked at each other, not sure what had just hit them.

Finally, Jeremy piped up, "Well, Daniel, at least she knows kickboxing, so she should be able to protect you."

When all their plans were finalized, Pastor Sergio said a prayer for God's protection, and for success in their attempt. Then he asked Abuelita to serve their meal, although no one was in the mood to eat.

After lunch, Daniel tried to focus on the construction work. He pulled out the sketches he'd drawn for the framework and went over them with Terrell.

Since it was a basic, square building, and not very big, the plans were simple enough. The team already had the framework for two walls up by dusk.

The tape over Paola's mouth itched and burned, and she was desperate to yank it off. But each time she instinctively tried to reach up for it, the rope cut deeper into her wrists.

She was no longer able to sing, but some of the courage and peace her songs had stirred inside of her remained.

Even though Stefan had been murdered, Paola felt a small measure of comfort in knowing that he was now in God's Presence. And though she was in pain, physically and emotionally, she found a small trace of hope.

She knew that God was aware of what she suffered. And God was good.

Drained, hungry, and more thirsty than she had ever been, Paola gingerly lowered herself to the floor and tried to sleep. She dozed some, but she kept hearing the men outside talking, kept breathing their stale cigarette smoke.

Paola tried to tune everything out, but with nothing else to focus on in her prison, her brain zeroed in on the muffled voices of the soldiers.

The men came and went. For a while, she heard only one guard outside the door, pacing restlessly and polluting the air with his foul smelling cigarette. Now there were two again, but their voices sounded different from the two she had been listening to earlier, younger maybe.

They still smoked, though.

Finally, Paola's exhausted body surrendered to the sleep she so desperately needed.

Daniel noticed Jeff hovering at the edge of the work area, where the team was attaching sturdy plywood to the new framework.

"Is it time?" Daniel asked.

"It should be dark soon," Jeff replied gravely. "Sergio is having Luís refuel the truck."

Daniel nodded and finished driving in the nail he was hammering. He saw Resha vanish into her dorm while he gave Terrell some final instructions.

As Daniel made his way towards Luís' truck, the girl re-emerged, wearing black jeans and a black T-shirt. She had removed her flashy earrings and had a small pouch clipped to her belt.

Daniel blinked in surprise at Resha's all black outfit.

Resha in turn looked in disgust at his grungy white T-shirt. "We don't have to advertise ourselves. That T-shirt is filthy, but it will just about glow in the dark. Don't you have anything less visible to wear?"

Daniel raised his eyebrows. "When I packed, I didn't know I was going to be part of a S.W.A.T. Team."

Resha folded her arms and glared at him.

Daniel meekly went into his own dorm and came back out a moment later buttoning his dark blue denim work shirt over his T-shirt. He hadn't been wearing it since a big corner of it had been singed off from the fire two nights ago.

"Better?" he asked. "It's the best I can do."

"Well, at least maybe you won't be a beacon of light," Resha grumbled.

"Isn't that what we're supposed to be?" he asked innocently.

Resha said nothing, just turned and strode toward the rusted blue Ford. Daniel followed, a small smile escaping in spite of the grim situation.

At Pastor Sergio's insistence, Resha sat in the cab of the truck with him. Through the recently repaired rear window, she could see Daniel sitting in the bed of the pickup, his long legs stretched out in front of him. He had his eyes closed, but his alert posture told her he wasn't asleep. Praying, probably.

Resha should be doing the same.

She felt trapped sitting in the truck – she liked to move around while she prayed. She bowed her head anyway, asking God for wisdom and protection for them and for Paola. She prayed for the success of their mission.

Forty minutes later, Daniel rapped on the window and pointed to the right. Sergio nodded and began searching for the hidden turnoff. It was difficult to spot in the dark, but Sergio saw it at the last second and pulled into it.

Daniel and Resha climbed out of the truck and Sergio leaned out the window, needing to say something to these brave young people who were about to risk their lives for his family's sake.

But he could think of nothing to say. In the end, he reached out and clasped Daniel's hand, saying only, "I will be at our meeting place in half an hour. God go with you both."

He watched Daniel and Resha disappear into the trees, then dropped his head onto the steering wheel and tried to pray some more. But all he could say was, "Jesus, Jesus, Jesus."

Once they reached the city, Resha hugged the walls, staying in the shadows as they made their way to the building where Paola was being held. She was glad Daniel had enough sense to do the same.

When they got near the end of one the muddy dirt roads, Daniel peeked around the corner of a building. After a moment he turned back to Resha.

"There's two guys guarding the door," he whispered. "There was only one earlier."

Resha shrugged. "Matéo said there were two before."

She pushed Daniel aside so she could have a look for herself.

Two young men stood guard with rifles slung over their shoulders. The smaller of the two guards was chewing gum, and the other one looked flabby and overweight.

She gave a contemptuous snort. "Those guys don't look dangerous."

"No, but their guns do."

Resha wasn't about to let a little thing like that discourage her. She said matter-of-factly, "Then we have to disarm them."

"Any ideas?" Daniel asked. "They didn't teach me this stuff in Sunday School."

Resha scrunched up her face, analyzing their surroundings. She wished they could look in the window to see if Paola was still in the room, but the soldiers would see them for sure if they tried.

Resha's eyes slid to a ruined car parked next to an obviously abandoned building adjacent to the warehouse, then to the flat roof of the building.

Squinting, Resha appraised the distance between the two buildings, then turned to study Daniel. She was annoyed to find him watching her curiously.

"How agile are you?" Resha demanded, frowning as she sized him up.

Daniel reddened under her stare, and his shoulders shrank in as if he were trying to hide. She halfway expected him to fold his arms over his chest protectively like a virginal schoolgirl.

She was about to bark that her assessment was entirely objective, but he recovered enough to shrug and reply, "Not bad, I guess. What did you have in mind?"

Resha was surprised he seemed open to her assuming leadership in this situation. Most guys would go all macho and plow ahead unprepared. She studied his face. Could she count on him?

Physically, he looked up to the task, but she suspected he could be an emotional marshmallow. "Look, Daniel, I need to know you're going to be with me on this."

Daniel fixed his serious gaze on her. "I'll do whatever needs to be done to help Paola."

Resha believed him.

Two minutes later, Resha had outlined her idea.

They climbed onto the tar and gravel roof of the neighboring structure, using the disabled car as a stepladder.

When they came to the gap between the two buildings, Daniel hesitated. The space looked wider than it had from below, and the ground looked farther away than the ten foot drop they had estimated.

Beside him, Resha took a deep breath, took two steps back, then flung herself forward. She made it with a few inches to spare, landing knees first on the opposite roof.

Daniel winced in sympathy, then followed suit. It was easier for him with his long legs, and he managed to land on his feet.

For several moments, they crouched in silence where they had landed, listening. Daniel didn't know how much noise they had made, or if the sound had carried through the ceiling, or even if there were other militants in the rooms below.

When they were satisfied that no one was going to come after them with rifles blazing, they began to creep forward on the rooftop, quietly making their way to a spot over the doorway they had seen the men guarding.

They cautiously lowered themselves onto the overhang above the door, which reduced the drop to the ground by three or four feet.

Silently, carefully, they peeked over the edge. The soldiers were still there, smoking and making idle conversation.

Resha had instructed Daniel that she would give him a count with her fingers, and they would both leap on three, catching the guards by surprise. But as he waited for her signal, the stocky guard made a comment that sent the other one laughing.

Resha's nostrils flared and her eyes flashed fire. She jumped without warning, landing directly in front of the shorter commando.

Caught off guard, Daniel hastily followed her lead and leapt from the rooftop.

Resha had already landed a kick to the guy's solar plexus, and when he bent over to clutch his ribs, dropping his rifle, she grabbed his head with both arms and pulled down hard as she jerked her knee up. His face slammed into her knee and he was down before the second man could react.

By the time Daniel's quarry realized they were being attacked, Daniel had landed behind him and wrapped an arm around his neck.

Dreading his own actions, Daniel quickly bent the soldier sideways and spun him around, slamming his head against the concrete wall.

Out cold, the heavy soldier slid slowly to the ground. Daniel snatched up the man's rifle and studied it, searching for the safety switch so he wouldn't accidentally fire the weapon.

"If you're trying to turn on the safety, flip it so you don't see the red dot," Resha's calm voice informed him. She had taken the other guard's rifle and now brought the butt of it down hard on the soldier's forehead, even though he was already unconscious.

Daniel grimaced at her brutality.

"Kind of extreme, don't you think?" Daniel asked quietly, flipping the switch so the red dot was hidden.

Resha set aside the rifle she'd confiscated and pulled her tools from the little pouch she'd brought. She began working the lock with her customized nail file. "He deserved it. Didn't you hear that crack about Paola?"

Daniel hadn't been worried about trying to interpret their mumbled Spanish. Instead of answering, he quoted, half in jest, "'Vengeance is mine, saith The Lord.'"

"Yeah, well, I was His instrument of vengeance," Resha snapped.

Daniel wasn't too sure about her theology, but he kept quiet. Especially after he'd seen what she did to the soldier. He dragged the unconscious men into the shadows, watching for signs of trouble while Resha tried different things with the lock.

"First rule of self-defense: 'Don't stop until the threat is neutralized.'" Resha sounded irritated. She stopped working and turned to frown at him. "You need to remember that, Chief. It's important."

She turned back to the job at hand and hissed in frustration after an unsuccessful attempt at popping the mechanism. After she made a few more tries, Daniel heard a click.

Resha turned the knob and eased the door open. She started to step into the room first, but Daniel put a gentle hand on her shoulder and shook his head.

She shrugged his hand off and glared at him, and Daniel was afraid she was going to argue. To his relief, she just clamped her mouth shut and allowed him to enter before her. He was sure he'd hear about it later.

Daniel slipped in, ready to use the guard's rifle as a club if necessary.

Paola was alone, sitting on the floor. She'd scooted into the corner and was staring at the door with wide, terrified eyes. She must have been confused and frightened from hearing the scuffle outside.

Not sure if the broken woman recognized him, Daniel held a finger to his lips, then turned back to give Resha the all clear, but Resha was already pushing past him into the room.

Daniel saw recognition flicker in Paola's eyes as Resha approached her. He felt a rush of fury toward the Black Eagles when he got a good look at Paola's battered face, and he suddenly felt more sympathetic to Resha's vengeful actions.

He couldn't imagine what Paola must have endured at the hands of Ortega and his men, but her eyes told a story of outrage and grief.

Without a word, Resha crouched beside Paola and carefully peeled the duct tape from her mouth. Paola closed her eyes and trembled at the pain, but she made no sound.

As soon as the tape was off, Paola asked hoarsely, "Matéo?"

Resha ignored the query as she pulled out her switchblade and began sawing at the rope that bound Paola's wrists, so Daniel whispered, "He's fine. He told us where to find you."

Resha finished cutting the ropes and gently peeled them from Paola's wrists. The rough cords had left deep, red welts on the Colombian woman's skin.

Paola flexed her fingers, then used her shaky hands to rub her wrists. Resha silently handed Paola her canteen.

Paola gulped thirstily through her bruised, swollen lips. She handed the canteen back to Resha, her eyes expressing her gratitude, and Daniel offered his hand to her. Paola hesitated, then allowed him to help her stand.

The three of them quietly made their way toward the door, Paola favoring the side that had been injured in the wreck.

Adolfo took on his first solo assignment with great pride. He had been given the task of patrolling the headquarters of the Black Eagles while El Tiburon took most of his men with him on an unspecified mission.

Adolfo had wanted desperately to go with them, especially after he had been included in last night's adventure. He had been the only new recruit allowed to go along when the Black Eagles ambushed the car last night, and he knew it was because Ortega was testing him, to see how he would react to bloodshed. Seeing the traitor killed only whet Adolfo's appetite for more action, and he made sure Ortega knew it.

He realized that Ortega left him in charge of tonight's patrol duty because the captain did not anticipate any problems, but Adolfo planned to take the job seriously anyway. If so much as a rat stirred, he would blow its tiny rat brains out, just to prove his loyalty to the Black Eagles.

Adolfo had been told to take two others with him. He chose Dario, because even though the two hated each other, Dario had proven to be an able fighter and would follow his orders. His other choice was purely for the pleasure of it – he selected Gloria as his third companion.

As they walked about the complex, Adolfo was amused that Gloria had deliberately positioned herself so that Dario was between her and Adolfo. Gloria knew of the hostility between the two enlistees, and she was flirting with Dario.

Adolfo realized she was doing it just to make him jealous, but he found it exciting. Let Gloria have her fun for now – he knew whose bunk she would sneak into when their shift was over.

Adolfo's mind wandered until he realized they were almost to Ortega's special headquarters, where he was keeping the woman prisoner. Benito and Ramiro were guarding her to make sure she didn't escape.

The fact that Ortega had selected two such inept recruits had let Adolfo know the woman locked inside was unlikely to make any attempts to break out. Adolfo relaxed his guard and tried to listen to what Dario was whispering to Gloria as the three of them rounded the corner.

Tense and alert, Daniel stuck his head out the door and looked around. Seeing no sign of trouble, he slipped back out onto the rutted street. Resha followed, guiding Paola.

They had stepped around the fallen guards and walked several paces when three more soldiers appeared around the corner of the building, two men and a woman.

All had rifles strapped around them, and the two men looked intimidating, especially the one on the end with the scar down the side of his face. The militants stopped in surprise when they saw the two students and Paola, then scrabbled for their weapons.

Daniel knew he had to act fast.

The female soldier was nearest, but he wasn't about to hit a girl, even if she was packing a firearm, so he chose the sturdy-looking guy in the middle.

He swung the previously confiscated rifle around, slamming it against the side of the stocky guy's head. The edge of his swing also caught the third commando, sending him staggering backwards.

The sound of metal hitting flesh sickened Daniel, and he tossed the rifle to the ground. From the corner of his eye, he saw Resha do some kind of flying roundhouse kick, her foot aiming for the rifle in the female soldier's hands. He didn't have time to see if she made contact.

The commando he had struck was dazed but still conscious. The soldier had fallen, but was now on his side, reaching for the weapon he had dropped.

Instinctively, Daniel stepped forward and ground his heel into the soldier's hand, causing him to cry out in pain as he released the weapon.

Remembering Resha's earlier advice about neutralizing the threat, Daniel used the same foot to deliver a swift kick to the soldier's head. The soldier fell back, his head bouncing off the pavement, and Daniel winced.

"Daniel!" Paola gasped from behind him.

He turned to see that the third soldier had recovered from the blow, his scarred face now contorted into a mask of rage as his finger hovered over the trigger of his rifle.

He was not aiming at Daniel, but at Resha, who had now bested her opponent, pinning the soldier's girlfriend to the ground and twisting her arm behind her back.

Seeing the threat to Resha, Daniel felt the same fury the soldier must be feeling. Without conscious thought, Daniel flung himself toward the soldier in a football tackle, ramming his head into the man's midsection.

The shot went wild as they both hit the ground, rolling on the wet pavement. The man tried to point the rifle at Daniel, but Daniel grabbed the barrel with both hands and they struggled for control of it, each of them straining in a life and death battle.

The soldier was younger than Daniel, but he was just as tall, and thicker, and he'd been trained to fight. The commando released one end of the rifle barrel and drove a brutal fist sideways against Daniel's ear, and electric shocks of pain nearly rendered him unconscious.

While Daniel tried to shake off the pain, the soldier rolled them over and now had the upper position. He shoved the rifle barrel lengthwise against Daniel's throat, cutting off his air supply.

Driven by panic as his windpipe was crushed, Daniel managed to dig one heel into the ground for leverage and twisted his body hard.

The move threw the man off balance, and his grip on the rifle loosened.

In desperation, Daniel threw a wild punch, catching the side of his opponent's jaw. When the man's head snapped back, Daniel jerked the rifle from his hands and shoved it to one side. Now Daniel was on top again. He had no idea what to do with the man he'd pinned down.

Suddenly, a rifle butt landed hard on the soldier's forehead in an all too familiar move. The guy's eyes rolled back and his head hit the street with a thud.

Daniel looked up in surprise to see Resha standing over him, looking smug.

Her female opponent was sprawled on the ground next to the first guy Daniel had dispatched. The soldier must have put up a fight, judging by the scratches on Resha's arms and face.

"Sorry to spoil your fun, but we need to go," Resha said, out of breath from the fight. "That gunshot will probably bring all their buddies."

Heart pounding, Daniel glanced at their fallen foes one last time, then scrambled to his feet. As Resha had predicted, there were sudden shouts from several directions and rapid footsteps headed their way.

The three of them moved quickly to the side street, Paola still limping.

"Great," Resha muttered. "How's Sergio going to come for us? Those scumbags will be all over the place now."

"Sergio?" Paola breathed. "He's coming?"

Ignoring them, Daniel looked around frantically for a place to hide and came up with only one desperate idea.

"Back on the roof!" he ordered, his voice raspy from the assault.

The two Americans rushed around the corner to the car they had used as a ladder earlier, pulling Paola along with them. Resha jumped onto the car effortlessly, then scrambled onto the rooftop.

Paola had never appeared very athletic to Daniel, and now she was beaten and bruised. She looked fearfully up at the roof she was expected to reach.

With no time to waste on gallantry, Daniel hauled Paola gracelessly onto the car, and Resha stretched out a hand to help her. Paola took her hand as Daniel gave her a boost from behind, and Paola managed to crawl onto the rooftop. Daniel dragged himself up right behind her, pulling himself out of sight a split second before the beam from a high-powered flashlight reached the street they had just vacated.

The three of them scooted backwards to the center of the flat roof, trying to get as far out of sight as possible. There was a rusted air compressor in the center of the roof, and they leaned against it, gasping for breath. They stared at each other wild-eyed while they listened to the angry conversation as the soldiers found their fallen comrades.

Daniel could hear the militants directly below them, checking the doors of the building to make sure no one had gone in. He hardly dared to breathe for fear of making a sound that would alert the soldiers where they were.

When the sounds of searching moved down the street, Resha couldn't stand it any longer. She whispered, "I'm going to see what's going on."

She ignored Daniel's warning look and slithered toward the edge, loose roofing material scraping her elbows and belly. Peeking over, she could see the street was deserted, but the beams of flashlights still played across everything on the next block. There was no sign of Sergio or the truck.

As Resha leaned her head over the edge, a big raindrop splatted onto the back of her neck. Disgusted, she wiped it off, but another came, then another, until it became a full-scale deluge.

While Resha watched, the flashlights on the street below blinked out one by one. Apparently the search was being called off because of the weather.

Wimps.

Resha crawled back to the others. Daniel had taken off his denim shirt and draped it over Paola's shoulders, but it offered scant protection against the downpour.

"They're gone," Resha said shortly, settling back against the air compressor and closing her eyes.

"What are we going to do now?" Paola asked, her teeth chattering from the cold rain. Her whole body trembled as rivulets of water streamed down her face.

"Sergio may have decided not to risk coming back tonight," Daniel surmised. "Matéo managed to run from here all the way back to the mission center to tell us what happened. If he could do that, then we can probably walk it in a few hours."

Resha twisted her lips to the side. "Slogging through the mud in this downpour will be miserable, but it looks like they won't be searching for us in the rain, so we should be safe."

They both looked at Paola with concern. Resha doubted the frail woman would be able to make it.

Paola stood up resolutely. "Then let us go. I want to go home to my family."

Suddenly a faint light flashed on and off a short distance away.

Daniel and Resha hurriedly grabbed Paola and pulled her back down.

"Are they still searching for us?" Paola's voice trembled, her momentary bravado gone.

"I don't know," Resha admitted with a frown, cocking her ears to listen.

The light flashed again, a little closer. Daniel slid himself across the roof and looked down. He stage whispered, "I think it's Sergio!"

Resha quickly crawled over next to him to look. Sure enough, the old Ford truck was slowly making it's way down the street about a quarter of a mile away, its headlights off. Every block, Sergio would flash the lights briefly.

"Let's get down there and try to catch him." Daniel was already working his way to the edge of the roof.

The exhausted, soggy trio made their way back down from the roof, which proved more difficult with the rain making their handholds slippery. The bruises from the fight were making themselves felt, too, so all three of them were limping now.

Soon they were on the street they had seen Sergio on. They remained in the shadows until they saw the lights flash again a block away. Daniel stepped out into the open and waved before quickly ducking back into the darkness.

The truck sped up, coming towards them with the headlights off.

When the truck drew abreast of them, Sergio flung open the passenger door and Paola fell inside. The pastor wrapped his arms around his sister, and the two of them clung to each other, weeping silent tears.

Were they tears of relief that Paola was safe, or grief over Stefan's death? Resha wondered. Probably both.

She traded a resigned look with Daniel, then climbed into the bed of the truck. Sergio appeared to have forgotten about them, and there was no room in the cab for them anyway. It was going to be a long, wet ride home.

The main thing was, Paola was safe.

At last Sergio released his sister and turned the pickup around, starting back the way they had come.

Daniel and Resha sat in the truck bed, rain pouring over their heads and dripping into their eyes. Both were silent, lost in their own thoughts, but eventually Resha turned her attention to the drenched man sitting across from her in the truck.

He looked miserable, but she doubted it had anything to do with the rain. Just to get him talking, Resha said, "You did pretty good tonight, Chief."

Daniel barely glanced at her. "Thanks," he mumbled.

"Was that a football tackle?" she pressed.

He nodded, clearly not in the mood to elaborate. Resha wanted to respect his need for silence, but she was too pumped from their adventure. Besides, he looked like he needed to be distracted.

"You're on the team?"

Daniel shook his head and grunted, "Played some in high school."

"High school? So why not now?" She tried to picture him all decked out in a football uniform.

"Didn't like it," Daniel said. At her questioning look, he added, "Too violent."

Resha snorted at the irony, then snickered, then started to laugh out loud, her teeth flashing in the rain.

Her mirth made Daniel laugh, too. They were cold, wet, and bruised, but it still felt good to release the tension that had built up in them the last several hours.

As soon as the mission center came into view, the rain tapered off to a light drizzle.

God's little joke.

Captain Ortega was furious.

When he returned from a drug deal gone bad, he had found one of his new recruits with a broken nose, two still unconscious, and two more with a tale of colossal failure.

"Idiots!" he screamed at them, but he knew the fault was his own.

Not expecting any kind of action from the spineless Christians, he had left inexperienced trainees behind to guard their headquarters. He had taken with him all of his more seasoned men, and had lost two of them in the process.

Now he discovered that his hostage and plaything was gone as well. It had not been a good night.

The mission center was dark when they got back.

Daniel wasn't surprised, since they were trying to conserve the fuel that the generators guzzled. But as soon as they pulled up in front of Sergio's house, Pastor Jeff opened the front door and Matéo came flying out, looking for Paola.

When he saw her, he hurled himself at her and clung to his big sister. She hugged him back, then murmured something to him, and he reluctantly let her go.

Abuelita appeared and draped a towel over Paola's shoulders as Paola trudged into the house. Matéo started to follow, but Sergio slowed him down with a hand on the shoulder.

"No questions tonight, Matéo," Sergio told his little brother. The firmness in his tone implied that the words were meant for the rest of them, too. "Tonight we will allow Paola to rest, and tomorrow she will tell us whatever she wants us to know."

Daniel hovered uncertainly beside Resha under the carport. He was ready to crawl into his cot, but he wanted to let some of the water drip off before heading to his dorm.

Sergio suddenly became aware of them again and rushed to them, clasping their hands.

"Resha, Daniel, I cannot thank you enough for what you have done for my family. Paola is back with us because of the two of you." He almost wept in his gratitude, but seemed oblivious to their soggy condition.

Thankfully, Pastor Jeff had scrounged up some towels and handed one to each of them.

Daniel mumbled something to Sergio about being glad to help, then stumbled towards the men's dorm. When he dragged his tired body in, he wasn't surprised to find Jeremy and Kevin sitting up in the dark, waiting for him.

"So did you get her back?" Jeremy asked, keeping his voice low so he wouldn't wake the others. Terrell stirred anyway, and propped himself up on one elbow to listen.

"Yeah, she's okay," Daniel said without elaborating. He dried his hair with the rough towel Jeff had given him.

"You sound funny," Kevin told him.

"Some guy tried to choke me." Daniel explained as he peeled off his wet T-shirt and dropped it on the floor next to the towel. He sat down to remove his shoes.

Kevin and Jeremy leaned forward, eager to hear more. Kevin asked, "For real? What happened, man?"

Daniel lay back on the cot, not bothering to remove his wet jeans. "My throat hurts, Kev. I don't feel like talking. I'll tell you about it tomorrow."

"Oh, okay, man, whatever." Kevin sounded disappointed, but he backed off.

In the dim light, Daniel saw Kevin and Jeremy look at each other and shrug. Then he closed his eyes and saw again the young soldiers he'd fought with.

Tired as he was, the memories would keep him awake for hours.

Scrubbing her head with the coarse towel, Resha slipped quietly into the girls' room and found her duffel bag in the dark. She felt her way down the hall to the little bathroom, leaving soggy footprints.

No need to shower, she thought cynically. She pulled a flashlight from the duffel bag and examined the scratches on her face and arms, then scrubbed them thoroughly with soap. No sense inviting an infection.

Staring at her dim reflection in the mirror, Resha remembered fighting with the female commando, who had seemed a couple of years younger than she.

Resha had knocked the gun out of the bigger girl's hands, but then the girl had caught Resha by surprise and lunged at her, arms flailing wildly as she screamed out curses in Spanish. Resha had grabbed one of the soldier's wrists and held fast, and that's when the girl had used her free hand to scratch Resha.

Resha was ashamed to admit she'd resorted to fighting like a girl herself then, grabbing the soldier's hair and using it to drag her to the ground. Fueled by anger, she'd turned the girl face down and beaten her forehead on the pavement.

That's when she'd seen Daniel take a flying leap and knock down the last guerrilla. She hadn't expected Daniel to have that much fight in him. Resha smiled at the memory, unaware that she'd been the gunman's target.

Satisfied that she'd cleaned the wounds as well as she could, Resha rummaged around in her duffel bag for some clean clothing.

She'd snapped off the flashlight to save the battery, so she couldn't tell what color the clothes were, but she didn't care as long as they were dry. She pulled on some baggy jeans and a T-shirt, leaving her sodden clothes and the towel in the bathtub for now. She'd deal with them in the morning. Right now she just wanted to lie down.

Back in her room, Resha could see the faint outline of Mindy sitting up in her cot and Selena standing beside her.

Great. Selena must have been listening for her return so she and Mindy could ambush her.

"Resha?" It was Mindy's voice. "Did you get Paola? Is she okay?"

Resha stuffed her duffel bag back into its corner. She didn't feel like talking, so she answered tersely, "Yes, we got Paola. No, she's not okay."

"Why not?" Selena demanded. "What's wrong with her?"

Resha glared at Selena for her obtuseness, but the gesture was probably wasted in the darkness. "Her boyfriend is dead, and she spent the night with the creeps who killed him."

"Oh." Mindy sounded chagrined, as if those things hadn't occurred to her.

"I'm tired. I need to sleep," Resha announced bluntly, hoping they would get the hint. She stretched out on her cot.

Selena gave an angry little huff at Resha's refusal to satisfy their curiosity. She vented her disappointment with sarcasm. "What, you're not going to stomp around and pray tonight?"

"I've had enough warfare for tonight." Resha turned her back on them. She heard Selena huff again and return to her own cot.

Then Mindy said softly, "Good night, Resha."

11

Day 10: Tuesday

Antonio was beyond frustrated.

Last night after he and Manny had finally returned from Cordoba, where they had waited for hours to have some roofing supplies released to them, Manny had crawled to his room in exhaustion.

Antonio had stayed up to have a smoke, a habit he kept hidden from Sergio. When the rain started, Antonio took shelter under an overhang of the old classroom, determined to finish his cigarette. As he inhaled the smoke deep into his lungs, he saw Luís' rattletrap truck pulling into the driveway.

Curious what had kept Luís out so late, Antonio extinguished his cigarette and crept closer. Two of the Americans, the skinny Black woman and the big dumb-looking man, climbed out of the back, soaking wet. He was surprised to see that the driver was not Luís, but Sergio. When Antonio saw the passenger, he knew he was in trouble.

Antonio had not bothered going to bed. He prowled in the shadows, smoking, until morning. He waited until all the Americans except Manny left the men's dorm. Glancing around to make sure there were no witnesses, Antonio slipped inside. He went to the only occupied cot and jerked the sheet off the sleeping boy.

Manny sat up groggily, spluttering.

"Get up, *estupido!*" Antonio hissed. "Do you not know what has happened?"

Still half asleep, Manny shook his head with his mouth hanging open.

Antonio fought the urge to knock him off the cot. Instead, he flung the sheet back at Manny with contempt. "Paola is here. Your friends have somehow gotten her back."

"Huh? How?" Manny sounded as stupid as he looked.

"I do not know, but we are in serious trouble." Antonio leaned in close so Manny could see the fury in his eyes. "You should have told me their plans so that I could tell El Tiburon. Your job is to keep us informed."

"But we weren't even here," Manny protested. "I was with you all day driving around. How was I supposed to know they were going to do something?"

Manny had a point, but Antonio was not about to admit it. He remained on the offensive. "Get your lazy self out of that bed and go find out what they are planning now. Maybe if I have some new information for him, Captain Ortega will be more forgiving."

"Okay, Antonio." Manny struggled to untangle his feet from the sheet.

Antonio curled his lip in disgust and walked out.

Manny was starting to think getting involved with Antonio and The Black Eagles hadn't been such a good idea, but he was in too deep to back out now.

He wondered if he should pray – that's what the others would do. But he didn't know how.

Maybe he shouldn't have slept through all those teaching sessions Pastor Jeff gave them.

During breakfast, Jeff was grateful his team didn't interrogate Daniel and Resha. The students seemed to realize the two didn't want to discuss the events of the previous evening.

It must be hard for the young people to curb their curiosity, especially when they couldn't help but see the nasty bruise on the side of Daniel's face and the scratches on Resha's cheek. None of them would be able to concentrate on anything else until some of their curiosity was satisfied.

When they'd finished eating, Jeff asked the students to meet in the sanctuary, where he led them in a prayer thanking God for bringing their four friends back safely, then prayed for Pastor Sergio's family.

After the prayer, Jeff sat on one of two folding chairs he'd placed on the small platform. He invited Daniel to sit in the other chair and give the students a report from last night.

Daniel shot his pastor a reproachful look as he hoisted himself from the front row and joined Jeff.

The young man's weak smile was forced, and his face was drawn and pale. Jeff didn't think Daniel's haggard appearance had anything to do with the beating he'd taken.

The problem with deep thinkers was that they sometimes thought too much. Daniel was definitely a deep thinker. Jeff made a mental note to speak to Daniel in private soon.

Daniel wished Pastor Jeff had asked Resha to give them a report instead of him, since she'd seemed to enjoy herself last night, but she sat in sullen silence. Everyone else was looking at him expectantly.

Sergio and Paola hadn't joined them yet – they were probably waiting until he'd filled the others in before they came in so they wouldn't be bombarded with questions. Resigned, Daniel took a deep breath, then told them what had happened the night before.

"For real?" Jeremy crowed when Daniel was done. "You guys took out five soldiers? All right!"

Jeremy reached over with both hands to do a double high-five.

When Daniel looked away instead of returning the gesture, Jeremy settled for exchanging high fives with Kevin, who was grinning at Daniel like a proud papa.

Daniel didn't feel proud at all.

Hands he had lifted in praise to God on Sunday had been used to pummel God's creation on Monday. He had kicked a man who was down, and his knuckles were bruised from punching another man in the face. He remembered the sound the first man's head had made hitting the wall and the sensation of striking the other soldiers with the rifle, and he felt sick.

Without looking up, he muttered, "Maybe you guys should be congratulating each other, instead, for praying so much. I'm sure the prayer is what did it, not...not what we did."

When Kevin opened his mouth to ask more questions, Daniel held up a hand. "Guys, my throat is still sore from last night. I don't feel like talking any more, okay?"

He returned to his chair on the front row and sat hunched over, making it clear he was through discussing it.

Sergio rapped lightly on his sister's bedroom door for the third time that morning. This time he had brought reinforcements – Matéo stood beside him, peering anxiously at Paola's door.

"Go away, Sergio." Paola's muffled voice came through the door. "I am not feeling well."

"Paola, I know you wish to be alone, but you need to be with your family," Sergio told her. When that produced no reaction, he added, "And your family needs to be with you."

He nodded at Matéo, and the little boy took his cue.

"Paola, please come out. I was so worried about you, and I want to see you to know that you are really safe. Please open the door." He waited a moment, then added plaintively, "I miss you."

Lying face down on the bed, Paola sighed. She wanted nothing more than to stay shut up in her room, alone in the dark with her sorrow and shame. She had no desire to be with anyone, did not want to hear words that would do nothing to ease her pain.

But Matéo had overcome his own terror to get help for her, and she owed him something for that. She thought of her little brother running all night through the dark and unfamiliar jungle to find his way back home, and then leading the others to where she was.

His courage made her ashamed of the way she was hiding. For Matéo's sake, she forced herself to sit up and wiped her eyes. Dragging a hand through her tangled hair, she opened the door.

Matéo rushed in and hugged her. "Paola!"

Sergio gave her a somber nod as she halfheartedly returned her younger brother's hug. "Thank you, Paola. I know this is very difficult for you, but I must ask you to please come with me to the sanctuary. The others are very concerned for you also."

"I will come," Paola said simply. She gave Matéo a final squeeze, took a deep breath, and braced herself to endure one more ordeal.

Resha could understand Daniel's reluctance to celebrate.

While she had no compunction about the pain she'd inflicted on the Black Eagles' flunkies, she recognized the possibility of retaliation. Paola's rescue was surely a blow to the Black Eagles' pride, and they wouldn't take it lying down.

"Okay, now that we're done patting ourselves on the back, what are we going to do to keep the Black Eagles from doing something worse?" Resha said. "These are some bad hombres we're dealing with, and we've ticked them off big time."

Everyone turned and stared at her, speechless at the implications of what she'd said. Finally, Jeremy quipped, "Resha, you sure know how to bring a party down."

"It wasn't a party for Stefan and Paola, was it?" Resha asked, more harshly than she'd intended.

Jeremy looked mortified when he realized how flippant he'd sounded.

Before anyone could respond, Pastor Jeff cleared his throat and cut his eyes toward the doorway. Everyone got quiet when they saw Paola.

If Sergio had not been standing behind her with a protective arm over her shoulders, Paola might have retreated back to her room.

After hearing the Americans' words, Paola was uncertain of her welcome. Did they blame her for the danger they were now in? Did they regret rescuing her?

She could tell they did not know what to say to her now, and that they were trying not to stare at her bruised face.

The next few seconds were awkward. It was Mindy who acted first. She rushed to Paola and hugged her, careful not to hurt the battered woman.

"Oh, Paola, we're so glad you're home!" Mindy cried, gently leading Paola to sit in the chair next to her.

After Mindy had broken the ice, the others added their verbal welcomes, and Paola nodded and smiled back shyly to acknowledge their greetings.

Paola had dreaded having to face anyone, but now, surrounded by other believers, sensing their love and concern, Paola was glad she had come. Her heart was still broken, but her burden felt lighter when she knew it was being shared by her new brothers and sisters in Christ.

She clung to Mindy's hand for strength, and soaked in courage from the brief touch on the shoulder Resha had offered. Releasing the breath she had been holding, she gave Sergio a discreet nod to let him know she was in good hands sitting between the two girls.

Sergio returned the nod, then joined Pastor Jeff on the platform and spoke to the young missionaries.

"First I want to thank all of you for your prayers, and especially you, Daniel and Resha, for your brave actions. My sister is not feeling well, but she wanted to see you all to express her appreciation also."

Sergio sighed before continuing. "We also need to discuss our plans. I have asked Abuelita to keep Matéo occupied at the house so that we can speak freely. As Resha pointed out, Paola is safe for now, but by defying the Black Eagles, we may have put the rest of us in greater danger."

Mindy frowned, worried. "Do you think they'll come here to try to get Paola back again?"

Paola laughed, but it wasn't a happy laugh. "I am not that important to them. But revenge is. If word gets out that two unarmed Christian college students were able to overpower some of their soldiers, the Black Eagles will lose the respect of the people. Since they rule by intimidation, that is unacceptable to them."

"What do you think the Black Eagles will do?" Daniel asked.

"I do not know," Sergio admitted. He sat on the chair next to Jeff's, shoulders slumped. "I fear for your safety. The Black Eagles would not have forgotten their interest in the mission center, but I had hoped that they would wait until you were all gone before they resumed their harassment. Last night's activities changed everything."

The worried students all looked at Pastor Jeff. The American pastor ran a hand down the side of his face, clearly upset.

Even as she struggled with her own grief, Paola felt terrible for the trouble she'd brought on the missionaries. She began to tremble again.

As much as he hated to do it, Jeff felt he had no choice but to abandon the Colombian pastor and his family. "Sergio, we don't want to leave you to face this situation alone, but I'm responsible for the students' safety."

"Of course," Sergio said quickly. "I understand that you must remove them from here as quickly as possible. Do not worry, our God is our Protector."

"God is our Protector, too," Daniel asserted. "I think we should stay and do the work."

Jeremy added, "Yeah, we're almost done, and we'll be leaving in a few days anyway. I think God would want us to finish what we started."

Jeff leaned forward in his chair and pushed his glasses up, kneading his forehead with his fingers. He didn't want to be having this discussion again.

His students were right, but they couldn't know the tremendous pressure he felt to keep them safe. His sense of responsibility battled with his faith, and he felt another headache coming on.

Resha didn't help matters any when she said, "Stefan just gave up his life trying to get Bibles to his friends. I can't believe we're even talking about leaving before we're done just to save our own skin."

Paola's shaky voice added to Jeff's remorse. "Stefan wanted so much for Raul to have the Bibles to give to the people. My heart breaks because he died for nothing. Raul did not get the Bibles."

Kevin shook his head. "Yeah, I don't get why God let them Bibles burn up anyway after He kept 'em from burnin' up in that shed."

Paola looked puzzled and Jeff shot Kevin a cautionary look. According to Matéo, Paola had been taken away before the Black Eagles torched Stefan's car. She didn't need to know that Stefan's body had been further desecrated.

Thankfully, Paola didn't ask Kevin what he meant. "The Bibles were not burned up. That evil man Captain Ortega has them locked up in his office."

"He's got the Bibles?" Daniel stood up in his astonishment, nearly knocking his chair over. Kevin steadied the chair with a foot and watched his friend curiously.

"But why would he have them?" Sergio looked dumbfounded, too.

"I think he had the Bibles brought back just to taunt me, and to make me give him information, but I had none to give him." Paola shivered, as if she was reliving the interrogation. "He also thinks that even if you were not willing to pay for my release, you might be willing to buy the Bibles back, and that when you delivered the Bibles, you would lead them to the others who rebel against their plans."

"I wonder if the Bibles are still there." A thoughtful frown crossed Daniel's face as he slowly lowered himself back into his chair.

"They are probably there." Paola became more agitated as she described her ordeal. "While I was locked in that other horrible room, I could hear some of them talking outside the door. They were to make a large cocaine delivery to someone important that night, and they suspected that a rival gang was going to try to intercept their shipment. They were so distracted that the Bibles are probably forgotten for now. There are people waiting for The Word of God, and the Bibles are just sitting in that horrible, evil place!"

The reminder that Stefan had died in vain seemed to overwhelm Paola.

"Please excuse me," she choked. She got up and hurried from the room.

Mindy started to go after her, but Resha clamped a hand down on her shoulder and forced her back onto the chair.

"She wants to be alone," she hissed, and Mindy nodded meekly.

"You know if the Bibles are still there, we can't just let those creeps have them, right?" Jeremy leaned forward in excitement. "We have to get them back."

Jeff was appalled by the idea, but Sergio wondered, "How?"

"The same way we got Paola back," Daniel said firmly. Obviously he'd already been considering what Jeremy had just voiced.

"You wanna fight them bad guys again?" Kevin asked. Maybe he'd noticed more than he let on while Daniel was talking earlier.

Jeff was struck speechless with disbelief at their suggestion, but the rest seemed to be mulling over the possibility.

Finally, Daniel ventured, "Maybe we won't have to deal with them at all. I don't think they'll be guarding the Bibles the way they did Paola. Matéo showed me the other building where they took her first, and we didn't see anyone standing watch."

"I bet we could do it." Jeremy nodded emphatically.

"So when we goin'?" Kevin wanted to know.

Daniel chewed his lip a moment before deciding, "The sooner we go, the more likely the Bibles will still be there. We should probably go tonight, as soon as it gets dark."

Jeff had been leaning forward in his chair with his head in his hands. Now he leaned back in the chair with his arms folded, his legs stuck straight out in front of him. He rolled his head back to stare at the ceiling and sighed.

Daniel finally seemed to realize that his pastor had not participated in the conversation.

"Pastor Jeff?" he said. "You're awfully quiet."

Jeff didn't move. He spoke with his head still thrown back, which made his voice sound strange. "It sounds to me like you've already made up your minds. Why should I bother to say anything? You never listen to me."

"We always listen to you, Pastor Jeff," Daniel objected, looking troubled.

"Yeah," Jeremy insisted. "We might not do what you say, but we always listen."

Daniel gave Jeremy a dirty look, then turned back to Jeff. "Does that mean you don't think we should try it?"

Jeff sat up straight then, and faced Daniel squarely. "No, Daniel, I don't think you should try it. Do you understand how dangerous this is? It's one thing to take that kind of risk to save Paola's life, but this seems like a foolish gamble. Even last night, you barely escaped. They won't be caught by surprise again, and they'll be out for revenge."

Daniel gnawed his lip some more. "But, Pastor Jeff, if we did it to save someone's life, shouldn't we do it even more to save someone's soul?

What if somebody's salvation is riding on those Bibles, and we have a chance to get them back and we don't take it?"

When Jeff said nothing, Daniel added in a small voice, "Isn't this what 'laying down your life' is?"

So they did listen to him, Jeff thought, just so they could use his own words against him. He threw his hands up in defeat, then crossed his arms and leaned back again to resume his contemplation of the ceiling.

Daniel stared at him. Jeff knew the young man hated arguing, so Daniel must feel strongly about this. Jeff refused to encourage what promised to be a futile and dangerous attempt, though.

Daniel turned to the other pastor. "Pastor Sergio, what do you think?"

Sergio hesitated, studying the floor. Finally he looked up and said, "I cannot say. It would not be fair for me to tell you not to do this thing when I allowed you to risk your lives to save my sister. And it would not be right for me to encourage you to do it against your pastor's advice. I will leave you to work this out for yourselves, but I will pray for you to have God's wisdom, and I will support you no matter what you decide." He stood and left quietly.

"How's that for waffling?" Jeremy cracked. When no one responded, he suggested, "I say we take a vote on it. Majority rules."

Daniel looked surprised by Jeremy's practical suggestion. "That's actually not a bad idea. That way everybody can weigh in."

Jeff closed his eyes, his head still hanging backwards. "Vote among yourselves, then. I'm going to follow Sergio's lead and opt out. It's obviously out of my hands anyway."

Everyone turned to Daniel, looking to him for leadership since Jeff had apparently abdicated. Daniel looked at his mentor again. "Pastor Jeff?"

Jeff remained where he was, but opened one eye and looked sideways at Daniel to show he was listening.

"Would you pray before we vote?" Daniel asked.

Under her breath, Resha muttered, "It's about time."

Jeff had seen the girl's lips moving in prayer since Paola had left. Ashamed of the way he'd been acting, Jeff nodded and leaned forward in his chair, resting his forehead on his clasped hands.

The students quickly bowed their heads.

After a moment, Jeff prayed, "Lord, You know the situation we're facing here, and You know the best way to proceed. I don't want common sense to get in the way of faith, but I don't want us to do something stupid, either. Please speak to the hearts of these young people as they vote on what to do. Let Your will be done here. We ask this in Jesus' Name."

"Amen," Daniel echoed with the rest of the group. He waited silently a couple of minutes to see if anything in him had changed, but he still felt an urgency to get the Bibles back.

More confident now that they'd invited God's input, Daniel addressed the team. "Uh, okay, I guess it's time to vote, then. Who thinks we should go ahead and try and get the Bibles back?"

He raised his own hand and looked around. Jeremy, Kevin, Resha and Mindy had all shot their hands up without hesitation. Already that made a majority, but Daniel wanted to sound the others out in case they saw something he'd missed.

Since Terrell looked uncertain, Daniel addressed him first. "Terrell, you don't think we should go?"

Terrell shrugged. "I'm all for getting the Bibles back, but it seems too risky. I'm not willing to take a chance like that."

"Ain't nobody askin' you to go, man," Kevin grunted. "Me an' Daniel will go."

"And me!" Jeremy wasn't about to be left out.

"In that case, I'm for it." Terrell lifted a hand without much conviction. That left three dissenters.

"Selena?" Daniel turned to Selena, who squirmed uncomfortably under his intense stare, then shook her head emphatically.

"No way. You guys are crazy. Let them keep them. Just get some other Bibles."

Daniel looked pained. "It's not that easy here, Selena, especially after the flood. That missionary, Mr. Novak, said it might be months before they get any more."

"Yeah, it ain't like there's a Walmart around the corner," Kevin reminded her.

"And those poor people really need the Bible now more than ever," Mindy added.

Selena wrapped her arms around herself as if she were cold and shook her head again. "I don't care. It's too dangerous. It's not worth it."

"Okay, so it's a definite 'no' from you, then." Daniel acknowledged her viewpoint, but his heart hadn't been swayed by her objections. "What about you, Samuel?"

Samuel's thick Nigerian accent didn't make his answer less definite. "No, I do not think you should go."

When the Nigerian offered no further comment, Daniel glanced around for the one remaining member of the group, but Manny had disappeared.

When Sergio returned to the house, Paola's door was open. She had pulled the curtains back and sat on the edge of her bed, watching through the window as Matéo helped Abuelita in the small vegetable garden.

Paola looked up and gave a faint smile when Sergio peeked in. "I am all right, Sergio. I needed to be alone, but I am glad I went with you earlier. It was good to be with them for a while."

Sergio nodded and left the room. He would not burden her right now with details of the discussion in the sanctuary. He sat in the small armchair and bowed his head to pray.

Where should he begin? So much had happened in the past weeks. He had lost his family, the mission center had been destroyed, and now his sister had been violated and he had lost a close friend.

His new American friends were helping to rebuild the mission center, and they had returned Paola to him, so Sergio would start with them. He had promised, after all, that he would pray for them.

Sergio prayed for their safety while they remained in Colombia. He prayed that whatever decision they made would be God's will. And finally he prayed for Pastor Jeff, because he could see the toll this was taking on the man he had come to respect greatly in the last week.

As a pastor himself, Sergio could understand how Jeff was torn between trusting God and protecting his flock. He also knew that no matter how uncomfortable Jeff was with his students' plans, he would still support their efforts.

Sergio prayed with more intensity. As he was running out of words, there was a tap on the front door.

Jeremy stood there, the impish grin missing from his face for once.

"Pastor Sergio, the others asked me to let you know that we decided."

Daniel glanced up from another crude map he'd drawn when Jeremy returned to the dining area with an anxious-looking Pastor Sergio in tow.

Jeremy plunked himself down at the table next to Kevin. Pastor Jeff sat at one end of the table, sulking, while Resha sat at the other end looking on with interest. Mindy and Selena fidgeted at the next table. Everyone else had left.

As Sergio approached the table, Daniel indicated the map. "Pastor Sergio, will you drop us off again?"

Sergio bit his lip. "Daniel, you may use the truck and anything else that we have, but I will not leave my sister and Matéo alone here when there is the possibility that the Black Eagles will come."

"I guess I could drive it," Daniel said skeptically, raking a hand through his hair in frustration. So many decisions had to be made. "But then we'll have to leave it parked somewhere while we go and get the Bibles."

"I'll drive you," Pastor Jeff offered, and everyone looked at him in surprise.

Everyone but Sergio. The Colombian pastor gave Jeff a knowing nod and patted him on the shoulder.

Jeff gave a resigned sigh. "Look, I said my piece, we asked God for guidance, and you've decided to go ahead. Since you're going to do it anyway, I might as well do my part."

Daniel should have known Pastor Jeff could never watch his students drive off into a life-threatening situation without getting involved.

Relieved his pastor was on board, however reluctantly, Daniel pointed at a spot on the map. "I think it would be better if we got dropped off here, just to make sure nobody recognizes the truck from last night. We'll have to walk a little farther, but we should be okay."

"That's gonna be a long way to walk back totin' them Bibles, though," Kevin pointed out.

Daniel appreciated Kevin's confidence that they would be carrying the Bibles when they left, but his friend had made a valid point. Daniel scrunched up his nose, trying to figure out a way around that.

Sergio had been rocking back and forth on his heels while they talked, and now he said, "If I may offer a suggestion?"

Daniel nodded. "Please."

"I know that Raul is anxious to get the Bibles, and he will do whatever we ask him. The Black Eagles have not seen Raul's van, so perhaps we could use that to our advantage."

Sergio paused, squinting. Daniel could almost see the wheels spinning in the little man's head.

"Pastor Jeff can drop you off at the place you say, and then he can drive on to Raul's home to let Raul know what is happening. Raul can come back in the van and pick you up closer to the building."

Sergio's hands flew in every direction as he explained his idea. "It will take you some time to walk there, so by the time you have made your way to the building and gotten the Bibles out, he should be there waiting for you and he will take you straight to his home, where you can meet up with Pastor Jeff again."

"That sounds like it might work," Daniel said a bit uncertainly.

"Hey, it's the only plan we've got," Jeremy reminded him. "I say we go with it."

They spent several minutes deciding on where to be dropped off, and then a pick-up point to meet the van. Soon the table was littered with roughly drawn maps, one to show Jeff how to get to Raul's home, one to show Raul where to pick them up after they'd gotten the Bibles, and one more of the building Daniel thought the Bibles would be in.

Their earlier efforts had been discarded as their plans became more cohesive, and crumpled pages were scattered across the floor.

They examined the sketch of the warehouse now, and decided they would have to get through the main door first, then get through the door to Ortega's office down the hall.

Resha frowned as she listened.

Since that was her usual facial expression, Daniel paid no attention to her scowl when he turned to her. "Resha, I think I can figure out how to use that little gizmo you used on the other door. Do you mind if I borrow it for these other two doors?"

"Why make it easier to get caught by trying to jimmy two doors and walk down a hallway?" Resha demanded. "Why not just go directly into the room through the window?"

They stared at her, then Jeremy snapped his fingers and pointed at Resha triumphantly. "See, now, that's what I'm talking about! We just needed somebody to tell us the right way to break in and steal something."

Resha ignored him. "I looked at the windows in that room where they had Paola. The windows where they've got the Bibles will probably be the same. If you take out one pane, you can just reach in and undo the lock. Before we go, I'll show you the best way to break in through one of those windows."

Jeremy and Kevin looked impressed, but Daniel had noticed the way she'd worded her comment. "Before 'we' go?"

"Don't worry, I won't try to be a part of your little raid," Resha assured them. "But I'm riding along with you in the truck. I want to see where the Bibles are going."

"Oh, but you can't be the only girl," Mindy gasped, her eyes wide with horror. "I'll have to go along, too."

"Whatever," Resha muttered.

Daniel wasn't happy with the idea of the two girls going along, but he couldn't very well forbid Resha to come. After all, she'd been instrumental in rescuing Paola, and even now she was giving valuable advice. But Mindy, too?

He looked at Pastor Jeff for help.

Jeff stared back at him, then sighed, stood up, and walked out of the room. The pastor nearly bumped into Paola, who had wandered in again, her hair combed and her face washed.

Paola's eyes widened in surprised when she saw the group gathered there. "Oh. Excuse me. I was only looking for Sergio."

She lowered herself into a chair near Mindy and Selena and glanced curiously at the papers in front of Daniel.

Great. He hoped Paola wasn't going to want to come along, too.

Sergio didn't look too pleased to see Paola, either. He frowned and pressed his lips together for a moment before saying, "Paola, your entrance was timed perfectly. I want you to hear this, also."

He faced the group again. "Now that the rest of the plans have been settled, there is something I need to take care of. I know that Stefan is absent from his body and present with our Lord, but I wish to put his body to rest. Daniel, will you show me where he is?"

That was the last thing Daniel wanted to do, but Stefan deserved a decent burial. Daniel nodded soberly.

Paola stood up and said, "I will go with you."

Behind her back, Daniel caught Sergio's eye and shook his head. He'd seen the Chevy after the Black Eagles had torched it. Paola had been through enough – she didn't need an additional horror imbedded in her memory.

Sergio acknowledged Daniel's signal discreetly with his eyes. "Paola, I need you to stay here and find a good spot to...to bury our dear friend. Get Antonio and Luís to dig the grave so that it will be ready when we return."

When Paola opened her mouth to protest, he added, "When things are back to normal, we will find him a more suitable resting place, but for now, we will keep him close to us here. Please, go and choose the spot."

Reluctantly, Paola acquiesced, going outside to find the workmen. When she left, Sergio asked Abuelita to find a blanket to wrap Stefan's body in.

Remembering the burnt out shell of the Chevy, Daniel didn't know if there would be enough left to wrap. He laid a hand on Sergio's shoulder and advised quietly, so the others wouldn't hear, "Take some gloves, too."

Can this situation get any more out of control? Jeff wondered as he headed to the kitchen to search for an aspirin. He found the first aid kit in a cabinet and rummaged around until he found the small white bottle labeled "*Aspirina*".

Guess they have child-proof caps in Colombia, too, Jeff thought after fighting with the bottle a few minutes. He carried it to the table and sat down to squint at the directions, then gave up and laid his head on the table.

"Lord, things have gotten so out of control. I feel like I'm failing You, and I'm failing them. I'm supposed to be their spiritual leader but they don't listen to me."

After a moment, Jeff smiled ruefully with his nose pressed against the table. "Or am I getting upset because they're listening to You instead of to me? Have I gotten so bogged down with trying to protect these kids that I'm not letting them grow?"

Jeff sighed and sat up in a more conventional prayer position, then continued his one-sided conversation that was somehow two-sided.

"They're not kids, are they, Lord? They're adults who are trying to serve You, and I'm not ready to let them go. Please forgive me if I've been standing in Your way."

"Pastor Jeff?" A timid voice came from the doorway and Jeff looked up to see Jeremy and Kevin hovering anxiously.

Jeff straightened his glasses, wondering how long the boys had been there.

"You a'ight, Pastor?" Kevin asked, his eyes round with worry.

Jeff looked at their concerned young faces and was reminded that God loved them more than he ever could. *Lord, please help me remember that they're not in my hands at all. These kids – excuse me – these adults are in Your Hands. I release them to You.*

"I'm fine, boys." Jeff smiled and stood with confidence. He noticed the bottle of aspirin was still in one hand and shook it. "I had a headache, but it seems to be gone now."

Jeremy and Kevin looked relieved that their pastor was okay.

Then Jeff noticed something was missing. "Where's Daniel?"

"He wit' Pastor Sergio," Kevin told him.

Jeremy hesitantly added, "They went to, uh – they went to pick up Stefan."

Jeff closed his eyes.

Your Hands, Lord. Your Hands.

When the two men returned from their gruesome task an hour later, both were pale and subdued. Pastor Jeff came out to meet the truck, and his eyes found Daniel's briefly before Daniel looked down at the ground.

Luís and Antonio approached and carefully unloaded Stefan's wrapped body while Paola stood by. She made a move as if to uncover the face, to see her beloved one last time, but Sergio took her hands gently to stop her.

Sergio said nothing, so Paola's eyes went to Daniel's, begging more information, but he just looked back at her sadly.

Understanding flooded Paola's face, and with a strength that was not her own, she lifted her chin and allowed the two men to carry Stefan to his resting place.

Soon, Pastor Sergio, Paola and Matéo were standing beside the fresh mound of dirt, which had at its head a wooden cross that had been hastily but lovingly made by Jeremy and Kevin while the others were retrieving the body. Their task completed, Luís and Antonio had left to give the family privacy.

Abuelita stood with Jeff and his team a respectful distance away while the Restrepos said their final goodbyes to a man who should have become a part of the family soon.

Although Jeff knew the sorrow was shared by everyone present, Mindy was the only one who wept openly.

"You should have contacted me as soon as you saw that the woman was back!" Captain Ortega's voice shrieked from the radio Antonio had hidden away.

Antonio had witnessed his comrades being berated enough times that he could picture exactly what his boss was doing. Ortega would be dragging the radio's mouthpiece with him, stomping in angry circles around his desk, causing the radio to slide ever closer to the edge as he screamed and gestured at the radio as if it were a live person.

"Those wretched gringos must pay for making fools of my men. I will hunt them down like the dogs they are." Ortega proceeded to yell out more profanities and insults at his subordinate.

El Tiburon's temper was the very reason Antonio had put off contacting him. When Ortega finally paused in his tirade to catch his breath, Antonio calmly delivered news that might curry favor with his boss again. "You will not need to come here to get your revenge. They will be returning to your headquarters tonight."

Ortega remained silent and Antonio imagined the captain had frozen in his tracks. Finally, Ortega demanded suspiciously, "What for?"

"They want their precious Bibles back." Antonio allowed a mocking tone.

"Hah! Maybe those cursed books will be good for something after all." Ortega laughed. Antonio heard the chair in Ortega's office creak as the volatile captain sat down. "Tell me more."

"There will be three men, including the one who helped take the woman from you."

"Will Sergio be with them?" Ortega asked. "I am eager for an excuse to do something to that annoying pastor."

"I do not believe so." To keep Ortega from dwelling on his disappointment about Sergio, Antonio quickly tossed out another tidbit that should please his boss. "But I know they will be doing it later tonight."

If Ortega recognized Antonio's attempt to distract him, he did not mention it. All El Tiburon said was, "We will be ready for them."

Manny looked around at all the long faces. *Wow, this is really depressing.*

Since Paola had disappeared into the house, Abuelita was on her own in the kitchen, so the students had stayed inside to make it easier for her to serve lunch.

Nobody was eating much, though. Daniel still looked shook up from his earlier jaunt with Sergio, and only managed to choke down three or four spoonfuls of the thin soup.

Even Manny had lost his appetite. He felt bad about Stefan's death, and he was scared somebody would find out he was the one who'd tipped off the Black Eagles that Stefan was delivering the Bibles.

And Antonio kept staring at him, like he thought Manny was going to tattle or something. Manny was glad Samuel and Luis were sitting at the table, too, so he wouldn't be alone with the Colombian man.

His hands were so shaky he dropped his spoon. When he bent over to pick it up, he noticed a crumpled piece of paper under the table. He picked it up just to give himself something to do.

Sitting back in his chair, Manny furtively opened it up. It was a map someone had sketched. When Manny saw the name "Raul" scribbled on it, he realized it was something Antonio would want to have.

For a fleeting moment, Manny considered stuffing the map in his pocket to destroy it later, but he felt Antonio's eyes on him and knew he would have to give it up.

After watching her companions pick at their food for an interminable length of time, Resha pushed her plate aside and stood up. "That's it for me. I'm going to go finish cleaning up around the new framework until it's time to leave."

Looking relieved, the rest of them quickly followed her lead. They stacked their untouched plates in the center of the table with apologies to Abuelita.

Since the two pastors were off praying or something, the students came up with their own assignments. Terrell and Samuel dragged Manny with them to help Luís and Antonio work on the roof of the new storage building. The other three guys stayed in the dining area finalizing their plans for the night's undertaking.

Resha went outside to sweep up the piles of sawdust and stray nails, with Mindy trailing her as usual.

Selena stayed to help Abuelita in the kitchen, but came out a few minutes later, complaining, "Abuelita chased me out."

"You probably got in her way." Resha thrust the broom at Selena to put away, then hauled Luís's heavy toolbox from the cinder block shed to round up some supplies the men would need that night.

Selena leaned the broom in the corner and flapped her arms around. "Well, great. Half of the guys are working on the roof, and the others are going after the Bibles, and you two are going with them. What am I supposed to do?"

Why do they always act like I'm in charge? Resha blew out an aggravated breath. "Why don't you go see if you can help Paola?"

"She doesn't need any help," Selena complained. "Matéo already cleaned the chicken coops for her, and Abuelita cleaned up the kitchen by herself."

"Not that kind of help," Resha snapped, plunking the toolbox onto the ground. Selena gave her a blank look and Resha rolled her eyes. "Just go talk to her. She might need somebody to talk to after what happened to her."

Selena squirmed. "I thought you said she wanted to be alone," she protested.

"She's been alone all morning." Resha squatted beside the toolbox and undid the latches. "By now she's probably going crazy in there all by herself with nothing to do but think. That's why she came in here when the guys were making their plans. She's getting lonely. She could use a friend."

Selena looked disappointed her excuse had been shot down. "I don't know what to say to her. I mean, I like her and all, but what am I supposed to talk about?"

Resha shrugged impatiently. "Nothing. I don't know. Talk about the weather. It doesn't matter. Just be there for her. If she wants to talk about it, you'll know. If not, she'll just be glad someone's there."

"Okay. If you say so." Selena still looked uncertain, but she wandered off to find Paola.

Mindy stood by with a sappy look. "Oh, Resha, you're so sweet to care about Paola."

"Whatever." Resha busied herself poking around in Luís's toolbox.

"You were so determined to rescue her, even when nobody thought you could do it." Mindy stared at Resha, her face scrunched up in intense concentration. After a moment, she murmured, "You know, you're so pretty, but you always hide it. And you're always practicing your self-defense moves. You really don't trust men at all, do you?"

She looked at Resha with sudden understanding. "Resha, did it...did it happen to you?"

Resha examined a screwdriver, discarded it, and kept sorting through the tools.

Mindy stepped closer and asked again, "Resha, were you...raped?"

Resha could hardly pretend she didn't hear Mindy when the girl was right in her face, so she stopped digging and faced her square on. "Yes." She didn't elaborate, and her scowl dared Mindy to ask any questions.

Mindy shuddered, and her eyes brimmed with the tears Resha had never allowed herself to shed over it. "I'm so sorry, Resha. You must have been so scared, and so angry."

She reached over to hug Resha.

Resha shrugged off the hug and the sympathy, going back to the toolbox. "Well, I was hanging around the wrong crowd, and I was hardly the innocent that Paola is. It was still tough for me, but Paola just lost her boyfriend, too. Imagine what she's going through."

"It must be hard on her," Mindy agreed, but her eyes still rested compassionately on the hard-as-nails girl in front of her. "Did they put him in jail?"

"The cops wouldn't have paid any attention to a druggie with a jail record," Resha said scornfully. She picked out a different screwdriver and examined the tip. "I was planning to get my own justice, but I was the one who ended up in jail for B & E before I could shoot that n-..." she caught herself, "...the scumbag."

Resha abruptly slammed the toolbox shut. Mindy, already shocked by Resha's blunt statement, jumped at the sudden bang. Resha saw Mindy's eyes fly open wider, so she tried to soften things by adding, "That's when that group from your dad's church came to the jail and I got saved. It took a while, but I forgave the guy who did it."

Resha secured the latch on the toolbox and walked away before Mindy could ask more questions. She was surprised at herself for sharing so much. She'd never told anyone about it before. She'd been too ashamed, knowing people would blame her for what had happened.

She hadn't even told her mother, because she'd been afraid her mother would either talk her out of killing him, or else she'd do the job herself. Ironically, it had been Mrs. Cummings who turned her in to the police before Resha could carry out her vengeful act.

Living on the streets, Resha had broken into her mother's house and stolen some of her jewelry, intending to trade it in at the pawn shop for a gun. Desperate to get her daughter out of her self-destructive lifestyle, Mrs. Cummings had chosen that time to practice tough love — she reported the burglary to the police and allowed Resha to reap the consequences of her actions.

Her mother hadn't known about Resha's plans for revenge, but God did, and in His mercy, He'd prevented her from spiraling even deeper into sin.

Resha had hated her mother then, screaming out curses and death threats against her as her own body was wracked with the torments of crack withdrawal. She refused to acknowledge her mother when she came to visit the jail, and tore up the cards and letters her mother sent.

Resha blamed her mother for everything that had ever gone wrong in her life, but deep inside, she knew her misery had been caused by her own choices.

For the first time, Resha acknowledged how powerless she really was, and in her self-loathing, she cried out to the God her mother had clung to through all the pain Resha had caused her. God's answer was to send several women from a prison ministry to conduct a service at the institution that held Resha.

When the service ended, Resha had been the only one in her cell block to respond to their invitation to accept Christ. From then on, nothing had been the same.

Two of the women had discipled her as much as prison regulations allowed, and she'd hungrily devoured all the reading material they left for her. She was determined that the woman who would one day leave the prison would not be the same woman who went in.

Resha suspected it was her mother's prayers that brought about the leniency at her trial and her subsequent early release. When she was freed, she'd gone to her mother and pleaded for forgiveness, which Mrs. Cummings willingly gave. In spite of some rough spots as Resha learned to walk in her new life, the two of them had made peace with each other, and were now closer than ever.

Resha's mother still didn't know about the assault, though, and here she was spilling her guts to a girl she'd only seen in passing until just over a week ago. Even though Mindy was an airhead, her compassion was so genuine that Resha had opened up more than she'd intended. In spite of all of Mindy's drivel with Selena, Resha trusted her to be discreet about something this personal.

In a strange way, Mindy was becoming a friend.

Following Resha's strongly worded advice, Kevin and Jeremy pawed through their clothes, looking for something dark to wear.

Jeremy yanked his black Tweety Bird T-shirt from his backpack and turned it inside out, then held it against him to see if it would work. Tweety's bright yellow face still showed through, so he discarded the shirt and dug some more.

Daniel dragged a dark green T-shirt over his head.

"You have to borrow clothes from Terrell now?" Jeremy teased. "Where's your dark blue shirt?"

"You mean the one you nearly burned up? With me in it?" asked Daniel testily.

Jeremy looked penitent for half a second, then grinned. "That's the one."

"I let Paola use it last night, and I have no idea what happened to it after that," Daniel sighed, letting himself sit heavily on his cot.

The others sobered at the reminder of what had happened to their new friends.

Daniel hated to think he might be leading Kevin and Jeremy into danger. "This is something I have to do, but you guys don't have to come, you know."

"Hey, you're not getting rid of us that easily, Boss Man." Jeremy buttoned a wrinkled dark gray shirt he'd tugged from the bottom of his bag. "Why should you and Resha have all the fun?"

Fun? Daniel stared at Jeremy, feeling even more uneasy about them going. Were they just in it for the adventure?

When Daniel didn't smile at Jeremy's remark, Kevin looked at him curiously. "Whassup, man? You was all fired up a lil' while ago."

Daniel considered his words carefully, not wanting to insult them by questioning their motives.

"I guess I'm nervous because Pastor Jeff doesn't want us to go," he admitted, which was true, anyway. "I don't want to just ignore his warnings unless it's really God telling us to go."

"Pastor Jeff worries too much," Jeremy said dismissively. His voice trailed off as he added, "There are some things he can't protect us from."

The last comment seemed out of character, and Daniel and Kevin exchanged puzzled looks.

Before Daniel could ask him about it, Jeremy plunked himself onto his own cot across from him. "Come on, Dude, Pastor Jeff would be the first one to remind us that 'we ought to obey God rather than man,' right? If God's telling us to go, we can't let Pastor Jeff talk us out of it. You know he's an old worrywart."

Kevin sat next to Jeremy and added, "It just ain't no coincidence that them Bibles nearly got burned up twice. The devil be fightin' this, he don't want them people to get The Word. But God didn't let them Bibles burn. He musta saved 'em for a reason. We got to do this, man."

Jeremy leaned forward, his face serious. "Did you ever stop to think that maybe this was the whole reason we're here? That maybe God brought us to Colombia just so we could get those Bibles back?"

Reassured by their sincerity, Daniel silently thanked God for friends who were sold out to Christ. He grinned at them and stood up.

"Well, let's do it, then."

With Mindy at her heels, Resha strode into the dining area to find Daniel, Jeremy and Kevin. The two pastors were with them. She noted with satisfaction that the three young men wore dark clothing.

She plopped a small leather bag on the table in front of them. All three watched inquisitively as Resha assembled a flathead screwdriver, a small rubber mallet, and a roll of duct tape on the table.

"Okay, first you have to decide how quiet you need to be. I saw a generator last night, but it wasn't running. If it's running, the sound from the motor will cover up a lot of noise, so you should be able to just knock out a pane of glass close to the lock with this." Resha held up the rubber mallet.

"If you want to be more quiet, just crisscross some strips of duct tape across the window first, four or five pieces, and it won't make as much noise when you hit it. If you really need to be quiet, and you have enough time, you can dig out the caulking around the window pane with that screwdriver. The caulking looked all loose and cracked, so it shouldn't be too hard, it'll just take a while. Once you get that pane out, you can just reach in and get to the latch."

The three guys stared at Resha.

"You got street smarts," Kevin grunted in admiration.

"And you can say more than one sentence at a time," Jeremy teased.

Uncomfortable being the focus of so much attention, Resha narrowed her eyes at Daniel and made him repeat the instructions back to her. With a vague smile on his face, he dutifully recited the directions without error.

Resha nodded her approval and swept the items back into the pouch. She handed the pouch to Daniel and he clipped it to his belt.

Pastor Sergio was solemn. "There is nothing left now but to pray for you before you go."

Resha and Mindy stood by in respectful silence while the three young men bowed their heads. Sergio and Pastor Jeff laid their hands on each of their shoulders, and Sergio began praying for each of them by name.

For Daniel, Sergio requested wisdom and strength to lead their operation. For Kevin, he pleaded for courage and protection. When he got to Jeremy, Sergio paused.

Curious, Resha stilled her own silent prayers.

Jeremy raised his eyes and the two men made eye contact for several moments, as if some communication was passing between them. Then Jeremy tilted his chin up resolutely, and Sergio squeezed Jeremy's shoulder. He quickly closed the prayer by thanking God for the students' willingness to do this. If the others had noticed the exchange, no one commented.

They all stood in silence for a moment.

Then Pastor Jeff squared his shoulders. "Shall we go?"

As Sergio followed his American friends outside, he saw Selena leave his house and head toward the girls' room. A moment later, Paola limped outside, too. It grieved Sergio to see how much his pretty sister had aged overnight.

She came to stand beside Sergio and watched the four men and the two young women walk across the compound to the truck. "Where are they going? It is almost dark."

Sergio hesitated, studying the dark circles under eyes swollen from crying. After a moment, he decided she deserved to know. "They are going to go back to Ortega's headquarters. They hope to get back the Bibles that Stefan wanted Raul to have."

Paola nodded slowly, soaking in the information. Suddenly her eyes flew open. "Sergio, I could hear everything that was going on while I was their prisoner, so I know what happened last night. The soldiers they fought with were young people that the Black Eagles forced to join them a short time ago. They were inexperienced and not as committed to their cause yet. Captain Ortega was not expecting any trouble, so he left only those recent recruits behind while he and his seasoned men went to do their business."

Sergio was troubled. "So this means..." he prompted.

"If they go back and try to get the Bibles tonight, the soldiers who murdered Stefan will be there, those who are experienced and trained to kill. These young Americans will not stand a chance."

Sergio groaned but made no move to call the others back.

"Should we not let them know?" Paola asked frantically as the six people boarded the truck that would take them into enemy territory.

Sergio closed his eyes, searching his heart for wisdom. After a moment, he opened them again, saddened by the answer he found. "We have prayed and asked God for direction. They feel this is what He wants them to do. It is in His Hands now."

"Ride up front with me, Daniel," Pastor Jeff suggested.

Daniel glanced at his friends, then got into the cab with Jeff, bracing himself for a lecture. Jeff was probably still upset that they were doing this against his advice.

Sure enough, when they had driven about half a mile, Jeff said, "You know I wasn't happy about you and your friends taking this risk."

Here we go, thought Daniel. He opened his mouth to apologize, but Jeff held up a hand and continued.

"I've been praying about it, and I want you to know that I understand this is something you feel God wants you to do. I want you to know I'm behind you on this."

Surprised, Daniel said, "Thanks, Pastor Jeff. That means a lot to me."

Jeff wasn't done, though. "But something else is obviously bothering you, Daniel. What's going on with you?"

Daniel shrugged and stared at his fingernails. He'd been on edge since his fight with the soldiers, and had had nightmares about Stefan's charred body, but he thought he'd hidden his anxiety. How did Pastor Jeff always know when something was up?

"Daniel, you don't have to do this," Jeff said, without a hint of condemnation. "If any of you has any misgivings at all about going tonight, we'll cancel this right now. No one will blame you."

"It's not that." Daniel turned to face his pastor. Tempted though he was by Jeff's offer, he couldn't let his fear keep him from obeying God. "I know this is the right thing to do. Just like it was right to get Paola back."

"Well, then....?"

Daniel turned away again to hide his distress. After a moment, he said in a small voice, "They were so young, Pastor Jeff. Those soldiers were just kids."

"So are you," Jeff muttered, more to himself than to Daniel. He pounded the steering wheel. "Even if I'm not supposed to believe that. You shouldn't be dealing with all this."

Daniel frowned, confused. His pastor seemed to be having an argument with himself.

With an effort, Jeff got back on track. "They were 'kids' with guns. They murdered Stefan, they kidnapped and...well, they kidnapped Paola, and they would have killed all of you without a second thought."

Daniel struggled with his own thoughts for a moment. He needed to snap out of this before starting another dangerous mission. Finally, he admitted, "I've never really been in a fight before. I mean besides messing around with Kevin and Jeremy. I didn't plan on doing what I did. I didn't even know I had it in me to hurt another person like that. I – I...."

Daniel broke off and stared at his hands. It almost seemed they no longer belonged to him.

Jeff's voice was calm again. "Have you considered that maybe God gave you the ability to do what you did?"

Daniel blinked. No, it hadn't occurred to him. He glanced at the group in back and gave a half smile. "Resha thinks He gave her the ability to clobber that one guy. She called herself God's 'instrument of vengeance.'"

They both laughed softly at the girl's audacity. Then Jeff asked, "What did David do to Goliath in the book of First Samuel?"

Daniel wrinkled his nose, then allowed a crooked smile. "He drilled through his forehead with a rock, then cut off his head."

"Pretty violent, huh? Who gave David the ability to do that?" Jeff pressed.

Frowning, Daniel tried to remember the exact words from the passage. "Umn, he said he came against Goliath in the Name of the Lord, and that the Lord would deliver Goliath into his hand. So I guess God gave him the ability. But that's David. I mean, Goliath was fighting against God's people."

"Isn't Paola one of God's people?"

Unconvinced, Daniel didn't respond.

Jeff tried another line of questioning. "Daniel, why did you fight with those soldiers?"

Surprised, Daniel stated the obvious. "So we could rescue Paola."

Jeff nodded. "Paola told me you also tackled one that was about to shoot Resha."

Daniel made a noncommittal sound.

Jeff treated it as an affirmative answer. "Do you think God wanted Paola to be kept prisoner, at the mercy of those men? Do you think God wanted Resha to get shot?"

"No!" Daniel blurted, then added with less confidence, "So you think God actually wanted me to...to hurt those people?"

"I can't answer that for you, son," Jeff admitted. He slipped a worn thinline Bible from his shirt pocket and handed it to Daniel. "Look up Jeremiah 22:3."

Daniel found the passage easily and read out loud. "'Thus says the Lord; Execute judgment and righteousness, and deliver the spoiled out of the hand of the oppressor: and do no wrong, do no violence to the stranger, the fatherless, nor the widow, neither shed innocent blood in this place.'"

He looked at Jeff reproachfully. "That's supposed to help?"

"Well, I'd forgotten about that second part," Jeff admitted with a rueful smile. "But their blood is hardly innocent. My point was, according to that first part, God expects us to do what we can to correct injustice. You need to read what God says to Cyrus in Jeremiah 51...I think it starts in verse 20, when He's using Cyrus to carry out His justice on Babylon."

Daniel found the passage and read, "'You are my battle axe and weapons of war: for with you I will break in pieces the nations, and with you I will destroy kingdoms; and with you I will break in pieces the horse and his rider; and with you I will break in pieces the chariot and his rider; with you I will also break in pieces man and woman; and with you I will break in pieces old and young; and with you I will break in pieces the young man and the maid...'" Daniel looked up at Jeff. "Okay, I see your point, but this is Old Testament."

"Does God's character change?" Jeff challenged. When Daniel shook his head, Jeff continued, "God still hates injustice, God still wants us to fight for the weak. You want New Testament? How about..." Jeff thought for a moment, then suggested, "Matthew 10:34?"

"I know that one." Daniel smiled. "That's were Jesus said He didn't come to bring peace, but a sword, right? But I'm not sure He meant literally a sword, and anyway, that's Jesus, not us."

"Aren't we supposed to be like Jesus?"

Daniel considered Jeff's words. "Are you telling me that God thought it was okay for me to do what I did? That the end justifies the means?"

"That's something you need to discuss with God," Jeff conceded. "You know I don't advocate violence. But the book of Ecclesiastes says there's a time for war. I'm asking you to consider the probability that God wanted Paola to be rescued, and that God wanted Resha's life spared, and if that's what it took to do it...." He let the words trail off.

Daniel wasn't ready to admit to Jeff that the thing that bothered him most was the rage he'd felt when he saw Paola's battered face, and when he saw the soldier aiming the gun at Resha. He hoped it was righteous anger that had gripped him, but he wasn't sure.

He looked down and pondered the verses some more while Jeff drove.

In back, Resha, Kevin, and Jeremy watched the exchange curiously while Mindy gushed about how wonderful it was that they were going to retrieve the Bibles.

After a while, Kevin asked, "What you think they talkin' about?"

Jeremy wiggled his eyebrows. "Maybe he's finally getting saved."

Kevin snickered. "Which one, Daniel or Pastor Jeff?"

They both burst out laughing.

Mindy gaped at them. "I thought both of them were already saved!"

That made them laugh even harder.

Resha ignored them all and stared stoically at the passing scenery. She had a pretty good idea what the men in the truck were discussing. She'd seen Daniel's face last night when he'd looked back at his handiwork. The marshmallow.

After a while, Daniel handed the Bible back to Jeff, knowing he and God would have to talk about it some more later on.

"Thanks, Pastor Jeff," he said. "That helps a little. I'll think about it."

Jeff pulled the car over to the edge of the road and said quietly, "We're here."

Daniel climbed from the truck while Kevin and Jeremy jumped out of the back, dragging some thick canvas sacks with them. They handed one of the empty bags to Daniel.

"Raul should be here with the van in two hours," Pastor Jeff reminded them. "That should be enough time for you to walk there and do what you have to do. Daniel, I think you saw the van when you went with Stefan. It's a rusted blue Ford van, with one of the doors painted gray."

All three of them nodded, eager to be on their way.

Mindy scrambled out of the truck and gave each of them a quick, watery hug. "You guys be careful, okay?"

"We'll be praying for you," Jeff promised when Mindy crawled back into the truck next to Resha, who said nothing.

Resha's eyes locked on Daniel's as Jeff reluctantly pulled the truck away.

The three flitted through the trees, staying in the shadows in case a vehicle came down the road. When they finally made it to the town, they crouched behind ruined cars and hugged the walls to avoid being seen.

But there was no one around to see them. That worried Daniel.

When he stopped abruptly before rounding a corner, Jeremy nearly walked into him.

"What are you doing?" Jeremy hissed.

Daniel held a hand up for silence, looking around nervously. "I don't know. It feels...different."

"What you mean, diff'rent?" Kevin grunted.

Daniel tried to put his finger on it, but words of description failed him. How could he explain that the whole atmosphere seemed more oppressive and sinister somehow? He finally pointed to the only tangible difference he could discern.

"There's no people, for one thing. When Resha and I came, there were a few people around, like normal people, at least until we got close to Ortega's hideout. Now there's nobody. It's almost like they're hiding or something."

Behind him, Jeremy shuddered involuntarily, as if he sensed for a moment the same heaviness Daniel was feeling. Then he shrugged it off and hummed the theme from "Twilight Zone."

Kevin snickered. "So we gonna keep goin', or what?"

"We'll keep going," Daniel said firmly, and the three continued their stealthy trek.

When the building came into sight, the three of them looked up and down the street. Still seeing no one, they quickly crossed the road and started peeking in the most likely windows. From somewhere behind the buildings came the grinding hum of a large generator.

"This must be it," Daniel whispered as he peered through the grime-covered glass at a rusted desk and chair. A radio like Sergio's was on the desk, and there were boxes stacked against the walls. In one corner was what appeared to be a pile of books on the floor with a dirty blanket thrown over them. "I think I see the Bibles in there."

The other two peered over his shoulder.

"What are we waiting for, dude?" Jeremy nudged Daniel. "Let's go get 'em!"

Even with the noise of the generator to cover their activities, Daniel wanted to be as quiet as possible. Kevin and Jeremy kept watch while Daniel carefully chipped away at the rotting caulking.

Resha's technique worked surprisingly well, and within minutes, they had slipped the pane of glass out and Daniel reached in to work the latch.

The latch was painted stuck, so he used the screwdriver to loosen it. He managed to free the latch, but when he tried to raise the window, the swollen wood was stuck fast from the humidity and years of disuse.

Impatient, Kevin jiggled the window back and forth, causing chips of paint to rain down on them.

"Careful, Kevin, you're going to make too much noise," Daniel warned. He pressed at the edges, which made faint cracking sounds as the paint began to give. Finally, he was able to force the window up enough for them to crawl into the room.

With a final glance up and down the street, they dropped one by one into El Tiburon's lair.

The first one in, Jeremy whipped the blanket off the stack of books with a flourish.

It was the Bibles.

The Spanish Bibles were piled haphazardly, as if they'd been dumped there in a hurry, but to Daniel, it was almost as if the Holy Books glowed, a light in the oppressive darkness around them.

The three friends stared in awe at the stacks of Bibles, wearing stupid grins, forgetting for a moment the danger.

Kevin whistled quietly. "Man, can you believe they're really here?"

Daniel snapped out of it first. "Okay, start grabbing them."

He quickly stuffed a handful into his canvas sack. The others wasted no time in joining him.

They had filled two sacks and had just started on the third when Daniel's head snapped up. He cocked his head, listening intently for a sound it should have been impossible for him to hear over the loud hum of the generator outside. He whispered frantically, "Listen, did you hear that?"

The others froze to listen. Faint, stealthy footsteps approached from the end of the hallway, and it sounded like more than one person.

"Oh, man, somebody's comin'!" muttered Kevin, eyes bulging.

Jeremy made a face. "Uh, oh."

Daniel hurried to the window, hauling a filled sack with him. "Come on, guys, it's time to go!"

He hurled the sack through the opening and climbed after it.

Kevin handed another heavy sack up to Daniel, then pulled himself up and out with Daniel's help. Jeremy hesitated, looking at the small pile of Bibles remaining on the floor.

"Leave them!" Daniel hissed, feeling exposed out on the dark street. He reached back in to offer Jeremy a hand up. "We have to go now!"

Jeremy slipped away from Daniel's grasp, scooped up a handful of Bibles and stuffed them into his bag. "There's only a couple left."

Standing on the street, Kevin glanced around nervously. "Come on, man, we should go."

As the footsteps reached the door, Jeremy grabbed the last few Bibles and clambered through the window, stuffing them into the bag as he went. Daniel and Kevin each grabbed an arm to pull him the rest of the way up as several armed men burst into the room, yelling and rushing toward the window.

"Go!" Daniel yelled, and the three started running.

Instinctively, Daniel spun around as he ran and swung his heavy bag against the window, shattering it. The weight of it nearly dragged him down, but his action had the desired effect. The spray of glass made the soldiers stand back in surprise, throwing their hands up to shield their faces from the flying shards.

Sorry, God. Daniel thought, struggling to regain his balance as he shifted the bag on his shoulder. Your Word's a sword, though, right?

Daniel's distraction had bought them a few precious seconds.

Thankfully, they had also gained a slight head start by being at street level – the gunmen had to go around to the front door or climb through the window before they could give pursuit.

The moonlight reflected eerily from the rain slicked street, and they slipped and slid as they ran, but they refused to drop their precious loads.

Rapid gunfire from automatic weapons shattered the night, giving impetus to the friends' flight.

These men weren't carrying rifles like the soldiers from the previous night, Daniel realized, but automatic weapons that spat out several rounds at once.

Jeremy lagged a few steps behind, trying to get a better grip on his partially filled sack. Daniel turned back to urge him to hurry.

At the same moment, Jeremy gave a small cry and Daniel saw him hit the ground.

Through the sound of rapid gunfire and his own pounding heart, Kevin heard a surprised cry behind him.

"No!" He started to turn back, but Daniel spun him around before he could see anything.

"Keep going!" Daniel yelled, propelling Kevin forward with his free arm.

"But Jeremy..." Kevin started to protest.

"We'll get him later. Move! Move!"

The adobe wall a few inches behind them shattered from the gunfire, convincing Kevin to obey. He stumbled and would have slammed into the ground if Daniel hadn't gripped his shoulder to steady him.

A slash of red appeared on Daniel's arm. Daniel winced but didn't stop.

Kevin ran as fast as his load allowed, ducking low to avoid the gunfire.

The men chasing them started to fall back, and Kevin thought the soldiers had given up. Then the sound of a car engine rumbled over the droning of the generator.

Aw, man, now they're huntin' us in a jeep!

Daniel led the way, dodging between parked cars.

A shiny, black truck appeared at the other end of the road, so now they were blocked on either side. The two froze only a second before plunging out into the open to reach an unlit side street.

Their dark clothing made them harder to spot, but the Black Eagles kept firing in their general direction. They managed to keep just out of range of the gunfire, running with the ground exploding inches away from their flying feet.

Sucking wind, Kevin zigzagged down a narrow alley behind Daniel, hoping they hadn't been spotted. The detour worked – the jeep sped past the opening, the driver momentarily confused. They stopped for a few seconds to allow it to pass, gasping for air.

"I...can't...carry this thing...no more," Kevin panted, letting the bag of Bibles drag on the ground.

Daniel nodded and reached for the bag. "Give it to me."

Kevin stared at Daniel.

Blood ran down Daniel's upper arm, and his breathing was as ragged as Kevin's, but he had refused to lose his grip on his own bag of Bibles.

Kevin set his jaw and shook his head. "Forget it, man, let's just keep goin'."

He threw the bag back over his shoulder.

Blocking out the horror of what he'd seen, Daniel headed for the opening on the other end of the alley and peered into the street. He didn't see what he was hoping for.

"Where's the van?" Kevin demanded, looking up and down the empty street as they emerged.

"Don't know," Daniel admitted nervously. "I got turned around back there."

The black pickup appeared around the corner and they started running again, back into the alley the same way they had come. When they came out on the other side, the jeep had passed. Daniel whipped his head from side to side, looking for a familiar landmark.

"This way." He sprinted forward with Kevin beside him. They turned down another street, ready to drop from exhaustion but too terrified to stop moving.

Relief washed over Daniel when he recognized the rusted blue van he'd seen at Raul's house, but it was driving away. The driver had probably seen the military vehicles and gotten spooked.

Panicked, Daniel ran after the van.

The driver must have spotted them, because the van stopped and began backing towards them. Thankful, Daniel forced his burning lungs to keep pulling in air, forced his rubbery legs to keep working.

When they reached the van, the back doors opened and a pair of hands reached out to help. Daniel hurled his bag through the doors, then shoved Kevin in, sack and all. He banged on the door as he hauled himself in, yelling, "Let's go, let's go!"

The van jolted forward, but the tall man who had opened the door lingered in the doorway of the careening van, clinging to the door handle to keep from being thrown out. "Are there not three?"

Pain crossed Daniel's face. "No," was all he said. He bent over, hands on his knees, trying to catch his breath.

The man nodded soberly, closing the doors. "I am Raul," he said, peering more closely at Daniel. "You are hit."

Daniel glanced down in surprise at his bleeding arm. Raul worked his way toward the front of the speeding vehicle and began rummaging through the glove box. There was a bench on one side of the van, and Daniel sank down onto it, gasping for breath.

Kevin had already slid to the floor across from him and was also panting heavily. He had listened to the brief exchange between Daniel and Raul, and he now glared at Daniel with resentment.

"We ain't goin' back for him, are we?" Kevin demanded accusingly.

Daniel closed his eyes and gave an almost imperceptible shake of his head.

Kevin stood up and yelled, "We shouldn't have left him!"

His outburst startled the driver, who glanced back at them warily. A word from Raul seemed to calm the driver, and he drove on without comment.

Daniel stared up at Kevin with hollow eyes. "It was too late, Kevin. He was already dead."

"How do you know?" Kevin's voice was angry, but Daniel knew he was just grasping for hope. "Maybe they're just holding him prisoner like they did Paola. You don't know he's dead!"

Daniel buried his face in his hands, trying to shut out the images. His friend being spun around by the impact of the bullets before he fell.

Jeremy sprawled on the ground, his blood soaking the scattered Bibles in a rapidly spreading pool. The terrorist laughing as he kicked the Bibles aside, then emptied another round into Jeremy's lifeless body.

Finally Daniel looked back up at Kevin, laying bare his anguish.

"I know, okay?" he managed to whisper.

Kevin stared at him a moment longer, as if reading the story in Daniel's face, then he whirled away and slammed his fist into the side of the van, causing the driver to look uneasily at him again.

Daniel sighed heavily. "Look, Kevin, Jeremy knew the risk we were taking. We all knew."

Kevin didn't look at him, but glared unseeingly at the wall of the van, swaying as the van made another fast turn.

"Was it worth it?" Kevin gestured angrily at the two bags of Bibles they had managed to escape with. The bags that had seemed so bulky and heavy moments ago now looked puny and pathetic.

Daniel stared at the sacks but said nothing. His entire arm was starting to throb now that the adrenaline was wearing off, and he absently clutched it as the van wove through a seemingly endless maze of side streets. He barely noticed the blood oozing through his fingers.

A few minutes later, Kevin slid down to the floor across from Daniel again. Still refusing to face his friend, he asked through clenched teeth, "How's your arm?"

Daniel accepted the olive branch for what it was. "Hurts, but I think it'll be okay."

Kevin nodded and returned to his brooding silence as Raul climbed back over the seats with a wad of semi-clean napkins in his hand.

He reached forward to clean Daniel's injury, but Daniel held up a hand to stop him, not wanting to feel someone's comforting touch when his friend lay dead in the street.

Raul studied him for a moment, then nodded in understanding and set the napkins on the seat beside Daniel. He said nothing as he made his way back to the front seat of the speeding van.

Daniel grimaced as he peeled back his bloody sleeve and pressed the napkins against his wound, but the physical pain was a welcome distraction from the anguish he felt inside.

Dropping into the seat beside his brother Javier, Raul glanced out the window and felt his heart drop. A military jeep carrying three men rounded the corner at breakneck speed. A shiny black Ram pulled alongside the jeep, both vehicles gaining rapidly.

Javier must have seen it, too. The old van didn't stand a chance of outrunning the other vehicles, but Javier floored it anyway, causing the engine to whine in protest.

The truck and the jeep pursued them briefly, the black truck looming in the rear view mirror, the soldiers in the jeep standing with guns at the ready. The driver of the jeep had a walkie talkie pressed to his ear.

Just when Raul was bracing himself for the gunfire, their pursuers abruptly dropped back. The men in the jeep lowered their weapons and simply watched them drive away.

Raul and Javier exchanged troubled glances. Why did the Black Eagles stop following? It was as if they felt no need to give chase.

That was an unsettling thought.

Jeff was waiting outside with Resha and Mindy as the van pulled into the small dirt driveway behind Raul's house. Relieved that the van had returned right on schedule, Jeff yanked the back doors open almost before the van came to a stop, expecting to see an exuberant trio celebrating their victory. What he saw instead stunned him.

A shaken Kevin sat on the bench, supporting Daniel. Daniel's face was gray, and he looked barely conscious.

"I had to hold 'im up," Kevin explained inanely. "He kept passin' out."

That's when Jeff looked down and saw that Daniel's left side was drenched in blood. His gaze swept the inside of the van frantically. "Jeremy?"

Kevin's voice came more strongly now. "Those bastards shot 'im! They killed Jeremy!"

No one noticed the swear word this time.

Behind Jeff, Mindy let out a little cry and clapped a hand over her mouth, tears already forming. Resha closed her eyes but said nothing.

Jeff groaned and ran his hand over his eyes. This can't be real, he pleaded silently. Please, not this.

But when he uncovered his eyes, he was still in the nightmare and Kevin was still propping Daniel up in a pool of blood.

Mindy pushed past Jeff and stood inside the van staring at the men. "Oh! He's lost too much blood! He needs to go to the hospital!"

Raul had climbed from the van and stood beside Jeff. He spread his hands in apology. "Señorita, if there were hospitals in operation, we would have taken him there. The nearest open facility is fifty miles from here, and the road to get there has been impassable since the flood. There are no medical facilities functioning in this area."

"Well, then, we have to get him inside!" Mindy exclaimed.

Resha poked her head in beside Mindy, took one look at Daniel, then turned and ran into the house. Jeff wondered if the sight of so much blood had made Resha sick, but when Raul and Javier carried Daniel inside, Jeff saw her tossing things off the worn, sagging sofa to make room for Daniel as she called out orders in Spanish to a frightened looking little woman.

As the men lowered Daniel onto the sofa, Jeff guided Kevin to a rickety wooden chair. Kevin just stared straight ahead, clearly in shock.

In shock himself, Jeff stood torn between comforting Kevin and going to Daniel's side.

He watched Mindy and Resha doctoring Daniel and decided Daniel was in good hands. Taking care of him was probably the girls' way of coping with the tragedy, and they seemed to know what they were doing.

He left Daniel's physical wound to Resha and Mindy and set about trying to help with Kevin's emotional crisis. That was going to be difficult, because his own emotions were ricocheting between grief, fear, and guilt.

Oh, God, he prayed as he sat in a chair next to Kevin, *This young man needs help, but I'm just as torn up as he is. Help me know what to say.*

"We have to stop the bleeding." Mindy tugged ineffectively at Daniel's T-shirt, her fingers made clumsy by panic.

"Here, let me." Resha pulled her switchblade from her pocket and skillfully sliced the sleeve open to expose the wound.

The woman Resha had commandeered brought a blanket and a damp towel. Mindy used the towel to wipe the blood off the wound and peered at Daniel's arm closely.

"Bullet go through or is it still in there?" Resha asked casually as she draped the threadbare blanket over Daniel's legs.

Mindy prodded at Daniel's shoulder with the towel. "Hard to say without an X-ray. I think it went through, but the skin is so shredded and there's so much blood I can't really tell...probably hit an artery or something..."

Her words drifted off as the severity of his wound registered. She pressed the towel firmly against Daniel's upper arm to try to staunch the bleeding. He moaned, but Mindy kept the towel in place.

Someone handed Resha a brown bottle. She opened it and peered in, then showed it to Mindy.

"Oh, goody, hydrogen peroxide!" Mindy cried, delighted.

She was so glad Resha was here to help. Mindy was used to taking care of people at the hospital she worked at, but she didn't have any equipment or bandages or anything here.

The lack didn't seem to bother Resha. She'd hustled the little Colombian lady off again, and now the woman came back with a glass half-filled with what looked like watered-down orange juice. Resha took the glass and sniffed at it.

"The Colombian equivalent of Tang, I think." She handed Mindy the glass.

"Perfect! Lots of sugar, I hope." Mindy was grateful, even if it wasn't ideal. Really, Daniel needed an IV, but giving him liquids was the best she could do here. "Here, Daniel, drink this."

Resha stepped closer to keep pressure on the wound with the towel, allowing Mindy to stuff the sofa's cushions under Daniel's head to prop him up. When Mindy placed the glass against his lips, he spluttered and his eyes came open weakly.

"Drink," Mindy urged again. "You need to replace some fluids."

She didn't think Daniel had swallowed any, but at least it moistened his cracked lips. She kept his head propped up and tipped the glass again, chattering the whole time. "This smells really good. Go ahead and try to take a little sip, Sweetie, so you can get your strength back."

Mindy was talking to distract Daniel, but it didn't look like he understood what was happening anyway. His eyes weren't focusing and his forehead was cold and clammy. Maybe she should stop trying to make him more alert right now – unconsciousness would probably be a blessing.

Resha let up the pressure on the wound and stepped back. "Bleeding seems to be slowing down."

Mindy swabbed on some liquid from the brown bottle, another medical no no. But how else could she clean it without clean running water? "We'll need to find something to use as a bandage."

Resha translated for the woman who had brought her the towel and the peroxide. Glancing at Daniel's pained expression, Mindy added, "Oh, and something for the pain."

Standing nearby, Raul timidly offered them a bottle of aspirin.

Resha waved him away. "Not aspirin. Makes the bleeding worse. See if there's any Tylenol."

The man nodded and wandered off to search for the requested item. Mindy looked at Resha curiously. "You know something about first aid."

Resha shrugged. "Hospitals call the police for gunshot wounds and stab wounds. I've had to patch up a few of my friends at my place."

Mindy nodded solemnly, saddened by the nonchalant way Resha spoke of her troubled past.

"What about you?" Resha asked, reaching over to brush back Daniel's wayward hair. "You look like you know what you're doing here."

"I hope so," Mindy smiled. "I'm in nursing school, and I'm doing my internship at a pediatrics ward. I've seen kids come in with much worse than this!" Then she sobered. "Of course, there we have running water and the right medicines and equipment and stuff...."

Kevin sat frozen in his chair, staring at the ground, one elbow resting on the table. He didn't look up when Jeff pulled up a chair next to him.

Jeff stared at the reddish brown stains on Kevin's clothes. "Are you hurt, too?"

Kevin glanced down at his shirt without interest. "Nah. That's Daniel's blood." After a moment, he asked, "Is Daniel gonna die, too?"

"I don't think so, Kevin. It looks like a shoulder wound. Most people don't die from shoulder wounds." That is, Jeff added to himself, not if there are emergency rooms and medical care and IVs and antibiotics. Or at least sanitary conditions.

Jeff looked woefully at the ragged, filthy blanket that covered Daniel's legs, and at the discarded towel, which was soaked with what seemed an impossible amount of blood. Daniel's body must be going into shock from the blood loss, and without a blood transfusion, he could die from it.

Once more Jeff tortured himself, asking how he could have brought these vibrant young people into this situation. But Jeff didn't voice his guilt or his doubts. Better to let Kevin hold on to some hope.

Jeff glanced back toward the sofa and saw that the two girls had bowed their heads and were praying for Daniel. He felt a glimmer of hope of his own.

"It's my fault he got shot." Kevin's soft words drew Jeff's attention back.

"Jeremy?" asked Jeff, confused.

Kevin shook his head. "No. Daniel. I tried to stop when Jeremy got hit, but Daniel made me keep goin', and then I kinda stumbled, and he grabbed me to keep me from fallin'. That's when he got shot, 'cuz he wouldn't let go of my arm."

Jeff nodded. That sounded like Daniel.

"If it wasn't for Daniel, I'd probably be dead, too," Kevin pronounced mournfully. "And I just yelled at 'im."

Jeff had nothing encouraging to say to that. He wanted to ask about what had happened – he needed more details – but this wasn't the right time. So he said nothing, just kept praying quietly for wisdom.

After a moment, Kevin spoke again. "He knew, didn't he?"

Jeff was having a hard time following Kevin's train of thought. "What? Who knew?"

"Jeremy. He knew he was gonna die."

Jeff frowned, not sure how to respond. Where was that wisdom he had asked God for? To stall, he answered with a question of his own. "What makes you say that?"

"This whole trip, Jeremy been actin' different, and he kept sayin' some weird stuff. He musta known somethin' was gonna happen to 'im."

Jeff pondered that for a long time, remembering some of the conversations he and Jeremy had had in his office at the church the last two months. Conversations that Jeremy had sworn him to secrecy about. He wondered if the confidentiality mattered at this point.

Not sure whether the truth would help or just cause more pain, Jeff decided to keep his knowledge to himself for the time being. He answered as honestly as possible without breaking his promise to Jeremy. "I can't answer that, Kevin. Only God and Jeremy knew what was going on in his mind this last week."

Under other circumstances, the young people's loving concern for one another might have warmed Jeff's heart. As it was, he just felt lost and empty as he watched them take care of their unconscious friend.

Daniel would never know that Kevin slept stretched out on the bare wooden floor in front of the sofa that night, or that Mindy slept sitting on the floor with her head resting on the sofa near Daniel's feet so she could keep an eye on him.

Resha paced between the tiny kitchen and the equally tiny living room for most of the night. Jeff heard the girl's murmured prayers for hours before she finally dropped in exhaustion onto a ragged armchair and dozed.

Jeff didn't even try to find a place to sleep. He sat outside on the floor of the back porch, back resting against the wall, too numb to pray, too numb to cry, too numb to even feel the mosquitoes that feasted on his arms.

He should be in there with the students, but what would be the point? He had nothing to offer.

When morning finally came, Jeff got stiffly to his feet and forced himself to go inside to see what other misery the day might hold for them.

Please, God, You take over, because I'm not up to this.

12

Daniel hovered between oblivion and agonizing awareness, shivering from cold. His brain told him he needed to pull the blanket from his legs and cover the rest of his body, but he couldn't make his arms reach for it. He heard familiar voices coming from miles away and struggled to understand the words.

"His breathing is so shallow." A musical feminine voice, sounding worried.

"At least he's still alive." Deeper, more cynical, but still feminine.

There was light pressure on his wrist, then his neck. A vague notion flitted through his muddied brain that someone was checking his pulse. Then that someone was patting his hand gently.

"Daniel, how are you feeling?"

Daniel lay there unmoving, struggling to force his heavy eyelids up so he could see who the cheerful voice belonged to.

The light hurt his eyes, and he squinted, finally focusing enough to recognize Mindy hovering over him. Resha stood behind Mindy with her arms crossed as she looked down at him, frowning as usual.

"I've been better," he admitted in a raspy voice. He licked his cracked lips and looked around him. When he got his bearings somewhat, he struggled to sit up, but Mindy held him down with a hand on his chest. Her hand felt warm and he wished she would leave it there because he was so very cold.

"Slowly, Daniel, take it slowly. We don't want you passing out before you meet your guests."

"Guests?" he echoed, hating how feeble his voice sounded. The blood loss had done a number on him, but he managed to sit up with Mindy's and Resha's help. The resulting dizziness made him wonder if that had been a good idea. Pain came in pulsing waves, and the light faded in and out with it.

"Yes, Raul went in the van and picked up some of the people who are getting the Bibles you saved. They're waiting outside." Mindy offered Daniel a glass containing more of the dreadful orange beverage.

He turned away and weakly held up a hand to ward her off.

"You need to drink, Daniel, you lost too much blood." She offered it again.

"Trust me," Daniel managed to croak, "if I drink that stuff right now, I'll lose more than blood."

Mindy quickly moved the glass out of sight and smiled brightly. "Okay, maybe later then."

"I guess this ain't a good time to offer you some of Manuela's soup, then, huh, buddy?" came another voice, trying to sound cheerful but failing. Daniel forced his eyes to focus until they found Kevin hovering behind Resha.

"What?" Daniel asked in confusion.

"Manuela here made some chicken and rice soup for you." Pastor Jeff materialized in his vision next, standing beside Kevin.

Jeff indicated a tiny Colombian woman who was staring anxiously at Daniel, holding a bowl with a spoon in it.

A nebulous memory floated across Daniel's mind – he thought he'd seen the woman before, but he didn't bother to try to figure it out. It was hard enough for him just to process the words they were all saying to him.

"Oh, uh, thanks," he mumbled to the woman. His brain finally churned out the word he was looking for. "*Gracias.*"

The little woman smiled and dipped her head, and Resha murmured something to her in Spanish. Manuela nodded and left with the bowl she was holding, much to Daniel's relief. At least there was one less person standing around him, and she had taken the threat of chicken soup with her.

It was still hard to breathe – all the attention was making him claustrophobic.

Jeff seemed to read his mind. After one last concerned look, the pastor walked away. "I'll see if anyone ever found any Tylenol."

Resha followed his lead, grabbing Mindy's arm. "Come on, Mindy, let's go let the people in now."

Kevin didn't leave. He just kept staring at Daniel with his face all scrunched up. The way everyone was acting, Daniel wondered if he was going to die, too.

Now Kevin lowered himself onto the sofa beside him, careful not to jostle the sofa. "Look, man, I got to make somethin' right."

Okay, that settled it. Kevin thought his number was up. The thought should bother Daniel, but it didn't.

Kevin fiddled with a loose thread on the sofa, not looking at Daniel. "I'm sorry for actin' like that las' night, man. It ain't your fault, what happened."

Daniel struggled to make sense of what Kevin said. He came up with what he hoped was an appropriate reply. "Don't worry about it, Kevin. We weren't thinking straight."

I'm still not thinking straight, realized Daniel. *I have no clue where I am. All I know is Jeremy is dead and my arm hurts like crazy and I feel lousy and there is a stack of Bibles on the table over there and everyone is talking about soup.*

The mental effort exhausted Daniel, and he let his head fall back against the back of the sofa. He was glad Kevin didn't try to talk to him any more. His friend just sat next to him, his silent presence saying what words could not. He'd have to thank Kevin later.

If he lived.

After Ortega had dispatched three of his men in the black truck, he noticed a teenaged recruit hovering nearby, the one whose nose had been broken by the American dogs. He would punish the boy, and toughen him up in the process. He pointed to the pavement where his soldiers had snatched up the American's body. The Bibles were still strewn about, sticking to the dried pool of blood.

"You! Come here and clean up this mess."

Ramiro took a few frightened steps closer. "What do you want me to do with them?"

Ortega snarled, "I do not care. They are worthless now. No one will pay for books dirtied with blood. Get rid of them."

And he stalked away, knowing that the coward would not dare to defy his orders.

Ramiro considered the task a moment. He found some work gloves and an empty cardboard box, then approached the scattered Bibles. Seeing the swarms of flies hovering over the dark stains, he was almost grateful for the heavy bandages covering his nose.

He knew he was being punished for his failure the night before. He had been doubly disgraced because his attacker had been a woman.

"But you did not see her!" he had tried to explain to his peers, but they only laughed at him. So Ramiro kept to himself the memory of her eyes, lit up by some inner fire.

The task was more tedious than he'd imagined because some of the Bibles were glued to the pavement with the congealed blood, and he had to scrape them up with a sharp rock he found nearby.

As Ramiro neared the edge of the mess, he saw that one of the Bibles was relatively clean, with only a few spatters on one corner.

Curious about the Book that had caused two men to die, Ramiro pulled back the cover and flipped through the Bible, noting the names of the chapters. Surprised, he found that a letter had been tucked into the pages.

He looked around furtively to see if anyone was watching. Seeing no one, Ramiro picked up the book and quickly tucked it underneath his shirt.

A moment later – or was it an hour later? Daniel had no concept of time right now – he heard the back door open. He raised his head and saw Resha beckoning to someone on the back porch.

Several Colombian men and women dressed in ragged clothing stepped into the house hesitantly, along with a couple of teenagers. When they saw the Bibles, their eyes lit up.

Most of the adults dropped to their knees in front of the table where the Bibles were stacked and crossed themselves. Others picked up the Bibles and kissed them with tears running down their cheeks. The teenagers picked up Bibles reverently, as if afraid to dirty them.

Daniel stared at the surreal scene, then glanced at Kevin. His friend looked as baffled as he was. Was the Word of God that important to these people?

Seeing their astonishment, Raul explained, "Most of these people lost everything in the flood, including their Bibles, and had no way of replacing them. Others are new believers who have never had The Word of God in their hands before. You have changed their lives by bringing these Bibles to us."

Raul let the people savor their treasure for a few more minutes, then he spoke to them quietly in Spanish. For the first time, the people seemed to notice Daniel and Kevin.

Raul told the people about Jeremy's sacrifice, and the people's curiosity turned to awe. They approached the two friends and began thanking them effusively in Spanish.

"Gracias, gracias!"

"Dios te bendigas!"

Jeremy would have loved being the center of attention, but for Daniel it was unbearable torture. The unwanted adulation, combined with his dizziness and the throbbing pain in his arm, made him desperate for escape. He looked pleadingly at his pastor, but Jeff was blocked from coming near by the crush of people. Just when Daniel thought he would pass out, or worse, something changed.

Almost in one accord, the people bowed their heads and began to pray in Spanish for them. His fuzzy mind couldn't grasp the words they were saying, but it didn't matter – he felt the Spirit behind the prayers.

A few of the people reached out to touch him and Kevin gently as they prayed, and Daniel felt a peace began to settle over him. And it might have been his imagination, but he thought he felt strength flowing into his body as the people interceded.

Outside, a shiny, black pickup truck pulled up to the front of the tiny, rundown house. The passenger started to get out but hesitated with his fingers hovering over the door handle, halted by a sudden overwhelming feeling that he was being watched. There was something inviting, almost welcoming, about the place, but terrifying at the same time.

"¿Que pasa, Miguel?" demanded the driver impatiently.

Lt. Rojas was a seasoned veteran, and Miguel was sure the man was disgusted that he had been ordered to chauffeur two new recruits for a simple delivery job.

Afraid to anger the man further, Miguel struggled to put his feelings into words. "I do not know. This place, it feels strange to me."

Rojas was not sympathetic. He waved an impatient hand. "Yes, yes. I once felt the same thing when dealing with the Christians. But I have hardened myself and it no longer bothers me. Now stop making excuses. Get out and do what we came to do. *¡Andale!*"

Miguel scrambled out and pulled himself into the bed of the truck, where another enlistee sat with their cargo. The other young man, Jorge, looked up at Miguel with frightened eyes, and Miguel knew that he was also experiencing the strange combination of longing and dread.

"Come, let us get this done so we can get away from this place," Miguel said.

The two of them grabbed their freight, which seemed inexplicably heavier than when they had loaded it into the truck, and flung it over the side, onto the wooden steps of the sagging front porch. From inside the truck, Rojas reached through the back window and handed Miguel a nail and a piece of paper. "Do not forget this."

Miguel took the note and jumped out of the truck. He did not understand how he had ever thought there was something inviting about this place, because now he felt nothing but an indefinable terror. He hurriedly attached the note to the doorpost.

The message delivered now, Miguel scrambled back onto the bed of the truck with Jorge. He did not want to sit near Lt. Rojas again; the man seemed immune to the unearthly atmosphere, and his callousness made Miguel even more afraid.

The truck drove away and Miguel was relieved that the feelings faded with distance.

He did not realize that this had been one of his last opportunities to respond to the Presence he was so eager to escape.

The prayers inside the house died out one by one as if the people had prearranged it. They quietly picked up their Bibles and filed out without speaking. Raul followed them out and closed the back door softly behind him.

There remained an almost tangible sense of reverence in the room. Resha, Mindy, Kevin and Jeff stood in silent awe, not wanting to disturb the Spirit. After a few minutes of soaking in God's Presence, Daniel was finally the one to break the silence.

"Uh, I think I could try a little bit of Manuela's soup now, if that's okay."

Jeff watched as Mindy coaxed Daniel to eat a few spoonfuls of the soup, cooing at him like he was a three-year-old. Resha stood by, watching with cynical amusement. Kevin still sat beside Daniel, as if he could make his friend recover by the sheer force of his will.

Raul slipped back into the room and caught Jeff's eye. Putting a finger to his lips, Raul tipped his head toward the door, then went back outside.

Understanding the unspoken message, Jeff discreetly joined the gaunt man on the back porch of the ramshackle little house.

Raul wasted no time. "You and your friends must leave at once."

Jeff was nonplussed. The plan had been for them to stay a few hours to allow Daniel time to get his strength back. Last night Raul had even offered to try to find a doctor in the neighboring village this morning.

"The Black Eagles know where we are," Raul hurried on. "We are all in danger here."

"They found us? How do you know that?"

Raul lowered his eyes. "They have delivered a message that cannot be ignored."

A strange, cold apprehension crept over Jeff. "What kind of a message?"

"Prepare yourself, my friend." Raul led Jeff around to the front of the house. He laid a hand on Jeff's shoulder and pointed. Sprawled across the steps was a barely recognizable body, bullet riddled and bloody.

Jeff turned away quickly. "Oh, God. Jeremy."

"This is El Tiburon's way of telling us that he knows where we are and that he is about to attack," Raul explained, leading Jeff away from the dreadful sight. "There is no time to waste, Jeff. You must take your team away from here. Now."

Jeff nodded his agreement, then indicated Jeremy's mutilated body. "I don't want them to know about this. They've been through enough. They don't need to see this. But I can't leave him here."

Raul handed Jeff some keys. "Take the van. It will be more comfortable for Daniel, and you may be able to … move your friend without the others knowing."

"But what about you and Manuela? You're all in danger here, too."

Raul shook his head as he guided Jeff back toward the rear of the house. "My brother and I were planning to leave here soon anyway until we are able to rebuild. We will take your truck and the Bibles that remain, and we will stay with Javier's friends near Campo Dulce."

As they stepped onto the back porch, Raul turned to face Jeff before they went inside. "You should know, Jeff, that since an American citizen is now involved, the Colombian authorities will have no choice but to cooperate with your government. You must contact the American Embassy in Bogota as soon as possible. That may buy us all some time."

Ten minutes later, Jeff was driving away in the van.

Kevin sat numbly on the floor in back. Resha sat next to Kevin on the floor, staring out the back window with cool detachment. Mindy had tossed a towel on the bench to cover the bloodstains from the previous evening, and she now had Daniel positioned on the bench with his head in her lap to keep him from being jostled too much. The young man's face was twisted, as if his feverish dreams were filled with pain and grief and dark, unspeakable images.

Jeff was the only one of the five who was aware of the tarp-wrapped cargo that had been hurriedly strapped to the top of the van. It was a heavy burden for him to bear.

As soon as Jeff drove the van away, Raul and Javier threw a few belongings into the back of the truck, starting with the remaining Bibles. Manuela hurried to gather food and water and stuffed it into a pillowcase. Then she rushed into the bedroom and began looking through the closet.

Raul grabbed the first three hangers and shoved them into Manuela's hands, then pulled her toward the door. "There is no more time, Manuela. Come."

She had no chance to argue. They ran out the door and squeezed into the truck, where Javier was already at the wheel. As Javier pulled away, taking the only road that led out of the small village, Manuela began to weep. "We are leaving so much behind."

"We are leaving with our lives," her brother-in-law snapped as he sped over the rough dirt road. Then his voice softened. "I am sorry, Manuela. I know such things are harder on women."

Raul took her hand and explained, "The Black Eagles have been watching us already. Now they know for sure that we are the ones leading the people to rebel against their wickedness, and they will waste no time in making sure we are gone, one way or the other."

Manuela already understood all too well why they were rushing desperately from their home. Her mind flashed back to less than a year ago, when she and Raul had fled their own home in a similar fashion.

Stefan Guzman had spared their lives then, and had become a dear friend to Raul. Now he was dead, and a young man she had never met had also died in an effort to help them spread the gospel to the people who lived under the oppression of The Black Eagles.

"Will it always be this way?" she wondered aloud. "We were not even able to say goodbye to our friends."

"We have taught them for many months, and now we have put the Word of God into their hands." Raul patted her hand gently. "That will have to be enough."

"You can start over in Pueblo del Sol," Javier suggested. "My friend will let us stay with him, and you can distribute the remaining Bibles to the villagers. A village nearby, Campo Dulce, was taken over by Las Águilas Negras, and their pastor was assassinated. Some of the people managed to escape to Pueblo del Sol, but they are like lost sheep, living in the shadow of The Black Eagles. They will welcome your teaching."

Manuela gasped. "Their pastor was murdered, and you want us to go there and take his place?"

Raul put an arm over his wife's shoulders. "Manuela, our time here is obviously over, and God has opened another door. We have no choice but to go through it."

Her objections were cut off by the growl of several vehicles approaching ahead of them. Javier stepped on the brakes and swung his head, looking for a place to hide. Raul pointed to an opening in the dense jungle that might be large enough for the truck to fit through.

Javier pulled off the road and forced his way across the uneven ground, squeezing the truck between the trees. When he could go no farther, he cut the engine. Manuela prayed they had made it deep enough into the timber to avoid detection.

The three of them turned around awkwardly in the front seat to watch the road they had just left. Within seconds, three jeeps thundered past, filled with armed men.

It was a full five minutes before any of them dared to move. With shaking hands, Javier started the truck and cautiously backed it out of the trees.

They continued on their way in silence.

The three jeeps roared up to Javier's now empty house, and several men jumped out of each one. El Tiburon watched as two of his soldiers ran around to the back door to prevent escape while two others kicked in the front door, screaming threats at any occupants.

Both doors splintered open and hung uselessly from their frames as the armed men rushed in and began yanking open closets and looking under beds.

After a thorough search revealed that no one was inside the house, the highest ranking officer saluted Captain Ortega. "The insects are all gone, Tiburon."

"Good. We will not have to waste any bullets here," Ortega approved. "Take anything of value, and then torch this place to make sure that they have nothing to return to."

A few minutes after they'd gotten back on the road, Raul turned to look back, then pointed wordlessly behind them. Javier drove with more urgency.

Manuela knew what the black smoke billowing in the sky behind them meant. She sniffled as she thought of the decrepit old house that had been her home for nearly a year, and she wished they could have taken more of their belongings with them.

Then the realization hit her that if they had stayed long enough for her to gather their things, they would have been inside the house when the soldiers arrived.

She shivered in spite of the heat in the crowded truck. Never again would she complain to her husband about their hasty departure.

Jeff had been told that the radio in the old van didn't work, but he punched at the buttons in frustration anyway. He wished he had some way to let Pastor Sergio know what had happened so Sergio could prepare the others. Since they weren't expected until later, Jeff hoped they might arrive unnoticed so he could talk with Pastor Sergio before breaking the news to everyone else.

When he arrived at the compound, though, everyone seemed to be working outside, and the sight of the unfamiliar van brought them all to the front.

Jeff stole a look at the young people in back of the van. Kevin and Resha sat silently, wearing blank stares. Mindy still held Daniel's head cradled in her lap, and her cheeks were wet with tears. Daniel looked only semi-conscious, his face a mask of pain, and the bandage was shiny red — the rough drive must have caused the wound to bleed again. None of them looked ready to face the rest of their team yet.

Jeff sighed and climbed over the seats to join them in the back, saying softly, "We're here."

They all turned vacant eyes to Jeff, and he reluctantly opened the back doors. Pastor Sergio stood there, concern etched on his face. Jeff shook his head in warning. "Let me get them situated, and then we'll talk."

Sergio stepped back to allow them room to disembark. Paola stood a few paces behind him, her hand pressed to her mouth, while Matéo clung to her fearfully, as if he knew something terrible had happened. The other members of the team clustered uncertainly off to the side.

Jeff and Kevin managed to rouse Daniel and helped him from the van.

Staring at Daniel's pale face and bandaged arm, Terrell burst out, "What happened?"

Taking several steps closer, Selena demanded, "Where's the truck?"

Less forcefully, she asked, "Where's Jeremy?"

Manny backed away, his eyes bulging and his face draining. Suddenly he turned and ran, but no one paid any attention. They were all focused on the shell shocked group that had returned in the van.

Turning his back on the group that had greeted them, Jeff addressed those he'd arrived with, giving orders with an authority he felt woefully stripped of. "Kevin, help Daniel to his cot. Resha, you and Mindy get the first aid kit from the kitchen and see if there's anything we can use."

Terrell stepped up to help Kevin with Daniel. Jeff gave Paola a meaningful look, and she led Matéo away.

As soon as they were out of earshot, Jeff turned to Sergio, whose eyes were filled with realization and shared grief.

"I'll explain everything, but first there's something we need to take care of."

Resha was grateful Pastor Jeff had given her and Mindy an excuse to escape a barrage of questions from the others.

Selena had her own ideas, though. She followed Mindy and Resha as they made their way to the kitchen area.

"Where's Jeremy?" she asked again, her voice frightened now.

Resha saw nothing to gain by sugarcoating it. She stopped in her tracks and said bluntly, "The Black Eagles shot him."

Selena looked horrified. "He's dead?"

It was Mindy who replied shakily as she rubbed fresh tears from her cheeks. "Yes."

"And Daniel?"

"They shot him, too." Resha was impatient to get on with their assigned mission. "He's not dead. Yet. If that wound gets infected or we don't stop that bleeding, he could die, too. So leave us alone so we can find what we need."

Selena sucked in a deep breath and shook her head in denial. Her face paled and her lips started to tremble.

Great. She's going to have a meltdown right here in the hall.

Resha's eyes met Mindy's, and in unspoken agreement, they each grabbed one of Selena's arms and detoured to their room. Resha hoped Selena would pull herself together quickly, because they had work to do.

"Why?" Selena was blubbering full force now. Mindy sat beside Selena on her cot, alternately patting and stroking the girl's hand.

Pacing the room, Resha demanded brusquely, "Why' what?"

"Pastor Jeff and Pastor Sergio told them it was dangerous to go," Selena protested, as if reminding them of that fact would change what had happened.

"Obviously they were right." Resha snatched a bandana from her backpack and tossed it to Selena, who blew her nose on it with a decided lack of decorum.

"But they went anyway!" Selena cried. "Why did they go when they knew it wasn't safe?"

"Because God said we're supposed to spread the gospel, and that's what they were trying to do. Do you think Jesus died on the cross so we could sit around in our church coffee shops and be 'safe'?"

"But Jeremy is dead now, and Daniel is hurt, just to save a bunch of books?!" Selena threw her arms out, her crumpled face a mixture of disbelief and despair.

Resha glared at her. "Not just 'books', Selena, the Word of God."

"I know, I know, but …" Now Selena clutched her head with both hands as tears squeezed through her closed eyelids.

"No, you don't know, Selena," Resha snapped, tired of playing games, tired of pretending Selena was okay spiritually. Maybe God had more in mind than just having them comfort the distraught girl. "If you really understood what The Word of God means, you wouldn't be asking why they were willing to risk their lives for it."

Selena looked down and began sobbing harder again.

Great. Why wasn't Mindy helping her out? Resha had never been one for subtlety, and she knew she lacked the tender touch Mindy would surely have with the hysterical girl.

Since Mindy just sat there sniffling and patting Selena's hand, Resha plunged ahead. "Jeremy and the other guys knew The Word of God can change these people's lives."

Then she stopped pacing and parked directly in front of Selena, looking pointedly at her. "It could change your life, too, if you let it."

A flash of anger quieted Selena's tears for a second. "You...but...I don't think my life needs to be changed," Selena stammered defensively. With less force, she added, "Not that much."

"Oh, please, Selena, stop kidding yourself." Resha waved a dismissive hand. "I don't care if the worst thing you've ever done is look cross-eyed at your momma, if you don't accept Jesus Christ, you're going straight to hell." As if she hadn't offended Selena enough, Resha had to add, "And I'm not."

Selena looked like she was going to object, but Resha didn't give her a chance. She got right in Selena's face. "I know what you think about me, and you're pretty much right. I was into alcohol, and not the soft stuff with the fancy names, either. I'm talking hard liquor. I was hooked on drugs. I've lied, cheated, and stolen from people, including my own mother, and I did jail time for it. I've slept with more men than you've ever lusted after."

To Resha's satisfaction, Selena actually flinched at that one. Resha was on a roll now. "I've committed sins you've never even heard of. But when I finally believed The Word of God, when I finally accepted that Jesus Christ paid for all that sin when He died on the cross, it changed me completely. All that stuff is gone."

Resha paused, giving Selena a chance to respond, but the girl just blew her nose loudly again and refused to meet her eyes. Oh, well, why stop now? "Guess what, Selena? If the Black Eagles came in here right now and blew us away, we'd all be standing before God, and He would find me holier than you, because I've been washed in The Blood. How far do you think you'll get then by saying, 'But I went bowling with the church Youth Group'?"

That must have hit close to home, because Resha's words finally got a response. Selena wailed, "Well, what am I supposed to do?"

"You know that 'book' Jeremy died for? It tells you." Seeing Selena wince, Resha tried to soften her tone. "The Bible says the only way to Heaven is through Jesus Christ. Not by going to church and pretending to be 'good.' The only way to get forgiveness is to believe that He died for our sins."

"I guess I've heard that," Selena admitted. "I didn't think anybody took it seriously any more."

"Jeremy did," Resha bit out. Her remark almost set Selena's tears off again, so Resha tried to forestall it by offering, "Selena, do you want to have the kind of faith in Jesus that Jeremy had? The kind of faith that gets rid of your sin instead of pretending it doesn't exist?"

Selena nodded mutely, staring at the floor.

Resha wasn't going to accept a token response – she needed a definite answer. "The book of Acts in the Bible says whoever calls on Jesus as their Lord and Savior will be saved. Do you want to call on Jesus to save you from your sins?"

Again, a tearful nod.

Resha struggled against her impatience. After all, somebody was passing from darkness to light right in front of her. God, thanks for working on Selena's heart, but couldn't You do this when somebody wasn't bleeding to death in the other building?

She passed the buck to their roommate. "Why don't you let Mindy pray with you?"

To her relief, the tearful redhead took over without hesitation. Mindy grabbed Selena's hands and gently coaxed her to repeat a prayer based on the scripture Resha had just quoted.

Relieved to be off the hook, Resha rummaged through Selena's things until she found the girl's barely used Bible. Thumbing through it, Resha flipped to the book of John. She wished she had Daniel's Bible now. He would probably have all kinds of notes scribbled on the sides that would help Selena. Oh, well, this one would have to do.

When Mindy and Selena had finished praying, predictably with lots more tears from both of them, Resha thrust the open Bible into Selena's hands, pointing to the first chapter of John.

"Here, read this," she ordered without further explanation. To Mindy, she said, "Come on, let's go make sure Daniel didn't die while we were in here."

At Selena's stricken look, Resha kicked herself mentally. Why had she said that? Now Selena would think it was her fault if Daniel died. She tried to smooth it over. "Don't worry, Selena, if he did, at least we'll know he's in Heaven."

Good going, girlfriend.

She all but shoved Mindy out the door, leaving Selena staring in confusion at the Bible.

Mindy was so worried by what Resha had said that she went straight to the men's dorm, forgetting to look for the first aid kit. She was happy to find Daniel hadn't died. As a matter of fact, he was sitting on his cot looking a little less ghastly. Kevin and Terrell were keeping him company, and he gave a wan smile when the girls came in.

Kevin pointed to a first aid kit that rested on a chair beside the cot. "Pastor Jeff brought that in, and he got Paola to bring Daniel somethin' to drink from some supplies they was savin'."

Mindy was thrilled to see a single serve Gatorade bottle next to Daniel with a few sips missing. "Oh, that's perfect. You'll need to finish drinking that, Daniel. But let me change that dressing first."

She pushed the first aid kit to one side and perched delicately on the edge of the chair to peel off the bloody strips of sheet they had used as a bandage last night. All three guys tried to look at the wound, but Mindy blocked Daniel's view with her head and waved the other two off with a dainty hand, tsk-ing at them.

They reluctantly backed off. But not before Terrell caught a glimpse of the way Resha had hacked up the sleeve of the bloodstained T-shirt.

"I think you owe me a T-shirt," he told Daniel.

"Sorry about that," Daniel said weakly.

Mindy poured antiseptic from the first aid kit on a wad of cotton and chirped, "You'll never guess what just happened." Without giving them a chance to reply, she went on happily, "Selena just gave her heart to Jesus."

"For real?" Kevin asked in surprise.

"One down, one to go," Terrell declared.

"That's great," Daniel murmured. His face turned ashen again when Mindy dabbed at his upper arm with the disinfectant.

Mindy wanted to examine the wound better, but she didn't want the others to see how bad it was. Besides, she couldn't do anything for now except keep it clean. She poked around in the first aid kit for some clean gauze, then expertly applied a fresh bandage and snipped off the excess. "You guys should have heard Resha talking to her in there. She's a wonderful preacher."

The three guys looked at Resha with new respect.

Resha frowned and changed the subject, pointing to a battered backpack sitting at the foot of the cot next to Daniel's. "Is that Jeremy's backpack? I'll bet there's still some protein bars in there."

"Oh, that's such a great idea!" Mindy clapped her hands. Why hadn't she thought of that herself? "Get one, Resha!"

Resha twisted her face to one side, as if regretting her suggestion. Crouching, she pushed aside rumpled clothes until she came to a few loose bars at the bottom of the knapsack. After scanning the wrappers, she chose one and handed it to Mindy.

Mindy read the label. "Ooh, lots of carbs and protein! Daniel, this will be perfect to help your body rebuild its blood supply!"

She offered it to him, but he turned away.

The reality of Jeremy's death slammed into Daniel again at the sight of his friend's things. Between the pain Mindy had inflicted on him and the prospect of eating Jeremy's food, Daniel's world started to go black again. He hoped he wouldn't disgrace himself in front of the girls.

Kevin must have read something in his face. He moved towards the door. "Come on, ya'll. Let's let 'im rest."

Terrell took the hint and left, but Mindy hesitated. She looked disappointed as she laid the granola bar on the chair next to the first aid kit. "Well, okay, but promise you'll take a few bites."

"Okay." Daniel nodded. Anything to make them leave.

Resha's eyes told him she didn't believe him, but she steered Mindy out the door.

After they'd gone, Kevin turned back. "I'ma go see what Pastor Jeff want us to do now. I'll check on you later."

Daniel nodded again, but mentally, he'd already checked out.

"He's got a fever now," Mindy said dully as she followed Resha from the men's dorm.

Great. That meant the wound was getting infected. Well, without antibiotics, there was nothing they could do for him except keep praying.

Resha needed to be by herself for a while. "I'm going for a walk."

Mindy nodded absently, the cheerfulness she'd maintained for Daniel's benefit all but evaporated now. For the first time since they'd been in Colombia, Mindy looked tired and dejected, and Resha felt sorry for her.

She should probably say something encouraging to Mindy, but she was tired and dejected, too. She just shook her head and turned away, leaving Mindy alone with her hopelessness.

As Resha headed toward the field behind the mission center, she saw Matéo slumped on the steps to his house. Resha had intended to get as far away as possible from everyone, to give herself a chance to collect her thoughts, but something made her stop and walk closer to the forlorn boy.

"Hello, Matéo." Her greeting was solemn.

He looked up at her with eyes red from crying. "Miss Resha, is Mr. Daniel going to be okay?"

Resha sat on the steps beside him and considered her answer carefully. "I hope so, Matéo. Are you praying for him?"

He nodded soberly. "Yes, Miss Resha. But when the Black Eagles attacked us, I prayed very hard, and they shot Stefan and took my sister and did bad things to her anyway. I have been praying for Paola, but I still hear her crying when she thinks no one is listening. And we prayed for all of you when you went to get the Bibles, and Mr. Jeremy got killed and Mr. Daniel..."

Matéo's voice broke, and so did Resha's heart, but she covered it better than Matéo did.

The poor kid was only nine and already he was being forced to face his doubts in a major way. She should wrap her arms around Matéo and comfort him, but somehow she couldn't bring herself to do it.

Instead, she patted him awkwardly on the shoulder and said words that were true but probably not helpful to a little boy whose mother was too many miles away.

"I don't understand it, either, Matéo, but I know God is good. We can't stop trusting Him just because He didn't do things the way we wanted Him to."

Resha saw the skepticism in his eyes but went on anyway. "This whole thing is horrible to us, but Stefan and Jeremy are in Heaven, and the people got their Bibles, so they didn't die for nothing. Paola is back home with you and Sergio. We just have to keep praying for her and Daniel and believe God is going to let them be all right."

Matéo nodded uncertainly and looked down at his feet. Frustrated that she hadn't been able to give him the comfort he needed, she gave Matéo's shoulder a squeeze and stood.

He didn't look up as she walked away.

The encounter with Matéo had drained Resha, and the idea of taking a walk no longer appealed. She hoped instead to find solitude inside the sanctuary. Resha could always find peace inside a church, even an unairconditioned building furnished with a ragtag bunch of rusted chairs.

She didn't make it inside.

The sight of Mindy sitting despondently on the ground, leaning against the cinder block shed, stopped Resha in her tracks. The girl's arm was draped over the dog as she rocked herself back and forth. Mindy must not be ready to face Selena again yet, either.

I'm really not up to this, Lord. Resha resisted the idea of going to talk to Mindy. After a brief inner struggle, she took a deep breath and strode toward the other girl. As Resha stood over her, Mindy looked up at her with watery, expectant eyes.

"You and Alfredo need to go give Matéo a hug." Resha jerked her head in Matéo's direction.

Mindy glanced toward Sergio's house, then scrambled to her feet when she saw the boy hunched over on the steps. "Oh, the poor little thing."

The redhead wiped her eyes and hurried to Matéo's side, the dog loping along beside her.

There, that ought to help Mindy and Matéo both.

Resha finally made it inside through the side door, intending to bypass Selena in their room and hide out in the sanctuary for a little while. Once again, her plans were delayed.

Pastor Jeff called to her from the dining area just before she reached her goal. Conditioned by her former experiences with authority figures, Resha's first thought was that she was in trouble – she put on an indifferent mask and braced herself for whatever was coming.

But Jeff placed a fatherly arm over her shoulders. "Resha, this has been a terrible situation, and I appreciate how you're helping to keep everyone together. And you did a fine job in there with Selena."

How in the world did Pastor Jeff know about that Selena fiasco? Resha wanted to melt into the floor.

"I was kind of hard on her," she admitted, discreetly easing out from under his arm.

If Jeff noticed how she'd ducked away from him, he didn't mention it. His mouth quirked ruefully at her words. "Sometimes that's what it takes. Selena's been to church enough times that she's probably heard at least some watered down version of the gospel. Maybe it took your....uh...more 'forceful' presentation for her to take it seriously."

Resha felt a flush of pride at his approval. It was a new experience for her, being appreciated by a man for her spiritual worth. She was surprised how much the pastor's acceptance meant to her, and she felt a need to escape her own emotions.

She mumbled something incomprehensible and hurried off as if she knew where she was going.

A faint, understanding smile crossed Pastor Jeff's face as he watched Resha scurry away. That young lady carried a lot of hurt and anger, yet God was using her in spite of herself.

Jeff had grudgingly admired her stubborn insistence on rescuing Paola, and had been thankful at how she'd taken charge of Daniel's care last night when they were all in shock over Jeremy's death.

He'd overheard her passionate, if tactless, tirade that finally helped Selena recognize her need for Christ. And he'd seen how she couldn't pass up a hurting little boy or a girl who needed comfort.

This last small act of kindness he'd just witnessed convinced him God was breaking down some long standing walls around Resha's heart.

At least that was one bright spot in this mess.

Still playing the part of the faithful laborer, Antonio helped Luís connect the wiring for the newly constructed storage building. He spotted Manny wandering around the compound listlessly, but ignored him until the overweight boy ambled toward the building.

Antonio quickly excused himself to Luís and accosted Manny before he got too close.

"You know better than to come to me in the middle of the day," Antonio growled. "What is wrong with you?"

"You said nobody would get hurt," Manny whined. "Then you said it would only be Stefan because he was a traitor. Now my friends are getting shot."

A quick glance around assured Antonio that no one was nearby. He could get rid of this lazy coward right now, but he did not want to face Captain Ortega's wrath again for taking things into his own hands. He would have to wait until Ortega gave him direct orders.

For now, Antonio made himself sound conciliatory. "Your friend's death was an accident. I know this is a lot for you to understand right now, but our goal is much bigger than you realize. We will talk later and I will explain everything."

Manny didn't look convinced, so Antonio decided to sweeten the pot. "El Tiburon is very impressed with all your help. He wants to meet you soon."

The chubby boy's face brightened, but only a little. "He does? Really?"

"Yes, really." Antonio nodded confidently, reassuringly. "I will talk to him tonight and find out how soon we can get you involved more with the business side. Meet me out by the fountain tomorrow night and we'll talk about it."

"Okay, Antonio."

Manny was far from satisfied by Antonio's assurances.

He'd been told too many lies, and had learned now what The Black Eagles were capable of. But he was in too deep, and after what he'd seen, he was too scared to cross Antonio. He no longer saw any choice but to go along with whatever the man said.

While Manny was wrestling with his guilt and fear, his sister had finally laid all of her own guilt and fear to rest. Selena lay on her back on her cot, hugging her Bible to her chest, marveling at the peace inside of her.

She hadn't really understood much of what she'd read, and she'd given up after the first chapter, but it didn't matter – for the first time, Selena knew she had eternity to figure out God.

She'd never felt so loved before, or so safe. Why had no one explained it to her like that before? Why had it taken Resha, of all people, to help her understand what this whole thing called "Christianity" was all about?

In a fit of honesty, Selena had to admit she'd heard the truth before. But back in America, she'd had everything she could possibly want or need – her days were spent in pursuit of fun, surrounded by friends who made her feel good about herself.

The only time she'd been confronted with the truth was on the occasional Sunday mornings when her pastor was in the mood to give a softer version of what Resha had told her. Selena had never felt a need to look deeper into her own heart.

It had taken being out here in this God-forsaken place, hearing Pastor Jeff's in-depth teaching, seeing the way the others lived out their faith, and the death of someone she'd grown to like a whole lot to finally get her attention.

Selena hated that Jeremy had died, but she knew only something that drastic could have forced her to finally admit to herself she was lost. Otherwise, she probably would have kept pushing aside the things Pastor Jeff tried to teach them, pretending they didn't apply to her, and then forgotten it all when she got back to her comfortable life at home.

"Wow, Jesus," she said, in her first prayer as a brand new child of God. "I can't believe I ignored You for so long. I'm really sorry about that. Thanks for loving me anyway. Thanks for showing me The Truth. I want to live for You now, okay?"

And though God didn't respond to her audibly, she knew He had accepted her awkward attempt at talking to Him. She'd have to ask Resha to teach her how to pray better.

Selena laughed to herself at the idea of asking the contentious girl for help, but for some reason, Resha didn't seem quite as scary to her any more.

With his team settled as well as possible, Jeff joined Sergio in the office, where the Colombian pastor was adjusting the radio. When Sergio had made contact with the American Embassy, he stepped aside so Jeff could talk.

Jeff took a deep breath. "My name is Jeff Harding. I'm an American pastor here on a mission trip with some young people, and we have a situation here..."

Feeling isolated and trapped in the men's quarters, Daniel dragged himself off his cot and wandered around the complex. He tried to stay out of sight so Mindy wouldn't send him back to the dorm.

The two pastors were sequestered in Sergio's office, and Daniel could hear them talking on the radio. Everyone else was walking around in a daze, trying to carry on with their tasks. It didn't look like much work was getting done.

Daniel managed to make his way to the kitchen and begged Abuelita to give him something to do. The old woman sat him at the table and put him to work sorting out a large box of mushy mangoes, demonstrating how to select the ones that were still edible.

Following her instructions, Daniel pawed through the fruit with his good arm, tossing aside the ones that were obviously beyond hope. The smell of rotting fruit didn't help his already queasy stomach, but he kept at it. At least he could make himself useful sitting down.

Mindy found him there, and urged him to drink more Gatorade. She started checking on him every hour or so, forcing him to swallow a few spoonfuls of soup each time.

She also fashioned a sling for his arm out of a pillowcase Abuelita had given her for that purpose.

By evening, Daniel was feeling a bit stronger.

In an effort to keep things as normal as possible, Jeff insisted on having their usual evening meeting. The atmosphere was so bleak he almost wished they hadn't come together.

Questions about what had happened hung in the air, but Kevin looked so forlorn and Daniel looked like he was in so much pain that no one had the heart to ask them. Resha's glower discouraged all conversation, and Mindy kept crying, so the curiosity of the rest of the group went unsatisfied.

The only one who looked remotely interested in what Pastor Jeff had to say tonight was Selena, but she kept getting distracted by Mindy's sniffling.

After a dispirited attempt at a devotional, Jeff gave up. "Let's just pray. We need to pray for Jeremy's family, and we need to pray for healing for Daniel, and we need to pray for safety for Pastor Sergio and his family."

The students bowed their heads. Even Manny, wide awake for once and looking jittery, bowed his head.

Unable to sleep, Resha lay staring at the ceiling in the girls' quarters, listening to the steady breathing of the others. She had run out of prayers, so all she could do was lie there trying to be quiet and trying not to think.

Around midnight, Resha heard a faint sound in the courtyard. Someone was moving around outside – had the Black Eagles caught up with them here?

She was swiftly and silently on her feet, peering through a small tear in the makeshift curtain.

It was only Daniel, pacing restlessly over the cracked paving stones. He'd taken off the sling but still held his wounded arm against him as if it hurt to move it.

Would he rather be left alone, or did he want someone to talk to? He'd probably prefer to be alone, she decided, but he shouldn't be. Besides, she was feeling a need for company herself. She shrugged her camo shirt over her tank top and slipped out to join him.

Daniel had stopped pacing and stood at the edge of the courtyard with his back to Resha, staring out into nothingness. He didn't react to her arrival.

In case he hadn't noticed her, she announced her presence, asking softly, "Can't sleep?"

Daniel didn't acknowledge her immediately, and Resha wasn't sure if he'd heard. She sat on the bench and waited.

A few moments later, Daniel said, "Kinda hard to sleep with Jeremy's empty cot right next to me."

"Yeah." What else was there for her to say? She waited some more.

Finally, Daniel continued. "I know we're Christians and all, and I'm supposed to rejoice or something because Jeremy's in a better place now. I mean, I know he is. He was goofy, but he loved God for real. But I keep thinking about his family."

Resha went to stand next to him, gazing out at the same nothingness, sharing his pain.

"Yeah," she said again. "I didn't really know Jeremy before this place, but I knew his sister a little bit from that reform school. We weren't exactly friends, and I wasn't saved, so I didn't pay much attention, but I remember seeing him when he came to visit her. He was just a wiry kid then, all skin and bones and eyes and curls."

Resha almost smiled at the memory of a much younger Jeremy. When Daniel didn't respond, she kept talking. "Natalie used to make fun of him for going to church all the time, but I could tell she really loved him. She just thought he was wasting his time doing all the churchy stuff instead of the usual fun teenager things, like he was throwing his life away."

Resha stopped, realizing what she'd just said. She sighed. "From Jeremy's prayers every night, I guess she's still not saved. I hope this doesn't push her farther away."

Daniel was quiet, contemplating Resha's comments. After a while, he said, "Kevin asked me if it was worth it."

"These people seem to think it's worth it." Resha frowned, remembering the people's reaction to the Bibles. "They risk their lives every day for being Christians, and they acted like it was an honor for Jeremy to die that way."

Daniel nodded. "They risk their lives every day just for breathing. They're used to living this way. Americans take our faith for granted, so this is totally foreign to us. We're kind of..." he trailed off.

"Spoiled?" she suggested.

Daniel actually smiled a bit. "Yeah. Jeremy was definitely spoiled. He was the last guy I figured would give up his music and his girlfriends and his Starbucks to come out here and do construction work in the mud."

His smile wavered and Resha could tell he was struggling against breaking down. She was losing her own battle as she remembered the impulsive young man who had brightened her days in the short time she had known him.

Without thinking, she turned and wrapped her arms around Daniel's waist, resting her cheek against his chest. "I'm so sorry, Daniel."

Her tears came quietly. She was embarrassed and angry with herself. She'd meant to comfort Daniel, but instead she'd thrown herself at him like some simpering, weak female and allowed him to comfort her.

What was she thinking?

Startled, Daniel froze for a moment, then reached his good arm around Resha's shoulders and pressed her head closer to his chest with his other hand, ignoring the pain that shot through his arm. Her short hair seemed strange to him, coarse and oily, but somehow it felt right.

It was comforting to hold her like this, to know he wasn't alone.

They stood that way for a long moment, drawing strength from each other.

After a while, Resha sighed and pushed away from him, not meeting his eyes. "You really should try to get some rest, you know. You need to get your strength back."

Daniel reluctantly released her. "Yeah. I think I can sleep now. Thanks."

Resha nodded and hurried back inside, discreetly wiping her eyes.

Outside, Daniel stood in the darkness for few more minutes, his memories of Jeremy now sharing space with thoughts of Resha's wiry hair.

Then he took a deep breath and went back to his room. He surprised himself by actually going to sleep.

13

Day 12: Thursday

Resha woke from her fitful sleep the next morning when Selena bounced playfully on the cot. "Hey, girl, I saw you and sexy Daniel out there hugging last night. Hubba hubba!"

Selena's good mood had apparently carried over from yesterday and she was trying to cheer everyone else up, but the small amount of sleep Resha had gotten had done nothing to improve her own frame of mind. She sat up and shoved Selena off the cot.

Mindy was staring at her in shock. "You mean you were alone last night with one of the boys?"

Leave it to Mindy to blow things out of proportion. As if the rules still applied after everything that had happened. Resha snarled, "Oh, please! What were we going to do, get it on out there on the broken rubble? Never mind that he can hardly move his arm. Get a grip."

Mindy and Selena both drew back at her tone, and Resha regretted her prickly attitude. Just a little bit. She tried softening her voice. "Look, the guy just saw his best buddy shot to pieces. He needed a friend, okay? A friend."

Then, before she could catch herself, she had to add, "So get your mind out of the gutter, Pastor's Daughter."

So much for being nicer. Resha saw the hurt in Mindy's face and quickly bent over to tie her shoes, more angry at herself than anyone. Mindy was irritating, but she wasn't a bad person, and Selena was, well...Selena.

After an awkward silence, Mindy apologized softly, "You're right, Resha. We shouldn't assume the worst about each other. We're all under a lot of stress here. Thank you for showing the love of Jesus to our brother."

Selena rolled her eyes behind Mindy's back.

"Whatever," Resha mumbled, feeling worse than ever about her outburst. She stalked out of the room, tugging her shirt on over her tank top.

While the team was suffering through breakfast, the sound of a helicopter hovering overhead mercifully gave them an excuse to put down their forks. Two no-nonsense agents from the American Embassy had arrived, introducing themselves as Richard Massey and Diana Cortez.

The agents quickly disappeared into Sergio's tiny office with the two pastors, shutting the door firmly behind them.

Since it was obvious they wouldn't be allowed to listen, the students reluctantly left the dining area and began installing the siding on the newly constructed building.

Although FBI Agent Richard Massey hated the violence that had necessitated his presence, he was optimistic this investigation would give him vital evidence against the ruthless drug cartel that had been operating with impunity because of corruption in the local government.

He'd been leery at first of the cold, impatient Colombian agent he'd been partnered with. Now he respected her hard-nosed competence as she questioned the Colombian pastor. Agent Cortez seemed especially interested in Sergio Restrepo's description of Stefan Guzman's former involvement with the Black Eagles and his subsequent murder.

Sergio handed over a wrinkled paper with a message the Black Eagles had delivered the day before the Americans had arrived.

"The FBI can't officially get involved with Guzman's murder," Massey told Sergio after examining the note, "but more than likely the same people who murdered your friend also killed Jeremy Andersen, so this information is helpful. If we can do anything with Andersen's case, Guzman may get justice indirectly."

The agents turned their attention to the American pastor beside Sergio.

Jeff Harding seemed remorseful as he described how his group had come to be involved in the actions that resulted in Jeremy's death. While Massey sympathized with the pastor's distress, the agents continued asking questions with detached efficiency.

After an hour of relentless probing, Massey explained, "We wanted to get as much information as we can from you so that we won't have to spend as much time interrogating the young men who were victimized. We understand this has been traumatic for them, and that one of them is injured, so we'll keep things as brief as possible."

At last the pastors were released and Kevin Gaines was brought in.

As promised, they didn't keep Kevin for long. They asked a few questions to confirm what Jeff had told them, then asked for a description of the men who had chased them.

Kevin's eyes bulged as he stared at them in disbelief. "Man, it was dark, an' they was shootin' at us, an' we was runnin' too fast to be lookin' at 'em. I didn't see nothin'!"

Agent Cortez smirked at Kevin's gauche way of expressing himself, but Massey remained professional. "I understand, sir, but if you can remember anything at all, it would be very helpful to us."

After Kevin had told them whatever he could, they called in Daniel Wescott.

They asked him the same questions they had asked Kevin and received the same responses, although Daniel's replies were much more concise and a lot less colorful. One notable difference, however, was that Daniel was able to give them a detailed description of the man who had shot Jeremy.

When they were done, Massey urged Daniel to ride back with them in the helicopter to a medical facility in Bogota.

The young man frowned and chewed his lip as he considered the offer. After a moment, he asked, "Could Kevin or Pastor Jeff go with me?"

Massey and Cortez looked at each other.

Massey replied, "I'm sorry, but we only have room for one passenger. We encourage you to come with us, but you would have to come alone."

He didn't want to tell him yet that the fourth seat would be occupied by a body bag. They needed to keep his friend's remains for the course of their investigation, but the American pastor had asked them not to share that disturbing information unless it was necessary.

After a few more seconds of contemplation, Daniel shook his head. "No, I'd rather stay here with my friends. We're going back to the U.S. in a couple of days anyway. I'll just wait and go to the doctor there."

Before they left, the agents apologized to Pastor Sergio for not being able to assign protection to the mission center. Many of the American Embassy personnel had left the area to escape the effects of the flooding. The ones that remained were stretched beyond capacity already, so there simply wasn't anyone available.

"But if the Colombian authorities will cooperate with us, we'll ask them to find some officers that are not in the Black Eagles' pocket and assign them to patrol the complex," Cortez promised. "They're overwhelmed with work after the flood, too, though, so that may take a few days, if we can do it at all."

As a consolation, the agents temporarily issued Jeff a satellite phone that he could use to contact whoever he needed to in the States.

Jeff's first call was to his senior pastor, Rob Davenport, to give him the bad news.

Pastor Rob took it pretty well, but Jeff knew he was devastated by Jeremy's death. The senior pastor still managed to give Jeff some much needed counseling and prayer.

When Rob offered to help in any way he could, Jeff was tempted to saddle the other pastor with the worst task of all. But while Jeff had no doubts that the senior pastor would be visiting the Andersen's soon, Jeff knew whose responsibility it was to notify Jeremy's parents.

It was the hardest call he'd ever had to make.

"Two people from the American Embassy have just left!" Antonio hissed into the radio's mike. Panicked and furious, he was anxious to take action.

Ortega's response was not any calmer than Antonio's.

"They were supposed to kill all three of the American pigs!" he shouted as if it were Antonio's fault. "If they had done that, we could have just gotten rid of the bodies. There would be no one to complain, no witnesses! Now we will have the authorities watching the place and snooping around."

Emboldened by Ortega's admission that his men had made a mistake, Antonio pointed out, "I told you we should have just moved in and shot them all immediately."

The long silence that followed gave Antonio plenty of time to regret his lack of respect for his boss.

"Have they questioned the fool who has been feeding you information?" demanded Ortega at last.

"No, they only questioned the two pastors and the idiots who got away." Antonio was relieved that the captain had chosen for now to overlook his transgression, but he knew it would not be forgotten. His next words would not earn back Ortega's favor. "They did not seem to suspect any of the Americans, but the fat coward walks around looking as if he is going to start crying at any moment. I do not believe he will keep quiet for much longer."

"Then kill him, too!" Ortega yelled. "It is too late to worry about leaving the gringos out of this, anyway. The best we can do is make sure that he cannot tell what he knows. Then get away from that place."

"Are we going to leave Restrepo and his family alone?" Antonio was disappointed.

"Of course not, *pendejo!*" spat El Tiburon. "As soon as the authorities have lost interest, we will go in and take care of all of them."

"Since the authorities are already involved, why do we not just do it now?"

"Because, *tonto*, they will be watching the place now and will notice if a jeep full of my men arrives. Just do what you are told, and do not get caught."

Antonio could tell he had pushed too far. He quickly back-pedaled, injecting a note of humility into his tone. "Yes, Tiburon, I will take care of the *gordito*, and then I will come to you in Campo Dulce to await further orders."

"You had better." The threat in Ortega's voice was unmistakable. "When will you deal with him?"

"Tonight," promised Antonio.

Jeff was finishing the last of several other unpleasant but necessary phone calls when Sergio came into the room. With him was an older Colombian gentleman carrying two leather cases. They both waited patiently while Jeff completed his call and hung up the satellite phone.

"Pastor Jeff, this is Dr. Mosquera," Sergio explained. "Luís went to pick up some siding this morning and asked Dr. Mosquera if he would ride back with him to check on our young friend."

"Gunshot wound, I understand," said Dr. Mosquera in excellent English as the two men shook hands.

Jeff nodded. "Yes, we don't know how serious it is, and he lost a great deal of blood. He should be resting in the other building."

Sergio excused himself as Jeff and Dr. Mosquera walked across the courtyard to the men's dorm. Daniel's cot was empty.

Confused, Jeff checked the other cots, but Daniel was nowhere in sight. Selena walked past the door, dragging a bucket of water across the courtyard for unknown reasons.

"Selena, have you seen Daniel?" Jeff called after the girl, frustrated.

Selena gave him a wicked grin and jerked a thumb toward the back of the property, where the team was attaching siding to the new structure.

Daniel, wearing the makeshift sling Mindy had made for him and moving slower than usual, was using his good arm to help unload the long boards Luís had just brought.

"Oh, no. Daniel!" Jeff sighed in exasperation. To the doctor, he said, "Excuse me a minute while I go get our patient."

The doctor smiled. "Do not worry, my friend. I know how to deal with recalcitrant patients."

He dragged a chair for himself beside the cot Jeff had identified as Daniel's.

A few minutes later, a sheepish Daniel sat shirtless on the cot as the doctor checked his heart and blood pressure. Jeff stood watching a few feet away, with Kevin hovering anxiously beside him. Daniel grimaced as Dr. Mosquera began poking and prodding at the wound with some kind of stainless steel instrument.

"The bullet seems to have exited the arm, but it chipped off some of the bone here," Dr. Mosquera explained as he smeared something on a white cloth he had laid on the cot. "There are bone fragments in the wound that are probably causing more pain. You may have to have them removed surgically when you get back to the states."

Daniel nodded, clamping his mouth shut to keep from making any sound as the doctor continued digging. Didn't they believe in local anesthesia in Colombia?

To his relief, Dr. Mosquera wiped his tool one last time and put it back in his bag. He stuck a thermometer in Daniel's mouth and pulled out a small penlight.

"Have you been drinking plenty of liquids?" the doctor asked as he shined the light in Daniel's eyes.

Daniel nodded again, unable to speak around the thermometer.

"Have you been able to eat?" He snatched out the thermometer and peered at it.

Daniel started to nod again, then realized he could talk now. "Yes, sir. A little."

"Good," said the doctor. "Any nausea?"

"Not too bad today," Daniel said uneasily. He squirmed in embarrassment as the doctor asked a series of questions about bodily functions.

If Jeremy were here, he would be making wisecracks to distract Daniel and make him laugh, but all Jeff and Kevin could do was pretend a sudden intense interest in looking out the window until the doctor got through the awkward stuff.

Finally Dr. Mosquera began putting away his instruments of torture. "Can you move your fingers for me, please?"

Daniel obliged, or tried to. His fingers wouldn't fully cooperate, but the doctor seemed satisfied with his feeble efforts, because he nodded in approval.

"Good, good. I understand you've been outside building houses in spite of your injury."

"Uh, well..." Daniel felt guilty for disobeying Jeff's orders, but he couldn't stand staying in the room all alone, just staring at Jeremy's things. "I was wearing that sling thing."

"And you will continue to use the 'sling thing' until your regular doctor tells you otherwise, but you are not to do any more construction work. Your body temperature is dangerously low, your heartbeat is weak and your blood pressure is far below what it should be. You must understand it is very important that you stay here and rest. The only way your body can replenish itself is when it is at rest." The doctor enunciated the last sentence slowly to emphasize the importance.

"Yes, sir," said Daniel meekly as the doctor began rummaging in his other bag. He watched warily as Dr. Mosquera filled two wicked looking syringes.

"This first one is for the pain." The doctor stabbed Daniel's uninjured arm with the needle. Daniel tried not to flinch as the liquid burned its way into him.

Discarding the first syringe, Mosquera held up the other one to the light, checking the amount. "This is an antibiotic for the slight infection that has started. Tomorrow you will start on an oral antibiotic."

Daniel nodded, trying to follow what the doctor was saying. For some reason the words weren't coming together in his mind. Maybe he'd worked out in the sun too long that morning. When the doctor inserted the second needle, Daniel was surprised that he could barely feel it. He stared, mesmerized, as the fluid drained from the syringe.

Dr. Mosquera held a small pill bottle in front of Daniel and shook it. "This is the oral antibiotic. You will take one pill first thing in the morning, and every six hours after that. It is very important that you finish the bottle."

Again, Daniel nodded mutely, but the doctor's face was becoming fuzzy. When Mosquera held up a second bottle, Daniel saw three bottles instead of one. He blinked.

"These are for the pain. You may take one as needed, every four to six hours, starting tomorrow."

"Uh, tomorrow?" Daniel's dazed mind grasped at the only word that registered. He couldn't figure out why the doctor looked amused.

"I doubt that you will need them before then. Now lie back on your cot while I apply a fresh bandage."

Yes, lying down sounded good. With relief, Daniel lowered his head to the pillow as the doctor assembled cotton and gauze and a tiny pair of scissors.

Dr. Mosquera shook his head with regret while he skillfully applied the bandage. "It is unfortunate that our medical resources are so limited right now. He needs a much more thorough examination to determine the extent of the injury. He should have had his fluids replaced intravenously as soon as it happened, probably a blood transfusion."

"Will there be...permanent damage?" Jeff was concerned about the lack of mobility he'd just witnessed. He heard Kevin's sharp intake of breath and realized the possibility hadn't occurred to Kevin before.

"It is hard to tell without X-rays," the doctor admitted. "The most immediate concern is the blood loss, but there is nothing to be done about that here. There is definitely some nerve damage, and he will have severe scarring. He will likely need a skin graft to close the wound, possibly some repairs to the bone. As to his mobility, well, he will need extensive rehabilitation when he gets home."

Jeff sighed heavily at the response. He hated the thought of the athletic young man being scarred and maybe permanently debilitated. Beside him, Kevin was clenching and unclenching his fists.

Mosquera snipped the bandage and gave it a final inspection before putting his things away. He must have noticed their downcast faces. "I am only a man. Do not underestimate the healing power of God. Daniel is alive. It is already a miracle that his organs did not shut down from the massive blood loss. It is a miracle that the infection is so minor considering the unsanitary conditions he has been in. It is a miracle that he is walking around doing things that he should not be doing without the benefit of pain medication. Do not lose hope."

Dr. Mosquera offered the two pill bottles to Jeff. "I will leave the medications with you. They should make him more comfortable and help with that infection. But please see that he gets proper medical attention when he gets home."

Jeff accepted the bottles and absently stuck them in his pocket. "Thank you for all you've done, Doctor. I'll make sure Daniel follows your instructions."

"And I'll try to make him stay here and rest," Kevin offered. "But he's pretty stubborn."

"I do not think that will be a problem." Dr. Mosquera smiled and indicated the cot. Daniel's head had lolled to the side and he was snoring gently. "He should sleep until morning. The first shot was only a mild painkiller, but in his weakened condition, it acts as a powerful anesthetic. I normally would not risk it, but the situation appeared to call for drastic measures."

Uncomfortable that the doctor had taken such liberties without his or Daniel's consent, Jeff smothered his concerned objections. After all, customs were different in Colombia and he shouldn't complain, especially with medical help so inaccessible right now. Besides, knowing Daniel, it was probably the only way to keep him in bed. He followed Dr. Mosquera out to the courtyard to take care of the bill, but the doctor waved away his offer of payment.

"We are brothers in Christ. You are here to help our people rebuild. It is the least I could do."

Jeff thanked him sincerely, and the men shook hands.

As Dr. Mosquera left, Jeff glanced back inside in time to see Kevin take a sheet off Jeremy's empty cot and drape it over Daniel's bare torso, protecting his friend's modesty.

Jeff's heart ached for them all.

Jeff didn't have it in him to give a devotional that evening. When the students gathered in the sanctuary after their chores were done, he just read to them Isaiah 41:10. "'Do not fear, for I am with you. Do not be dismayed, for I am your God. I will strengthen you and help you. I will uphold you with My righteous right hand.'"

Then he asked them to gather at the front to pray, and they all joined hands, clinging more tightly to one another than usual. Paola and Sergio had joined them, but the circle still seemed incomplete without Jeremy asking for prayers for his sister, or Daniel's quiet, contemplative prayers.

Jeff somehow got through it. As soon as the group uttered "Amen," Jeff excused himself and went to the house, dejected and feeling more ineffective than ever.

Sergio followed Pastor Jeff out, leaving the students to linger in the sanctuary, restless and worried.

Paola stayed with them, sitting between Mindy and Selena. She'd had her fill of solitude and took comfort in being around the life and energy of the young people, even though they were now reeling from the shock of their own loss.

Without Daniel around, Kevin finally opened up and shared the details from their tragic adventure.

"It's like they knew we was in that room," he finished, sounding bewildered. "We didn't make no noise, but they came straight to that room we was in, chargin' in with their guns already out."

His words triggered a memory in Paola. "When they attacked Stefan and me, it was like they were expecting us, too. At first I thought they were lying in wait to rob anyone who passed, but they would not waste their time on such a deserted road. Besides, they are cocaine dealers, not highway robbers, so they must have been expecting us to come that way. And they knew who Stefan was. They said his name and called him a traitor before they...before they killed him."

She shut her eyes tightly as the emptiness welled up in her again.

Mindy patted her hand sympathetically, then wondered aloud, "But how could they have known you and Stefan were going to Raul's that evening? How did they know the boys were going to be there last night?"

The group was silent for a moment. Then Kevin suggested, "Maybe they was listenin' to the radio transmissions."

"No, Sergio has been careful not to give away any information on the radio ever since the Mexican volunteers were killed," Paola assured them. "Besides, Raul does not even have a radio, so there was no one to discuss our intentions with. No one mentioned our plans on the radio, I am sure of it."

"Then somebody here must have given them the information directly," Resha pointed out.

"Like a spy or somethin'?" Kevin asked.

"It's creepy thinking somebody's watching us." Selena shuddered. "Could it be Luís or Antonio?"

Behind her, Manny grew more and more fidgety.

Paola shook her head, certain that her brother's helpers could not have done such a thing.

Terrell seemed to agree with her. "Luís and Antonio couldn't have had enough information to tip off the Black Eagles. They're hardly around, and they weren't anywhere near us while the guys were planning that stuff. They hardly even speak English."

Realization hit them all at once. Paola and the students stared at one another until Mindy spoke their thoughts out loud. "Does that mean...one of us is responsible?"

"Seems like the logical explanation," Resha drawled.

Selena frowned. "But why would any of us be involved? We're not even Colombian."

Paola couldn't imagine that any of the students secretly had any ties to the Black Eagles, but they all studied each other appraisingly.

Inevitably, the students' eyes slid to the only member of the team who seemed hostile. As usual, Samuel had not contributed to their discussion.

When he saw their suspicion, he laughed without mirth. "You suspect me because I appear different from the rest of you. I do not talk like you or dress like you or laugh at the things you think are funny, but inside I am the same." He thumped his chest to indicate his heart. "You need to stop looking for someone who is different on the outside and look for someone who is different on the inside."

They all just stared at him. Samuel laughed again and walked out of the room.

The young Americans looked frightened now, especially Manny. The chubby boy had gone white.

Pobrecito, Paola thought. *Now that the evidence seems to point to one of the students, Manny is probably afraid he will be sleeping next to the traitor responsible for Jeremy's death.*

Fully dressed, Resha tossed and turned on her cot, trying not to wake the others with her restlessness. Her mind wouldn't stop churning with muddled thoughts and there was no way she'd get to sleep any time soon. Excitement about Selena's conversion, memories of Jeremy, apprehension about what The Black Eagles were planning – all competed for space in her sleep-deprived brain.

She was still pondering Samuel's cryptic words, wondering if they had meant anything or if he had just been lashing out in anger because they suspected him. The Nigerian man's ways were so strange, but what he said had reminded her of Pastor Jeff's lesson on judging.

Samuel had suggested they look for someone who was different on the inside.

What was that scripture Pastor Jeff had quoted? Something about not judging according to appearance, but judging righteously. That went right along with a verse Daniel had showed her the next day, about how we tend to judge others by the way they look, but God looks at their heart. Was that what Samuel had been getting at? But how could they tell whose heart was different?

As Resha lay staring at the ceiling, a faint sound from outside reached her ears. She frowned and listened carefully.

There it was again. Someone was definitely walking around in the courtyard.

Glancing at her watch, she saw it was nearly midnight. It couldn't be Daniel again. Kevin had told them how the doctor had drugged him. Had it worn off already? She peered out the window but saw no one.

Resha slipped out the door, carefully closing it without a sound.

346

There was movement at the end of the courtyard, a person making his way to the far corner of the main building, where he stood looking around uncertainly.

Manny?

Manny fidgeted nervously. Antonio had promised to explain everything tonight, but Manny no longer trusted him. Too much had gone wrong.

He thought of how Antonio had slapped him when he'd stupidly burned down the storage building. Okay, that had been a dumb thing to do, but couldn't Antonio tell Manny had done it to show his loyalty to the Black Eagles?

Obviously loyalty was important to them – they'd killed Stefan for being disloyal. Manny tried to convince himself he had nothing to worry about – he wouldn't betray them. Not because he believed any longer in the promises Antonio had made, but because he was too scared to betray them.

Stefan's and Jeremy's deaths weighed heavily on his conscience. If Manny hadn't passed information to Antonio, the Black Eagles wouldn't have known about their activities, and maybe none of it would have happened. Manny tried to convince himself they would have found out some other way.

Besides, Antonio had assured him everything would make sense after tonight. He'd even said Manny might get to meet with El Tiburon soon, and then things would start looking up for him.

Maybe they were ready to get him more involved so he could start making money from their drug trade. If Manny made enough money, he might be able to forget about his own guilt.

He glanced around apprehensively. Where was Antonio?

It was obvious Manny was waiting for someone.

Resha tried to decide whether to confront Manny or to wait to see who he was meeting. The door opened behind her and Selena ambled out, barefoot and disheveled.

Great.

"Resha?" Selena asked sleepily, raking her hand through her tousled hair. "What are you doing? Are you meeting Daniel again?"

Resha tried not to show her irritation. "It's not Daniel, Selena. It's your brother."

"You're meeting Manny now?" Selena's eyes grew wide. She'd been hanging around Mindy too long.

"Not me, dummy. It looks like he's waiting for someone, and I'm trying to find out who."

"Well, let's just ask him." Selena was wide awake now.

Resha hissed at her to wait, but Selena started marching toward her brother. Resha followed quietly, staying in the shadows.

At least Selena had enough sense not to yell at Manny across the courtyard and wake everyone up. As she drew even with Manny, she demanded, "Manny, what do you think you're doing?"

Manny jumped, startled. Evidently whoever he was expecting was supposed to come from the other direction. "Selena? You don't need to be out here. Go back to bed."

"No." Selena folded her arms and planted her bare feet. "I'm not leaving until you tell me what you're up to."

Manny sighed. "Look, what I'm doing is none of your business, okay?"

"It is my business," Selena argued firmly, straightening to stand at her full height and putting her hands on her hips. "Mama told me to keep you out of trouble, so you have to tell me what's going on."

"Okay, but keep it down, huh?" Manny glanced around nervously. "Antonio and I have a little side deal going, that's all."

In the shadows, Resha crept closer to hear better. Was Manny the traitor? Suddenly Samuel's words from earlier made sense. Manny and Selena had been the only ones who had not accepted Christ, and now Selena had become a Christian. So only Manny was different from the rest of them "on the inside." Of course!

Selena, meanwhile, made no attempt to honor Manny's request that she "keep it down." She flailed her arms and her voice rose in agitation. "A side deal? What kind of side deal, Manny? I'm going to tell Pastor Sergio."

"Pastor Sergio does not want what is best for the Colombian people." Manny spoke in a monotone, like he was quoting a phrase that had been drilled into his brain over and over.

Selena rolled her eyes. "Oh, please, what kind of garbage is that? He stayed here and is doing all this work for free just so the other people can come home. He's telling people about God."

"But he's keeping them poor, Selena," Manny insisted, sounding more like himself again. "The people could be making money, lots of money, but he convinces them it's wrong."

Selena gaped in disbelief. "Are you talking about drugs, Manny? Growing cocaine? How stupid can you get? That's not only illegal, it's flat out wrong!"

"Not growing it, Selena," Manny said contemptuously. "I'm no farmer. The money is in exporting it."

Resha was tempted to go out there and smack Manny for his stupidity, but Selena would probably take care of that herself in about another minute. Resha kept still. Maybe she could learn something that would be helpful to the two agents who had come by earlier.

Then Resha noticed someone else hidden among the trees behind Manny and Selena, listening to every word. Antonio!

Only tonight, Antonio looked nothing like the passive workman he normally presented himself as. His face wore a derisive sneer, and without his usual loose-fitting workshirt covering his sleeveless T-shirt, Resha could see strong muscles rippling in his arms. A lit cigarette dangled from one of his hands.

Manny and Selena must be too distracted to notice the smoke from it. Resha pressed herself deeper into the shadows, hoping Antonio wouldn't see her.

"What do you know about exporting drugs, Manny?" Selena demanded. "You're just a little punk kid."

Manny flinched at her remark, then drew himself up. "I know a lot more than you think. I'm not talking about being a sleazy drug dealer on the corner making pocket change. This is a powerful organization with international connections. Antonio's been teaching me, and I've already had a part in some of their operations."

The truth hit Selena hard. "Antonio? Oh, my God, Manny. You're the one who's been giving out information! You and Antonio are responsible for getting Jeremy killed!"

"That wasn't supposed to happen." Doubt crossed Manny's features. "I think that was an accident."

"Oh, please, Manny, even you're not that stupid!" Selena was starting to look scared. "You better not get involved with these people. They're dangerous!"

"It is too late, *mijita,* he is already involved." Antonio stepped out from the shadows, speaking perfect English. He flicked his cigarette aside calmly. "And now, so are you."

From her hiding place, Resha could see the gun Antonio held slightly behind him, just out of sight of Manny and Selena. Terrific. What was she supposed to do with that?

Resha considered going for help, but getting to either Pastor Sergio's house or the men's dorm would force her out into the open where Antonio could easily see her.

Besides, there might not be enough time. Resha toyed with the idea of confronting him herself, but for some reason, the thought of fighting with Antonio terrified her, even though a few nights ago she'd taken on several armed soldiers without hesitation. Maybe it was because Daniel had been at her side that night, or maybe it was because the soldiers they'd fought with had been younger and clumsier. Antonio moved with the confidence of a master martial artist, and his eyes held an evil intelligence that had been missing from the young commandos they'd attacked. Resha remembered the look of hatred she'd seen in Antonio's eyes the day he'd dodged the falling pipe, and her heart started to pound.

Selena wouldn't be much help if it came to a physical confrontation, and Resha couldn't count on Manny's assistance. He was gawking at Antonio, obviously scared and confused.

So she continued to listen, hoping the situation would somehow end peacefully.

"Your brother has placed you in an awkward position, *chicita*," Antonio said. "Now you know too much."

"I know enough to know you tricked my little brother into helping you." Selena put her hands on her hips and glared at him with more guts than Resha would have given her credit for. Then again, Selena wasn't on her own any more – she had Someone Else inside of her now, giving her the courage to continue. "And since you're standing there speaking English, I guess you've been lying to Pastor Sergio, too, making him think you're just some poor working peasant. Well, you won't get away with this."

Resha felt like cheering at the way Selena stood up to him, but she wondered if Selena realized how dangerous her predicament really was.

Antonio's next word's erased any doubts. "That is too bad. I do not enjoy killing beautiful women, but you leave me no choice." He whipped out the pistol and pointed it at Selena's head, and she and Manny both gasped. "Come, let us step away from the buildings."

Eyes fixed on the gun, Manny and Selena both backed up in the direction Antonio indicated.

"Oh, come on, Antonio, that's my sister," Manny whined, but from the way he was cringing, he was clearly not about to physically defend Selena.

Antonio laughed. "Am I supposed to care about that?"

Don't go! He's going to kill you! Resha's mind screamed as they moved farther away from the compound so that gunshots wouldn't be heard by the others. Antonio was clearly planning to shoot them both, then probably dump their bodies into the ravine, which had swollen again after the recent rain. They would be carried downstream and not be discovered for days, giving Antonio plenty of time to disappear.

And Resha was the only one around to help.

God, do You really expect me to do something?

Cold sweat prickled her scalp as she considered it. Her breathing became shallow and her heart beat so hard she thought it might pop out of her chest, alien-like. As she struggled to figure out what to do, all of her senses in overdrive, Resha heard a faint sound from the side.

Mindy was making her way across the courtyard.

Oh, no, thought Resha, Not her of all people. Lord, why couldn't You have sent me someone who could actually help?

Mindy stared pointedly into the darkness where Resha had hidden herself, as if she were trying to communicate something. Then she began walking noisily and stubbed her toe. She yelped aloud. "Ooh, that hurt!"

Three sets of eyes turned to Mindy, and Resha realized the other girl was deliberately providing a distraction. Still uncertain, Resha took advantage of the diversion and slipped several feet closer to the trio, careful to remain in the shadows. She positioned herself behind a flowering shrub to watch.

Mindy waved cheerfully to Selena and the others, seemingly oblivious to the tension. "Hi, you guys. I couldn't sleep either. I guess I'm just so excited that we're almost finished."

Antonio moved behind Selena to keep the gun from Mindy's sight, but he kept the barrel pressed firmly against Selena's back so she wouldn't cry out a warning. Resha could see his jaw tighten and knew he was losing patience.

"Oh, Antonio, you're here, too!" Mindy sounded delighted to see him.

The pretty redhead was nearly even with them now, blocking Antonio's view of Resha. Resha used the moment to move in closer still. She slid quickly and quietly behind the thick trunk of a tree and crouched, hoping for an opportunity to do something, although she had no idea what.

As soon as Mindy was within range of the gun, Antonio acted. He suddenly twisted one of Selena's arms behind her, causing her to gasp in pain. At the same moment, he pulled the gun from behind her and pointed it at Mindy, keeping a firm grip on Selena.

"Go stand beside her brother," he ordered.

"Antonio!" Mindy exclaimed as if surprised at his naughtiness, but Resha was glad to see that she obeyed him. "I didn't know you could speak English! And what are you doing with that gun?"

"Solving a problem." Without warning, Antonio whipped the pistol around and slammed it into the side of Selena's head.

Selena crumpled to the ground. Manny's mouth dropped open in shock. For once, Mindy didn't burst into tears, but ran to Selena's side and knelt beside her.

Cold sweat streaked Resha's face as she tried to slow her breathing, psyching herself up for what would surely be an uneven battle.

Satisfied that the two girls were occupied for now, Antonio pointed the gun at Manny. "You fool. My orders were only to get rid of you tonight, but because you could not keep your mouth shut, I will have to kill both of them, too."

Manny opened and closed his mouth like a fish. "But, Antonio, I've been helping you. I'm supposed to be one of you." When Antonio only sneered, Manny continued desperately, practically in tears. "I thought...I thought...you said I was special, that you could use somebody like me..."

Antonio curled his lip in disgust. "We did use you, *baboso*. You think I picked you because you were better than the others? I chose you because you are weak and lazy and would believe what I told you. We used you for information, but I have no more use for you."

Antonio cocked the pistol, no longer concerned about their distance from the buildings.

Okay, Resha thought, The guy's not kidding. I either have to do something or stand here and watch Manny get his head blown off. It's now or never, Lord. Help!

Pushing her fears to the side, Resha spun out of the darkness and put every ounce of her strength into the roundhouse kick she aimed at Antonio's wrist.

The gun flew out of Antonio's hand as Resha's foot impacted it, but the element of surprise lasted less than a second. Although Antonio had always played the part of a docile helper for Sergio's benefit, he now revealed himself as a conditioned warrior. Resha suspected he had more than a few martial arts moves of his own. He also had a good hundred pounds over Resha. And he was angry.

That last part scared her the most.

With a vicious curse, Antonio lunged for the gun. Resha had to keep him from getting it. She raced Antonio and beat him to it by a millisecond, giving it a swift kick that sent it sliding across the bumpy stones of the courtyard.

Antonio gave a furious growl and changed his direction to attack Resha. He landed a kick to her ribs which sent her to the ground, but she ignored the pain and managed to roll out of his reach and bounce onto her feet before he could land another.

Fear threatened to immobilize Resha as Antonio came at her with his arms slicing the air in deadly arcs, but she had to keep moving if she wanted to survive this encounter. Any hope she had for going on the offensive quickly evaporated and she fell back on defensive maneuvers, blocking and ducking as she deliberately moved away from the others and closer to the buildings.

From the corner of her eye, she spied Mindy going for the gun, but she had no time to see what would come of that. If another of Antonio's blows hit, Resha would go down for sure, but she managed to keep dancing just out of his reach, feeling only the edge of his strikes.

Tired of shrinking back, Resha ducked under a particularly vicious jab from Antonio and managed to get in a quick body blow to his rib cage. The only effect it had was to make him angrier, and she quickly spun away from him again.

Antonio's mouth poured out vile curses in Spanish, but the blood pounding in Resha's ears kept her from making out all the words. As near as she could tell, it was something to the effect that he was going to rip her heart out and feed it to the dog. She dodged another thrust, twisting out of the way just before it landed on her neck.

When Resha found herself backed against the pile of concrete that had been the fountain, Antonio smiled. He paused as if to savor the moment, but it was enough time for Resha to whip her switchblade from her jeans. Antonio narrowed his eyes and took half a step back as she slashed at him in rapid motions.

Feeling a sliver of confidence, Resha lunged forward with the knife, sending him back another step.

But Antonio was not retreating. He had taken the step back to better aim his kick, which knocked the knife from Resha's hand and sent hot sparks of pain through her hand and wrist.

She tried to retaliate with a kick of her own, but he was too fast. He caught her foot and twisted hard, and she hit the ground face first.

Ignoring the stars exploding in her head, Resha made herself roll over, hoping to kick at him before he could pin her down. Antonio was already on her, striking the side of her head with his fist. The blow dazed her, and she knew she had no chance of winning this fight.

Survival was her only goal now.

Seeing Antonio's fist pulled back to strike again, Resha tried to scramble out of his way but found herself blocked by the fountain.

Well, Jeremy, I guess I'll be seeing you soon. Resha scrunched her eyes shut.

Instead of feeling the crushing blow, Resha heard a gunshot. Had Mindy actually figured out how to fire the thing?

Antonio spun around to face whatever new threat had approached, and Resha used the opportunity to quickly back-crawl out of his reach.

"Antonio, if you touch her again, I will not hesitate to use this on you."

It was Pastor Sergio's voice, not Mindy's. Through bleary eyes, Resha saw Sergio wielding the gun like a professional. He looked fearsome in his anger in spite of his small stature. Exhausted, Resha leaned her aching body against the broken fountain and curled up, hoping the reprieve would last.

Antonio crouched as if to lunge at Sergio.

Sergio shook his head in warning. "There are several bullets left in this gun. It will only take one to kill you. And if that is not enough, look around you, Antonio. No matter how skilled you are, you cannot fight all of us."

The rest of the men emerged from the shadows, wielding makeshift weapons. Mild mannered Pastor Jeff looked out of place brandishing a three foot length of metal pipe, but it was clear he was ready to use it if necessary. Terrell and Kevin stood by with pipes of their own, and even

Samuel was wielding a two by four. Every one of them looked ready to kill Antonio on the spot for what he'd done to Resha, but they managed to hold themselves back.

Luís, unarmed, looked at Antonio sorrowfully.

"How could you do this, Antonio?" Luís asked the man he'd treated as a friend. "We have worked side by side as brothers this last month. Pastor Sergio took you in and gave you a home when you lost everything."

Antonio spat. "You fools, I did not lose anything! You Christians are so trusting you believed everything I told you, but I was sent here by the Black Eagles to find that traitor Guzman. They hoped I would be able to persuade Sergio to cooperate without violence, but he is too blinded by his ignorant beliefs."

"It is not ignorant to serve God, Antonio," Sergio told him. He nodded at Luís, who approached Antonio with a rope in his hand.

Antonio snarled and made a move as if to strike Luís when Luís came near. Sergio took a step closer, cocking the pistol, and Antonio reconsidered. He allowed his wrists to be bound behind his back, cursing at them the whole time.

"You will pay for this, Sergio," Antonio growled. "The influence of Las Águilas Negras is everywhere. I will not remain a prisoner, and when I am free, you will pay."

Sergio looked at him sadly. "You misjudge the loyalty of your comrades, I am afraid. Their concern is not for your welfare, but for what you will reveal about them to the Colombian authorities. Not everyone in the government has been bought."

Fear crossed Antonio's face for a moment, but he quickly reverted to cursing at Pastor Sergio and swearing vengeance by the Black Eagles.

"You will stay here until help arrives," Sergio informed his prisoner. As soon as Antonio was securely tied, Luís and Sergio led him forcibly into the sanctuary.

With Antonio subdued, Jeff, Terrell and Kevin tossed their metal pipes to the ground and rushed to Resha's side as Samuel stood back and watched. Mindy appeared from somewhere and beat all the rest of them to Resha. They crouched beside her, peering at her anxiously.

At that moment, they all looked beautiful to Resha.

"Resha? Resha?" Mindy cried, grabbing at Resha's hands. "Are you okay?"

Peachy, Resha wanted to say, but it took too much effort to be sarcastic, so she said nothing.

She was still dazed from the assault. Blood trickled from her nose, and her cheek was scraped from landing on the jagged stones. She tried taking a deep breath to clear her pounding head, but stopped because it hurt too much to fill her lungs. She wondered if her ribs were broken. She felt sure her knuckles were.

Mindy cooed at her and dabbed at her face with a napkin, trying to wipe off some of the blood. Resha worked her jaw, assessing the damage. Not too bad, considering. At least she still had all her teeth.

"How...?" Talking was too painful, so Resha didn't finish her question.

Pastor Jeff understood what she wanted to know. "Mindy came and told Pastor Sergio what was happening, and gave him the gun. I rounded up the rest of the men to help."

"Do you think you can stand up?" Terrell asked her.

Resha was surprised to see genuine concern on his face. She managed to nod, and he and Kevin gently helped her to her feet while Jeff looked on with a worried frown. She swayed, but they steadied her until she got her bearings.

"I'm okay now." Resha tried to make her voice firm. The men released her but stayed close as she took a few steps.

"Come on, let's get you inside," Mindy chirped, placing her arm around Resha's waist to support her. She shooed the three men away. "Go on. Resha and I will take it from here."

Inside their room, Resha dragged herself to her cot. She sat and allowed Mindy to apply antiseptic to her cheek. As much as Mindy's cheery prattling grated on Resha's nerves, she was thankful for the girl's skillful ministrations right now.

"You look worse than me," a familiar voice drawled without sympathy.

Resha looked up and saw Selena sitting on her own cot, holding an ice pack to her head. Resha had been so intent on getting out alive that she'd forgotten about the others. Mindy was poking at Resha's side now, feeling for broken ribs, and Resha pushed her away impatiently.

"Where's Manny?" she demanded, her voice tense.

Selena laughed, but stopped abruptly and held her head, grimacing. "Ow, that hurts. Manny ran away right after you got the gun away from Antonio. What a guy, huh?"

Resha wasn't interested in analyzing Manny's character right now. She'd just taken a serious beating to save his life.

"Somebody better find him before the Black Eagles do."

14

Day 13: Friday

The next morning Terrell and Kevin stood over Daniel's cot, watching him snore.

"Guess that shot hasn't worn off yet," Terrell observed.

"Daniel gonna be mad when he finally wakes up," Kevin remarked.

They left for breakfast without him.

With most of the team out of action, it was a sparse group that gathered in the dining room. Only Samuel, Kevin, Terrell and Mindy joined the pastors and Luís at the tables.

Resha was too sore from her battle with Antonio to get out of bed yet, and Selena was too embarrassed to show her face after learning that her brother had betrayed them. Antonio had been taken into custody by the American Embassy early that morning, along with Manny, whom Terrell and Kevin had found last night, lost and whimpering in the jungle across the arroyo.

None of them had much energy for the work that morning, but thankfully there was very little left for them to do. Samuel began painting the fresh siding they'd put up on the new building while Terrell and Kevin finished up the sheetrock on the inside. Mindy swept up the mess they'd made. When Resha and Selena joined Mindy after lunch, the three of them put a coat of paint on the interior walls.

With the new building finished except for the wiring, the team's job was complete. When the students had first arrived in Colombia, they'd expected to celebrate when the work was all done, but after everything that had happened, they felt nothing but a vague sense of relief.

Even Sergio was subdued by the events of the past week, but he still seemed pleased and appreciative that the work was finished. He walked around the mission center admiring the job they'd done and nodding his approval under the watchful eye of two Colombian police officers that had been stationed at the mission center for the time being.

"Now I am certain that the mission center is ready to reopen, and soon it will be filled with volunteers from a relief organization, and with local workers and their families as they rebuild their homes and recultivate their fields," he told Pastor Jeff. "You and the students have all worked so hard and sacrificed so much to help make it possible. Words cannot thank you."

Daniel peeled his crusted eyes open. Was it getting dark already, or was something wrong with his eyes? He licked dry lips and looked around in confusion.

It sounded like someone was running the sink in the tiny bathroom. Daniel turned on the cot, trying to see his watch in the fading light.

A moment later, Kevin came out of the bathroom drying his face with a dingy towel. "Hey, you finally up?"

"Where's the doctor? Did he leave already?" Daniel's tongue felt thick as he forced out the words.

Kevin grinned. "Yeah, buddy, the doctor left. Yesterday."

"Yesterday?" Daniel hauled himself to a sitting position, then shut his eyes as dizziness washed over him. "Whoa."

"Take it easy, man." Kevin opened the half-finished bottle of Gatorade that was still sitting beside the cot and handed it to him. "The doctor left you some kinda pain medicine. Want me to ask Pastor Jeff for it?"

Daniel's arm hurt, but not enough to make him swallow a pill. He shook his head, but the movement made his head spin again. He took a sip of the Gatorade and felt a little more coherent. "I've been asleep since yesterday? It's Friday already?"

Kevin hovered around Daniel, watching him closely. "Yeah, man. I think you was fakin', just to get out of work."

Daniel stared at him, too befuddled to appreciate Kevin's attempt at humor. He frowned. "I need to get up and help. We have to get everything finished today."

He leaned over to reach for his shoes and nearly toppled all the way onto the floor.

"Relax, man, it's all done." Kevin gripped Daniel's shoulder to steady him. "You woke up just in time for dinner."

Daniel ran his hands shakily through his hair, absorbing the information. "Dinner? It's that late? What happened?"

"That doctor gave you somethin' to knock you out 'cuz you wouldn't stay in bed." Kevin snickered. "You comin' to eat?"

The thought of food repulsed him. "Bleah. I think I'll pass."

"Just come out there an' sit with us, then," Kevin urged.

Daniel didn't want to be alone, but he wasn't up to facing the whole group. He reached under his pillow for his Bible. "No, I think I'll stay in here and read awhile."

"Okay, man." Kevin reluctantly headed for the door.

Daniel stood up cautiously, then waited until he stopped swaying before making his way unsteadily toward the little bathroom. When he finally reached it, he noticed Kevin was still standing in the doorway with a worried frown. Aggravated, Daniel said, "Kevin, I'm okay. Will you just go and eat?"

Kevin gave a sheepish grin. "Okay, I'll go before you start callin' me Jeff Jr.. But I'ma come get you after we eat. Man, we got a lot to tell you!"

The group, minus Manny and Selena, had gathered for their final debriefing before their departure the next morning.

Resha sat on a chair at the end of the row so she could prop her aching body up against the wall. Mindy had wrapped the hand that Antonio had kicked, but the fingertips that peeked out from the bandage were swollen and purple. Her face was swollen, too, and scraped raw where she'd skidded across the stones. It was an effort to maintain her usual poker face as Kevin and Terrell recounted for Daniel the events of the previous evening.

"I can't believe I slept through all that," Daniel groaned, running a hand over his head in frustration. He turned to Resha with sorrowful eyes. "I should have been there."

Feeling his gaze on her, Resha guessed what Daniel was thinking. He was undoubtedly feeling guilty and useless. That was ridiculous, of course. With that winged arm, he'd probably have just gotten in the way if he'd tried to help, maybe gotten them both killed. She hadn't needed Daniel's help, anyway – God had sent Mindy to rescue her.

Resha laughed to herself at God's sense of humor. She gave Daniel a wink, causing him to draw back in surprise.

When Kevin and Terrell had finished filling Daniel in, Jeff resumed his chair on the platform.

"What's going to happen to Manny?" Mindy asked.

"Manny is safe for now at the American Embassy," Jeff explained. "They'll have to turn him over to the Colombian authorities, of course, but they felt like he'd be in danger if they let him go to the general prison. They'll have to make arrangements to make sure he's protected before they release him to their custody."

Terrell frowned. "So he's going to be charged with something?"

Jeff sighed. Manny had been difficult to get close to, but he was still one of them. Jeff hoped things would go well for the boy. "Probably. He was involved in criminal activity, after all, even if he was just a pawn to them. Their government isn't as lenient as ours. But for now, I think they just want to get as much information out of him as they can."

"Selena told me she was going to stay in Colombia to be with her brother," Mindy told them.

Jeff had already discussed that with Pastor Sergio. "Well, I don't know if she'll be allowed to visit him, but he'll probably feel better knowing she's still close by. I talked to their parents, and they'll be here as soon as they can catch a flight. Hopefully they'll get it all sorted out."

"What about you, Pastor Jeff?" Daniel asked.

"I'll have to stay here at least a few days, too, to answer any more questions they have." He paused, looking at Daniel and Kevin. "And I promised Jeremy's parents I would stay here until the authorities release his body."

An uncomfortable silence settled over the group. Finally, Daniel said, "I didn't know they had his body."

Wanting to protect them as much as he could from more grief, Jeff responded with the impersonal wording he had seen on the paperwork. "The Colombian authorities have possession of Jeremy's body. They'll make sure he's shipped home as soon as their investigation is complete."

"How do they investigate something like this?" Mindy asked tearfully. "I thought the government was all corrupt."

Sergio stood up from his chair on the front row and joined Jeff. "No, the president of Colombia is trying to rid Colombia of the drug traffickers who have controlled much of the country for so long. There are many good men here who are working against the illegal activities of groups like The Black Eagles, but smaller, less civilized areas such as ours are often overlooked, allowing for much corruption in the law enforcement agencies here."

The little Colombian pastor began to pace on the platform. "If there is anything at all good about this situation, it is that your friend's death has gotten the attention of the authorities in Bogota as well as drawing attention from your own country's authorities. While government officials have not previously concerned themselves with the activities of the drug dealers in our region, they are now forced to become involved because an American citizen was murdered."

Sergio stopped pacing and faced the group. "Perhaps... perhaps Jeremy's sacrifice will result in finally crippling the operations of The Black Eagles in this area."

A sturdily-built, bearded guard unlocked Antonio's cell. Antonio glowered at him threateningly, but the guard was not intimidated.

"Antonio Moreno?" he inquired without expression. "Come with me, please."

Antonio swung his legs off the metal cot and narrowed his eyes. "For what purpose?"

"An agent from the American Embassy is here to question you," the guard said indifferently. Then, so that only Antonio could hear, the guard leaned in and said quietly, "My name is Diego. El Tiburon sent me."

At that, Antonio got up quickly and followed the man out of the cell and down the hall.

As soon as they were out of sight of the other prisoners, the guard discreetly slipped Antonio a gun. "Captain Ortega told me to give you this. He said to tell you not to worry, you will not spend one more night in that cell."

Antonio grinned as he accepted the gun. El Tiburon must think very highly of him to send a personal escort, and so soon. He checked to see that the weapon was loaded, then slid it into his waistband, keeping one hand on the grip as they rounded a corner.

Suddenly he was looking into the barrel of Diego's gun.

In spite of his confusion, years of training enabled Antonio to move at lightening speed. He whipped the pistol from his waistband, but he wasn't fast enough. Diego had been highly trained, too – he had pulled the trigger before Antonio could fully raise his weapon.

At the report from Diego's gun, several others came running, including F.B.I. Agent Richard Massey, who had been waiting in the interrogation room.

Diego put on a frightened look. "I was bringing him to the room for questioning, and he pulled a gun on me!"

They stared at the prisoner's fallen body, trying not to look at what was left of his head. Sure enough, Antonio still clutched a gun in one hand. Shocked, one of the other officers asked, "Where did he get that gun?"

Diego shook his head in fake bewilderment. "I do not know. But when he pointed it at me, I had no choice but to shoot him. It was self defense!"

More and more uniformed guards were pouring into the hallway towards the gory scene, but one man walked away. It was obvious what had happened here, but he knew there would be no proof, no investigation.

Agent Richard Massey left the building in resignation, knowing that no information would be forthcoming from a dead man. Antonio had reaped the consequences for his evil actions, but in doing so, had left Massey without a link to the others who'd been involved.

God would have to find another way to carry out His justice on the rest of them.

"I have one more thing to tell you all," Jeff said.

Sergio excused himself at once. With regret, Jeff watched him go. Moral support from the other pastor would have been nice, but after much discussion, he and Sergio had decided it was best for Jeff to be alone with his team.

He looked at the floor for several moments, mustering his courage. This wasn't going to be easy, for any of them. Would Jeff's revelation comfort them, or would it make things worse? Either way, Jeremy's parents and Jeff had agreed that the group deserved to know.

"There's something you all need to know...about Jeremy." Jeff took a deep breath, then just said it. "Kevin, you were right. He did know he was going to die."

Mindy gasped. Kevin gaped. Daniel swallowed hard. They all waited for more.

"He just didn't expect it to be like that. When I talked to Jeremy's parents yesterday I asked them if it would be okay to share this with you and Daniel, Kevin. They told me I should tell the whole group if I wanted to, since you've all become close on this trip."

Now that he'd gotten started, the story came tumbling out. "A couple of months ago, Jeremy came to me with some distressing news. He'd been diagnosed with an incurable form of leukemia. It was in the early stages, so he probably had a couple of years, especially if he'd gotten treatment, but he hadn't decided yet if he was going to have treatment or not."

Daniel dropped his face into his hands, unable to speak. Kevin shot up from his chair and yelled angrily, "'Course he was gonna get treatment!"

As if that made a difference now. Jeff just looked away.

Kevin walked a few steps, then sat down again abruptly, as if he didn't know what to do with himself. Finding the real source of his hurt, he yelled again, almost accusingly, "Why didn't he tell us?"

Jeff dragged his eyes back to Kevin, wanting to offer what little reassurance he could. "He was going to, Kevin. He was going to wait until he couldn't hide his symptoms any longer."

Kevin was on his feet again. "We was like brothers! We could'a helped him through this. He should have told us!"

Jeff agreed with Kevin, but he'd honored Jeremy's request for secrecy. Later, they would have questions about Jeremy's illness, but for now they just felt betrayed. He tried to alleviate some of it. "He was afraid you would start treating him differently, and he wasn't ready for that. It was really important to him that the three of you had this trip together without you and Daniel worrying about his sickness the whole time. I didn't think he should come because of his illness, but he insisted, so Pastor Meyer and I convinced the board to approve his application."

The last admission almost choked him with guilt. If he hadn't allowed Jeremy to come, Jeremy wouldn't have been killed.

Kevin now sat stoically, glaring straight ahead, arms folded angrily across his chest.

Daniel still hid his face behind his hands, like a child pulling the covers over his head, as if that would protect him. The rest of the students were silent, absorbing the news.

Jeff forced himself to put aside his self-condemnation for now. There was still one more thing he had to say. "There's something else I should tell you. At my last meeting with Jeremy before this trip, Jeremy shared with me that it wasn't the thought of dying that bothered him. He told me he was secure in the knowledge of Christ, and he wasn't afraid to die. What he was afraid of..." Jeff had to collect himself before continuing. "What scared Jeremy was the thought of watching himself wasting away, of becoming a burden to his family. He said he was okay with dying, he just wished...he just wanted it to be fast."

Daniel gave a small groan and sank even lower in his chair. Kevin got up, gave his chair a vicious kick, and stormed from the room.

After a moment, Terrell looked at Jeff questioningly. When Jeff nodded permission, Terrell went to find Kevin. Mindy sniffled. Although Resha's face showed no emotion, tears glistened in her eyes. Only Samuel sat impassively. Jeff wondered what the Nigerian man was thinking.

The students seemed to recognize that the meeting was over. Resha stood up quietly and headed for the door. She stopped beside Daniel's chair, opened her mouth as if to say something to him, then thought better of it and just left. Mindy followed Resha's lead, giving Daniel's good shoulder a gentle squeeze on the way out.

He didn't react.

When Samuel walked out without a word, the pastor was alone with Daniel.

Jeff knew Kevin would need to blow off more steam, but he'd be okay eventually. It was Daniel he was more concerned about. On top of the grief of losing Jeremy, Daniel would be consumed with misplaced guilt because he'd always felt responsible for his two younger friends. And the young man tended to bottle things up.

The pastor sat in the chair next to Daniel. "I'm sorry, son."

Daniel finally raised his head. Surprisingly, his eyes were dry. "I saw what they did to him, Pastor Jeff. I saw everything. Am I supposed to believe that dying that way was better than whatever this disease would have done to him?"

Jeff remembered the condition of Jeremy's body when it was dumped on the steps. What must it have been like for someone as sensitive as Daniel to watch it happen? He wished he had solid answers for the anguished young man, but he had nothing.

"I don't know, Daniel. I just know that this didn't come as a surprise to God. He knew what was going to happen on this trip and for His own reasons, He allowed it to happen."

Daniel nodded, but Jeff knew his words had brought no comfort.

He'd thought he was a decent shepherd, but he'd felt more inadequate in Colombia than he ever had before. He could help his students deal with the usual trials and tribulations of college life, but when it came to a real crisis, he came up empty. Jeff sat silently beside his young friend, at a total loss.

"I guess it's down to the wire now, huh?" Daniel's words caused Jeff to look at him quizzically. "You always taught us that it's easy to trust God when everything's going okay, it's easy to serve Christ when all our needs are being met. You said we find out where we really stand when everything falls apart around us and there's nothing left but Him. It must be time to find out where I stand."

Had he said that? Jeff wondered.

"I'm going to be okay, Pastor Jeff," Daniel told him, his clear blue eyes radiating sincerity. "I really am. I just kind of need some time alone, okay?"

Jeff hated to leave Daniel alone right now, but he had nothing to offer if he stayed. He stood and walked away, patting Daniel clumsily on the back.

When he reached the door, Jeff turned to sneak a glance behind him. Daniel had fallen to his knees in the small sanctuary, seeking comfort from the only One who truly understood his pain.

Yes, Daniel was going to be okay. Jeff closed the door quietly.

Although Selena hadn't wanted to face the group yet, she seemed eager to get the details about the meeting from Mindy. Resha lay on her back on the cot and closed her eyes, hoping they would think she was still recovering from last night's beating so they wouldn't try to include her in the conversation.

As Mindy finished describing what they'd learned, voices floated in from the courtyard. Selena tiptoed to the window and lifted the corner of the curtain to peek out.

"Looks like Terrell found Kevin," Selena observed. "They're both going inside now."

"Oh, good." Mindy sighed in relief. "Kevin was so upset. Daniel, too."

Selena squinted into the darkness outside. "I don't see Daniel. Wonder where he is."

"Oh, I'm sure he'll be okay, too," Mindy said hopefully. "Pastor Jeff was with him."

Lying still on the cot, Resha didn't bother to point out what her keen hearing had picked up a few moments ago. The thick wooden door to the sanctuary had opened and closed, but only one set of footsteps had gone down the hall, towards the back exit that led to Sergio's house where Jeff was staying. That meant Daniel was still in the sanctuary, alone.

She considered joining him to see if she could offer some comfort, but she hadn't done much for him the other night when she'd talked to him. Maybe it was a guy thing, and she hoped Pastor Jeff had been able to help him. But Jeff had left too quickly, so probably it would take a bigger "Guy" than Jeff.

Resha wondered why it even mattered to her.

Before she got saved, Resha had pretty much lived for herself, not caring at all about anyone else. To her, other people were there to be used or ignored. Since becoming a Christian, she'd first started to become aware of other people's problems. Then that awareness turned to compassion, and that compassion grew into a genuine desire to help them, and Resha realized that God was beginning to develop His character in her.

Still, that didn't explain why her heart ached so much for Daniel's pain, why his suffering touched her so deeply. It must be another step in that journey, she supposed. Better to blame God for her feelings than to explore any other ridiculous possibility why she should be so concerned about the man.

Resha's lips twisted into a cynical smile. If this trend kept up, soon she'd be like Mindy and burst into tears the next time she accidentally stepped on a bug.

She waited until the other two had dropped off to sleep, then sat up and began to pray for Daniel.

Kneeling on the hard clay tiles, Daniel longed to feel God's comforting Presence as he had so many times before, but his emotions were too raw. He was surprised at the intensity of the anger that washed over him.

The piano stood silently in the corner, a stark reminder of how Jeremy and Paola had brought the sanctuary to life with their worship just a few short days ago. Now Jeremy was dead and Paola's life was in ruins, and the echo of their praises was a mockery in Daniel's ears.

His heart cried out the question that had tormented him for three days. "Why did it have to be Jeremy, God? He was so happy and full of life and he didn't deserve that. The sickness, the shooting, any of that. Why Jeremy?"

Instead of an answer, a question rose up inside Daniel. *Would you rather it had been Kevin?*

Shocked at the question, Daniel answered aloud. "No! Of course not! Kevin is just as important to me as Jeremy was."

The voice came again, and this time Daniel recognized it as the Holy Spirit searching his heart. *One of the others on the team, then?*

The thought of one of the girls being shot to death sickened Daniel.

One by one, he thought of the other members of the team and realized that even though he wasn't as close to them, he wouldn't have wanted any of them to die. Not even cowardly, misguided Manny, who was indirectly responsible for Jeremy's death.

Daniel shook his head against the idea of anyone else in the group dying. "No, no, no, none of them."

Who, then? came the Voice.

For a moment, Antonio's face flashed into Daniel's mind, and the gunman who had pulled the trigger, and Captain Ortega, whom Matéo had described to him. But for some reason, even the thought of them dying instead of Jeremy brought no satisfaction. That surprised him.

"Why did it have to be anyone, God? Why did anyone have to die?"

There was no answer. Instead, the question came again with quiet persistence. *Who would you have chosen to die?*

Finally, Daniel's heart acknowledged the bitter thought that had been lurking in the back of his mind all along. Jeremy had brought life and joy and laughter everywhere he went; all Daniel did was stumble through life and make a fool of himself. He would have gladly traded his own life if it would have meant Jeremy could live.

"Why couldn't it have been me, God? I would rather have died myself than for Jeremy to be the one. Jeremy didn't deserve to die. Why didn't you take me instead?"

There was silence for a moment, and then a Bible passage from the last book of John gently came to mind. In the passage, Daniel recalled, Peter apparently did not like what he'd been told about his own future, and had the audacity to question his Lord's will for someone else's life. Jesus didn't answer Peter's question, but instead basically replied, "What business is that of yours? Your job is to follow Me."

Daniel acknowledged the point with a grunt, but he wasn't satisfied. "But Jeremy was the better man, God. So again, why him and not me? Why am I still here when Jeremy had so much more to offer?"

Less gently this time, Daniel was reminded of the book of Job, in which Job questioned God's will. God's response to Job was to rebuke him for several chapters. In the end, Job was shamed into admitting, "I am unworthy..."

And, like Job, Daniel recognized that he had no right to question his Father's will.

Still kneeling on the ground, Daniel forced himself to raise his hands to God, ignoring the pain the movement caused his injured arm, and prayed, "I'm so sorry, God. I hate what happened, but I guess...I mean, I know...that You know best. It's about Your will, not mine. I'm sorry for being angry at You. It just...hurts so much."

With that humble admission, the Presence Daniel had longed for enveloped him, and his tears finally found release.

He cried with convulsing sobs, weeping out his anger and his grief and his guilt over not being able to save his best friend. Weeping for Jeremy's family, and for Pastor Jeff, who had shouldered the responsibility of informing them about their son's death. Weeping for Kevin and for himself, who would never again laugh at Jeremy's offbeat humor. And weeping that Jeremy had not felt free to share with him and Kevin, and so had carried the burden of his illness alone.

And he wept for Resha, his tiny friend who'd been the victim of Antonio's brutality, and for Paola and Stefan, whose dreams of a life together would never be, and for the young soldiers he'd fought with, who were deceived by a false ideal and whose souls were lost.

And finally, for his own lost innocence.

His tears finally spent, Daniel picked himself off the ground and stared up at the wooden cross. He was exhausted, but he felt a peace he hadn't felt before. He was still confused and his heart was still torn, but he found he was unable to stir up the anger at God he had felt earlier.

And as he sat, gazing at the cross that spoke of the ultimate sacrifice, aware that his own wisdom would never be adequate to grasp the reasons for what had happened, a simple answer came.

Jeremy fought the good fight and finished his course. He kept the faith. Will you do the same?

In the quiet, dark sanctuary, Daniel nodded and lifted his hands again, surrendering to his Father's love. "God, You are good, no matter what. Thank you for letting me have Jeremy as a friend."

A faint smile found its way onto Daniel's face as he pictured Jeremy doing his trademark moves on streets of gold, dancing for an audience of One.

"I'll see you again one day, buddy," he promised, then stood up and dusted himself off. It was time to get back on course.

15

Day 14: Saturday

Resha made one final pass around her sleeping area to make sure she didn't leave anything behind. As she hoisted her duffel bag onto her shoulder, she noticed a small bulge in one of the side pockets.

She reached in to find out what it was and pulled out her gold hoops, the ones Jeremy had salvaged for her after she'd pulled Matéo from the ravine. She must have slipped them into her bag and forgotten about them.

She sat down on the cot and studied the earrings. Jeremy had wiped every trace of mud off of them, and they were gleaming, at least as much as dollar store earrings could gleam. Resha hadn't noticed it before, but one of them had cracked, probably trampled in all the confusion that day. Jeremy had welded it back together so the damage was barely noticeable. So much trouble for a dollar pair of earrings.

Resha shook her head, remembering some of Jeremy's antics. The way he'd danced with Selena, the way he'd made Matéo laugh, the way he'd made a game out of everything. He'd teased them all, especially Daniel, but it was never mean spirited. Now who was going to break Daniel out of his melancholy shell?

There had been another side to Jeremy, too. Resha thought of how he'd worked shoulder to shoulder with them in the sweltering heat, never complaining, never letting on he was sick. How he'd led them in worship that day, stepping out of the spotlight he loved so they could focus on the God he loved more. How he'd prayed for his sister every night.

She remembered the first time she'd seen Jeremy, when he'd come to visit his sister at the school years ago. He'd kid around and make Natalie laugh, but he always ended his visits by telling Natalie that he was praying for her. Jeremy had kept his word to Natalie, and Resha hoped his prayers would be answered.

Jeremy, you were one of a kind. I'm sorry I didn't get to know you sooner.

"Resha, are you ready to go?" Mindy's anxious voice came from the doorway.

"Yeah, I'm coming," Resha said, but she made no move to get up.

Mindy's eyes went to the earrings in Resha's hand and she said wistfully, "He was a nice guy, wasn't he?"

A rare smile transformed Resha's face. "Yeah. He was."

Samuel had already seated himself in the passenger seat of the waiting pickup truck, holding his grimy satchel on his lap. He didn't look up when Resha flung her duffel bag into the rusted bed of the truck.

Only one truck was needed for the return trip. Four of the original ten would not be going back with them. Selena and Pastor Jeff would be staying with the Restrepos for a while, Manny was in some jail cell somewhere, and Jeremy....well, he wouldn't be going home now, either.

Behind Luís' dilapidated heap, Agent Diana Cortez stood next to an official vehicle, tapping an impatient foot. Waiting with her were two Colombian police officers who had been hand-picked for their trustworthiness. As a protective measure, the trio would follow the American students to the bus station in Cordoba, where the team would board a bus bound for the airport in Medellin.

Two other officers would remain behind to guard the mission center, and in a few days, the compound would be filled with returning families and a work crew from a humanitarian relief organization.

Mindy tucked her pink backpack next to Resha's army green duffel bag, then ran back and hugged everyone who would remain at the center, crying hard.

Selena hugged her back fiercely, then shocked Resha by hugging her, too. "Thank you so much for everything, Resha."

Uncomfortable with the show of affection, Resha patted Selena awkwardly on the back before inching away. She almost backed into Matéo.

The little boy looked her steadily in the eye. "I will be praying for you, Miss Resha."

Resha understood that he was telling her that he still had his faith. He must have been listening to her that day after all. She crouched down so she could be face level with him. "Thank you, Matéo. I'll be praying for you, too."

Suddenly he threw his arms around her waist. "I love you, Miss Resha."

This time, Resha was able to return the boy's hug. To her surprise it actually felt good.

"I love you, too, Matéo," she said, meaning it. They held on for several seconds before Resha pulled away to see Mindy watching them, all misty eyed.

Excited by all the affection going around, the dog chose that moment to start barking and wagging his tail, trying to get in on the action. Mindy laughed and hugged Alfredo, getting her face slobbered on in return.

Daniel had paused in his round of handshakes to watch Resha's exchange with Matéo. Strangely touched, he looked away before she caught him staring.

He and Jeff exchanged a quick embrace. "See you when you get back to Houston, Pastor Jeff."

Breaking the hug, Jeff pointed a finger in Daniel's face. "See a doctor about that wound."

"I will," Daniel promised.

All the farewells had been said now, and the rest of the students had boarded the truck, arranging themselves around the duffel bags and backpacks piled in the truck bed.

Daniel took one last glance at La Vida Nueva Mission Center, feeling like he was leaving a huge chunk of himself behind. Then he climbed in and Luís started the truck. As they pulled away from the complex, the Colombian police car fell in behind.

No one said much on the long drive to the bus station.

Alone in a Colombian jail cell, Manny Gutierrez lay on a thin mat on the bottom half of a metal bunk bed, cringing each time he heard footsteps in the hallway. He hoped that F.B.I. agent had been telling the truth when he assured Manny that he would be protected. In spite of Richard Massey's words, Manny couldn't help being scared. He kept imagining the gun that Antonio had pointed at his head.

Agent Massey had also told Manny his parents had been contacted and would arrive in Colombia in a few days to help deal with the mess he'd created with his greedy, blind ignorance. Manny was ashamed to face them, but at the same time, he couldn't wait to see them.

The agent promised he would try to arrange for Pastor Jeff and Selena to visit him sometime today. Manny didn't understand why Selena had bothered to stay behind to be near him while the others went back to America. Especially after he'd betrayed the group and then abandoned her and the other two girls to Antonio's mercy.

Maybe it had something to do with the God the rest of them all prayed to. Before they'd taken Manny away, Selena had told him she'd become a Christian. He'd thought they were already both Christians, but something had obviously gone very wrong in his case.

Manny wondered if it was too late for him. If Pastor Jeff really did come to visit him, Manny would have to ask him about that.

Because travel to and from Colombia was still sparse, the airplane was practically empty except for a few scattered businessmen and a couple of families. With all the seats available, the airline staff didn't bother to enforce the seating assignments.

It irked Resha that Mindy had to park herself right next to her. Still, Resha had learned by now how to tune out the constant chatter, so she really didn't mind it much any more.

Samuel, of course, seated himself alone on the other side of the plane. Terrell and Kevin sat together, leaving Daniel alone with his thoughts.

Daniel stared out the window, his eyes fixed on the clouds. Resha wondered what he saw in them.

Looking out her own window, she thought she figured it out. Instead of the sky, all Resha could see was Jeremy's smiling face. She could almost hear his infectious laugh over Mindy's endless jabbering. Memories and regrets simmered in her mind for most of the six hour flight.

It felt almost anticlimactic when the plane touched down on American soil again. Resha's most overwhelming emotion as she stepped off the airplane was self-consciousness about her appearance.

She'd gotten used to a lowered standard of grooming in Colombia, and now she became painfully aware of her unwashed hair and wrinkled clothes. She shivered in the chilly mid-December wind, having grown accustomed to the steamy tropical climate of Cuenco Verde.

As soon as the group had left the terminal, Samuel, true to character, vanished without a goodbye to anyone.

Mindy gave each of them another quick hug, promising to stay in touch. Then she waggled her fingers at them and ran into the waiting arms of a handsome young man Resha assumed was the boyfriend she had mentioned.

Terrell and Kevin looked at Daniel and Resha, then looked at each other.

"Hey, Daniel, me and Terrell fixin' to go get a Coke. We'll meet you at the car, okay?" Kevin said.

"Oh, uh, sure," Daniel mumbled distractedly.

Daniel's friends melted discreetly into the background and Resha found herself standing alone with a man she'd grown to admire.

With an effort, Daniel dragged himself back into the present. His eyes focused on Resha, who stood there in her rumpled camouflage shirt with her duffel bag slung over her shoulder. Her face was scabbed and still a little swollen, but she'd put her dangling gold earrings on again. Why had he never noticed before how pretty she was?

He wasn't sure what to say. "Uh, did you need a ride home?"

Resha shook her head. "No, my momma and my sisters came for me." She pointed her chin toward a faded gold Camry that was idling across the parking lot.

It was strange to think of Resha having a mom and a normal family. He wondered what she was like in everyday life. Somehow he doubted she acted much different in their own world, but it would be nice to see her dressed in something other than her grungy camouflage.

The two stared at each other. Daniel was confused by his emotions, not sure how to say goodbye.

Finally, Resha spoke. "Well, Chief, I guess I'll see you on the next mission trip."

She stood on tiptoe and gave Daniel a quick peck on the cheek, catching him by surprise. She abruptly turned away and hurried off with uncharacteristic shyness.

Daniel couldn't let her go like that. Not any more.

Too much had happened on this trip for him to take anything for granted. He reached out with his good arm and caught one of her hands before she could make it too far. "Hey."

Resha turned back to him, looking surprised by his unexpected boldness. Daniel was amazed to see that her cheeks were flushed and her eyes sparkled with unshed tears.

"Why do we have to wait till we're across the world? We only live across town from each other," he heard himself say.

Resha's cocky mask snapped back into place. She shrugged and said, ultra casual, "Sure, Chief, get my number from Pastor Jeff and give me a call sometime."

Then she gave him one of her patented dazzling smiles and walked away with a confident swagger that made Daniel's heart jump. When she reached her family's car, she turned and gave a saucy little salute before ducking inside.

Daniel watched the car drive off with a silly grin on his face. Then he picked up his bag and headed toward Kevin's car, where his friends were waiting to drive him home.

EPILOGUE

Houston, TX

Pastor Jeff had been back in Houston for nearly a month, but he still hadn't quite readjusted to his fast-paced schedule. There were times when Jeff would almost prefer the long, hot days of backbreaking work in Colombia over the stressful demands of his hectic life at home.

He'd just returned to his modest apartment after a frustrating day of trying to teach disinterested students at Woodrow Christian University. Now Jeff had only a few minutes of respite before he had to leave for church, where a group of rambunctious young people would be gathered for his Wednesday evening Youth Group activities. Afterward, he would grade papers late into the night.

While he leaned back on the kitchen counter waiting for the coffee maker to do its work, Jeff sorted through the stack of envelopes he'd grabbed from his mailbox on the way in. Mostly junk mail. Annoyed, Jeff tossed aside the brightly colored credit card offers and grocery store ads.

A thick envelope with a Colombian postmark on it caught his attention and he tucked it under his arm. Jeff poured himself a cup of coffee and carried it, black, the few steps to his small living room, where he settled onto his comfortable, well-worn sofa to read the letter from Pastor Sergio.

Jeff smiled to himself as he unfolded the three-page missive. He knew most of Colombia had electricity again now, and he'd seen a high-powered computer at the mission center, but the old-fashioned Pastor had penned the note by hand rather than sending a quick email. Jeff took a sip of coffee and began to read the spidery handwriting.

Dear Pastor Jeff,

I trust that our Lord and Savior Jesus Christ is keeping you in His loving care. He has blessed us exceedingly here at La Vida Nueva Mission Center.

We were able to reopen officially a few days after you left. There are many workers staying here now, some of them local and some from the charity group, and they have already rebuilt many of the homes that were destroyed by the flood. People are returning to the area and Paola and I have been able to share the gospel with them. Several have accepted Christ's offer of forgiveness and we have baptized seven new believers so far.

We are thankful to God for allowing us to be used in this way, and we are thankful that He sent all of you here to help bring it to pass. If not for your team's hard work, we would not have been able to finish the work so quickly and our little village would most likely have been forgotten.

And if not for young Jeremy's death, we would most likely still be living in fear of The Black Eagles. Because of Jeremy's murder, the American Embassy here in Colombia has been able to draw the attention of our government to the illegal activities of The Black Eagles in Cuenco Verde and in the surrounding areas.

I am still saddened that Antonio was murdered in prison. Antonio betrayed our trust and had a part in the death of two beloved friends, but my heart is heavy for what I fear must be his eternal destiny. My only consolation is that I know that Antonio heard the gospel presented clearly many times during his stay with us, so his blood is not on our hands.

Even though Antonio will not be supplying information as we had hoped, he had been bragging to young Manny Gutierrez, and by God's grace, Manny was able to give the authorities more information than he realized he had. As you probably know, Manny was released last week and has returned home with his family.

Another young man has come forward also, a teenaged boy named Ramiro Calderon who was forcibly recruited by the Black Eagles. Ramiro somehow obtained one of the Bibles that was dropped when Jeremy was killed, and he believed in Christ after reading part of the Bible and a copy of the letter we had placed in it. He managed to escape from Lt. Rojas and turned himself in to the authorities who were guarding our mission center.

He is staying here with us until we are able to locate his family, who moved away after their village was razed by The Black Eagles.

Manny's and Ramiro's testimonies, along with statements from Raul and Javier and the information provided by Paola and Matéo, gave the Colombian police adequate reason to arrest Captain Ortega and Lt. Rojas and several others. They are now in custody awaiting sentencing for their drug trafficking activities, and possibly for their part in the murders of Jeremy and Stefan.

With their leaders in prison, the rest of The Black Eagles have abandoned their efforts to take over the mission center and have mostly vacated this area, and so many of the villagers are free again to live their lives without oppression.

They come to me unhindered now, and I am able to give them God's Word. Each one leaves with a Bible just like the ones your students rescued, and each one leaves with the story of how one young man gave his life in an effort to make the Word of God available to them.

Jeremy's death has not only helped to bring many evil men to justice, but has also helped many to know Christ. I hope this knowledge brings you comfort in some way.

Again, I thank you all for what you did for the Lord and for our family.

Please know that you are ever in my prayers, as is each member of the team who came with you, and the family of the young man who sacrificed himself for the cause of Christ.

In Him,
Sergio

Jeff refolded the letter and sat in thoughtful silence, his cup of coffee now cold.

He remembered how Jeremy had come to his office at church before the trip, begging Jeff to let him go to Colombia in spite of his illness. Jeremy had said he wanted to use his remaining time on earth to make a difference. He'd made more of a difference than he would ever know.

But then, Jeff realized, Jeremy probably did know. He imagined Jeremy now, grinning smugly down at him from Heaven, saying, "See, Pastor Jeff? I told you I was supposed to go to Colombia! Is God good, or what?"

Raising his mug in a little toast, Jeff grinned back. "Yes, Jeremy, God is definitely good."

Oh, taste and see that the LORD is good;
blessed is the man that trusts in Him.

— Psalm 34:8

DISCUSSION QUESTIONS

1. Pastor Jeff's first inclination is to leave Colombia as soon as he learns of the danger, but the students talk him into staying. Do you think he made the right decision?

2. Pastor Jeff hopes this missionary trip will help Daniel grow into a more effective leader. Do you think this happened?

3. What qualities does Daniel have that make him a good leader? Which of his qualities detract from his ability to lead?

4. Do any of the other students become leaders during the trip? If so, which ones? Was it intentional, or did he/she just fall into a leadership role?

5. Terrell thinks that Resha should not have been allowed to come because of her past. Daniel believes that God had a purpose for each person being there. Who do you agree with?

6. How has Resha's opinion of men been colored by her past? Does her opinion change by the end of the trip? Why or why not?

7. When the team realizes that there is a traitor among them, they automatically suspect Samuel. Why? Is Samuel partly to blame for their suspicions?

8. Why is Manny singled out by The Black Eagles? What characteristics does Manny have that make him an easy target for their plans?

9. Mindy gives the impression of being hopelessly naive. Do you believe she is as empty-headed as she seems? Do you think she deliberately puts on a facade?

10. At the beginning of the book, Jeremy tells Pastor Jeff that he believes God wants him to go on the mission trip. Do you think Jeremy said that to manipulate Pastor Jeff, or did he really believe God wanted him there? Do you think it was God's plan for Jeremy to go on the trip?

11. As Pastor Sergio prays over the young men before they leave to retrieve the stolen Bibles, Sergio and Jeremy share an unusual moment. Do you think Jeremy knew what was going to happen? Do you think Sergio knew?

12. Do you think things would have turned out differently if the team had known all along what Pastor Jeff revealed about Jeremy at their last session? Why or why not?

Dear Reader,

Thank you for reading Like A Flood. I hope you enjoyed it, and that reading it impacted you as much as writing it did me. My hope is to write stories that not only entertain, but that also help readers in their own walk with Christ, or maybe even introduce them to my Lord and Savior and very best Friend.

If you want to know more about me, please visit my webpage at www.elizabethproske.com. You can send me a message from there, too, or just email me at Elizabeth@elizabethproske.com. I'd love to hear from you, and answer any questions or comments you might have.

Blessings!
Elizabeth Proske

NEXT IN THE MISSION FIELD SERIES

Part 1: Daniel's Odyssey

Daniel Wescott is not handling grief well. After his best friend's death, Daniel's guilt and depression drive him into a lonely, downward spiral. His friends are fed up with him. His pastor doesn't know what to do with him. It seems even God isn't on speaking terms with him. So Daniel turns to the only source of comfort he can find, but the relief he finds might cost him his soul.

Part 2: Saving Natalie

Before his death, Jeremy Andersen had prayed relentlessly for his sister Natalie to get saved. Now that he's gone, her brother's faith is far less appealing to Natalie than finding her next fix. She finds herself being sucked into a dangerous world of drugs and prostitution. Her new friends Mindy and Resha are determined to see that Jeremy's prayers for Natalie get answered, though, even at the risk of their own safety.

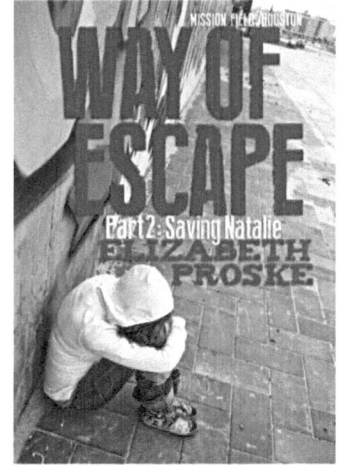

EXCERPT FROM WAY OF ESCAPE, PART 1
Chapter 1

Icy roads, freezing wind, and a steady drizzle; only a fool would go out on a night like this. A fool, or someone desperate.

It was both foolishness and desperation that brought the little Toyota to the deserted corner of a shopping strip that had closed for the evening. A skinny girl with wispy, brown hair climbed out of the car, her pale face turning left to right as she searched anxiously for the person she'd arranged to meet.

"Cruz?" she finally called out in a small voice, wrapping her thin arms around herself to ward off the chill.

A few feet away, someone lit up a cigarette, briefly illuminating the thick, dark-skinned man she was looking for. A wide doorway sheltered Cruz from the worst of the weather, and he wore an expensive fleece-lined coat far better suited to the chill than the frayed denim jacket the girl wore. He greeted the girl as if there was nothing unusual about either of them being in such a desolate place, and on such a frigid night.

"Hey, Sweet Thing. How's my favorite girl this evening?"

Although Cruz had adopted the lingo of the Houston streets he serviced, his accent was unmistakably Puerto Rican. The girl studied the man's ebony features, hungry for the affection she found there even though she knew it wasn't real.

"Not so good, Cruz." Her shoulders drooped and she stared at her feet. "My little brother died."

Cruz did a near perfect imitation of sympathy. "Ah, I'm sorry, Babe. Life on the streets is hard, ain't it? How can I help?"

"Jeremy wasn't on the streets," the girl objected, confused. "He was....never mind. I need a fix, Cruz. Can you hook me up?"

"Don't I always deliver the goods, Baby?" purred Cruz. He took a long drag on his cigarette before asking, "How much you got on you?"

The girl fished in the pocket of jeans that were too loose on her and came up with a handful of rumpled twenties she'd stolen from her mother's purse that evening. A fleeting moment of guilt tugged at her as she remembered how her parents struggled to pay their bills, but her need for the temporary relief the money would buy was stronger than her conscience. She handed over the cash.

Cruz flicked his cigarette away and counted the bills, then gave her a huge smile, his gold teeth reflecting the streetlight. "Nice. You got enough here to upgrade to something better."

She hesitated and Cruz poured on more sympathy, more persuasion. "You're going through a bad time, Baby. Might need a little extra help to get you through, you know."

After a moment, the girl shook her head. "No. The usual, I guess."

His smile didn't fade. "You got it, Sweet Thing." He pocketed the money and counted out three little packets.

The girl licked her lips subconsciously when she saw them. Cruz resisted the urge to taunt her, knowing that wasn't the way to earn repeat business. He pressed the packets into her grasping hands. "You go on and enjoy that, now."

"I will," the girl promised, backing away with her treasure. Before turning to trot back to her car, she called, "Thanks, Cruz."

Cruz almost laughed. The fool had just thanked him for ripping her off and destroying what was left of her brain!

As she drove away, two more figures emerged from the shadows, a young Puerto Rican with a slight build and a taller, darker man sporting dreadlocks and shades, even in the darkness. They had watched the entire transaction, ready to jump in to protect their boss if anything went wrong.

"Is that the last one, Cruz?" the short, Hispanic teenager whined. He had his hands jammed deep into his pockets to protect them from the cold, but he still shivered. "Can we go now?"

The charm Cruz had manufactured for his customer vanished as he barked at his latest recruit. "What's wrong with you, Emilio? You better toughen up if you want to hang with the big boys."

Emilio cringed and stammered through blue lips, "I'm okay, Cruz. I just want to learn, that's all."

Cruz swung his glare to the tall, grinning Jamaican. "What about you, Tony? You getting cold feet too?"

He laughed at his own play on words. Tony's smile grew wider and he answered in a distinct Jamaican patois, "Yuh de boss man, Cruz."

Tony's calculated flattery and Emilio's fearful submissiveness were exactly what Cruz wanted, needed, to make him feel like the man he was. Pacified by the adulation, he answered Emilio's question. "We have one more meeting tonight, and then we can all go home with fat pockets. The boss lady is sending us another dealer. She wants us to supply him. That means we're movin' up in the ranks, boys."

Tony said nothing, just kept grinning, but Emilio couldn't hide his eagerness to be done for the night. "Are we gonna meet him pretty soon, Cruz? Is he gonna come here?"

"I'm already here," a deep voice said from directly behind Cruz. Cruz whirled to find himself with his nose inches from someone's chest. None of them had noticed anyone approach.

His hand discreetly going to the weapon he had tucked into his waistband, Cruz turned his gaze upward and looked into the face of a light-skinned African American man in his twenties.

Cruz had dealt with plenty of street thugs before and the one standing in front of him now looked like any other, with his chunky bling and low-riding baggy jeans. There should have been nothing intimidating about this dealer, but when the tall man smiled, the dead look in his eyes sent a chill through Cruz that rivaled the bitterly cold wind pounding his back.

Cruz wondered if his boss realized that she had signed on with pure evil.